Valley of SHADOWS

Phoenix Emrys

Dreamspinner Press

Published by
Dreamspinner Press
4760 Preston Road
Suite 244-149
Frisco, TX 75034
http://www.dreamspinnerpress.com/

This is a work of fiction. Names, characters, places and incidents either are the product of the author's imagination or are used fictitiously, and any resemblance to actual persons, living or dead, business establishments, events or locales is entirely coincidental.

Valley of Shadows
Copyright © 2010 by Phoenix Emrys

Cover Art by Paul Richmond   http://www.paulrichmondstudio.com

All rights reserved. No part of this book may be reproduced or transmitted in any form or by any means, electronic or mechanical, including photocopying, recording, or by any information storage and retrieval system without the written permission of the Publisher, except where permitted by law. To request permission and all other inquiries, contact Dreamspinner Press, 4760 Preston Road, Suite 244-149, Frisco, TX 75034
http://www.dreamspinnerpress.com/

ISBN: 978-1-61581-545-6

Printed in the United States of America
First Edition
July, 2010

eBook edition available
eBook ISBN: 978-1-61581-546-3

To everyone who's ever believed in me
Especially Spencer, for putting me on this path

With a suggestion
And four little words:
"You can do this."

Chapter 1

"Congratulations, Ellery. *The Warrior's Tale* has topped the best-sellers lists for the third week in a row. Copies of your book are flying off the shelves. Hanover House is very happy with its hottest property."

"How alliterative of you, Max." I can hear the dollar signs in her voice. "Are you sure you aren't considering a career change?"

"Not on your life." The sound of her light chuckle tickles my right ear. "I'll leave the writing to you. I'm quite happy to stay in your shadow managing your career. It might not be as glamorous, but so far it's proven extremely lucrative."

No arguments there.

"My shadow, my ass!" Now it's my turn to chuckle. "Max, please, you're about as shy and retiring as a barracuda!"

"All the better to get you the best deal possible, my dear," she airily ripostes.

"Of which you take a generous cut!"

"Ellery, I earn every percentage point! Quit complaining. I've made you a very rich man."

"Okay, I'll give you that." I take a quick sip of my tea. "On both counts. Just think: but for you—and your endearingly nosy niece—at this very moment I might be anonymously languishing away in a garret somewhere in glorious, anonymous poverty."

And definitely not having this conversation. Hmmm. Considering the circus my life has become as a result of the entrance of the redoubtable Maxima into it, the garret option sounds pretty good. On both counts.

Max giggles. Not a sound one often associates with her. Trust me on this one.

"Oh, Ellery, get over yourself already. Languishing is not your forte, and while a garret probably seems romantic to someone with your unique sensibilities, there's nothing glamorous about poverty."

"I never said there was. Anyway, how the hell would you know? Being born with a silver Porsche in your mouth hardly qualifies you as an expert on the subject."

"Admit it, Ellery," Max continues, "Carrie's curiosity about her fiancé's mysteriously reclusive roommate and the equally mysterious manuscripts he was so protective of—her going behind your back and going through them was the best thing that ever happened to you. To both of us, actually."

"Oh, yes, lucky, lucky me." I roll my eyes, serene in the knowledge she cannot see the visual expression of my total lack of enthusiasm for my supposed fortune. "What an incredibly serendipitous stroke I drew a college roommate engaged to a charming young lady with no concept of personal space, boundaries, or property. And what were the odds, her aunt happening to be a hungry literary agent looking to make her mark."

With luck like this, I shoulda booked passage on the Titanic.

Sarcasm is wasted on Max. The idea someone—namely me—might not actually enjoy being routinely victimized by the Machiavellian media publicity engine in which she has me ensnarled doesn't figure in her reality. Power mad beast that she is.

Pull my life over; I want to get off now.

She blathers on about how bleeping lucky I am to be me. I tune her out and check my watch. Nine fifteen. No sign of the other significant female in my life. That's odd. I wonder what's up. She's not usually tardy. It's not like she would have slept in or anything. Maybe she's finally moved on. Pushed off, cleared out, flown the coop, decided to find some peace and leave me to mine. Not that I'll get any, even if she has headed off for greener pastures, but a man can dream.

"Five best sellers in a row." Max again. Oops, is she still talking?

"The movie rights and DVD residuals alone are keeping me up nights. You, Ellery Joyce James, are one supernova of a hot literary commodity. I don't know how you do it."

It's a secret, and I plan to keep it that way.

"The detail in your stories is incredible; it's like you've actually been there. In the past, I mean. The events you describe, the people, the places, everything you write; it's all so… well, it's almost spooky how real you make it all. I don't even want to think about how much time you spend researching. Then there's the actual writing. You do sleep, don't you, Ellery? You crank these babies out so fast! Especially this latest one. Ellery, I swear, it reads like you actually lived Marcus's life!"

Well, someone did, all right, that much is true, but it wasn't me.

Pop goes the bagel! It's about time!

"That's great, Max, I'm pleased you're pleased." And I'll be pleased as soon as I sink my teeth into this little bakery beauty here. "But I sense you're not calling to dazzle me with a deluge of praise and award me another laurel wreath to rest on."

'Kay. Bagel has been fished out of the toaster and plated. Whee. Excellent, we are mere seconds away from achieving breakfast. Next step, cream cheese.

Oy, this poor fridge is ever so bare. Nothing much left of the odds and ends I picked up to tide me over until I make a proper re-provisioning run. I've been back now almost forty-eight hours, and I still haven't gone outside. I will, I will; it's just…. I have to keep reminding myself I'm not in New York anymore. It's okay to leave the house. This is sleepy little Birchwood. I'm not gonna get swarmed by paparazzi the second my foot hits the sidewalk.

I hate big cities. New York in particular. Damn publicity tours! Every time I get conned into doing one, I swear it'll be the last. Maybe this time it'll finally be true.

The solution to making it all go away is simple. I must cease feeding the beast. When I stop pumping out the moneymakers—if there are no more big, shiny books to bally-hoo—I'll no longer be useful to those making a killing selling little pieces of me. I'll drop off everyone's radar. The world will forget me and move on. Ah, bliss.

Definitely something to look forward to. Can't quit yet. As much as I hate the machine, the cash it's cranking out is largely funding the work I really care about. My other really big secret. That won't always be so; all that insider info has been turning my investments into gold. A little while longer and I won't have to write the books any more.

Soon, soon. I'll hang it up and fade back into my wallpaper, here. No more touring, no more book signings, no more stupid interviews and talk show appearances. No more getting the crap scared out of me turning a corner unsuspecting and seeing my face plastered all over the newsstand on the cover of some stupid tabloid.

Calm down, Ellery, it's all over for now. The big, bad city is behind you, and you're back home, safe and sound in good ol' Birchwood. Breathe and focus on the task at hand.

Cream cheese, where's the cream cheese? Aw, don't tell me I'm out of cream cheese!

"You know me too well, Ellery," Max sighs. "Why, yes, now you mention it, I did have an ulterior motive for making this call. I was wondering when we were going to get a peek at your current masterpiece in progress."

Ah! There it is! Cream cheese! Yum! Step three, flip the lid, insert knife, and spread.

"Not yet, Max." I wedge the cell between my chin and shoulder so as to expedite lid-lifting. "I'm not ready to let anyone see it yet. It's kind of... uh... experimental."

Yeah. Experimental. Sure, why not. That works. Sounds good too. Way better than owning up to not having even started the damned thing yet.

Aw nuts! The container is empty! This is not happening.

"Not even me?"

I can hear her pouting from three thousand miles away.

"Nope, not even you," I heartlessly return.

No cream cheese. I am officially bummed out here.

"Now I'm really intrigued. You're not usually this mysterious about your work, Ellery. This one must be something extra special."

You just keep on thinkin' that. Me, I have to cut this conversation short. There is no way I'm eating this stinking bagel without cream cheese. I don't have to and I don't want to. However, the cream cheese shortage means my toasty friend here is destined to be a discard. The trashcan gets a bagel. My stomach gets squat.

I have no breakfast. *Dommage.*

That's French for "woe is me."

Well, this bites. Big, big appetite. No bagel. Bummer.

Now what?

Oh boy, I really don't want to go back to Dinah's Diner yet, but being hungry enough to start gnawing on the knotty pine is a powerful motivator. I can't keep avoiding the place forever, especially as their reopening has removed my excuse for not making an appearance. Other than being chickenshit, that is. I'm not ready to return, but I'm really, really hungry. And you know what else? Even when I have crummy cream cheese, these stupid bagels are a lousy substitute for their lovely breakfasts to which I've become not so much accustomed as addicted. My mornings haven't been the same without Norma's utterly divine Eggs Benedict.

God, I've missed that place, and Norma and Molly and—the unfortunately late and deeply lamented Martin.

"You writers," Max laughs, snapping me back into the conversation. "You're all such prima donnas. Fine, suit yourself; be mysterious. As long as you produce, I don't care if you want to hole up in your ivory tower and remain completely incommunicado for the next six weeks."

"Is that your not-so-subtle way of reminding me of my deadline?"

"Ellery, would I be so obvious?" She laughs again. "All right, I've wasted enough of your time; I'll stop talking and let you get back to work. Be brilliant, and see you in a couple of weeks?"

"Looking forward to it, Max."

Please let her be done. I don't ask for much, but definitely asking for this.

"Oh, Ellery, before I forget, there's just one more little thing."

Argh. Of course there is. Hunger is making me hallucinate. I swear I see bagel-shaped spots in front of my eyes.

Without any cream cheese.

"Now I know every time we've talked about this you've refused to listen to reason, but you know me."

Indeed.

"I'm willing to give you another chance to see things my way."

Now there's an offer I can't refuse.

"Ellery, I really think you should reconsider the bodyguard issue."

Absolutely not.

"No, Max."

"Not even after the incident in New York?"

That was New York. The Big Apple. This is Birchwood. The Small Potatoes. I've lived here long enough to be on speaking terms with almost everyone in town. I'm fine with them, they're fine with me. We're all fine. Birchwood is good, and so am I, as long as I'm here. End of discussion.

Honestly, I don't know why she thinks I need "people." Things are complicated enough around here already; adding additional warm, nosy bodies to the population of my happy haven is the last thing I want. Or need. Yet for some unfathomable reason, Max seems determined to encumber me with an entourage. Personal assistants, secretaries, gophers, researchers, bodyguards—you name the species of superfluous lackey, she's had a go at running them by me and inciting me to employ them.

I don't get it, but I won't have it—or them—either. No matter how much she nags. But so far it hasn't stopped her from trying. She has been going on, and on, and on, about this bodyguard issue for the last six months. Still not gonna happen. It's bad enough I let her run my public life. I'll be damned if I'll put up with some no-necked bruiser telling me what to do once I've escaped the fishbowl and returned to my private domain.

Especially a no-necked bruiser she's handpicked and programmed to be her puppet proxy. Anyway, the whole idea of me needing personal protection is ridiculous. I don't know what the heck she thinks could happen to me in Birchwood.

"No, Max." Geez, give it up, already.

I hear an impatient hmph on the other end of the line. Max is becoming miffed. She's not used to resistance, especially from me. I don't often dig my heels in—with good reason. Brooking Maxima Collins is not to be embarked upon lightly. Nor is it for the faint of heart. Trust me, when going head to head with a mega-diva of truly epic proportions, you pick your battles.

Every one I do, I win.

"Well, we'll leave it for now, but this isn't over, Ellery."

Yeah, it is. Deal with it.

"Seeing as how you've suddenly become so tediously unreasonable, I suppose there's no point in discussing disposing of that backwater monstrosity you're living in?"

Hey, don't diss my digs. It's a very nice monstrosity. Loaded with atmosphere, lousy with history, oozing quirky charm and character, all with a foyer you could bowl in. Aside from the fact I dropped a bundle to restore it to its former glory and a little more besides, after having barely survived the insanity masquerading as my most recent New York experience, backwaters suit me just fine.

"La, la, la, got my fingers in my ears."

"Seriously, Ellery, even after what little you've done to it, the place is too hideous for words. It gives me nightmares just looking at it. You're absolutely adamant about living in the creaky old place?"

Oh, I am, I am.

"We could still gut the entire interior, and then possibly I could persuade Darren to pop down there, inspect the building, come up with a floor plan that would make the place habitable."

In your dreams, sweetheart.

"La, la, la, I can't hear you."

"Mind you, the property isn't a total loss. The grounds are lovely, and it is a good location. For the middle-of-nowheresville. How about this, demolish the old, in with the new, we could completely do away with that shabby old eyesore and put up a beautiful new, modern building."

"You need to stop talking now, Max."

Speak to the phone, the El has stopped listening.

"Honestly, you're such a child," Max wearily scolds me. "I can't talk to you when you get like this."

I know. That's the idea. Bad, bad Ellery.

"I'll get back to you when you're prepared to be more reasonable."

That would be... never!

"Kiss, kiss," Max signs off, and breaks the connection.

"You should marry that girl."

Ah, there she is. The other woman. So much for my hopes of having a completely normal day for the first time in....

God, I don't even remember how long it's been since she hasn't been....

Haunting me.

"Good morning, Mrs. Sheridan," I sigh, tossing my cell phone on the kitchen counter and the bagel and empty cream cheese container in the trash. "Don't you ever knock?"

"Most amusing, my darling boy."

I turn and see all five feet of her, from the top of her silvering head to the fuzzy pink tips of her over-sized slippers. Her sparkling eyes are set like ironic agates in the comforting creases of her time-tracked face as she stands in the middle of my kitschy country kitchen, smiling indulgently at me.

"Marry Max? That's possibly the most bizarre thing you've ever said to me." I cross my arms and frown at her. "And given some of the odder conversations we've had over the years, we're talking a whole lot of bizarre, here!"

"You need someone in your life, dear," she says with a sad smile.

"Whether I do or not is neither here nor there, and also none of your business," I irritably retort. Thankfully we don't have this conversation much, well, not much any more, that is; even so, I'm growing more than tired of it. Max and I have a successful business relationship. So far we haven't killed each other. I relate to her on a personal level as personally as I've ever been with anyone living and breathing. The relationship is what I need it to be. Comfortably functional. Max is definitely not a touchy feely kind of person. And she's far too preoccupied with running my life to expend much energy actually discovering who I really am or what I can do.

Exactly what I need her to be.

"Max is a good friend, and an even better agent. She's also the last person I'd consider getting involved with."

If I were considering getting involved with anyone. Which I'm not. Life is complicated enough without adding intimacy to the insanity. No, it was made clear to me a long time ago it's better for me and everyone else to never, ever go there.

The price I pay for being me.

Marry Max. Mrs. S. should take her act on the road; she'd totally knock 'em dead in the Twilight Zone. I'm not in the market. Not now, not ever. Even if I were, she wouldn't be on my short list. Not simply because she's Max. Or because she's engaged. Again. She's… she's not the right one.

If I weren't half-dead from hunger, I wouldn't be thinking about this at all, and I certainly wouldn't admit that for all my "I walk alone" bravado, I *do* have a short list. It's short. Only has one name on it. No, that's not right; it's not a name, because I don't know it. Not a name. A face.

I try not to let it happen, but sometimes, despite my best efforts to keep it away, when I lie awake late at night or surface in the morning, caught in that twilight state between the world of wakefulness and dreams—I see it. The face. Just a hint, teasing, ephemeral features dancing in the recesses of my awareness, not long enough to be able to pick him out in a lineup, yet leaving enough of an inner impression for me to be certain I know him. I know I've never met him, he probably doesn't even exist, and yet….

Forget it, and him. Stuff all this nonsense back in the oubliette in your head and have done with it.

"It's not like you know a lot of other women, darling." Mrs. Sheridan gives me a pointed look over the tops of her wire-framed glasses. "Or any other people for that matter. You spend far too much time with—"

"And whose fault is that?" I snap at her. I know, I know, I shouldn't be getting so irritated. She means well, and God only knows, if it weren't for her tirelessly running interference and helping to keep certain things under some semblance of control, my daily existence would bring fresh new meaning to the concept of "living hell." All the same, being a constant in my life for over twenty years doesn't give her the right to run it!

"Have you had breakfast yet, dear?" she soothes. "No, of course you haven't," she confidently carries on before I can reply. "You wouldn't be this grumpy. You can be quite rude when you're hungry, you know. There's obviously no talking to you at the moment, dear, so scoot now and eat something, and why don't you take the morning off? We'll postpone the appointment until after lunch. How does that sound?"

"That sounds fine, Mrs. S." I sigh and rub my eyes. "Now, buzz off so I can shower and get dressed. Go… go knit something."

"Now, dear, you know I can't knit anymore." She blinks, favoring me with an ingenuous smile. "I'm dead."

Poof, she disappears.

Thank God, I thought she'd never leave.

Oh, I'm sorry; did I not mention Mrs. Sheridan is a ghost?

Yes, it's true, I'm crackers. Ever since I was a boy, I've been seeing and hearing this sweet, little old dead lady hanging around, constantly popping in and out of my life. Why? I dunno, you tell me. But for whatever reason she's here, seems like I'm stuck with her, or her with me. I've kinda gotten used to her and the whole talking to a dead person all the time schtick, and it wouldn't be so bad if she were the only one.

Oh, God, if only she were the only one!

Step out of the shower, quickly toweling off, yes, I will take the time to shave, dammit. It's my face, and if I want to shave it, I will. Screw Max and her "Now Ellery, I thought we settled this, you look so much sexier with the scruff. We're going to forget about the razor for the rest of the tour."

I hate stubble. It itches like crazy, and I don't like the way my face feels when I don't shave. I hate it almost as much as I hate this hair. Black and straight and way too long. I want to drag a towel over my head and go. Not stand here staring at myself with a blow dryer. I hate blow dryers. I hate my face, my black, supposed bedroom eyes, my chiseled, dimpled chin and all. I hate the entire "Ellery, it's all about image. You're the whole package. You not only write it, you could be on the cover. We're going to give you a total Fabio makeover. You can carry it off, and the public will love it. Just… give it a try. Especially the hair. You'll learn to live with it. Trust me."

While I've been blowing, foaming, scraping, frowning, and frothing at the mouth, I've moved way past hungry and into frankly freaking starving. I hurl myself into my closet and throw on some clothes. Now I finally need to commit to where we're heading next.

Eat out or fetch provisions and cook in? Truth be told, I'm equally unthrilled with door number two. The grocery store option. Especially after the last encounter I had at the deli counter. Not something I'm anxious to risk repeating. Certainly not on an empty stomach.

Grocery shopping could prove to be an equally unpleasant alternative to daring Dinah's, depending on who's hanging around whom while they're prowling the produce aisles hunter-gathering, completely oblivious to the fact they're being relentlessly stalked by their recently dearly departed.

Lucky bastards.

So, what's it going to be, the deli or Dinah's? Either way, I really need to go out. I checked out the obits in the paper this morning. It's been pretty slow on the death front recently, so maybe I can get to wherever I decide to go and back again without encountering any spectral stalkers.

Oh, Ellery, just suck it up and go already!

I slip on my jacket and grab my cell and the manila envelope for my mailing service: a week's worth of wrapping up loose ends messages from the out-of-towners. I've lost track of how many of these post-mortem missives I've sent out over the years. Literally thousands of cards and letters along the lines of, "Hello, you don't know me and I prefer to keep it that way, but Fred wants you to look in the tool shed under the third brick from the bottom. I don't know what that means, but he says you will. Have a nice life and sorry for your loss, but if it's any consolation, he's looking well."

Or similar variations on the same basic theme. Beyond-the-grave instructions, blessings, and words of love, last good-byes from those taken before they could be spoken, pleas for the bereaved to let go and move on. So many things left undone, unsaid, postponed until a tomorrow these souls took for granted and never got to have. Most of these other-side supplicants were basically good people, their requests well meant and worth fulfilling, but as in life, so also in death, some, but not all. Occasionally I've run across some bad ones, twisted and bitter while they were alive, death evidently not evincing any improvement in their character. They come to me reeking with envy and resentment, still wanting to strike out and hurt the ones they've left behind. Those kinds of messages I don't pass on. Hey, I don't have to do this at all, and I certainly don't get a postage allowance for it!

I've often wondered what effect these little metaphysical missives have had on the recipients. I hope they've done something good for someone out there, but as I have no plans to do any follow-ups on this end, I guess I'll never know. Maybe it's just as well. I don't know anything about them or their lives, and they are equally unaware of me and mine. That's what works best for me, and that's the way I plan to keep it.

So far, so good. No one—that is, no one living—knows I can do this. Not that it's been easy to keep this so-called "gift" under the radar. Hey, you try to carry on a conversation with a real person while a dead one is attempting to flag you down. Eventually the haunts I encounter during the course of my daily existence work out badgering me non-stop is akin to flogging a dead horse. If you pardon the expression. I'll deal with their dead baggage for them, but I'll do it in my time and on my terms. If they don't bother me until I'm ready to deal with them, I tend to be much more co-operative.

As for the ones who come from all over the frigging world—and I haven't a clue how they find me—Mrs. Sheridan does an excellent job keeping them at bay. Nothing like having my own personal otherworldly secretary and spectral screener at my service twenty-four seven. Thanks to her, nobody and nothing bothers me when I'm at home. My personal living space is sacrosanct, my sole refuge from the otherwise constant bizarreness also known as my life. She keeps the magnificent and Max-maligned mansion-slash-mausoleum-slash-former-B&B I was bequeathed off limits and out of bounds to anything not breathing. They don't get to waft through my walls unless they've got an appointment. Seriously.

While this little arrangement, for which I'm quite grateful, gives me sanctuary from the psychic storm constantly swirling about everywhere else outside these ivy-covered walls, it also means I don't get out much. 'Cause as soon as I venture outside my—literal—comfort zone, I'm fair game.

Oh well, let the games begin.

CHAPTER 2

I ARRIVE at the top of the grand front staircase, taking a moment to admire the view down its sinuous, imposing length. With definite emphasis on the length. I love this gleaming oak behemoth. Who knows how many ancient acres of stately, now deceased oaks were deforested so I could one day enjoy such an elegant and stately way to convey myself from floor to floor.

I'm standing on a shitload of arboreal corpses.

You know what? I spend entirely too much time dialoging with the dead. It might be making me strange.

I'll leave off contemplating my eccentricities and go downstairs. If I start now I'll make it all the way to the foyer by lunchtime.

Yeah, this place is pretty ginormous, absurdly oversized for one person, but that's a large part of why I like it so much. There's just so much to do and see in here. Hours of entertainment walking from room to room. I fixed it up and modernized the plumbing and wiring, but I tried to keep the essential quirky character of the place intact. It came with a few original inhabitants and several residual imprints on the ether scattered here and there, but nothing I couldn't handle. Couple of crossovers and a thorough psychic house-cleaning later, and we're all good now.

But not entirely alone, or so it would seem. I wasn't here long when I discovered the house also had an additional, unadvertised extra. It came not only furnished, but with a resident domestic. At least, she used to live here. Mrs. Potts, bless her Alzheimer-ized old head. Thirty years she ran this place for the woman who last owned it. Until the disease reduced poor Mrs. P. to a vacuous but completely innocuous shell of herself.

And speaking of the last owner, when I took possession, I was really hoping Jemima Jones would still be here so I could ask her why she left The Boarding House to me. At least, that's what the sign I inherited along with the house proclaimed the former Birchwood Manor was redubbed when she put it into service as a bed and breakfast.

Perhaps it was the entertainment value inherent in the irony of that appellation. Given mine, that is. Joyce James? James Joyce? *The Boarding House?* I certainly got a hoot out of it. So much so, I repainted the sign and rehung it.

Hey, it makes me laugh. Not a lot does, these days.

And here comes Mrs. Potts now, teetering on shuffly little old lady feet across the expensive imported Italian tiles that comprise the stunning mosaics splayed out all over the foyer floor.

Sometimes she slips through the casual constraints of the old folks' home three streets over to somehow always make her way here. She's harmless, hardly ever breaks anything, and is occasionally lucid enough to bake the most amazing blueberry muffins you've ever tasted. I'll bet in her prime she was a culinary force truly to be reckoned with.

And here she is, once again, some part of the woman she was briefly resurrected and drawn here by no longer binding ties of responsibility and obligation. The disease retired her a decade ago, but she doesn't know that. She doesn't know much anymore, bless her, and yet her sparse remaining fragments periodically shine through the confusion obscuring what's left of her. Putting together what little remains leaves me with a tantalizing personality puzzle. I wish I'd known her when she was younger. But that will never happen. That woman is mostly dead and gone. Although the body is still very much living. It's sad to see what's left of her walking about like this, literally a living ghost.

I'd better let her keepers know she's slipped their surly bonds once more. They probably haven't even missed her yet.

I commence my descent and pull out my cell to make the call. I've got The Shady Rest Retirement Home on speed dial. They pick up on the first ring.

"Cal is on his way, Mr. James," Virginia's resigned voice informs me before I can get a word out.

Oh, so I was wrong. Someone's paying attention today. Excellent.

"Thanks, Virginia."

"At least we always know where to find her."

"Yeah, thank goodness for that."

Not the first time we've had this conversation.

I re-holster my cell and hit the main floor. Mrs. Potts seems oblivious to my presence and intent on plotting a course for the kitchen, although her trajectory could change at any moment. She could just as easily end up in Albuquerque as anywhere in my house. At first I think she's going to teeter on by without so much as a "Who the heck are you again?", but then her birdlike head floats around on her scrawny neck and she gives me a vague, inscrutable smile.

"Good morning, Khnumhotep," she quavers and nods knowingly.

She always calls me that. It's a no-brainer it's Egyptian, so I tried Googling it and actually got a hit. Apparently Khnumhotep was the name of one of the two male occupants of a tomb in Saqqara who may or may not have been Ancient Egypt's first gay couple on record. The archaeological jury is still out on their orientation. And they were manicurists. Some things never change. Anyway, that's the origin of the name, but why she insists on applying it to me—bit of a mystery. My background is strictly Anglo-Saxon, but I've had many other ethnic origins erroneously attributed to me because of my coloring. "Dusky" is a descriptor I've heard more than once. But being taken for a possibly gay ancient Egyptian hairdresser, or whatever, is one for the books. In an attempt to track down where this nickname—and Mrs. P.—is coming from, I've asked around, attempting to find out if either Mrs. Potts or Jemima Jones had any Egyptian inclinations, but that doesn't seem to be the case. Nothing in the remaining effects in the house would lead one to that conclusion, either. Maybe it's nothing more than her memory dredging up something randomly whimsical to label me with. The way her mind is now, it's really hard to say.

"I'm just on my way to feed the cat," she wispily warbles.

That's nice. Would be even better if I had one.

I'll leave her to it, then. Satisfying the nutritional requirements of nonexistent felines should keep her out of trouble until Cal comes to collect her. Me, I'm outta here to see to mine.

Breakfast, breakfast, must have some breakfast.

On the other side of my front door, I encounter yet another impediment to my intentions and progress. Bert, my UPS guy, arriving for the envelope I'm toting. Bert's a great guy, quite the character. A regular person, not like most of the lunatic residents of the asylum I recently escaped from. He loves to talk. Boy, does he love to talk.

Our paths don't often cross. Not that I wouldn't welcome the opportunity to spend more time in conversation. Chatting with Bert is actually a lot of fun. But I don't do it often. I keep to myself, mostly, when I'm in town. Normally, whenever he comes, I don't see him at all. On the mornings when he makes his scheduled pickup, I'm usually down here earlier. I leave the envelope in the box for him, he takes it and goes. But this morning the conversation with Max put me behind schedule.

This could be a problem. He looks way too pleased to see me. No way I'm gonna get away with a mere handoff. I see a lengthy conversational interlude in my immediate future.

"Morning, Mr. Jim." Bert blasts me with a grin. "A bit early for you big city types, isn't it? I thought you celebrities didn't get out of bed until noon."

Did I mention he really likes to talk? Ugh. My stomach is threatening to storm up my throat and take prisoners. But, what the hey, it's not gonna kill me to starve for a few minutes longer. Bert's a good guy. I'll play the game with him.

"Oh, you know us celebrities," I shrug. "Haven't even been to bed yet. All that partying, you know."

Bert's weatherbeaten face cracks even wider. We do this schtick almost every time we talk. My public profile is all a big joke to him and the rest of the town now, but when I first showed up here five years ago, the prevailing negative reaction to the James Invasion was no local laughing matter. Fairly harsh and hostile critics, these folks were. Until they got to know me.

We've all subsequently successfully weathered their initial

apprehension of and objection to my presence in their hallowed hamlet. When Birchwood first got wind the last surviving member of their founding family had left the mansion to some fancy-pants writer, there was much weeping and wailing and sharpening of pitchforks in the town hall. Apparently fears—and imaginations—were running high regarding my possible nefarious intentions for the ramshackle remnants of what had once been the grandest building in town. Their apprehensive speculations ran the gamut from drug lab to casino to playboy mansion and every imaginable variation of absurdity in between.

Time, patience, schmoozing, and throwing a lot of money into civic improvements and community services went a long way to winning the townsfolk over and putting the boots to both their fears and over-the-top imaginations. I just wish they hadn't insisted on putting my name all over half the buildings in town. A public humiliation I'm resigned to living with while being eternally grateful the Town Council agreed to confine themselves to those expressions of their gratitude in lieu of the statue thing. Mind you, if Art Baker reintroduces the statue proposal in one more Town Council meeting, I'm going to sneak over to his house in the middle of the night and spray-paint his porch Pepto pink.

Don't mess with me, I'm bad.

But not exactly a social butterfly. Monks do more entertaining than I do. And a sight more drinking. Bert knows damned well the closest I've come to partying in Birchwood in the last year was when I made a cameo appearance at the Founders' Day town fete six months ago.

Didn't stay long. Those riotous revels in the town square? Grandmas drinking Gatorade in public, dogs and cats dancing together. Mass hysteria.

Way too much excitement for me.

"Partying!" Bert guffaws. "Gotcha, Mr. Jim. Nice to see you back. Oh, by the way, the missus wanted me to ask you, next time I saw you. How's that Ellen keepin'?" He winks conspiratorially at me.

Don't remind me.

"Saw that one, huh?" I barely suppress a weary sigh and hand him my envelope.

"You know it." He smiles again, a huge, warm, gap-toothed grin. "The missus taped it for me. We're getting quite a collection, ya know."

Preserved for all posterity. Me doing the limbo on Ellen. Great.

"Matter of fact, we've taped every show you've ever been on. Every single danged one!" He puffs his chest out proudly. "Listen, if you ever want copies—"

"No!" I quickly raise a hand and cut him off. "Thanks, but it's… it's…."

I hate being a performing media seal, and I'd rather stand on my head and fart fish than see visual proof of some of my more absurd public antics. Bert doesn't know that. Why would he? Who wouldn't want to watch themselves on Ellen? Or Oprah, or The View, or… or….

God, man, stop before you scare yourself to death.

Gotta let him down nicely. He means no harm, and I take none.

"I… I'm hardly ever home. And when I am? Work, work, work." I force a smile that makes my face creak. "When would I watch them?"

I wonder how many years I'd get if I stole into their house in the dead of night and ignited their cinematic proof of my public ignominies.

Ah, they'll have to catch me first.

"Ya know, we still can't get over it, Betty and me, somebody as famous and high-faluting as yourself settling down in our pokey little town."

Oh, Bert, not so "faluting." And the fame thing? If I could do what I do without it, I'd do it. Without it.

That sentence made sense when I started. Definitely have to eat something.

"Don't sell your town short, Bert. It's got a lot of things going for it. Starting with the people who live here."

Great people. Best in the world.

His ruddy complexion flushes up a noticeable notch, and he oozes honest pleasure from every pore.

"That's a real nice thing to say, Mr. Jim." He beams at me, doffs his ball cap, and wipes it across his brow. "But then, you're a real nice man. What with takin' the time like you do to answer your fan mail." He taps my envelope nestled against his slightly damp armpit. "Real nice."

Fan mail? An honest enough assumption. If only he knew what that soggy manila envelope actually contains.

I wonder if he'd be so comfortable standing on my front porch and chatting with me if he knew what I can really do.

Accepting his praise dishonestly makes me uncomfortable, but it's not like I can tell him the truth. He doesn't know he's given me credit for something I haven't done, nor is he aware the good he meant me has had the opposite effect. Not his fault, and yet the unfortunately misdirected accolade is settling on me like a major emotional damper. I try to shake it off by turning things around.

"So are you, Bert," I tell him sincerely. "And by the way, it's James, not—last names aren't like first names; you can't use a—tell you what, why don't you call me Ellery."

"You got it, Mr. Jim." Bert reseats his hat on his head with an audible plop, rocking it back and forth on his cranium as if searching for some arcane, optimal resting position. After a couple of seconds he finds it, then sniffs and gravely gathers himself for the formal farewell.

"Well, can't stand here jawin' all day. That's not what they pay me for. Have a good one."

You too, Bert.

I walk him back to his truck and wave him on his way. Stand in my drive, watch the truck round the corner. Make it to the sidewalk, take a deep breath, look cautiously left and then right.

All clear. Not a spook in sight.

I love this town. Low population. No crime rate to speak of outside the occasional shoplifter or DUI. Very low profile on the specter density meter.

My idea of paradise.

If I were in a larger metropolitan city chock full of folks crowding each other in and killing each other off, I'd already be up to my armpits in dead people by now. Growing up in rural New England did not prepare me for the psychic tsunami awaiting me in every major city I've been forced to visit since this rollercoaster ride commenced. I was just about to go insane from the omnipresent otherworld and seriously needed to get away from it all when Jemima Jones's executor contacted me and informed me I was the sole beneficiary of her will. I now owned a big, old, run-down, honest-to-God mansion in a little town I'd never heard of. Exactly what the author ordered. I didn't understand it, but I didn't question it, and as soon as I stopped turning cartwheels of joy, I was on the next plane to Denver.

One SUV rental and a two-hour drive later, and I knew I'd found both an answer to my prayers and my heaven on Earth.

Five years later, my affection for this town and its denizens has not diminished. And while I've been on my nostalgic mental meander, my feet have found their way to the town center. The only other soul I encountered during the ten minutes it took me to get from where I was to where I am was quite corporeal. I will admit his resemblance to Peter Lorre made me do a double take, but I let it go. I've been on the receiving end of far too many "Hey, do you know you look exactly like" comments to inflict one on anyone else.

I've made it to the intersection across from our picturesque village square-cum-city park. The light's red, but this time of the morning there's no traffic to speak of, so call me crazy, but I'm going for it.

Two seconds after I step off the curb, my blissful reverie is interrupted by a painful reminder that this town most of America's forgot is not totally exempt from senseless, random tragedy. Paradise is only an illusion, after all, and the proof not even Birchwood is perfect stands invisible to all but me and weeping inconsolably on the other side of the street.

Dammit, I hate it when it's a child!

This is bad, this is really bad. I can't believe she's still here. It's my fault she's still here. Fine, maybe the accident happened while I was on tour, but I shouldn't have assumed she was safely gone, especially given the way she died. But oh, no, I was in such a damned, selfish hurry to get back to my hidey-hole I couldn't spare Becky five lousy minutes. All I had to do was swing by, take a look, make sure that poor little girl had made it to the other side okay.

Here, it was right here in this intersection is where it happened.

Look at her, over there, poor little lamb, crying and calling out. Her mommy, she's calling for her mommy.

Her mommy won't ever be coming for her.

Mommy buried her two months ago, after she was killed while running out into the street after her dog. She was mowed down by a big, big truck driven by an impatient out-of-towner in such a hurry to get back to the interstate he didn't see her or the puppy.

The dog made it across the street okay, but Becky....

Sweetheart, I'm really, really sorry.

She's still sobbing inconsolably and calling out for her mommy, trying to get someone's attention, but the sole passing soul she appeals to walks right by her like he doesn't see her.

Because he can't.

Hang on, honey, I see you. You're not all alone any more. It's going to be okay now.

A blaring horn and the deafening sound of a roaring diesel engine snap me back to the alarming awareness I've zoned out a couple of steps away from the curb. I'm planted in the intersection, staring at Becky, and the light is still red.

You know what? Unless I want to end up becoming similarly creamed, I'd better move.

Fast!

My heart hammering, I leap for my life, hurling myself frantically back onto the sidewalk as a huge, black pick-up plows through the intersection, slashing the spot I was occupying a split second ago. Too stunned by my narrow escape to do anything but sit on my ass and stupidly blink at the juggernaut roaring by me, I have a brief but surprisingly clear view of the occupants of the cab. During those few seconds, the image imprints itself on my shell-shocked consciousness.

The man with the leather jacket and Foster Grants in the driver's seat has close-cropped russet hair. Not quite buzz-cut short, but close. He's staring straight ahead, his starkly handsome profile so chiseled you could slice bread on the angles, jaw clenched so emphatically the sound of his teeth grinding together is probably registering on seismic detectors in the next state. Whoever this guy is, he's definitely more than the epitome of grim, and obviously not easily distracted from whatever dark thoughts he's obsessing over. He has to know he nearly smeared me all over the street with his big black monster of a truck, but he roars relentlessly on by without giving me either a glance or the finger.

The same cannot be said for his passenger. The redheaded girl riding shotgun beside him is plastered to the window, staring at me, her eyes wide with wonder. Our eyes lock, I have a scant second to process their amber depths, realize she's just figured out I can see her, and oh, God, I so don't believe this.

She's dead too.

Wow, this really is a red-letter morning. I've seen two ghosts, almost become one, and I still haven't had breakfast.

All in good time. I might have had the life scared out of me, but I'll live to screw up another day. I'm still here, and so is Dinah's. And it'll be there ten minutes from now. Postponing my breakfast a few minutes longer will not be the death of me. I know I keep saying that, but it's true.

We'll cross Becky over, then we'll think about noshing.

Becky stops crying, watching me hopefully while I cross the street on the next green, her huge, drowning eyes devouring me with every step I take toward her.

"M-mister?" she sniffs when I reach the opposite curb. "Can... can you help me find my mo-mommy?"

My heart cracks, and I have to blink fiercely to keep back a few tears of my own. Before I answer her, I take a quick look around. The early morning pedestrian traffic is starting to pick up; there are a couple of people heading toward us from both directions, not to mention two more on the other side of the street, waiting to cross. I can't talk to her here; I have to get her to come with me, somewhere more private further in, in the park.

"Mister," she quavers. "I know I'm not supposded-ed to talk to... to strangers but my mommy is lost-ed. I've been looking for her for a long, long time, and I can't find her. Can you help me?"

"It's okay, Becky," I quickly assure her. "Your mommy sent me to find you."

I'm sorry, I'm so sorry for the lie, it's cruel, but I've got no choice, and it'll be okay once I make her understand, but I can't do it here.

"She did?" Becky sniffs, her tiny, tear-stained face pathetic with hope. "Do you know where she is?"

"Don't be scared, honey. I'm going to help you. But I need you to come with me, now. Just come with me, and everything's going to be okay."

"Are you going to take me to my mommy?" she appeals to me, her lower lip quivering.

Dammit, busybodies at six o'clock, closing fast. Manny Parker and his wife Irene. If I let her latch on, I can wave bye-bye to at least thirty minutes of my life while she relentlessly pumps me for insider info about all the beautiful people I've recently been forced to rub elbows with.

You know what, Mrs. Parker? Not today. Pick a number and come back later. I'm booked.

I turn my back on the Parkers and focus on Becky. I have to think fast and move even faster. Not too proud of myself, lying to this child yet again, but she has to follow me. Now.

"Yes, honey, I know where your mommy is. Come with me now, okay?" I don't wait for her answer, striking out swiftly for the center of the park and my ultimate destination. I see her flickering faintly on the periphery of my vision and breathe a sigh of relief.

Got her. She believes me. She's coming.

"Oh, Mr. James!" Irene sings out behind me. "Mr. James, we didn't realize you were back in town! Yoo hoo, Ellery!"

"Dammit, Irene, leave the man alone. He gets enough of that crap in the big city," I hear Manny scold his wife. "Why do you think he decided to settle here if not to get away from people pestering him?"

Yeah, Manny, that too.

The sound of the bickering Parkers swiftly recedes behind me while I hustle through the park, making for one of my favorite spots. It's a very special place, an isolated bench tucked underneath one of the majestic oaks brooding over the perimeter of this placid swatch of green. I pass one occupied bench, then another—oh, that's odd, there he is again, the Peter Lorre wannabe.

Something not right about that. Seeing a stranger twice in one morning. Heck, in less than an hour, even. Come to think of it, there's something—odd—about him, too.

Get a grip, Ellery, this town is so small if you picked out a spot and parked it for an hour the entire population could troop by you, twice, no problem.

I've reached my bench, sheltered and secluded beneath the oldest oak in the park. Even better, it's blessedly vacant. Nice, quiet, concealed. I can help Becky now, with no interruptions.

The second after I plunk my ass down, she appears by my side. I'm looking into her sad, spectral face, mentally marshalling for what must come, but there's this noise on the edge of my consciousness, messing with my concentration. I can't seem to screen it out; it's like mental sandpaper rasping away at my awareness. Loud, obnoxious, alarmingly familiar, behind and off to the right, getting louder.

What the hell is that noise?

Oh, I know! Diesel engine!

A large, dark shape crawls past my peripheral vision. Like a big, black truck slowly circling the park.

Why am I paying attention to this? So it's a truck, so what? I gotta get back on task here. Becky needs me, and if that little lip starting to quiver once more is any indication, she's figuring out I've told her a white lie or two.

"Mister," the poor little ghost pleads. "Where's my mommy? You said you were taking me to my mommy."

"Yes, honey, I did." I swallow my own tears, lean forward, and put my heart into every word. "Believe me, if I could take you to your mommy, if I would."

Not going to do it, not going to tell this child another lie, not for anything.

She's quiet for a moment, processing. Calming down, though. Trusting me. Sensing I'm telling her the truth. Good. That's good.

"Mister...."

"My name's Ellery, sweetie."

"Ellery," she corrects herself and smiles shyly at me. "Do you know where my mommy is?"

"Your mommy is okay. She misses you, and she's sorry she left you behind, but she had no choice. I'm here, because she couldn't be, to tell you about a place where you need to go, now. It's a good place, a safe place, and she wants you to be a good girl and go there."

"Is that where my mommy is, Ellery?" she softly whispers.

"No, sweetheart," I tell her honestly, gulping and blinking. "She can't go there yet, but you know what? You can, and you have to be a big, brave girl and go to the nice place first. Your mommy will be along, to be there with you, as soon as she can, and while you're waiting for her, you'll meet a lot of nice people who'll look after you until she comes. She will come, as soon as she can. I promise, sweetie."

"Mommy wants me to go?" The big brown eyes examine my face, searching for truth, hope, and direction.

"Yes, she does, baby."

"And... and she's coming for me? Soon?"

"I promise you, you'll be together again before you know it."

"This nice place, are you taking me there, Ellery?"

"No, honey, I can't go there either. Not yet. Now, I want you to look for a really bright light. The brightest, bestest light you've ever seen."

"I see it!" she suddenly exclaims. "Ooooh, it's so pretty, Ellery, don't you see it?"

"No, honey, I don't. But you see it, and that's good. Now, I want you to go into it. Just walk straight on through the light, and the nice place is on the other side."

"Ellery, there's a pretty lady in the light!" Becky excitedly points.

Thank God, I was hoping there was going to be someone waiting for her. I shouldn't have any trouble getting her to cross over now.

"She says she's my grandma. My mommy told me my grandma went away to live with the angels a long time ago, before I was bornded. Is this where she went?"

Okay, here we go. I was hoping she would just cross over, and then she'd be safe and where she belongs before she had to deal with the whole death thing.

Please don't let this scare her.

"Yes, Becky, that's where she went. And now she's come back for you, to look after you, while you wait for your mommy."

"If I go there, will I see angels too?" she quietly asks me, her sweet face sad and serious, understanding gathering in her trusting eyes.

"Yes, baby." I nod, barely able to get the words out. "Lots and lots of angels."

"I'm going to heaven, aren't I?" Her voice is so soft and brave. "My mommy and daddy can't see me anymore, all those people walking by me on the street, they couldn't see me because something bad happened and I'm not... I'm...."

It's too big a word for someone so young and small. But she knows; she understands what's happened to her.

I think she's gonna be okay.

"Please, Becky," I plead with her, my voice breaking. "You have to go now."

"Okay," Becky looks at me wistfully, her eyes full of wondrous new wisdom. "That's what my grandma says too. I'll go with her. You're a nice man, Ellery. Thank you for helping me."

"You're welcome, sweetie." I can hardly see her through the curtain of tears.

"Tell my mommy and daddy." Her voice is already starting to fade. "I love them."

I will, Becky. I promise.

"I love you too, Ellery."

And with a soft sigh and a shivering whisper of an otherworldly breeze rustling the leaves overhead, she's gone.

You know, sometimes this thing I have, it's not so bad.

I wipe my eyes and blink hard to clear my vision. Several hundred yards away, the Emerson sisters are walking past me on their way to the library. Cecilia gives me a snooty stare and then turns away, whispering to her sister.

Yeah, it's wacky Mister James, the eccentric writer, spooking the squirrels again. Nothing to see here, ladies; keep on moving.

I have to devote a few more seconds to putting myself back together before I can even think of getting off this bench. Wipe my eyes again, blow my nose, breathe, breathe some more, ooh, listen to that, stomach rumbling loud enough for them to hear clear across town.

Okey doke, I'm good. Dinah's, here we finally come.

I push myself to my feet and prepare to make the trek back across the park to my ultimate destination. Call me crazy, but I can't help briefly scanning the street behind me.

There's no sign of a big, black truck, but then, I didn't think there would be. Whatever I thought I saw before was undoubtedly a figment of my famished imagination. Mr. Speedy Grim-soles, whoever he is, he's probably long gone down the interstate, on his way to wherever at about a hundred and fifty miles an hour. Hopefully not racking up any fatalities on the way.

Taking his young, unsuspected passenger with him.

Fine by me. I've done my good deed for the day.

CHAPTER 3

MY MOUTH to the gods' ears, as the saying goes.

Oh man, I was afraid of this. I was hoping, so hoping when I didn't see Martin haunting his funeral, that he'd already crossed over, but oh no, no such luck. Ta-dah, behold, the previously departed former owner of Dinah's, recently deceased after succumbing to a myocardial infarction, but now he's back, large as life, if you'll pardon the expression. His wife Molly's normally sparkling blue eyes are dulled with grief while she listlessly pushes a damp hank of checkered terrycloth in vague circles across the black Formica surface of the lunch counter, utterly oblivious to the frantic gesticulations of her former spouse. He's right by her side, putting on a floorshow no one but me can see, so desperate to get her attention he's all but stripping off and prancing naked on the lunch counter.

And I thank whoever happens to be listening I've been spared that spectacle at least. However, as long as I've got your attention, is it too much to ask to be allowed to have a little breakfast before I have to deal with another one who's missed the regularly scheduled pick-up?

I can't not speak to Molly, but I'm definitely sticking with pretending I don't see Martin. What the hey; it's worth a shot. Just because it's never worked before, well, there's always a first time.

Keep telling yourself that, Ellery. You're good at denial.

"Ellery!" The hollow tinkling of the door chime draws Molly's attention, and the instant she sees me, her mournful face morphs into something a lot happier-looking. "Oh, Ellery, we've missed you. Thanks goodness you're back!"

I'm buffeted by the naked affection in her gaze. She means it. She missed me. I mean—really—missed me.

Me?

I really don't know what to do with that.

Martin, on the other hand, has eyes only for his wife. He's unremitting in his efforts to attract her attention. Maybe I can use that. To keep from blowing my cover, I mean. If he stays focused on her, I might slip by him and actually get something to eat without any further interruptions.

Here's hoping.

"Hey, Molly." Look at Molly, only at Molly, pay no attention to the dead man in front of her bobbing, waving, and grimacing. "How are you doing?"

Here's a thought. Giggling at the faces the ghost is making might not be a good idea.

"Molly, honey, please look in my desk," Martin despairingly begs his wife.

He doesn't pay me any mind. Why should he? As far as he knows, I'm just another dumb living stiff who can't see or hear him. An impression I don't have any intention of disabusing him of, at least not until I've had my breakfast!

"Please, honey, you don't have anything to worry about," Martin moans. "Look in my desk, the bottom left hand drawer. The papers are all there."

Of course they are. Dammit. Okay, this is awkward. And giving me ideas I have no business entertaining in this context. Especially if I don't plan on outing myself to either the living or the dead.

Yet I can't help thinking about it. Martin's office is only a few feet away. Just before the kitchen, in the back, on the way to the bathroom. There are no customers in the diner, Molly's alone out here, so I'm guessing Norma and the others are in the kitchen. So close. I could do it. I'd have to be really quick, but I could pull it off. I could pretend I was going to the can, and then pop in there while no is looking, grab it out of the desk and….

And then what? Drop it on the floor somewhere and pretend I found it? That wouldn't work! Slip it in the pocket of Molly's sweater?

Mail it to her anonymously? Wouldn't be the first time I've done that. But I could get caught—either in the office, coming out, or—or something. Then how would I explain how I knew about it and didn't tell anyone?

It's too risky. I can't take the chance. No way I'm doing or saying anything that might bring any of this home to my doorstep. It hurts to see Molly tied up in knots with worries she doesn't know she doesn't have, but I'm gonna have to live with it. Unfortunately, so is she, for a little while longer. Fretting a few extra days won't hurt her.

Keep telling yourself that, pal.

It'll be fine, and so will she. As soon as I have my breakfast, I'll go right back home and take care of it. I'll dash off one of my standard anonymous letters to Molly with all the details. But I won't make her wait a whole 'nother week and then some for Bert's regular run to the re-mailing service. I'll take it in to Denver myself this afternoon and mail it there. That much I can do for her.

It's gonna be okay, Molly. I promise. Lest we forget Martin; I haven't. I'll find some way to talk to him alone, or—no, no wait. I know. I'll ask Mrs. Sheridan to tell him for me. That'll work. She can pass the message on that he needn't worry; Molly will be getting a letter telling her about the policy. Knowing Martin, he probably won't take her word for it; he'll likely hang around until he sees Molly with the policy in her hands, but then he'll go. It'll be good. It'll work out just fine for both of them.

Me too, because there'll be no way to connect me with any of it.

Sounds like a plan.

"Oh, Ellery, it's hard, so hard." Molly lopes around the counter, heading straight for me, Martin hard on her heels. She slams into my chest, craving comfort like an addict. I hold her, feeling awkward and awful, her distress hitting me like a fist to the heart. "I miss him so much. I can't believe he's gone. I can't thank you enough for everything you've done. I have no idea where we'd be if you hadn't helped with the funeral expenses, but everything we had, we put in this place, and we still owe so much money."

"It's okay, Molly," I hug her tightly and try not to see the envious hunger in her husband's eyes. It's killing him to watch another man do his job. "Martin was a good man. You're both my friends. If there's anything else I can do, anything at all, don't hesitate to ask."

Money, sympathy, a shoulder, big box of Kleenex, whatever you need. Oh, wait, maybe not. The thing that would mean the most to you right now and do you the most good? Can't help you there.

Martin hovers anxiously at my right elbow, agony bleeding off him in waves while he watches Molly start to sob into my chest.

"This wasn't supposed to happen; we were supposed to grow old together," Molly wails. "He had no insurance; we've got no savings."

"No, baby, no!" Martin yells ineffectually into her ear. "I would never do that to you. Never! I'm covered; I have a huge policy! You wouldn't talk about it with me, but it's my job to take care of you, no matter what. I promised you, you'd never have to worry about nuthin'. So I went ahead and got the policy on my own. I was gonna tell you about it, but I never got around to it. But I got it, baby. I keep my promises. It's in my desk. Bottom drawer, left hand side."

I really wish he hadn't said all that. Even better, I wish I hadn't heard any of it.

I don't hate my life but, God, sometimes, I swear it hates me.

This is breaking all the rules. I learned a hard and painful lesson a long time ago: never, never, ever pass messages on in person. That resolve has kept me safe—and kept my secret for over twenty years. But dammit, this isn't some anonymous stranger I know nothing about, will never meet, and whose suffering is abstract and will never impact on my reality. It's Molly. She's in real pain I can see and feel, and you know what? I'm a selfish jerk. The hell with the self-imposed safety protocols. I can't stand to see either of them like this, especially when I can make it stop by simply opening my mouth.

And improvising as if my life depended on it. Ha, ha.

"Listen, Molly, Martin once said something to me about life insurance. He was thinking about getting some. Maybe he did and didn't tell you. You know how he was. Have you looked in his desk? I'm thinking if he did go through with it and got a policy you obviously don't know about, that's where it would be."

Martin stops yelling at Molly and stares at me suspiciously.

"Ellery, can you hear me?" he barks at me.

I give him a little nod. His astonished eyes expand to twice their size, and he immediately abandons Molly to round on me.

Oh, goody.

"No," Molly sniffs. "No. I haven't. I… I know he's gone and it sounds silly, I know, but he was so territorial about that office and the desk. I haven't had the nerve to go in there. Don't laugh at me," she begs, her lower lip quivering.

Never, dear.

"Tell her!" Martin vehemently instructs, so in my face if he were breathing, he'd be steaming up my glasses. That is, if I still wore any. Lasik surgery is your friend. "Tell her she's got to look in the bottom drawer!"

"I think you should. I think you should look in the desk, particularly in the bottom drawer on the left hand side. I really do."

"What?" She looks up at me, her face tear-stained and confused.

"Trust me, Molly." I smile at her and wipe a tear from her cheek. "Just go and do it now. I'm sure Martin wouldn't mind. What have you got to lose?"

"If you say so." She shrugs and smiles tremulously.

"I do. Now go."

I open my arms, release her, and off she scampers, making tracks for Martin's private sanctum. Martin throws me a crooked grin of thanks and wafts off after his wife.

Me, I'm off too, bound for my customary booth by the windows in the back corner of the restaurant, where the morning sun is particularly pleasant at this time of year. I sit myself down in the radiant golden pool bathing the booth and wait for Molly to finish shaking down Martin's desk, sincerely hoping my immediate future involves a nice pot of tea and a heaping plate of Eggs Benedict.

Please, please, feed me! God knows I've earned it!

"Oh! Oh! Oh!" Molly screams from the office. "Bless you, Martin, bless you!"

I'm guessing she found it. Better brace myself.

Molly erupts from the back room, bounding happily toward me, a packet of folded papers—probably the coveted policy—tightly clasped in her fist. Martin materializes beside his wife, beaming from ear to proverbial ear while Molly bounces ecstatically in front of my booth.

"Oh, Ellery, oh, Ellery, thank you!" she bubbles, gulps, and burbles, joyful tears streaming down her cheeks. "How did you... how did you know?"

A little birdie told me. Goes by the name of Martin.

"Lucky guess." I shrug. "Does it really matter? What's important, Martin's looked after you. You're gonna be okay now, right?"

She nods vigorously and bites her lip. "How can I ever thank you?"

Hmmm, I dunno, that's a tough one. Let me think about this for a moment.

"I could really go for a pot of tea right now. Not to mention a nice order of Eggs Benedict. Hash browns extra crispy?" I finish hopefully.

"Oh, oh," she blurts, then claps her hand to her mouth and starts to sob. It may be a few more minutes for that order.

I get to my feet, pull her in for another hug, and let her cry it out. She'll be okay in a minute or two. Then I'll get what's coming to me.

I peer over the top of Molly's head and see Martin standing patiently beside us, waiting until he has my attention.

"Thank you, Ellery," he says to me, his eyes resting longingly on Molly. "Please tell her I love her."

I nod. I will. Don't know how quite yet, but I will.

"I have to go now."

I know. Safe journey.

One instant he's standing there, grateful tears gleaming in his eyes and then....

He's gone.

Godspeed, my friend.

Two down, hopefully none more to go.

At least not 'til after breakfast.

MMMMMM, so, so good! It's about time, but more than worth the wait! Gonna savor every single scrumptious morsel.

"Coffee."

The curt sound of a deep male voice startles me out of my ecstatic absorption with my breakfast. I thought I had the place to myself!

My sanctuary has been invaded. How did this happen? I swear I didn't hear anyone else come in. Oh, wait, wasn't exactly focusing on the front door chime during the Martin and Molly floorshow. This guy must have slipped by me while all that was going down.

Odd. Not exactly sure why I'm getting all weirded out by the idea of someone being in the restaurant at the same time as me. It's a public place; people have a perfect right to come in here and be here, and I knew that coming in. Never been a problem for me before.

Yet there's something.

You know what? I don't care. Man eating, here. Finally.

I ingest another forkful, chewing appreciatively, look up, and get my first eyeful of the interloper.

He's sitting with his back to me at the front lunch counter. Close-cropped auburn hair, leather jacket and jeans. Really expensive leather jacket straining across a set of well-muscled shoulders Atlas would envy. Very impressive. Hmmm. Who the heck is he? I'd remember shoulders like that, and no way that jacket came from Dexter's Big and Tall. And directly under it—wow—that's one nice ass. Not one I'd have forgotten any time soon. Not that I spend all that much time looking. But even so, unfortunately necessary celibacy resolutions aside, there are times when you can't help... seeing.

Like right now.

Definitely a memorable gluteus maximus.

Anyway, whoever this guy is, I'm positive he and his ass are not from around here. And yet, the more I study that broad-shouldered back, in addition to feeling suddenly lightheaded, I'm getting this creepy-crawly déjà vu feeling niggling in the back of my brain. I know there's no way I could possibly know him, and yet, I have seen him before. That makes no sense, I know, but there it is.

Oh, wait. No way.

No, it couldn't be, couldn't be him. Not Captain Grim and Run.

A quick glance over my right shoulder out at the parking lot and whoops, whaddya know, there it is, a big, black truck. Arizona plates. Whoever this guy is, he's a long way from home. But never mind that now. Last time this guy flashed by me, he wasn't alone. Where's his diminutive deceased stowaway?

"Hey, mister. You can see me, can't you?" A little dead girl with a shiny chestnut bob and wide amber eyes is suddenly sitting across the table from me.

Nooooo!

"Hi! My name's Carly, what's yours?"

Sighing, I put down my fork, fish my cell phone out of my jacket pocket, flip it open and dial my home number. No, I'm not calling myself to have a genuine heart-to-heart with my machine; even I'm not that pathetic. At least not yet. However, I don't know a better way not to look like a crazy person having a conversation with someone no one else can see than by pretending to use a cell phone. To ensure the pretence holds up, I usually pull an E.T.

Sadly, Max aside, I'm pretty much the only one who phones my home.

"Hi, Carly, pleased to meet you," I say into the phone while looking at the girl. "I'm Ellery."

She looks about ten years old. No more than that. Maybe a little younger, but no, I'm thinking ten. Her almost boyishly short hair is the same color as her dad's, her sparkling eyes like clear amber. She has a smattering of freckles across her miniature up-turned nose and the most endearing gap-tooth grin. A red striped T-shirt and a Yankees ball cap complete as much of her ensemble as I can see, more than enough to get that this young lady probably was happiest up a tree, knee-deep in dirt, or hanging out with her dad.

Nice-looking kid. I wonder what happened to her. There's no way to tell from the way she's currently presenting. She looks like a perfectly normal child, except for the being dead part. That could mean a lot of things: she didn't die in a messy or disfiguring way or, if she did, is choosing to manifest in a pre-mortem aspect, she doesn't remember how she died, or she doesn't know she's dead. But the fact she's aware no one can see her but me would seem to rule the last one out. As for the other possibilities, guess we'll have to find out.

"That's my dad over there." Carly points back to the man at the counter.

Kinda had a feeling.

"His name's Boone. Boone Dantrell." She smiles proudly at me.

Is it now? Whoa. There's so much testosterone potential packed into those syllables, any well-meaning parent who off-loaded a name like that onto their unsuspecting baby boy was unintentionally setting him on a predestined path to mega machismo.

Whatever this guy does for a living, betcha it involves guns. Yikes.

"I guess that would make you Carly Dantrell then, wouldn't it?"

My food is getting cold, my tea even colder, but I can't take my eyes off this pixie-faced charmer. She's not the first little dead girl I've ever seen in my life, not even the first one today, for God's sake, but even though I've barely met her, I'm thoroughly enchanted.

I want to know more about her and the angry man a few feet away from us.

Even if he does have a name so howlingly butch it's scaring the shit out of me.

"Please, Ellery, you have to help me talk to my dad." Carly's earnest plea cuts through the minutiae dancing in my head and hits me soul-center. "I'm really worried about him. Ever since I... I...."

She can't quite get it out. She knows what she is; I think she remembers how she got this way, but while knowing is one thing, actually admitting it? Entirely different story. I've been through this with hundreds, maybe thousands of dead people before her; I know what I'm talking about.

"I'm really worried about him. He's been going kinda sick and... bad... inside. Ever since I... um...."

Bless your heart, baby. Take your time. I'm not going anywhere.

"What do you want me to tell your dad, Carly?"

Her small, innocent face grows solemn. "That it wasn't his fault. What happened to me, I mean," she murmurs.

"And what was that?" I've got to take this really slow. The facts of death aren't exactly an easy thing to make anybody face. In my experience, while the moment of mortality epiphany can be extremely traumatic for anyone, it's especially so for children.

It's possible she's honestly blanked out the details of her demise. If that's the case, I might be able to talk her back to the moment of her death if necessary, but bottom line, whatever she knows, whatever she ultimately remembers, does she trust me enough to tell me?

I honestly don't know. Some people can never go there. That's why they get stuck here.

Not this little girl. Never going to happen.

"Ellery, my dad has a gun."

Um… what?

You know that cliché about blood running cold? Well, mine's near freezing.

I was just kidding about the gun thing before, but she's not, and I believe her. Knowing my mysterious stranger of the spectacular shoulders and equally impressive ass is also concealing a weapon is extremely alarming, but what's even scarier to contemplate; is he thinking of using it?

Shit, I don't want to sound like a gutless coward, which coincidentally is kinda the way I'm suddenly feeling, but I'm having an abrupt change of heart. In light of the additional information I have just received, I question the wisdom of continuing this conversation. It's not that I don't want to help this child. I'm all for sending her on her way. But engaging in any sort of interaction with a guy with a gun—possibly on him—in order to accomplish that?

Getting involved with the living is way outside my comfort zone. Especially live ones who might be just as inclined to shoot me as look at me. And can put their muzzle where my mouth is.

I might talk to ghosts on a daily basis, but I'm in no hurry to become one. And if that makes me a gutless wonder, bring it on.

"He feels really bad," Carly explains, innocently oblivious of my craven mental back-pedaling. "'Cause he wasn't there... when it happened."

Whatever "it" was.

"He blames himself," I prompt. "For ...?"

I'm presuming her death, but I still don't know for sure. But one thing I do. Boone Dantrell has guilt issues and a gun, and his daughter wants me get into it with him—for her.

Let me think this over. Ghost, guilt, gun. Not a great combination. Man with guilt can use gun to make a ghost of messenger. Like that even less.

I stare silently at her, my brain still furiously ticking over all the pros and cons of spending one more second in this booth. As freaked as I am by the prospect of an armed response from her father to any input from me, I can't help feeling sorry for the guy. Boone Dantrell, I don't know you and probably never will, but you have my deepest sympathies. I've never been a father, but I know what it is to lose someone who's your whole world.

Two someones, actually. Funny, I was only a little younger than Carly is—was—when it happened.

Some wounds never heal; they just get easier to live with.

"My dad blames himself for what happened to me," Carly murmurs, lowering her eyes. "To make me like this."

So she does know. That answers that.

I want her to elaborate, but she's keeping her head down, not making eye contact. Whether that means she's not ready to share or not ready to say, I don't know.

"Like what?" I ask her quietly.

"Dead." She lifts her head and bravely blinks at me. "My dad says it's his fault, but he wasn't even there when it happened. My mom tried to talk to him about it, but he wouldn't listen. He would just sit in his truck in the garage with my catcher's mitt and his gun and stare at them. Then my mom got real sad and went away. I don't think she's coming back," Carly finishes in a small, sad voice.

Unfortunately, she's probably right, and it's too bad. Sorry to hear that, honey, sorry for your dad, too. And your mom. I'll probably never meet her, but I wouldn't wish such a loss on anyone.

"Carly, do you have any brothers and sisters?"

"No." She shakes her head sorrowfully.

Their only child. Damn.

I don't know why, but suddenly I'm feeling anxious and antsy, like I'm being swarmed by a moldering horde of vengeful phantoms busting free from the deep sepulcher where they've been long and safely buried.

I'm talking to a dead girl mourned and missed by two parents who lost everything when they lost her. Once, I was a boy who watched his whole world vanish in a single, horrific instant when his parents were taken from him in an accident only he survived.

We were in the car, going home after spending a sunny Sunday at the beach. The wind was blowing Mom's hair in her face, and she was laughing. I remember the sound and how much I loved to hear it. I was laughing too. Then she wasn't laughing any more, she was screaming, and the car was spinning and whirling. There was this weird, bright light in my eyes and a strange, roaring, growling sound, and then I couldn't hear or see anything. When I woke up later, I was alone in this big white bed in a scary white room. I called for my mom and dad, but the doctors, the nurses, the big guy with the long face from Child Services said they were dead. They said my parents were gone, they were dead, and I would never see them again, but… but….

No, no, there was nothing else, they were dead. They died in that car. Anything else, the other thing, only a dream, just a dream, a stupid dream, years ago, long gone, over and done, nothing more to it, nothing to remember.

"Will you help me, Ellery?" Carly leans imploringly across the table. "Will you talk to my dad, for me, tell him I'm okay and he doesn't have to be sad anymore?"

"Sure, sure, I'll… I'll…."

I don't know why I said that. I feel for the kid, but I can't do it, can't break the rule ever again, not even for her. I have no intention of going anywhere near Boone Dantrell, never mind attempting to pass on a message from his dead daughter. I don't know why, but this conversation is making me uncomfortable. I want to stop talking to her now. Don't want to be here. I can't... I can't even think about this anymore. Thinking about her—and him—dead children, dead parents, feelings so raw and vivid, grief, cutting so deep, hacking fresh hunks out of my soul like it's happening all over again.

Something inside, rising, swelling, battering at the backdoor of my consciousness for admittance, badgering me to remember.

I don't think so.

Nope. Can't, won't do this now, whatever hoary hunk of mnemonic sludge is attempting to escape the swamp of what's best left dead and forgotten, it can take a number and get back to me later.

"Thank you, Ellery." Carly grins. Before I have a chance to disabuse her of my impulsive and completely incomprehensible vow, she abruptly disappears.

Dammit!

"Carly!" I hiss, hoping she's still within, well, range. Dammit, I have to get the kid back so I can take it back! "Carly!" I give it another shot, louder this time.

I got nuthin'. Great, now what? You know damn well what, Ellery: you take five and write Boone a "Dear Dad" note from Carly. Then you pay the bill, you get the heck out of here, leave the note on the windshield of the truck, and run like hell for home. Then hope him seeing it does the job for both of them. That's all you can do, all you need to do. And once you're home, you're safe. Problem solved.

As long as you stay inside your bolthole for the rest of your life, you'll never be troubled by them again. You'll never have to worry about what happens next, never find out if Boone gets on with his life or if Carly's love keeps her tied to him and she fails to cross over, thereby joining the pathetic ranks of the lost and forgotten souls wandering the Earth. That's the ticket, son. Hole up in the Boarding House for the rest of your days and you'll never be bothered by what your decision to turn your back and keep yourself safe does to this girl and her father today.

It's not fair. Why is it always me who has to make things right for all these people? I didn't ask for this. I didn't ask for any of this. I only wanted breakfast.

I'm seriously contemplating vigorously applying the front of my forehead to the cheap veneered surface of this table—repeatedly—when the back of my neck starts to prickle with that creepy crawly feeling I get, and believe me, I get it a lot when someone or something is watching me. It's happening now, big time, eyes, eyes are on me.

I glance over toward the lunch counter and see Boone still sitting on the bar stool, but now he's turned around, sipping his coffee, watching me.

What the hell? Why is he doing that?

I've still got the damned cell in my hand!

Cold, his eyes are so cold, echoing sinkholes of unending pain. The eyes of a man on death row, marking time until the bitter end, self-condemned, his own judge, jury.

And executioner?

Oh, my God, Carly, please, please, please forgive me, but I'm sorry. I'm in way over my head. Sure, I've consoled tons of bereft people in my time, not like I've had a lot of choice, but I'm not even close to being a professional grief counselor, and besides, no one I've dealt with in the past has been as dangerous or as far gone as I'm thinking this guy is, and I'm reasonably certain none of them have been armed.

Check please!

Boone is still studying me like he plans to draw a picture of me later from memory. Okey doke, we've passed creeped out and are officially moving into shit-scared. I'm thinking I should actually use this cell phone for more than a convenient prop and give the sheriff a call, see how fast he can get over here.

Gun, the man has a gun. I wish I didn't know that almost as much as I wish I knew whether he was planning to use it.

Or not.

Boone drains his coffee cup, placing it firmly back on the counter beside him.

"I know you," he unexpectedly announces. "I knew I'd seen you before, but I couldn't place you 'til now. You're... you're that writer guy Eve's so nuts about. James." Boone Dantrell nods, thoughtfully stretches his long, denim-clad legs, and then slides off the stool. "Ellery James," he finishes with a frown. "I knew I knew you," he ominously concludes and starts toward me.

Okay, so he recognizes me. Like that's never happened before. There's a People magazine with my face on the cover on the news rack across the street in Drucker's. Stupid picture, even stupider article. Max made me do it, and one of these days, I'm gonna get her good for it.

The "Michael Crichton of Romance." What the hell is that supposed to mean?

And they're *not* romance novels!

Super, staring mystery solved, I can start breathing again. I'm freaking out for nothing, and this tall, grim vision in denim and leather hasn't been scarily surveying me because he's contemplating going postal and taking everyone in the diner, including me, with him. He doesn't want to shoot me, he wants my autograph. Oh. Vaguely disappointing in an I'm-not-exactly-sure-why kinda way, but way better than the shooting scenario I've been spooking myself with.

"I've had critics try to take me out in the press before," I quip, going for humor while this dead-faced, dead-eyed man approaches me. "But never with a truck."

There's a brief, faint spark in the lifeless depths of his scary, empty eyes, which are the most amazing shade of green I've ever seen. A scintilla of a sparkle, desperately fighting to ignite.

No, must have been imagining things, this man's emotional shop is not only closed, it's been demolished, asphalted over, and made into a parking lot. My half-assed joke would have gotten a bigger laugh from a slab of granite.

"Oh, that." He hefts one leather-clad shoulder like he's shrugging the incident off. "Didn't mean to scare the crap out of you on the street there, but I had the right of way."

"Indeed," I carefully reply. "I make it a point never to argue with a man with a two ton truck pointed at me."

Not to mention the gun. Complete with shoulder holster. I can see the faint outline under his jacket. I guess that answers the is-he-or-isn't-he-packing question. Who is this guy, what does he do that he needs to carry a gun, why has he come to my quiet little town, but most importantly of all, why has he come over to my table?

Well, I think I know why, but what I really want to know is:

Why me?

Chapter 4

BOONE DANTRELL looms over my booth, hands stuffed in the pockets of his to-die-for leather jacket.

"I'm Boone," he flatly announces without extending his right hand for me to shake. "Boone Dantrell."

"I—" I catch myself just before the "I know" slips my lip. Stupid, Ellery, really, really dumb! Way to almost freak the guy out letting on to info you shouldn't know!

"I'm Ellery. Ellery James." I immediately switch on my Pro-Am Book Signing Smile. "But you already knew that. So, do you want me to make this out to you, or…?" I reach for the nearby dispenser to get a napkin.

"What?" He stares blankly at me while I fish a pen out of my coat pocket. I always carry one. Occupational hazard.

Comprehension dawns when he sees me poised to write.

"No, no." He shakes his head and squares his shoulders, momentarily mesmerizing me with the motion. "No, that's fine; I don't want—one of those—that's not why I'm here."

He takes a small step back, like he's being pushed by a blow to the solar plexus, and for a slight, shimmering second, micro-fractures rupture in his formerly impenetrable façade, spewing screaming shards of vulnerability, loneliness, and unimaginable grief all over me.

Horrible, howling grief blankets him like a skin-tight shroud.

For as long as I can remember, I've seen dead people haunting the living, desperately coveting what they have and take for granted. The ability to live and breathe. It's not a pretty sight. Those poor, dead bastards would gladly sell the rest of their eternity for a single second of what they can see but no longer be a part of, but here's a reality wrinkle I never saw coming: the tragic flipside of the mortality coin.

How's this for irony?

I'm currently confronted with a guy on our side of the final divide I'm pretty sure would jump at the chance to trade places with any one of them. I was wrong about this man; he isn't dead inside at all, but he sure as hell wants to be. He'd sell his still-corporeal soul for the respite from the raging inferno of grief inside him even an instant of final oblivion would grant him.

So far, he's not having much luck.

He's still breathing, but he doesn't dare try to live.

God help me, I remember what that feels like.

Then, just as quickly as it slipped, Boone's shield slams shut.

"I'm sorry," I blurt. "I just assumed.... I mean, usually, when people walk up to me and tell me their name, it's because they want...." I shrug and tap the napkin with the pen. "Comes with the whole best-selling, semi-celebrity author package."

"Sounds rough." The corner of his mouth gives a slight, ironic twitch. "So how is Oprah these days?"

Still trying to get me to come on her show again. Once was enough, thanks.

"She's... ah—"

"Nah, I'll pass." His muttered comment cuts me off. Good thing, because I had no idea how I was going to finish that sentence. His gaze slides off to the side; he clears his throat and ups the volume. "My ex-wife's the fan. She's got every book you've ever written. Haven't read 'em myself, but I've seen your face around my house so often I feel like I've known you forever."

I don't know what my face is saying now, but I'm definitely OMG-ing on the inside.

"Your face. On the dust jacket. Of the books. Your books," he blurts. "My wife would leave them all over the house, and I was always picking them up and...."

Looking at you.

He doesn't actually say it, but I see it in his eyes.

Interesting.

"That's what I meant. Nothing weird or anything like that," he concludes his explanation with a weak smile.

"Thanks for clearing that up." I manage a wan reciprocating grin.

Okay, so, not an autograph then. So what does he want?

Me?

Whoa, now I really am seeing things. The air around Boone is sparkling, forming a shimmering corona around his head and shoulders like they're draped with a fine mesh studded with diamonds.

Oh, no. Tell me I did not see what I just saw!

I think I know where Carly went.

"Mind if I sit?" Boone inclines his head towards the empty side of booth.

As a matter of fact, I do, now I know what a certain little ghost is up to. I know what she wants, but you know what? I want no part of it.

She's asking too much, it's too close to home; this man is too steeped in grief. The nearer he gets, the harder it is to stop feeling it pounding a sympathetic symphony inside me I need to call on account of pain. I don't want to get involved, don't want to feel this again, but most of all, I don't want to remember.

"Seat's not taken," I hear myself say.

Boone glances uneasily back towards the door of the diner, looks down at his shoes, shifts back on his heels like he's making up his mind, then sighs and slides, easing his long, lanky frame into the booth and along the opposing banquette.

I have no idea why I invited him to sit down, and now he has, now he's actually across from me, I know real terror. Apparently I'm not the only one. Those penetrating malachite eyes fix squarely on my face, widening slightly with uncertainty. It's a subtle signal, but enough tell me he hasn't got a clue why he's sitting in my booth.

If I didn't think there was a real possibility he'd blow out my brains for trying, I'd throw him one.

Boone, my friend—and I use the term in the figurative sense only—relax. You're not losing your mind, you're just, well, you're not quite in the driver's seat right now. There's a pint-sized phantom puppeteer pulling your strings.

Very good she is at it too, apparently.

I've only encountered this once or twice before. Pretty darned impressed to be seeing it now. It goes like this. Despite what you see in the movies, it's very seldom the dead can directly influence the living. Your average just-passed-over soul, no matter how desperately they want to get their message across, doesn't have the energy to do much more than ineffectually waft around and yell at people. One of the main reasons someone like me, who can see and hear them and thereby be entreated to become their flesh and blood proxy for their post-mortem purposes, becomes a Mecca for the dead. Whether we want to or not. Believe me, once the word gets out a live one is online, the needy dead come a-runnin', and, well, it takes some getting used to. Not everyone can. Lucky for me, I had help. If Mrs. Sheridan hadn't taken me under her wing, I'm not sure how I would have turned out. Or ended up. Not at all convinced I'd have made it this far without going insane or doing myself in.

Not so far out there, believe me.

But back to the dead and why they can't push the living around; near as I've been able to figure out, it's because we're not supposed to stay here, on the level of the living, once we snuff it. Hanging with us breathers isn't good for those newly passed into spirit; there's very little to sustain a ghost on this plane energy-wise, and sooner or later, believe it or not, if it stays here much past its departure-by date, it gets hungry. It's not long before it goes from wafting about watching and wishing it could interact with the living to actually needing to leach energy from its former loved ones in order to sustain itself. Which is when the haunting and the creaking and the scaring starts. All that spectral sound and fury is intended to manipulate the living into generating the emotional energy the hungry ghost feeds on. Usually negative energy, like fear and hate and anger, very potent stuff, tasty in the short term and easy to get the living to exude but, like the dark side of the Force, not good for anybody.

Once they start down this path, the dearly departed get even more lost, growing fainter and farther from what they used to be and where they need to go. They become increasingly warped and frustrated by all the reminders of living they can see but can no longer be a part of and maintain their twisted, twilight existence by feeding on the emotions and energy of anything living in their area of influence.

After a few decades stuck in one place mainlining every scrap of psychic scrud it can wring out of its victims, you have one really nasty piece of work indeed.

So really, having your dead Aunt Bessie haunting you, not a good thing for either one of you.

Happily, though, because most people who die really do get to where they need to go, the percentage of those who hang around and go bad is extremely small. Although I have, on occasion, crossed over the odd hard-core haunt, mostly I encounter short-timers who only need a little help letting go. I do what I can for them. We make it work.

Carly qualifies as a short-timer, as long as she doesn't stay too much longer, but apparently she also belongs to a very select sub-set who *can* affect the living. In my experience, altruism and innocence can sometimes give spirits a very special power to do what Carly is doing to her dad. It's like the universe has a loophole for the pure of heart.

Carly has to have both of those qualities working in spades for her, because I've never seen a spirit overshadowing a living entity as successfully as she's working her dad. Not possess. Not control. Think of it like extremely effective subliminal suggestion.

Really, really effective. Unfortunately.

I blink and there she is, parked on the bench beside her father. I'm very glad to see her on the outside of her father, as opposed to the inside.

I can't believe I just said that.

"I got him to come to you, Ellery," she proudly announces.

I know you did, you sneaky little spirit, you. I can't thank you enough. Now you're no longer pushing him to be where neither of us want him to be, here's hoping he'll make tracks for his truck and get the hell out of my town.

God.

"Talk to him, tell him you can see me!" Carly frowns at me.

Oh, I don't think so!

Boone is still sizing me up like he thinks him being here is somehow my fault. Hey, don't look at me; I didn't have anything to do with it. Wasn't even my idea; I was just sitting here, minding my own business, trying to have my breakfast.

Which, by now, is colder than a literary critic's heart.

Those of them who actually have one.

"You should eat up." Boone's eyes dart down to my much-awaited and barely tasted repast, now regrettably congealing on the plate. "It'll get cold."

"Too late," I toss back at him. "Listen, Boone, I don't want to be rude, or anything."

"Tell him!" Carly again. The pout is fierce, but it ain't working.

Not on your life. Or mine either.

Bad analogy.

"Ellery, can you give me the name of a good motel nearby?" Boone abruptly demands.

That much I can do.

"Morrison's Motor Inn. Only one between here and the interstate. Go west on Main Street, keep going. It's about a mile out of town, you can't miss it."

"No, Ellery!" Carly's expression is stricken. "Don't tell him to go there; that's where he's going to do it. The bad thing. I know it is!"

Oh, no. Man with gun plus bad thing equals bad news for all concerned. Mr. and Mrs. Morrison are good people. Sending this guy over there to blow his brains out all over one of their nice little rooms?

Not exactly neighborly.

"If you don't mind the extra drive, there's a Holiday Inn about twenty miles further down the interstate," I helpfully add. "They've got satellite TV and a pool."

Although I'm thinking you're not planning on doing much swimming.

"Thanks," Boone awkwardly replies. "The place in town is fine. That's all I wanted to… I guess I'll be…."

"Please, Ellery, please!" Carly desperately pleads, her eyes welling with tears. "Help my dad!"

Okay, okay, I wasn't gonna let him go, not really—stop crying!

I hate this, I frigging, freaking *hate* this, and by the way, this is a big, big, huge mistake. I never get involved, never, never, ever. Broke that rule only once before, nearly ruined my whole life. Got a bad, bad feeling history is about to repeat itself. Thanks ever so much, Carly, for making me cross this line, and as for you, Boone frigging Dantrell….

Screw you too!

Here goes nuthin'.

"Boone, don't do it." I lock eyes with him and start to speak to him in a low, soothing voice. "Don't go over to that motel, check in, and then use the gun you've got under your jacket to blow your brains out. I don't want you to do it, the Morrisons wouldn't be too thrilled having to clean up after you, and Carly doesn't want you to do it either."

If I'd reached into his holster, pulled out his gun, and shot him between the eyes, he couldn't look more astonished. He slumps against the back of the booth, the air whooshing out of his lungs in a startled rush; his face white with shock, eyes blank and staring.

That went well. So far I'm still alive.

Okay!

I've barely concluded my mental pat on the back when the petrified man across the table revives with a vengeance. The blood rushes back into his face like a roaring red tide of unreasoning fury. His eyes smoke and spark with dangerous rage, and before I can blink, he swarms across the table like an avenging juggernaut intent on coming right through me. After viciously fisting the front of my shirt and rising rapidly out of his seat to meet me, he yanks hard, pulling me up and out from behind the table, then halfway across it. Plates, mugs, utensils fly and globs of late, lamented Benedict squish beneath me and squirt all over the booth, but I don't have time to worry about any of that, no, not me, I've got bigger problems. I'm nose to nose with a homicidal maniac, and I'm thinking I've got about ten seconds to live.

Yep, there's definitely a reason I don't do this in person.

"What kind of sick bastard are you anyway?" Boone spits into my face. "Who the hell are you and what the fuck do you know about Carly? I oughta beat the crap out of you, you sick, sick fuck!"

No good deed goes unpunished. Gotta keep reminding myself of that one.

"Dad!" Carly wails. "Please don't hurt him! Ellery's our friend; he's trying to help us! Dad! Please, listen to him!"

Thanks for that, kid. Really. Nice try. You get "A" for effort. Would probably work better if he could hear you.

"What's going on out here? What's with all the racket?"

Norma! That's Norma in the kitchen! Norma, hey! Over here! Call the cops, call the fire department, call me a cab!

Help!

"Hey, shit-head!" she roars. "What are you doing to Ellery?"

Next thing I know, two hundred pounds of incensed, grease-covered womanhood brandishing a Louisville Slugger is barreling down the length of the restaurant, rapidly galloping to my much-appreciated aid.

"Let go of him, you bastard, or I'll knock your block off!" she hollers at Boone while chugging toward us like a short-order cyclone. I've never seen anything so beautiful in my life. I just might marry that woman. That is, if Hank doesn't mind sharing.

"Ernie, call the sheriff!" she bellows back toward the kitchen. "Mister, you better let go of him now, or I swear to God I'm gonna start swinging!"

Boone growls in frustration and flings me back into my seat. While I bounce off the back of my bench, he leaps over his and onto the table of the booth behind us. The second he hits the ground, he ducks to narrowly avoid Norma's roundhouse swing, then nimbly skirts her and starts backing down the aisle, hands held in the air.

"Okay, okay, no need for violence, you can put that away. I'm going," he tells her in an easy, engaging voice, flashing her a warm, roguish smile so utterly unexpected and so… so….

Oh, my God, he's gorgeous!

"That's right pal, you are," she snaps at Boone, brandishing the bat for emphasis, her enormously fleshed frame positioned strategically between us. Obviously this is a woman completely impervious to the effects of the charm card being blatantly waved at her.

I wish I could say the same. Whoa.

"And you keep on going 'til you hit the interstate, you hear? We don't need out-of-town trash like you in here. I ever see you in my place again it'll be the biggest mistake you ever make!"

The engaging grin vanishes, and Boone's face contorts as if someone's just driven a splinter into his heart.

"Too late," he grates. He retreats backwards for several more steps, snapping his head my way. After burning me with one final scathing stare he whirls, and bolts from the restaurant. Norma thunders after him all the way to the door, her bat held at the ready. Behind me, I hear the din of the huge truck being kicked into aggressive life, the angry squeal of tires heralding its peel out of the parking lot.

And that, I sincerely hope, is the last I'll ever see of Boone Dantrell and his pesky dead daughter.

I slump with relief against the side of the booth, pretty much where I landed once Boone dropped me and I stopped bouncing. I'm shaken and way past rumpled, the front of my shirt an orange smear of a mashed-up amalgam of ketchup, eggs, hash browns, and hollandaise.

I'm quaking, sweating, and covered in goo, but damn, I'm alive!

Woo hoo, I'm alive!

"Hey, Ellery, you okay?" Molly comes hurtling out of the kitchen in response to Norma's bellows, her daughter Grace and Ernie the busboy hot on her heels.

"I got the shit-head's license number," Norma proudly announces from the front door. "You want me to phone George and have him pick him up, Ellery?"

"Aw, Ellery, look what he did to your shirt!" Molly exclaims. "That's never gonna come out. And he spoiled your breakfast! Norma, let's get this boy another plate. Ernie, clean up this mess. Come on, Ellery, honey, sit over here and we'll get you all fixed up."

I'm being swarmed and subjected to the most concerted fawning and fussing I've experienced in recent memory. I'm touched they're so concerned about me, but I wish they'd back off, let me breathe. I'm fine, really, no harm done. Had the crap scared out of me, sure, but he wouldn't have hurt me, not really, I don't... I don't think....

What am I saying? If Norma hadn't intervened.... He could have killed me!

Oh, my God, he had a gun, he had a gun, what if he'd—Norma coming at him with the bat, trying to protect me, she had no idea he had a gun.

What if he'd shot her?

Killed her?

I feel sick.

"Here you go, Ellery."

Grace plops a cup of coffee in front of me, and I latch onto it, wrapping grateful, albeit slightly shaking, hands around it, raise it to my lips, and take a brief, scalding sip.

You know, normally I can't stand this stuff, but right now it tastes like ambrosia.

"Just be a couple more minutes with your breakfast, Ellery," Norma sings out from the kitchen. "What do you say, you want me to sic the sheriff on the shit-head?"

No, definitely not. Good riddance to Boone Dantrell. With any luck, he's halfway to hell via the next hole-in-the-wall motel that'll suit his suicidal intentions. Go ahead, blow your damned head off.

Whatever. Not my problem anymore.

I raise my head from my coffee cup to see Molly seated across from me, her pretty face full of concern.

"Are you sure you're all right, Ellery? That guy didn't hurt you, did he?"

"No, no, it's okay, I'm fine," I reassure her, at the same time hoping she'll just leave and leave me alone. No more questions.

"What happened? Why did he come after you like that?"

"I… I don't know." I shrug and try to take refuge in my coffee. Say something, anything. Lie. "He asked for an autograph and then just went nuts."

"You think it was some kind of weirdo stalker thing?" Grace pipes up, her eyes dancing with excitement and curiosity.

Bless. Grace is Molly's youngest daughter, and she's all of nineteen. She's lived in this sleepy little town her entire life, and this is probably the most exciting event she's ever participated in.

I can't believe what I almost did to these people. They have no idea how close they came to dying today. I brought it here. My fault.

If anything had happened to Norma, or Grace, or any of these kind, lovely people, I'd never forgive myself. This thing I can do, I've cursed it, I've tried to deny it. Okay, it's true I've also used it to my advantage at times, but I've always been so careful never to let anything I see or do or know blight anyone else's life. Only mine.

Oh my God, what if I've been fooling myself all these years by thinking it was okay to live this way, even on the edges of other people's lives? Maybe I was wrong. Maybe I need to go even farther away, keep totally to myself, stay away from people altogether. It's the only way to be sure something like this never happens again. Only total detachment can guarantee these things I draw to me don't spill over onto anyone else.

"I don't know, I don't know what it was all about." I barely hear my reply to Grace. "Thanks for your concern, but it's over now. Let's just let him go and forget about the whole thing. No harm done."

"It's your call, Ellery, but you ask me, I think you should press charges," Norma humphs, sliding a steaming, overflowing plate of Eggs Benedict in front of me. "There ya go, pet," she purrs and then shoves into the booth beside Molly to watch me partake. "You eat up, now."

Whatever appetite I might have had has quite deserted me, but I smile uncertainly at the ring of expectant faces rounding me, jab a tentative fork into the prodigious mound of food in front of me, and take a bite.

CHAPTER 5

AN HOUR and a half later, I've been fed and entertained by the kind denizens of Dinah's, and now I'm homeward bound, hopefully to put the events of this morning firmly behind me. Yep, that's what I'm gonna do: go home, move on, get down to business, forget all about Boone and Carly Dantrell.

Sounds like a plan.

Only one thing wrong with it: I can't get either one of them out of my mind. It would be too damned easy to write Boone off as a grief-crazed psycho on a collision course with his own immolation, but I'm convinced there's more to him than that. Besides, I can't stop seeing his eyes and that ephemeral but oh-so-charming smile.

Then there's Carly. The second she made her first appearance in my booth, the kid got under my skin, and I can't shake her any more than I can forget about her father. Boone couldn't have brought forth such a delightful ray of sunshine, raised her to be such a bright and caring soul, and not have some of the same goodness inside him.

I know what grief can do. I know how it can twist you and drive you to insane places. Now I'm slightly farther away from being on the receiving end of Boone's wrath, his behavior in the diner doesn't seem so dangerously demented.

Come on, Ellery, do you really blame the guy for going off on you?

No, I don't. That's the hell of it. Especially if I think about exactly how I provoked his extreme response. Here's me, a total stranger, shouldn't know squat about him, certainly shouldn't know the name of his deceased daughter or that he's considering killing himself, and I hit him with, "Don't mind me, and don't take this the wrong way, but I'm about to push your most personal, private buttons."

It's a wonder he didn't rip my head off.

But he didn't. He scared the crap out of me and murdered an innocent shirt, but actual violence inflicted on my actual person? Not a scratch, for all the grabbing and smearing and swearing.

Of course, Norma running him off before he could really, seriously get into it might explain why I'm still alive. Perhaps, but I don't think so. I know what the man *said* he was going to do to me, but I don't believe it. I won't deny he did an excellent impression of going totally postal. But that's all it was. Sound and fury. Lots and lots of fury. But not, I think, true homicidal intent.

I have absolutely nothing to base this on save my own instincts, but they've served me extremely well so far. And what they're telling me now is bashing me into the middle of next week was not Boone's prime objective. Of course, I could be letting myself be taken in by a pretty face. There's a first time for everything, even for me.

What do you know about that?

He was amazingly handsome. Along with the ass, not a face I'll be forgetting any time soon either.

But if I'm not simply falling for his face and my instincts are right and hurting me wasn't what that sorry scene was all about, then what? Hmmm. Let's think about this for a moment. He had questions, and he wanted answers. Answers he didn't get. He doesn't strike me as a man who suffers the word "no" gladly. Or with any grace whatsoever. Just how determined is this guy to get what he wants?

Boone's unsatisfied curiosity. Should I be concerned about it?

What's yer gut telling you now, smartass?

He's probably hundreds of miles from here by now, but just the same, I'm gonna pick up the pace. I'll be fine once I get home and behind those thick stone walls.

One of the few upgrades to my lovely mansion Max insisted on, and I grudgingly agreed to and paid for, was an over-the-top security system. Oh, sure, I appeared appropriately docile while submitting to the installation, but the second she was safely out of town I promptly reasserted my masculinity by refusing to use the ridiculously redundant thing. My personal version of passive resistance.

This is Birchwood. The last serious crime wave we experienced hereabouts was when a family of second-story raccoons pulled a series of daring daytime break-ins. They'd worked their way through half the homes on Beaker Drive, ruthlessly relieving them of their Cheetos and bling, before the Daryl twins cleverly trapped the whole thieving kit and caboodled them into the next county. It was all the town talked about for weeks.

Given the extremely rare occurrence of events as heinous as those in these environs, you'll forgive me if state-of-the-art security systems weighed in right on the bottom of my list of must-haves.

Only… that was then, this is now. My post-Boone perspective has me radically rearranging my priorities. It is also occurring to me that declining Max's persistent offer of my own personal rent-a-thug wasn't so clever, either.

Way-hey Ellery, feeling paranoid yet? Jinkeys, I haven't had this much fun since my last root canal. Becoming quite the adrenaline junkie, here. Maybe I'll take a recuperative nap and then head on over to the Shady Rest and play chicken with the old folks creaking up and down the corridors with their walkers.

Let it never be said I don't know how to show myself a good time.

Good luck to you, Boone Dantrell, wherever you are. No hard feelings. As strange as it sounds, I'm honestly sorry I'll never get to know you. I wish what happened between us had ended differently. That maybe you'd listened instead of freaking. You'd be a lot happier right now.

Maybe I'd be too.

Dammit.

I know you think that gun you're carrying is your best solution to ending the pain tearing you apart every waking moment of every single day, but I hope you don't use it. It isn't the answer, and if I had another chance, I'd tell you that. No otherworldly bullshit needed, this would be man to man. That unanswerable ache inside you, I know how much it hurts, and while it never goes completely away, it does get better.

You just have to give it time.

That much I know for sure. That's what I'd tell him.

Oh well, too late now.

Ah, home sweet home!

I heave a huge sigh of relief when I slip through the wrought-iron gate marking the entrance to my property. Boy, am I glad to see this place! Thought I'd never get here. The hedges are slightly mangy, and so is the sprawling lawn, but you know what? To a man in the throes of a mild fit of unaccustomed paranoia, they've never looked more beautiful.

A sudden, mournful gust of wind scuds across my path, driving a thigh-high cloud of dust laced with withered leaves before me. I sprint across the worn flagstone circle that decades earlier had rung with horses' hooves and steel-banded wooden carriage wheels. The house's ivy-covered granite façade, normally welcoming, now seems vaguely gloomy and brooding.

Then again, maybe it's just me.

The huge, overhanging balcony hulking over the front entry casts an inky curtain across my final destination. The only remaining obstacle between me and certain safety. Behind this massive, black hunk of antique timber lies my carefully constructed, most certain refuge. Can't wait to step through that door and close it, thereby putting the entire outward world of insecurity behind me.

My hand surrounds the cold latch, clenches, and pushes. No resistance. Not locked. Oh my God, it's open! Well, it would be, on account of I left the house without locking it. Like I always do.

Any other morning, coming home to a house unsecured, unoccupied, and completely undefended the entire time I've been gone? Wouldn't give it a second thought. In fact, remarking about any of the above upon arriving chez moi wouldn't even occur to me. I leave my house unlocked all the time. It's fricking Birchwood, what's the big deal?

Wow.

Has immersing myself in this placid, sleepy little town really made me so complacent? I close the house up when I'm away on tour, but when I'm in residence? I don't remember the last time I locked door behind me. I don't even carry the key anymore. I think I threw it in the junk drawer in the kitchen, but I'm not entirely sure. What's the problem? This is Birchwood, remember? The last time they locked and barred their doors here was during the Civil War.

What could happen to me here? What indeed. I seem to remember making a similarly naïve observation earlier this morning prior to embarking on what I thought was going to be a routine breakfast stop.

We all know how that turned out.

All right, fine, whatever, we're home now. Maybe we haven't been doing it much lately, but it's never too late to start locking the barn door behind us.

"Any homicidal maniacs come to call while I was out?" I impudently challenge the foyer while I slide the deadbolt home. Only echoes answer me. Phew!

So much for frightening flights of fantasy. Birchwood, remember? Nothing ever happens here.

I enjoy occasionally freaking myself out with improbable possibilities. Gets the adrenaline flowing, reminds me I'm still actually a part of the human race. Well, sort of.

I face the grand foyer and holler out again. "Hey honey, I'm hooooome!" The acoustics in this wood and marble expanse would make a concert hall envious. It took some experimenting to find the optimal spot to send the sound waves straight up and then ricochet them off the stone and plaster angels roosting along the crown molding. But if you stand—right here—and yodel? Hours of fun.

I'm not losing my mind. Really. Just temporarily letting it off the leash. It'll be fine; it knows the way home.

Okay, enough messing around. Back on task, here. Alarm system, alarm system. Turn it on. How do you do that, again? Not exactly sure. Guess it woulda helped if I'd actually paid attention during Max's how-to demo. Maybe next time.

You're not taking this very seriously, are you, Mr. James? Not really. Not now. Now I'm safely surrounded by my solid, familiar, stone security blanket, all my Boone-related paranoid fantasies?

Rapidly going bye-bye. Not unlike him.

With the evaporation of my apprehensions, I'm becoming uncomfortably aware of how uncomfortable this damned shirt is becoming. Not to mention disgusting. The encrusted gobs of the remains of the Benedict Boone hauled me through have subsequently solidified and are now cracking and flaking off with every movement. Blech. Also not nuts about the feel of the crunchy texture against my skin.

The shirt is officially toast. Ironic, in that I didn't have any. I'll shed it, have a shower, and fetch a replacement. By then it'll be time to get to work. I should endeavor to actually accomplish something today. Max's earlier and less-than-subtle reminder I'm required to put out another book shortly was not lost on me. The source material may come from the other side, but I must also do some actual writing in order to transition ghostly memoirs into the form the public eventually receives. I have slightly more to do with the process than simply taking dictation.

I move across the foyer floor, heading for the staircase, unbuttoning my shirt and sliding it down my shoulders.

"About time you got back," a cold, deep voice sounds from the landing the same time my foot hits the bottom step.

Cold, deep, and distinctly male.

The sound yanks my head up by the ears. I freeze, stupid with shock, gaping at the russet-haired man in jeans, dark button-down shirt, and leather jacket lounging casually against the subtly curving oak balustrade defining the entire length of the upstairs landing. God, look at him, the arrogant bastard, lounging around like he owns the place, completely at his ease, as if he came with the house. The confident, smarmy smile on his face, large brandy snifter in his left hand, an even larger gun in his right.

The business end of which is currently pointed at the middle of my chest.

Oh look, we've got company.

Merde.

"Hi, Boone," I nervously acknowledge him. "This is a surprise."

"You know, you've got no food in this place," my impudent interloper drawls dangerously, then takes a slow sip of the amber liquid in the snifter. He studies me for several seconds, mocking me with his confident, glittering, super-scary eyes. Love the green, hate the glare.

Sorry we're short on snacks. But I see you found the bar.

"I haven't had time to shop. Too busy dodging trucks and unprovoked diner attacks. But thanks for reminding me I need to stock up."

Huh? Why did I just say that? Possibly the cannon aimed at my chest is interfering with my thought processes? Such as they are.

Boone emits a subtle snort, peels himself off the banister, and starts down the stairs.

"You lied to me," he accuses. Ominously.

What's he talking about? Lied to him? I hardly even know him!

"There is another place to get a room in this town after all." His mouth contorts in a grin that bypasses ironic and goes for a head-on gallop straight into cruel. "Funny you failed to mention it."

I'm completely lost and becoming increasingly preoccupied with not soiling my drawers while Boone and his gun descend ever closer. When did the topic of room rentals enter into our previous one-and-only conversation?

Rooms. Oh, oh, wait, I get it. It's weird, but I get it.

"Oh." It's not much, but it's all I've got at the moment. Boone's booted feet hit the foyer floor. We're on the same level.

"The place is big enough, but I don't rent out rooms. The previous owner did, but I don't. This is a private residence now. I live here... alone."

Oh, way to go, genius. Now he knows there's little to no likelihood anyone is going to walk in on us, inconveniently interrupting his intentions, whatever they are. Not unless Mrs. Potts pulls a Houdini for the second time today, but even if she did show up unexpectedly, I doubt her unwitting intervention would slow him down much.

"Then maybe you should take the sign down," Boone observes in a shockingly silken voice.

Sign? Oh, right. Sign. Good idea. I'll get right on that. As soon as you're gone.

That is, if I'm still breathing.

His sensuous, menacing tones are giving me palpitations. Terrifying, and yet oddly exciting. He faces me, his eyes flitting up and down my body, lingering briefly on my mid-section before recommencing their restless roaming. Awareness of the visual caress sucks all the moisture out of my mouth until my tongue feels as dehydrated as a piece of beef jerky.

Whoa.

He's doing it again. Staring at my chest.

My very bare and over-exposed chest.

"Don't stop on my account," he murmurs, baring his teeth.

Damn! Practically naked, here. At least from the waist up. Armed and possibly psycho stranger with dilated pupils and creepy grin pointedly eyeing all exposed skinage. I am aware I have led an extremely sheltered life—by temporary pop celebrity standards, that is—but even I know this is probably not a good thing.

He's really staring at me. Why is he doing that? Okay, not so much me as my—he did *not* just lick his lips!

Is he...? He is!

He's checking me out!

"Do you mind?" I hastily shrug my shirt back on with as much dignity as I can muster. I'm not going to let some grinning goon make me feel like a piece of meat in my own home.

Even if he does have a gun.

Now there's something I never thought I'd hear myself ever say.

"Fine, suit yourself." Boone gives his shoulder a casual toss and his wrist a more deliberate flex, lightly swirling the amber liquid in the glass in his grasp. "Down to business. I can do that." He uses the snifter to wave me past him, toward the breezeway leading to the west wing. Not the gun. The gun doesn't get waved anywhere; it stays on me, not wavering an iota. "Now, I want you to walk this way."

It's out before I can stop myself.

"If I could walk that way…." I manage to regain control of my tongue, and my senses, before I commit further oral inanities.

Boone stares at me, utterly expressionless. The only thing moving is a small muscle in his jaw, rhythmically ticking.

"Are you done?" His green eyes gleam. I think he's amused, but I can't tell yet. This man doesn't wear his heart, or anything else, on his sleeve. I wonder if anyone ever got behind those eyes and really got to know him. I wonder if I could.

I wonder if he'll let me live long enough to try.

"I think so." I nod. "Yeah. I'm sure. I'm definitely done."

"I'm so glad to hear it." The sarcasm coating every syllable is hard to miss. "Now, would you mind?" He waves the snifter again. "If it's not too much trouble."

"If it were, would you care?"

No, I don't have a death wish. At least, not one I'm consciously aware of. I do, however, seem to be suffering from a sudden bout of can't-shut-up-itis.

Hopefully it's not terminal.

Boone hacks out a harsh, barking laugh. "Your instincts for self preservation suck, but you've got spunk."

"Don't tell me, you hate spunk."

Shut up, shut up, *shut up*! Why I can't I shut up?

Boone's eyes narrow in a curious parody of playfulness. "Normally, I'm kinda fond of it. Not right at the moment, however. That being said, you need to stop farting around, now, and do what I tell you."

Okay, point taken. I think I've pushed this particular envelope just about as far as it will go.

"Oh, and by the way, nice and slow," Boone warns. "No sudden moves."

Is he kidding?

"What do you think I'm gonna do, throw myself on your gun?"

"I wouldn't advise it," he dryly retorts.

Neither would I.

I stalk proudly past him without attempting any heroic disarming maneuvers.

"Head for your rumpus room at the end of the hall," he instructs from behind. "We'll sit, have a nice chat. You'll spill your guts. I'll decide whether I'm gonna let you live or not. It'll be fun."

By whose definition?

The parlor. He must mean the parlor. Returning to the scene of the crime? Or just wants a refill? He's obviously been in there once already, the proof he located my bar, such as it is, sloshing around in his left hand. I hope he confined his snooping to rifling through my liquor stash and hasn't violated any other rooms on this floor. Particularly the library.

Wait a minute, he was upstairs when I arrived. What was he doing up there? How long has he been here? How did he find out where I lived?

Don't be stupid, that probably only took him all of five minutes. All he had to do was ask. My well-meaning neighbors wouldn't hesitate to helpfully point out my domicile to any well-mannered axe-murderer who wandered into town and made a few polite inquiries.

It's not their fault. They were raised that way.

If I get out of this alive, I owe Max one hell of an apology. She wants me to take on a bodyguard, hell, I'll let her kit me out with a whole herd of 'em.

If a bunch of geese is a gaggle, would a bunch of guards be a gargle?

When we enter the parlor, I'm accosted by the striking sight of the afternoon sunlight liberally flooding the room, the gauze curtains—pardon me, window treatments—garnishing the intervening French doors barely diffusing the radiant invasion. A golden corona spills onto the huge oriental carpet adorning the dusky walnut floor under our feet. The original wood, thank you very much. I don't want to tell you what refinishing it cost me. The carpet imperceptibly but inevitably fading under the glorious ultraviolet assault wasn't exactly cheap, either.

It's a nice room. Large, but warm and welcoming. Spared no

expense restoring the extant furnishing I inherited along with the house, as well locating the additional, complementary contemporary pieces. The room is a thoughtful and loving amalgam of old and new.

It'll make a fabulously photogenic backdrop for the forensic photo shoot.

My captor doesn't seem at all swayed by the expensive aesthetics of our surroundings. Maybe he's not into traditional.

"Okay, over there." Boone points his snifter at the long leather couch nestled against the originally oak-paneled wall opposite the French doors. I head there as directed and carefully sit myself on one end while he takes station on the other.

I take a deep, shuddering breath and start re-buttoning my shirt.

"Hey! Don't move!"

What's his problem now? "I just wanna button my shirt!"

"I said don't move!" he snarls.

He's serious. For the first time since this started, a frisson of fear creeps along my spine.

This is bad; this is really, really bad. I'm entirely alone and utterly defenseless in this big, massively decorated funhouse with no possible hope of help or rescue, being held at gunpoint by the scariest and yet sexiest man I've ever met in my life. A combination I find simultaneously alarming and stimulating.

Kinda your M. Night Shyamalan version of your basic good news-bad news scenario.

We engage in a silent but deadly game of visual chicken, something my opponent has the perfect face for. I can't get anything from his chilly, chiseled façade. If he's going for intimidating, he's totally nailed it. He doesn't say a word, stares some more, and then a strange, disquieting confidence overtakes his eyes. Like he knows something he's not saying.

Or plans something he's also not sharing.

The staring gets even more intense, and personal, while he slowly, deliberately drinks me in and takes a savoring sip from the brandy snifter.

Now what?

My life experience up to this point has been woefully shy of encounters with homicidal maniacs, so I'm unsure as to the proper victim protocol applicable to this situation. What do I do now? Is there an underlying pathology—or deadly predilection—behind that dead-eyed stare I should be seriously concerned about? Should I be mentally preparing to beg for my life?

Is all of this staring and slurping supposed to be scaring me? Someone throw me a clue, here!

I'm tired of sitting here in my assigned ostensible victim position. I assume that's what's supposed to be going on, but you know what? I'm just not feelin' it. Boone seems quite comfortable playing the menacing thug, so I'm guessing he's used this particular pose to good effect before. One slight flaw in his smug scenario: he doesn't realize he's dealing with someone not so easily intimidated by yer standard threat of death.

After all, he can only kill me once. Though I'm not crazy about the prospect, I'm not totally terrified of it either. It's the unique perspective thing. I might not know everything about what happens next, but I do know enough not to fear it.

What the hell is he drinking, anyway? It had better not be the Courvoisier! That stuff's a hundred and sixty bucks a bottle, and I was saving that one. Don't ask me for what, exactly, but I'm sure something would have come up. Eventually.

I think it's just about time to break this up this stare-athon. And show Mr. Dantrell he's not the only one who can play this game.

I go on the offensive, hoping I'm plenty offensive. "Please tell me that's not the Courvoisier!"

Let's get this party started.

Chapter 6

THE snifter pauses during its latest transit to Boone's lips. Lucky glass.

Where did that come from?

"What do you care?" He's puzzled but still confident he has me completely cowed. "For all you know, you're gonna be dead in the next two seconds."

Time to take you down a peg or two, bucko.

"You're assuming I find that threatening." I lean back, assuming an easy, uncaring posture, exactly mirroring his. "That would be a mistake."

Faint, responding flare of interest registering in opposing adamantine glare. A hit! A palpable hit!

"Maybe sooner, if you don't start talking." Boone rolls over my remark, refusing to admit to uncertainty.

Crankin' it up a notch!

"Listen, I don't know where you acquired your social skills, but trust me, there are easier ways to initiate a conversation. You dropped by for a chat, all you had to do was say so; you didn't need to bring a gun. I love talking; I could do it for days. You want to pick a topic, or shall I? The weather do it for you? The stock market? Global warming? The price of tea in China? How about them Yankees? Read any good books lately? We already know your reading list doesn't include any of mine. How'm I doing so far? Feel free to jump in any time you hear something you like!"

The stone face imperceptibly cracks; a specter of a smile

momentarily haunts Boone's features, and he emits a soft, amused snort.

"You're good," he nods thoughtfully. "Don't spook easy. Spunk and guts. Liking you more and more… Ellery."

The way his voice softens right down, caressing the syllables of my name, like speaking it is a spiritual act.

Oooooh. That's so hot.

Stay on track, stay on track, don't get distracted now, you're supposed to be doing the psyching, not vice versa.

Show no fear, show no fear. Keep your mind where it belongs, not where it wants to go.

"I'm so happy for you," I rev up the sarcasm. "As long as you're leaving the topic selection to me, apparently, I have to ask: who do you think you are, breaking in here and… and—"

Boone snorts. "What break-in? The place was wide open."

Oh, yeah. I forgot.

"But just for the record, your lock wouldn't have given me any problems, even if the place had been properly secured."

"But you did come here, fully intending to break in."

Boone lifts his right shoulder to concede the point.

"So whether you needed to or not, simply a technicality. Locking the door would have made it harder for you—"

"Slightly harder," Boone corrects. "But not by much. And that security system you've got? Waste of money."

That's nice to know. Gonna enjoy saying "I told you so" to Max. I hope.

"So what you're telling me is any effort I made to keep you out would have only slowed you down, not stopped you."

Another amused nod.

"Okay, you've made your point, I concede no physical breaking in was actually required. All you had to do to was open the door."

And help yourself.

"Pretty much." Boone nods, leans back, and rests the snifter on the back of the couch. "Still, if your aim is to keep people out, locking up and turning on your fancy and overpriced security system would prove to be more of a deterrent. For all but the most determined. And skilled," he finishes with a confident grin. "Try it sometime."

How utterly fascinating. I'll mull it over later. Right now, I've got to move on.

"Locking the place up. Gotcha. The second you're gone, top of my list. But getting back to my original point, entering my house, while I wasn't in it, locked or not, without my permission, is technically considered breaking and entering. I know what the sheriff would consider your uninvited presence here, should I choose to call him and ask his opinion."

Boone's escalating eyebrow telegraphs the unlikelihood of that event occurring. "Hellooo, man with a gun here," he patiently explains, waggling the weapon in question for emphasis. "How exactly are you going to do call anybody if you're dead?"

Sweetheart, you have no idea what you are saying. I know you think the question is rhetorical, but I can give you an answer, even though I highly doubt you'd believe it. What an interesting scenario! How would I put the post-mortem finger on him? I could, I actually could! All I'd have to do is hang around, do some scouting, and find someone like me. I can't possibly be the only one who can do this; I'd never get any sleep if I were, for starters. Maybe Mrs. Sheridan could point me in the right direction. She has probably has a list; she seems to know almost everything else, why not where other Communicators are hiding.

It's not an official designation or title or anything, simply a label I bestowed on myself. I had to call it something.

Oh, and speaking of my dear, dead Granny, where is she? It's well after lunch, and by now on any other given day, Mrs. Sheridan would be leading a line of the lost and confused through my living room, but today, I got nothing. Nada. A total negative on the specter-detector. Not even a stray strand of random ectoplasm.

Now I'm really losing it, getting mad at a ghost. Even if she were here, what the hell could she do? Throw herself in front of the bullet? Boo Boone to death?

Yeah, that'd work.

"Why do you keep threatening me?" He probably won't tell me, but I'm interested. "What did I ever do to you?"

Oooh, wrong thing to say, if the sudden blotchy red spots spontaneously erupting all over his tanned face are any sort of reliable barometer of his emotional state.

"I should shoot you right now," he mutters, his voice so low and laden with menace the threat is making my bones ache.

Things just got extremely serious. Possibly terminal for both of us. He looks fully prepared to shoot me and then turn the gun on himself.

I've got to stop thinking like this. No one is getting shot today, especially me!

"Dad, please don't do it! Don't hurt Ellery!"

Hello, thank you, and it's about damned time somebody showed up! Carly pops in, placing herself on the couch between us. I don't know how she got past Mrs. Sheridan, but whatever, I'm very glad to see her. I could definitely use the help.

She doesn't waste time asking questions; she goes straight to work, immediately mounting a massive innocence intervention. That's one major whammy she's laying on her father. Here's hoping she's still got some pull when it comes to psychically pushing her dad around.

You go, girl!

"Daddy, Daddy, please put it down!" she fervently but ineffectually pleads with the dread-eyed man with the gun, and my fate, in his hands. "Daddy, you have to listen to me."

So much for that idea. Sorry kid, the lines are down, your call cannot be completed as dialed.

"I'm sorry, Ellery." Carly turns remorseful eyes on me. "I tried, but I can't make him stop. He won't hear me."

I know, sweetie. Thanks anyway. I'm sorry your Dad hates himself so much he only has ears for his own self-loathing. But somehow he made you, and here you are, putting your fate, your future, and your entire afterlife on hold—for him. You have such faith in him.

I hope you're right.

I hope he's worth it. Only one way to find out.

"Listen, Boone." I take my attitude down several notches and go again. "Can we crank this conversation back a few stupid threats or two and maybe start over?"

I crank my eyelids apart and bleem him with the widest, most trustingly optimistic expression in my repertoire. I haven't used it in years; I'm praying I haven't forgotten how.

I know, I know, I'm slightly on the mature side for the wide-eyed innocence routine, but desperation can make you do bizarre things.

Boone stares at me, real bewilderment momentarily ghosting his gaze. "Who *are* you?" he throatily demands.

It's such an abrupt switch from hostile to haunted that I'm rocked back as well.

And then the moment is gone as swiftly as it bloomed.

Boone rebounds, louder, accusing. "Ellery Joyce James," he sneers. "Is that your real name?"

What?

My name? He's asking me about my name?

Okay, whatever.

"Sadly, yes," I sigh. "My parents drew their inspiration from two of their favorite authors. Serendipitous for them the James part came pre-supplied."

Boone nods and takes a thoughtful swig. Calming down again. Oookay....

"How about your folks?" Personal nomenclature seems a safe enough subject. "Did they have a soft spot for American frontiersmen with a penchant for lost causes?"

Boone languidly waggles the gun—and his eyebrows—at me.

Hmmm. Obviously he intends to limit his conversational contributions to asking the questions, not answering them. It's a start. On the bright side, as long as he's grilling me, he's not drilling me.

Wow, that's a great line. I ever branch out into detective novels,

I'll definitely find a way to work it in.

"You're nothing like I was expecting," Boone murmurs, his eyes gentling, becoming almost kind.

Um... ah... what? What is this guy, an emotional yo-yo? Ten seconds ago he looked like he wanted to kill me; now he's all nicey-nicey? What is going on here? Is Carly still working on him? Maybe, maybe, she hasn't taken her eyes off him in the past few minutes.

Breathe, breathe, and go with it. You're still alive. So far, so good. We just might get through this in one piece.

"Ellery Joyce James." Boone chews the side of his cheek. "Reclusive, slightly mysterious alleged writer of hugely popular bodice-ripper romance novels. The masses can't seem to get enough of them, and him, rocketing him practically overnight from the bottom of the obscurity barrel to the top of the celebrity treat of the week list. Mind you, there's no accounting for taste," he finishes with a taunting grin.

Alleged writer? Who's he calling alleged? And they're not romance novels!

"I write historical fiction," I sniff. "Not romance. Most people fall in love during the course of their lives. Usually there will be some in the story, but they're not about romance, per se, it's only an element in the plotline."

"Oh, excuse me!" Boone sarcastically rebuts. "My mistake! Not that anyone gives a rat's ass one way or another."

"I do!" I bristle at him. "And so do a lot of other people who aren't gun-wielding, hostage taking...."

Boone takes another sip. I wonder how much he's already had. He doesn't look inebriated, but that doesn't mean anything. Depending on when he got here and how long it took him to find the bar, he potentially had the time and opportunity to make a serious dint in the bottle.

Whaddya think, is he a happy drunk or a mean one? Given how this day's been going so far, what are my chances?

"So." Bone bears up manfully beneath my scathing stare for several seconds and then breaks our silent stalemate. "Ellery Joyce

James. What's a hip guy like you doing in a place like this?"

Trying to survive?

"I woulda thought a media darling like yourself would prefer spending most of your time in New York or LA, hanging out in all the hot spots and rubbing elbows with the beautiful people. Not slumming in the sticks with us regular folks."

It's a fair question. I'm not surprised he's asking it, actually. He's for sure not the first. However, it's not the one I've been both anticipating and dreading ever since he appeared at the top of the stairs. Me and my 'tude may have somewhat forestalled his original intention, but I'm not kidding myself why he's really here.

When is he going to ask me about Carly?

"That was quite the fox you had on your arm last week when you were at that red carpet thingy—"

"The Grammys."

"Whatever."

Fox, fox, now what is he talking about? Oh, he must mean Max! He thinks Max is attractive? I guess you could call her that. Attractive. In an over-achieving, over-privileged, old money kind of way. Of course, I never have. Thought of her that way. To me, she's Max. Full time agent, part time escort, and sometime friend. And that's about it.

But why bring her up now?

"Is she just a friend or are you doin' her?"

What?

"Boone," I sigh. "Listen, I don't know what you're fishing for, and frankly, I don't care. Not that it's any of your business, but Max is my agent. Nothing more. I applaud her taste in writers, but when it comes to the men in her personal life, her judgment really sucks."

That gets a short, sharp bark of laughter out of Boone.

"How about you?" He leans forward, and his eyes flit down to my crotch and then away again. "What do you like in a man?"

Is he serious? Or simply messing with my head?

Want to hear something crazy? Not sure which option I'm hoping for.

"You were the last thing I expected to see when I walked into that diner."

I can't read his expression, and the tone of his voice isn't giving anything away either. What's going on behind those shuttered eyes? Amusement, scorn, indifference?

It shouldn't matter to me, what he thinks. It shocks me that it does.

"You think you're really something, don't you." His eyes are hard, his tone cutting. No mistaking the disdain in his expression this time.

His visible censure hits me hard; again I'm shocked how much. Why do I care? Why am I so disappointed he's standing in the same erroneous judgment over me as pretty much everyone who's ever met me and been oh, so very wrong? Not that I've anyone to blame for their low opinion of me but myself. It's my own damn fault for honing my shallow celeb schtick to such superficial perfection.

Fooled another one. Only this time, what this one thinks matters, and I don't know why.

I've never cared a whit about anyone else's opinion. Quite the contrary, the more people who thought I was a waste of space and stayed away, the better it suited me.

Why do I want this guy to be different? Why do I want him to look deeper, to see further, to find the real me? Why do I think he could, and would?

"You don't know anything about me," I mutter, glaring spitefully at him.

"I know there's something hinky about you." Boone's return glare is equally frigid and unfriendly. "And I'm not leaving here until I find out what you know."

"That could take years," I snap. "I actually know quite a bit!"

"Clever," his mouth says, but his eyes are completely devoid of mirth. "But don't push it. And don't piss me off. I've cut you some slack so far because you're cute, but I'm starting to lose my patience."

What did he just say? I'm cute?

He thinks I'm cute?

That's it. I've officially crossed the last frontier of my sanity. I'm ecstatic because my possibly homicidal home invader thinks I'm cute. But it is kind of exciting. In a lunatic fringe sort of way.

"Don't let my dad scare you," Carly interjects encouragingly. "He can talk like a big, bad meanie, but he's a good guy. He only hurts bad people."

Out of the mouths of babes.

All right, taking an enormous chance both Carly and I don't really suck at character assessments, but it's time to move this conversation along. Not only am I starting to get hungry again, but I could pee right now.

Yup, a couple of pots of tea will do it to you every time.

"Listen, this has all been very entertaining, as well as slightly intimidating, and I just might use it in one of my books, but we've already established I'm not renting out any rooms, and my cupboard is bare so I can't feed you or bed you...."

That didn't come out right.

Boone's green eyes gleam, and the corner of his mouth twitches. "I don't recall asking," he drawls. "But then again, I don't have to."

Right. Now that's just downright creepy.

"Writer, huh?" At least he didn't say "alleged." He downs the last of my booze and sets the empty snifter on the end table. "Are you any good?"

"Depends on who you ask," I shrug. "My latest has been on the best sellers' list for the last three weeks. Draw your own conclusions."

Am I answering his question or bragging? Sounded a bit like bragging to me. Ah, ego, thy name is Ellery. However, it is obvious my answer has not impressed my intimidator.

"So a bunch of suckers followed the herd. So what? All that proves is there's a shitload of people out there with questionable taste and money to burn."

That was mean!

Boone's green eyes glow mockingly. "Save it." He holds up his hand before I can squawk out a defense. "Whatever your game is, you seem to have done all right for yourself."

I'm comfortable. In a material sense only. I wasn't kidding about needing to pee.

"You got all of this from writing a few books." He surveys the opulent splendor of my parlor with a slight sneer. "Really?"

Damn, you caught me. My entire literary career has been a clever cover. I'm really a drug lord. I smuggle heroin in hollowed-out copies of my books.

"I've made a few bucks, so what?"

Why are we talking about money now?

"I'll bet you have," Boone squints at me. "You're probably rolling in it."

I can't believe what I'm hearing. Have I got it—and him—completely wrong? It would certainly explain why he hasn't asked me about Carly. If he doesn't care about her, if she isn't the real reason why he's come, not asking why I said what I said to him in the diner would make perfect sense.

Money? Is that what he wants? Robbing me? Is that why he's here?

No, I won't believe it. It can't be true, can't be that mundane. And depressing.

But what if it is? What if he's just like all the rest of them after all, him and his damned, superficial ass? Only after what he can buy, beg, or steal. Wouldn't that just serve me right? And be the biggest practical joke of all.

I should stick to the dead. I suck with the living.

"Listen, if money's what you want, you can have it. The safe is in my study. I'll be happy to open it up for you so you can rifle through it to your heart's content."

The corner of Boone's lip curls like he's just caught a whiff of something putrid and insulting. "I don't care about your money," he lowly murmurs, his voice deep and dangerous, like molasses laced with strychnine. "All I want is for you to cut the crap and tell me who you really are and what's really going on here."

And here we go again, back into the Intimidation Zone. The way he's been flipping back and forth between friendly and freak-me-out, it's a wonder he doesn't have emotional whiplash. As it is, I'm getting dizzy trying to keep up with the reality shifts.

For his latest trick, he's pulled conspiracy theory out of his sleeve. What's next? Aliens?

I picked a fine time to run out of tinfoil.

Can this day—or conversation—get any weirder?

It's time to wrap this puppy up. My back teeth are doing the backstroke.

"Listen, Boone, this has been a total hoot. I can't remember the last time I had so much fun at gunpoint, but you know what? I've got a life I'd like to get on with, I'm sure you do too, so why don't we move it along, get to the bottom line. Shoot me, rob me blind, whatever the hell you came here for, let's get on with it and get it over with right now!"

I start to rise, but Boone anticipates my intention, surging to his feet, brandishing his gun in a white-knuckled grip. "*Siddown!*" he roars.

I do what I'm told. You would too.

Boone's face is a study in granite while he makes a slow, cruel show of cocking his gun.

"You wanna get it over with?" he grates, deliberately leveling the gun at me. "Fine by me, I'm easy."

Wait a minute, that's not what I meant.

"Don't worry," he smirks, no doubt moved to offer cold comfort by the stark shock on my face. The not being scared of death thing? While technically true, doesn't mean I want to experience it any time soon. And definitely not in the next few seconds.

"I'm not going to kill you. Yet."

Did I say cold comfort? Try frigid.

"I need answers first."

Finally!

"I have a few. Ask away."

"That was some slick trick you pulled off in the diner. I want to know how you did it. I want to know how an alleged writer I never met who spends half his life in the tabloids and the rest of it holed up in an updated knock-off of the Munster's mansion in Nowhere, Colorado—how you know about me and my dead daughter."

Ah, at last. I've been waiting for this question the entire conversation and have no more idea how to answer it now than when we first started.

"Lucky guess?" I bleat.

"Say anything stupid like that again and I'll put a round right between your eyes." Boone's eyes are as merciless as the syllables he spits at me. "Don't think I won't, because believe me, Mr. Writer, I've got nothing to lose."

"It's gonna be okay, Ellery." Carly's quaver barely registers on my consciousness. Oh, right, she's still here. She kinda got lost in the threats. "He won't really do it. And besides." She juts her chin out with endearingly juvenile defiance. "I won't let him hurt you."

Bless you, sweetheart. Thank you for trying, but I think I'm on my own, here.

I look Boone squarely in the eye and take a deep breath.

I can do this.

"Tell me!" he demands in a low, ominous rumble.

"Tell him, Ellery!"

What? Tell him what? I talk to dead people? Oh yeah, that'll go over great.

"I'd love to, but you won't believe me."

Well, he won't.

"Try me," Boone snarls, his upper lip curling back from his teeth in a feral grin doing its best to convince me my life expectancy isn't going to extend much beyond the next thirty seconds. Ah well, it is what it is. The truth isn't always pretty or what we want to hear, but it's all I have.

"I know about you and Carly because she told me."

"What are you talking about?" Boone's eyes are mere slits now. I sense he has just taken skeptical to a whole new level.

So long, it's been nice knowing you.

"Just what I said. I see dead people, Boone. Just like the kid in the movie. Hear 'em too. All the time, all over the place. Carly came to me in the diner and asked for my help communicating with you. She's the one who told me you had a gun and what you were planning to do with it. Oh, and by the way, she's sitting right beside you."

And with those few words, my life is over.

Chapter 7

BOONE is a silent missile of doom hurtling toward me. He grabs me and slams me into the couch cushions, pressing a knee to the middle of my chest to pin me down. His bent leg carrying his full weight, he leans over, pressing the barrel of the gun to my forehead.

"That is a sick, goddamned lie." Boone's voice is strangely calm, incongruently soothing, his face close enough to mine to kiss. A bizarre notion at a time like this, but there it is. "Tell me the truth or I'll kill you." He draws back, his mouth smiling serenely, his eyes glittering green orbs of malice, promising to deliver me into a world of hurt. "What does Carly say about that?"

Actually, not much. Which kind of surprises me. Don't see her any more either. Fine time to bail on me, girlfriend, what with me putting my life on the line for you. Typical. After everything I've done for everyone else, now, when I really need spot of divine intervention, I'm hung out to dry.

"Be still, my darling boy."

Oh, wait, perchance my expectation of my expiration was slightly premature? I can't see her, but there's nothing wrong with my hearing; that definitely was Mrs. Sheridan's voice. Ah, there she is! Peeking over Boone's shoulder! Yoo hoo, Mrs. S.! Pardon me if I don't get up! Nice of you to drop by! Do me a favor and save me a seat on the next celestial shuttle?

"I am with you." Her soft utterance is sweet. Not much good to me in the practical sense, and neither is she, but I appreciate the thought. Illogically reassuring. "Don't be afraid. He will not harm you."

Oh, really? Who's going to stop him? You? Small flaw with your plan. You're dead! Dang, so much for the rescue, but thanks for stopping by!

Weird, this is weird. The specter of imminent death looming largely in my immediate future is making me hallucinate. Either that, or Boone has become radioactive. If I'm not seeing things, then a soft nimbus of liquid golden light is coating his head and shoulders. Not sure where it's coming from or why, but it is definitely there, and it's getting stronger, spreading outward, spilling over his body like a dreamy, golden haze.

Weird.

"So soon you forget everything I've taught you," she lightly scolds me. "Never mind, I'm here, now. Be still."

Sure, whatever you say, no problem. Like I've got a choice?

The glow is softly roaming over Boone's skin as if driven by an animating intelligence. It flows gently over his body with purpose, on a mission, seeking something specific.

Oh, wait. Of course it is. I know exactly what it's looking for and why. And where it's coming from. Boy, do I feel stupid. I'm sure Mrs. S. would smack me good upside the head if she could. I deserve it.

I can't believe I let this happen. Boone's ass must have gone to my head; I should have scanned him the second I saw him at the top of the stairs. The emotional shifts were my first clue, and I missed them. Damn, I know better! I almost deserve to have my brains blown out for being such a dumbass.

Um... just kidding!

But all is not lost; Mrs. S. is here to save the day. And me.

Thanks, ma'am.

Carly hasn't been the only one messing with Boone's head, although her meddling was a sight more kindly meant than the nasty thing riding in under my radar on his coattails. But I will give the guy some credit; although I have no doubt the constant ghostly goad in his ear was the major escalator to the current extreme, Boone's been fighting the homicidal impulses being injected into his subconscious ever since he got here. The whole time he's been pushed, he kicked back.

Now, I'm not entirely excusing him responsibility for his behavior, but I should have picked up on his passenger and sent it packing. Then maybe our interaction wouldn't have gone so far south I should be issuing iceberg warnings. Oh, well, appearances to the contrary, things are not nearly as dire as they seem. Thanks to Mrs. Sheridan's timely intervention, we may yet pull my nuts out of the fire.

She will take care of the monkey on Boone's back. Establishing a rapport with what remains is up to me.

Trusting my invisible ally will do her part, I find Boone's haunted gaze and lock on tight. Gotcha now, not gonna let go.

Boone's eyes, whirling pools of rage and pain—sucking me down—strike a resonant cord deep inside me. I don't understand; I feel like I've been here before. What he knows, what he is, what he feels whirls and swells inside me. It's all so familiar. So is he. I own his pain like it's my own, burn equally with every self-inflicted wound searing his soul. This has never happened to me before, this almost total identification with another, and the eerie empathy terrifies me, burgeoning until it threatens to burst me asunder. The resonance, the remembering, grows and deepens, surging along the tenuous gossamer connection between us, drawing ever closer to my awareness, daring me to reach for it, to pull it into the light, to finally recognize it and remember.

"Ellery?" A tiny, breathless voice close to my ear. Another ally only I can see.

Carly. Carly is kneeling beside me.

"Ellery, say this to my dad, quick!"

"Kid Slick to Colonel Cool," I obediently repeat. "Prepare to receive a Top Secret transmission, over."

Boone's face turns a sick, rice pudding white, and the gun barrel pressed to my forehead quivers. For a second he doesn't move, doesn't blink. The phrase means nothing to me; I definitely don't get it. But from his pole-axed reaction, I think it's safe to say Boone sure does.

His features slacken, his eyes fill with impenetrable frost, and the connection between us snaps when his awareness recoils from me, clawing back to a dark place of asylum and digging in with a vengeance. His hand moves slowly, languidly, like the air around it has solidified, lifting the gun up and away from me until the barrel is pointed harmlessly toward the ceiling.

"Colonel Cool ready to receive." Boone's voice is charged and cracking with grief. "Give it to me kid, over."

I have no idea what I'm saying, but it's working, so I keep repeating everything I hear. "Roger Dodger fourteen, seventy-three, twenty-five, acknowledge, over."

A single tear trickles down the side of Boone's nose. He's so far gone I don't know if he's even on the same planet any more.

"Colonel Cool, reading you loud and clear," Boone whispers. "Seven, eight, niner, twice in Carolina. Colonel Cool, over and out."

He wavers over me, his eyes filling. "Carly," he murmurs.

It's okay, it's going to be okay now. Carly's code has turned the tide. Boone won't stop me if I go for the gun.

Boone's knee remains jammed into my chest. He continues to reside in Zone City, seemingly having no conscious involvement with the pinning process. I'll get the gun first and then I'll worry about how to get him off.

Off. Off me. As in letting me up. Releasing me. Letting me go.

Slowly, carefully, I reach for the weapon. He doesn't blink, twitch, or otherwise react when my trembling fingers close on his hand and carefully, oh-so-carefully work the gun from his grasp.

Got it, I've got it, got the gun. Thanks, guys. Both of you.

All right, that happened.

Now for the next problem: how to persuade the shell-shocked statue parked on top of me to let me up. The knee caving my chest in? Really starting to hurt.

"Um. Hello? Can you get off me, please?" It's worth a shot.

Nuthin'. He's not moving, barely breathing, just hunkering there on my chest, staring out into space, slowly compressing my sternum into my spine.

Must make him move now, getting hard to breathe.

"Boone!" A little louder this time. "Hello?"

The lights are on, but nobody's answering.

I'm about to resort to bucking him off when he emits a low grunt, shakes his head, then pushes off me. Moving like he's sleep-walking through molasses, Boone gropes his way down the couch until he finds the other end and then collapses. He hunches forward, pillowing his head on his folded arms. He doesn't make a sound, but I can see fine tremors rippling through the fine leather stretched across his shoulder blades.

I need to get off this couch. Stretch my legs. Run around the house screaming a few times. Nothing major, just a little stress relief.

Oh, yeah, and hide the gun.

I quietly rise, scooping his gun and the brandy snifter, and head for the bar by way of the little writer's room. Fine, I'll come clean. Stashing the gun isn't the only thing on my mind. I could definitely use a belt right now.

As I approach the antique credenza housing my liquor, I spot the plundered bottle left impudently on display. The Courvoisier, of course.

I knew it.

Oh well, the bottle's already been breached, might as well join the party.

I squat down behind the credenza, reach behind the bottles on the bottom shelf, and stash the gun. That out of the way, I secure my own snifter and slosh some brandy in both glasses. I slug mine gratefully back while rubbing the sore spot in my chest. Tender, but not terminal. I'll live.

Ah, the brandy definitely hit the spot. Feeling slightly flushed and much better equipped to go another round with Boone.

I pour myself a refill and head back to my still-silent companion, who's exactly where I left him. He's sitting up now and mutely staring, doing a fair imitation of a man in a fugue state, completely oblivious to Carly pressed up beside him.

Oh, boy, he's really out of it. I hope the vegetative state isn't permanent. He's way too pretty to spend the rest of his life as a planter. Although I wouldn't mind keeping him around. He's very decorative.

I'd even water him.

God, I need to get a life.

One glance at Carly and my manic mental meanderings go right out the window. Talk about your heartbreaking tableau. She's pressed up against her oblivious and unresponsive father, her little spectral head resting on his shoulder. She's touching him with such aching tenderness, softly stroking his arm while she murmurs gentle words of love and pours her whole little heart into talking him back.

She could do it. Those staring, empty eyes would light right up if he could hear her. If he knew she was by his side, we'd see one hell of a resurrection.

But unfortunately, even though she has plenty of will, there's no way it's going to happen. All the love in this world and the next will avail her naught if he can't see or hear her.

I guess this is my cue. I'll take a shot talking to him again. Now he's no longer in a position to take a shot at me.

Only one problem: I'm not exactly sure what to say.

I stand over him, a snifter in each hand, wracking my brains for an appropriate approach.

"I'm sorry about the gun."

The sound startles me so severely I almost drop the snifters. That I was not expecting, but I'll take it.

"You have no idea how much," he mournfully continues. He sounds sad. Genuinely contrite. I believe him. "I know I don't deserve your understanding or your forgiveness, but I really am sorry for busting in here the way I did and…." He runs a despairing hand through his hair and hangs his head. "I never meant to hurt you. I wouldn't have… honestly… no matter what it looked like. I'm not a bully or a monster. I don't do shit like that. I don't know what came over me."

An interesting admission. Especially the last bit. He has no idea what he just said, but I don't think he's ready for the explanation for his behavior I could give him.

"Here." I extend his refill to him. "You look like you could use this."

He glances up at me, looking me over. This time the visual assessment is strictly business. He's trying to get a read on me. Get inside my head.

Figure out what I'm going to say and do next.

Good luck with that one.

"Thanks." He accepts the snifter and stares morosely into the swirling amber fluid it contains. "I won't give you any more trouble. I'll sit here quietly until the sheriff comes."

"You'll have a hell of a wait." I resume my former spot on the opposite end of the couch. "I have no intention of calling him. Or pressing charges. Although I'm fully aware I could. And should," I remind him, taking another sip of my brandy.

Oy, I'd better slow down. I need to keep a clear head.

"Thank you." His quiet response bleeds with honest gratitude. "That's kind of you. I don't deserve it, after the way I treated you."

"You'll get no arguments from me." I'm aware I'm being a bit harsh, and he wasn't entirely to blame for what he did, but I'm feeling the need to draw a faint line in the sand, here. "Thank Carly for my clemency. I'm cutting you this slack for her sake, not yours."

The second the words are out of my mouth I regret them, especially when I see how deeply I've cut him. He takes my verbal slap without a sound, and the quiet dignity of his next confession racks him up some major impression points.

"All I can say in my own defense is I've spent so many years acting like an over-the-top action hero I've forgotten how to be anything else. I've been running on crazy ever since she... she died, and it's done stuff to my head. What I used to do for a living, it makes you nuts. Hard, mean, seeing spooks around every corner. I walked away from it, but it's not as easy to leave behind as I thought."

I don't think he's talking about the same sort of spook I deal with. And the nature of his former employment? I wonder what it would be. Questions to be asked and hopefully answered another time. Later.

Assuming there will be a later. Or you even want one.

Do you, Mr. James?

Nope, nope, not going there now. Stay on topic. This is about Carly, not you.

Boone gives me a wan, weary smile and tilts the liquid in his snifter toward his mouth. I try to refrain from screaming at the speed with which he tosses it back.

"That stuff's not bad," Boone comments while setting the empty down. "Think I'll stick to beer, though."

So much for the good stuff. Whine.

"So, you ready to talk about this now?"

Boone nods but doesn't speak.

It'll come. When he's ready.

"That was our secret code," Boone tells the hands clasped in his lap. "Carly and me. She made it up. No one else knew about it. No one. There's no possible way you could."

"Yeah, there is." I put my snifter down and lean forward, focusing full on him. "Only one way. From Carly."

"Carly is dead!" Boone grates, his fists clenching.

"Yes, Boone, she is. But she's not gone. She's right here, sitting beside you. Just like I told you. I can see her and hear her. I don't know why. I don't know why I can and you can't, but there it is, and so is she. Now, if you don't believe me, if you absolutely insist, I'll play the 'prove it' to you game. I'll ask her anything you want, have her tell me any little piece of trivial information only you and she know, but I'm hoping that won't be necessary. Will you trust me?"

"You're taking a big chance with me," he murmurs. "It'd be a lousy way to pay you back, to not grant you the same consideration."

"Why would I lie?"

Boone stares at me, his eyes haunted with horrible longing. "You can see her? Really... see her?"

"I can."

"What does she look like?" His voice is barely audible.

"She wasn't much for bows and lace, was she?"

Boone smiles crookedly and shakes his head.

"'Cause the girl I'm seeing looks like she'd be happy up a tree or out fishing with her dad."

Boone drops his head. His shoulders shake. "I tried to take her fishing whenever I was home. Which wasn't nearly often enough."

I look over at Carly. Her eyes are glistening, and she's bravely blinking back tears.

"Her hair's the same color as yours, and not much longer."

"That was her idea," Boone tells the floor. "Eve used to beg her to grow it out, but she wouldn't. She didn't want to look like a girl."

"She's wearing a red jacket, a blue-and-white striped T-shirt, jeans, and a really cool pair of Nikes. They look brand new. Must have cost a bundle."

"They did. She begged me for them for a month. Bought them for her before I went out on my last mission." Boone's face and voice shatter. "She hadn't even broken them in. Eve and me, we… we buried her wearing them. The outfit you just described? It was her favorite."

"Daddy, don't be sad!" Carly sidles closer to her father and puts a small, phantom hand on his shaking shoulders. "It's okay. It didn't hurt." Her lower lip starts to quiver.

Okay, here we go. Is this where I find out what happened?

"Is she talking to you?" Boone turns toward me, his red-rimmed eyes heavy with envy.

I nod.

"I wish I could hear her," he chokes.

"I wish you could too."

His eyes clamp violently shut, his lips compressed together in a thin, white line, he curtly nods his comprehension. "Thanks. Would you… would you tell me what she's saying? I know I've got no right to ask, but…."

"It's okay, I don't mind."

"Thanks." Boone sniffs and clears his throat. "Thanks for helping my little girl."

"Boone."

It takes a moment, but he finally makes eye contact again.

"I'm not doing it just for her."

"Something else I have no right to ask for," he murmurs, quiet gratitude growing and faintly glinting through the mantle of shame he's wearing like an ill-fitting suit. "Or expect from you."

"Start again?" I smile at him. "Carly said she doesn't want you to be sad. She also said it didn't hurt."

I don't know what that means, but Boone clearly does.

The brief pulse of pain streaking across his face as quickly switches to self-loathing.

"It's my fault she's dead!" he chokes. "I killed her!"

He can't mean that literally—what he said—it's just an expression. It has to be! He didn't… actually….

Carly must be seeing what I'm feeling, because she's quick to jump to her father's defense.

"Oh, no, no, Ellery! Daddy didn't hurt me. He wasn't even there when I died."

I feel almost physically ill from the relief rushing through me.

"Daddy thinks God killed me to punish him for a bad thing he did."

Does he, now? That's really creepy. And from everything I know, understand, and believe about how the universe works, completely wrong.

But it explains a lot. Oh, yeah. It's all making sense now.

"What do you think, baby?" I smile kindly at her, inviting her to confide in me.

"What's she telling you?" Boone demands. "What's going on?"

I hold up my hand to silence him, giving Carly my full attention. "I'll get to you in a sec. I want to talk to Carly first."

Boone meekly accepts the slap-down. I don't know whether to be impressed or alarmed by the degree of tractability he's displayed since the tide turned.

I'll worry about it—and him—later. Carly is all I care about right now.

"Honey? It's okay, you can trust me. What happened to you?"

"I...." She eyes me uncertainly. "God didn't make me die and my daddy didn't either. Nobody did, it just happened."

I still don't know what "it" is, but that's okay. I'm not going to push it. I'll find out one day, I'm sure, whenever Boone decides to tell me.

Bless you, baby. You're going to be fine. As soon as I straighten your dad out.

"I think you're right." I smile at her. "Now let's help your father see it the same way."

"See what the same way?" Boone suspiciously demands.

"You're both carrying around some emotional baggage you need to kick to the curb."

"You have no idea what you're talking about," Boone mutters.

"You're right, I probably don't. But I'm willing to listen."

"I..." Boone starts to say, and then his jaw clamps shut. "Forget it. I can handle it."

"Really? Forgive my skepticism, but I think I've got cause. Would you call what you did to me 'handling it'?"

I didn't want to rub the recent past in his face, but if he clams up on me now, I can't help either one of them.

"I already said I was sorry," he protests.

"So you did. Apology accepted. Now, shut up and listen to me unless you want to land in more 'sorry' than you ever want to know. Boone, let me fill you in on a few facts of the afterlife. I'm very worried about Carly's future, and you should be too. In fact, you should be scared shitless. There's a very real chance that innocent little girl who right this very minute should be getting issued a set of wings and signing up for soccer on cloud nine is going to end up stuck down here instead, roaming the Earth as a lost soul, and if she does—it'll be your fault!"

Boone stares at me through moist, startled eyes. That rocked him. Good. It was supposed to. "What the hell are you talking about?" he hisses. "I'd never do that to my little girl!"

"No?" I fire at him. "Then why is she still here?"

"I... I don't understand."

I know you don't. Welcome to Afterlife 101. Here beginneth your first lesson.

"Carly shouldn't be here. She needs to cross over, to go to the other side."

"What, you mean heaven?" Boone blinks.

"I don't know if it's heaven or not, I've never been there, I only know there's a place, another dimension, plane of existence, whatever you want to call it, where we all need to go after we die. Staying here, becoming earthbound, is bad, but while the transition isn't optional, it's not automatic. Souls get stuck on this side of the curtain if they don't realize they're dead, if they don't want to let go of the living, if the living don't want to let go of them, or, and this is the one applicable to this situation, if they've got unfinished business. You see where I'm going with this?"

"I might have a clue," he grudgingly admits. "You're saying Carly didn't... cross over... like she was supposed to because she has unfinished business? With me?"

"Yes," I nod at him. "Pretty much. She's worried about you, Boone."

"What's to worry about? I'm fine." He glares defiantly at me as if daring me to disagree.

If I didn't think he'd punch me silly, I'd smack him upside the head.

"You see, that's what I'm talking about, that—what you just said is exactly why she's here, and she's gonna stay here, stuck to you like Krazy Glue!"

"Tell her I'll be fine and she should...." He makes a vague, dismissing gesture. "She should just go."

"She's right here, and she can hear every word you're saying. Besides, maybe you don't mind lying to her, but I'm not going to!"

Carly sits silently between us, her huge, innocent eyes

shimmering with sorrow. She watches me imploringly, a helpless witness to the struggle for her father's soul.

She has no idea his fate is not the only one on the line here.

She's counting on me. So is he, although he doesn't know it.

No pressure.

God.

"What are you talking about?" Boone eyes cut sharply to mine, glittering malachite animosity.

"Carly's been hanging with you ever since she died, watching you beat yourself up with the blame stick you've been hauling around. She came to me at the diner because she was terrified you were gonna use that gun I just took off you."

"I said I was sorry about that."

"I heard you. Shut up and let me finish."

"Fine. So finish."

"Thanks, I will! She thinks you're gonna shoot yourself."

"I thought about it," Boone grudgingly admits.

"Why?" I bluntly demand. "Would it change what happened? Would your self-immolation make the world a better place?"

"Some people might think so."

I ignore him and press on. "Would it bring her back?"

"Of course not," he chokes.

"What will it prove? What universal imbalance do you think sacrificing yourself will address?" I'm really getting revved up here.

He stares at me, clearly shocked by the concepts I'm flinging in his face. Exactly like I planned.

"That's... that's crazy. Makes no sense at all."

"It makes about as much sense as killing yourself." I gentle my voice down. "And trust me when I tell you, it would not be an end to anything. Including your problems. Death is not a 'get out of life free of your shit' card. It also does not mean oblivion. The proof is sitting between us, waiting for you to set her free."

"I don't know how to do that!" Boone cries out, in genuine pain.

"Yeah, you do." I edge a little closer. "You've got to let go of whatever you're blaming yourself for. And you must let go of her and move on with your life. Promise her you'll go on living and try to be happy."

"Happy! Are you kidding me? I don't even know what the word means anymore. Without her, I never will."

I've got him on the ropes, and I can't let up now. He's feeling mighty sorry for himself, and he's had so much recent practice he's a virtual self-pity virtuoso. He has to understand this particular boo-hoo fest will come at a terrible price.

And he won't be the one paying it.

"Get over yourself and be a man! If you can't do it for yourself, do it for Carly. She needs to cross over, and she can't as long as you're determined to throw yourself a life-long pity party. I don't know you very well, that might be your thing, but you know what? This isn't about you, pal. Suck it up and get on with it already before you doom your little girl to an unending afterlife of hanging around in your sorry shadow watching you whine your life away!"

Renewed rage flares in Boone's green eyes. Oooh, I've made him mad again. Good.

Here's hoping he doesn't hit back.

"What the fuck do you know about it?" Boone snarls at me. "What do you know about losing a child?" He crosses his arms and continues to glare at me, but it's not the mindless, murderous rage of before. Yeah, he's pissed at me. Good and pissed, but it's because he knows I'm right.

The wave of rage crests and then breaks as abruptly as it arose. I don't know if he's conceding or simply calling a truce, but for now the fighting is over.

"You got any beer in that thing?" He tosses his head back toward the bar.

"You oughta know, you've rifled though it already," I throw over my shoulder en route. "Any preferences?"

"Surprise me," he grunts.

I snag a couple of Coronas from the bar fridge and head back for the conversation pit.

"Here you go." I hand his off, sit back down, take my time snapping the cap off mine.

"You got any real beer in that thing?" He eyes the bottle skeptically. I ignore him.

"What do I know about losing a child?" I take a sip and swallow. "Admittedly, nothing. I've never had any. I can't even begin to imagine what you must be feeling, but you know what else someone should never have to experience? They shouldn't have to live through being a child and watching their parents die. What do you know about *that*, Boone?"

CHAPTER 8

A STRIDENT voice shocks me into silence. Yelling. I'm yelling at Boone. Why?

Embarrassed and angry, I snap my jaw shut, putting the brakes on my puzzling and far too personal tirade. I don't know why I've let any of this slip, especially to someone who's still essentially a stranger, even if we have recently shared an intense session of high-caliber male bonding. Exactly what caliber, I couldn't tell you. I'm a writer, not a sniper.

I hate talking about my past, hate remembering it even more. It's ancient history and has been duly relegated to the dusty repository of all things long gone and best forgotten. Some old bones should stay permanently interred. Nothing to be gained by disturbing their rest.

"Shit," Boone breathes, obviously equally startled by my over-the-top reaction. "I'm sorry, I had no idea." He takes a nervous swig from the bottle. "Are they still, you know, around?"

Nuts. Now that the can of worms has been cracked, they're crawling all over the table. I don't want to talk about this, but I have a sinking feeling denying his curiosity will only serve to incite it further. No way I'm getting away with dodging this particular conversational bullet.

I guess fair is fair. Acting as an intermediary between him and Carly has given me an unfair advantage, as well as access to his dirty laundry. Now he sees an opportunity to pry the lid off my hamper, of course he's gonna go for it.

"No." I shake my head and sink back down on the couch. "I never saw them. They must have crossed right it after it happened."

That's right. That's the truth.

Isn't it?

All of a sudden I don't feel so good.

Cold. I'm freezing. Like someone walked over my grave.

"Hey, you okay?" Boone leans forward, genuine concern on his face. "You look like you've seen a ghost."

"Oh, ha ha. That's droll." I rub my brow just above the bridge of my nose. I've got the beginnings of one mother of a headache digging in behind my eyes. Ow. "Seen a ghost. Wokka wokka. Rolling in the aisles, here."

Boone grimaces. "I can't believe I said that. Guess you hear that one all the time."

"No, as a matter of fact, I don't. So far you're the only one who knows I can do this. And I'd be deeply grateful if you kept it that way."

Boone gives me a long, thoughtful look while he mentally digests the juicy nugget of information I've just fed him. It hits me how much power this man now has over me. Holy hand grenades, this is so not good.

But hang on, this isn't exactly a one-way power-over situation. I might have dealt him one hell of a trump card, but he can't afford to use it. He needs me. I'm his Carly connection. He won't risk that. So that should keep me and my secret safe until I can figure out what my next move should be.

Actually, I already know what I should do, but I'm not crazy about the idea, especially with an incipient headache complicating things. I'm not fond of opening myself up this way. But if I want to get a proper read on him, I don't have any choice.

"Deal," he eventually nods. "Besides, even if I did squeal, who'd believe me?"

Oh, only every lunatic fringer and strung-out stalker-obsessive nut-bar wack-job between here and the here-after. The story would make him millions—and my life a living hell. When I'm in a particularly masochistic mood, I have oftentimes wondered how this constant state of weirdness I live in could possibly get any worse.

Hello! Wonder no more. Here we are!

"Hopefully no one, but let's not test the premise, 'kay?"

Damn. The demolition men in my head have switched from shovels to jack hammers. Must be the booze. You'd think I'd have learned my lesson by now. I can do a lot of things, but drinking is not one of them. As much as I enjoy indulging in the occasional quality libation, the stuff simply does not agree with me.

No matter how much I pay for it.

"Why are you doing this?" Boone's abrupt interrogative interrupts my escalating agony. "Cutting me some slack, I mean. Don't get me wrong, I'm really happy I'm not being extended an invitation to check out the inside of your local detention facilities."

"We actually do have a jail, believe it or not. It's brand new. Barely broken in. The most dangerous felon it has sheltered to date has been Grover McPhee. Whenever the sheriff hauls him in to sleep off the occasional bender."

Okay, deep breath, ignore the rave in my head, dial down the visual filters, and look.

"Town drunk?" Boone politely masks his amusement. He fights back a grin, but there's a definite sparkle in his eye.

"All his life. We're proud of him."

Is he flirting with me? Is that—no way! The aura does not lie. Tendrils of mustardy yellow are spidering around his head and shoulders, like veins in his energy field swelling with desire.

"Well, at least I'd have company." He turns the grin up a notch and boosts the sparkle to twinkle.

He is! He is flirting with me! A tiny, trembling ball of nervous excitement I'm not solely responsible for generating is commencing to coil in my belly. Oh, boy, lowering my screens is not without consequence. Feedback is a bitch.

I should squash it flat. Before it gets out of hand and takes me places I dare not go.

I don't want to.

"I can still make the call, if you're keen for the experience."

"I'll pass." The animation drains out of his expression, and the hunted, guilty look is back.

I didn't mean to shut him down. I was teasing. I guess he doesn't know me well enough to tell. Or I don't know how to do it right.

The savagery of his contrition is not an act. Definitely not faking it. He's flaying himself alive from the inside out. I can see every strip he's peeling off his soul playing out in his aura like metaphysical mood ring.

It's a hell of a seat I have here, front row centre to Boone's every emotion.

I settle in to listen and assess the show.

"I really am sorry," Boone meekly admits. "I don't know what came over me. Property invasion and armed intimidation is not my style. I'm not saying I'm an angel or anything, but I've been through some serious shit, and I've never gone dark side like that before. Not once, but twice. I don't get what made me go nuts like that. I don't understand any of this."

Boone takes a swift slug of beer and rubs the back of his neck. Now things have calmed down and so has he, I can really feel his pain. And that's not just a figure of speech. He's utterly terrified by everything he's seen and done here and convinced he's losing his mind. His uncertainty is hard to watch, even tougher to experience, but in a funny way, his inner ordeal and self-doubt is curiously refreshing.

I know how that sounds, and I can explain. I've been immersed in this spooky sideshow for so long, so accustomed to considering this continual state of freakiness normal, I'd forgotten how surreal my reality really is.

So this is how normal people see things.

Wow.

Ow! I really need to take something for this pain in my head.

"Is Carly still here?" Boone's soft inquiry interrupts my introspection.

Carly! What's wrong with my head! Boone, Boone, I've been so obsessed with Boone I've forgotten about Carly. How long has it been since she first manifested?

I don't see her. Obviously it's been over time, or she wouldn't have done a fade. Great. Way to go, Ellery. How am I going to explain this to Boone? I kept his daughter waiting too long and she had to leave before they could finish talking to each other.

"I'm sorry, I don't see her now."

"No?" He looks stricken. "She left me? Did she do the crossover thing? Already? Why didn't she say good-bye?"

"No! It's not like that. She hasn't crossed over yet. She's just not here right now."

"Why? If she didn't do the cross over thing, then where did she go?"

What do I tell him? I have no idea. I've never had to explain any of this before; I don't know where to begin.

"She didn't necessarily go anywhere. She could still be here. I simply can't see her now."

Boone is not finding it easy to assimilate what he's hearing. I can't say I blame him. I've had twenty odd years to deal with this stuff, and at times I still struggle.

"What do you mean, she's still here, but she's not? I don't get it."

Join the club. Even with Mrs. Sheridan's assistance, I'm still trying to work out the ground rules. I finally figured out it's easiest to simply go with what works.

"Manifesting isn't easy. It takes a lot of energy. Most spirits can only do it for short periods of time. Ten to fifteen minutes is usually the maximum. I wasn't exactly watching the clock, timing her from when she first appeared, but I'm sure she did at least that much and then some. I'm not surprised she had to… to dial it back and do a fade."

"Is she okay?" Boone asks apprehensively. "It doesn't hurt her… to… to be with me?" He swallows painfully, obviously distressed over the possibility the effort of reaching out to him might have caused his daughter pain. He's terrified the gift of getting her back, even for a short time, might have come at too high a price.

He should be scared. He's closer to the truth than he knows.

"She's fine, Boone. For now. But she needs to move on. We

should talk about that, how we're going to help you... help her do that."

"I miss her." Boone's distress deepens, grief dulling the vibrant malachite of his eyes. "She was just a baby."

He winds his arms around himself and bends forward, his face contorting with soundless agony. A strange, surreal lethargy washes over me; I feel like an out-of-body spectator to my every movement while I edge along the couch toward him. I still don't know what I'm doing or why when I reach Boone, take him in my arms, and pull him into my chest.

His body wracked with dry, sobbing heaves he doesn't attempt to stem, he sags limply into me like his spinal cord has been severed. I tightly embrace him, feeling the weight of his head heavy against my chest. He's eerily silent, his breathing labored and erratic, warm, moist puffs of air beating a syncopating rhythm against my naked neck.

"I know it hurts, I know it hurts." Soothing sounds pour out of my mouth. "And it'll keep on hurting 'til you think you can't stand it anymore. But you can, Boone, you can get through it. I know it doesn't seem that way now, all you feel is this awful, aching emptiness you think is never gonna get any better, but it will. I promise you, there is life, and hope and peace, on the other side of the agony. You just have to hold on, keep on going, push your way through the pain. Let yourself grieve, get angry, get crazy, whatever you need to do to get through one day and then the next. I don't know exactly when it will happen, but one morning you'll wake up, and it won't hurt quite so much. The morning after that, it'll hurt even less, and every morning from then on in, it'll get easier and easier."

His arms slowly wrap around me, tightening almost to the point of pain, his breathing slowing down, evening out.

We sit. He breathes. I wait.

"Does it ever go away?" I almost don't hear the faint, mournful murmur.

"No. Not completely. But it gets small enough you can live with it."

"How old were you when you lost your folks?"

I didn't expect the question, but I'm touched by the concern implicit in the asking.

"Eight. I was eight."

"Almost the same age as Carly." He takes a big, shuddering breath, releasing his claustrophobic clasp on me long enough to pat me awkwardly on the back. "How did you do it?"

"Just like I said," I softly answer and risk patting him back. "One day at a time."

"It's not that simple," he whispers. "You don't know what I did."

No, but I'd like to.

I don't know how to ask or offer. I don't know what he needs or wants from me. And then the brief window of opportunity so tantalizingly dangling in front of me is snatched from my grasp.

Boone pushes me away, straightening up with a self-conscious snort.

"Guess I should stop snotting up your shirt and get my shit together. Oh," he blurts with a pointed glance at my chest like it's the first time he's laid eyes on it today. "Damn, did I do that?"

Shirt. He's talking about the shirt. Omigawd. The nasty, egg-encrusted shirt I was intending to change before this all started.

Oh. Ick.

I finger one of the uglier portions of the garment and make a face. "Yeah, I guess you did."

"That's not gonna come out," he intelligently observes. "Hope you weren't too emotionally attached to it."

"Nope," I shrug. "I have one or two more where that came from. I should probably…."

I break off, feeling awkward and unsure. I need to change the shirt, and that means leaving the room. And him.

Not crazy about either alternative.

"Yeah," he nods, looking away. "And seeing as how you're not going to have me arrested, I should stop pressing my luck… and…."

Exit stage right, go away, depart the premises never to be seen again?

He's the one who brought it up, the leaving thing, I mean, but he doesn't seem in any hurry to actually do it.

I'm in even less of a hurry to watch him. Or make him.

Leave.

The idea of him going makes me feel sad, and scared, and small, and like I want to scream and break things. I've never felt anything like this before. I wish I knew what it was.

I stare at him; he stares at me. Whole lot of staring going on. One of us needs to say something.

Boone breaks first, lowering his eyes, fixating on his hands while he rubs them together.

"I don't have anywhere to go," he haltingly admits.

The fear, loneliness, and naked need lance along the pathways forming between us. I've left myself open, and I'm completely unprotected from the emotional assault.

"Hold that thought," I blurt, springing to my feet. "I have to change my shirt. Have another beer. I'll be right back and we'll.... we'll talk."

He's too close, the feelings flooding into me too intense—too much, it's too much. I have to get away, put some distance between us so I can raise shields again.

Oh, yeah, also really need to pop some Tylenol now. Going full-spectrum for even a short time has turned up the volume on my headache big time. It's like having tiny fingers scraping the inside of my skull just behind my eyes. Little bitty fingers wearing huge, honking, steel-toed boots.

I don't wait for either a yay or nay from Boone, immediately beetling out of the room and hurtling down the hall towards the stairs like I've got afterburners up my ass. I want to put some serious distance between us, and I want to return to the man in the parlor twice as fast. My head is pounding, my senses are screaming. I'm seriously messed up.

He'll wait for me. He's not going to leave. He said he'd stay. When I walk back into the room where I left him, he'll still be there.

By the time I reach my bedroom, I've dialed my senses back enough to reassert some emotional control. My head still hurts, but things are making sense again.

I ball my ex-shirt up and fire it into the trash beside the sink, then rifle around in the vanity drawer for the Tylenol. After dry-swallowing a couple of capsules, I head into the adjacent dressing room.

New shirt, here we come. I have about twenty, give or take, exactly like the one I just disposed of. Off the rack, nondescript, kicking-around-the-house, nothing special button-down shirt. I do have nice clothes. Max made sure of that. Damned nice, and three times as expensive. Normally, when I'm hanging out here, I don't bother with dressing to impress. I only trot out the good stuff for public relations purposes—book tours and interviews, premieres and openings—all the folderol unfortunately accompanying the semi-celebrity territory I loathe and despise. But when you've gotta do what I've sometimes gotta in the name of selling myself, I mean, my books, occasionally you gotta walk the walk and wear the stuff.

In a pinch I can turn out with the best of them.

Now, returning to my wardrobe options, I could replace one boring shirt with another, or I could trade up.

Hmmm....

No, not that one, that's a little too... not exactly a subtle statement. Don't want to look like sex on a stick. Nope, nope, nope, definitely not, nope, hang on, hold the phone. That one, I think. Max says it's her favorite. Flattering without screaming "Fuck me, please."

That's what she says! Should I change the pants too? No, that would look weird; I've got an excuse for redressing the upper half, but the lower, not so much.

What am I doing? Am I losing my mind? I'm standing here in my closet agonizing over what to wear like I'm getting ready for a date!

That's quite a leap, considering the object of my interest, while undeniably attractive, is still barely this side of homicidal, not to mention suicidal! Sure, I caught him giving my assets the eye, and my sneaky aura scan left little doubt as to the extent of his interest, but what I'm supposed to do with it, or him, or any of this? Haven't a clue.

Gah, I'm current with the latest dealing with the dead protocols, but interfacing with the living? Do they hand out manuals for that, and if so, where can I get one?

I yank the shirt I've selected off the hanger, throw it on, and start working the buttons while walking back into my bedroom. Thus engaged, I nearly bang into Boone, who is planted smack-dab in the middle of the doorway. Blocking my exit from the closet.

What the—didn't I leave you downstairs?

Apparently not, 'cause there he is, obstructing my exit; a larger-than-life vertical speed-bump impeding my progress. Just standing there. Smiling. Standing. Smiling.

Really strange smile. Like he's savoring a mouthful of whipped cream. I've already shut down, so I can no longer secretly scope his aura for clues as to what's going on in his head, and after what the previous scan did to me, when there was half a couch between us? No way I'm opening up again when he's standing close enough to....

How long has he been there?

Is he is he staring at me?

"Are you staring at me?"

Boone shrugs, avoiding the question. "Got tired of waiting."

I stare at him. He stares at me. I can't help but notice he's not moving out of the way.

So now what?

"Are you going to stand here all day?" Boone lifts his eyebrows expectantly.

"Well, I hadn't planned on spending the afternoon in the closet, but there's this guy in my way."

Boone points at himself and gives me a "you mean me?" expression.

"We definitely don't want to keep you in the closet." His response is low, silky, and laden with innuendo. "Do you want to come out now?"

His warm, intriguing voice sends an alien but not unwelcome frisson of excitement rippling down my spine.

"Yes!" I squeak. My mouth is saying yes, but in my head I'm thinking….

You have to stop thinking what you're thinking. Just. Stop.

Now.

"Well." He flashes me a roguish smile. "All you had to do was say so."

Despite seeming to comply, he doesn't entirely clear out of my way. He repositions himself against the side of the doorframe, barely allowing me an adequate escape corridor past him, and then throws me an impudent grin as if daring me to go for it.

Off-balance, nervous, and strangely excited, I quickly slip by him.

"Good choice," he murmurs, his eyes on the portion of my chest revealed by my still only half-buttoned shirt.

"Bastard," I mutter and flee, my face flaming.

I mutter myself halfway through the bedroom, fingers fiddling with buttons I can't seem to fasten. I'm acutely aware of the man following hard on my heels, but I'm still not sure how I feel about it. Or him. Or where this, or either of us, is going next.

A scratchy, noxious growl emanating from the general area of my bed abruptly cancels my incipient panic attack. As if I didn't have enough going on already.

Now what?

I look toward the sound, already knowing what I'm going to see, and sure enough, there it is, skulking on my duvet, the author of the aural interruption. A black, writhing ball of dispossessed ectoplasmic ugly is cluttering my counterpane, sniffing and snarfing and frantically casting around for the nearest passing two-legged energy buffet.

Well, hello there, you fugly little scrud! What are you doing in my bedroom? Or, an even more interesting question, what are you still doing in my house? Mrs. S. obviously evicted you, but apparently didn't take out the trash while she was at it. No worries, I don't need her to dispose of the likes of you. You, I can handle.

I wonder why she left you here. Oh, I get it, this must be her way of telling me I'm out of practice. She thinks I'm getting rusty, bless her. Whatever. She's wrong, and I'll take it up with her later. Right now, however, I'd better wrap you up before you get wind of Boone and attempt to reacquire.

Too late!

With an excited, triumphant shriek, the uninvited guest I don't want hanging around makes a galloping beeline for the one I do. Boone innocently exits my walk-in, having no idea he's been selected as catch of the day by a dislocated, free-roaming, energy-seeking ball of badass negative energy.

Try saying *that* three times fast.

Oh, no, you don't.

You can't have him. I saw him first.

Okay, I probably didn't, but you still can't have him.

"Don't move," I instruct, inserting myself between Boone and the etheric ball of ick barreling toward him with gluttonous speed.

"Okay," he grins playfully. "What have you got in mind?"

"Not what you're thinking." Lacking my unique perspective on the situation, he has no idea of the nature of the fray I'm about to throw myself into on his behalf. I don't know what base impulse of Boone's either hatched this thing or drew it to him, but in order to protect him from falling back under an outside malign influence he's not aware of but probably created and was definitely sustaining, I first have to stop it from latching back on.

Then we'll permanently pop the ectoplasmic pimple.

Problem solved.

I ignore another suggestive remark from behind and concentrate on what lies ahead. I close my eyes, breathe, and flex my will to extrude the barbed energy cord that'll connect me to the zoink in order to remove it from both of our lives. My target hasn't a clue what's about to happen; it's mindlessly fixated on reattaching itself to its former meal ticket. The oblivious man behind me unable to seeing it coming.

I launch the cord, the glittering terminator sailing cleanly across the intervening space, neatly penetrating the outer membrane of the noxious loping mass. A mental push drives the barb, and the cord it carries, deep into the zoink's energy body. Now my cord is properly anchored, I give it a mental shake and settle a couple of shining loops around the soon-to-be-ex-ick before it realizes it's been hooked, lined, and about to be sunk.

Or should I say transformed. A zoink is a very basic etheric creature. Just about as basic as they come. A baggie of semi-sentient, barely animated energy with only one prime directive: to suck up even more energy in order to perpetuate its miserable existence.

Energy. Not very nice energy at the moment, but still, only energy. You can't destroy energy, but you can make it better. By increasing the vibrational level. Bust the sow's ear by making what's inside more suitable for a silk purse.

The weapon of choice? Good vibrations. Which is what I'm going to pump this thing full of now, via my handy-dandy little etheric cord. Subject it to a vibrational transfusion, whether it wants one or not. That will step up the frequency of the energy inside the membrane, and when its ambient internal positive level peaks past a certain critical point, the zoink simply ceases to exist. Pretty basic stuff, but it's been a long time since I've actually done it. I don't have much contact with this class of wiggler any more. They don't get in here, where I live, and when I'm out there, in the midst of their progenitors and hosts, I screen so I no longer see them everywhere I look. I learned to tune them out a long time ago. I had to, or I'd have gone nuts. There's simply too damned many of them. You can't fight them all. Believe me, I know; there was a time when I tried.

You, you, little mothersucker, this is your unlucky day. You picked the wrong guy to hitch a ride on. Kiss your ugly ass good-bye. You're on my turf? You're automatically toast.

The instant it senses the good vibes I'm pumping into it, the zoink starts howling like a banshee in a blender. I harden my heart and my ears against its frenzied expressions of fury and keep making with the good energy infusion. Almost instantaneously, a smear of gold erupts around the barb pulsing dimly in the zoink's murky centre. The blot of brilliance rapidly expands, displacing and transforming the roiling, dirty muck whirling inside the zoink's swelling, blistering outer membrane.

This isn't going to take very long. We should reach critical mass....

"Hey!" Boone's hand clamps on my shoulder. His touch sends a wild electric shock sheering through me, racing down the cord and into the pulsating mass of swiftly morphing psychic pest. With a brilliant, soundless flash, the former zoink's outer membrane completely shreds and pristine, pure white light spills joyfully into the universe.

And that, kiddies, is how EJJ cleans house.

Perhaps my self-awarded accolades are slightly premature.

Normally, when you do an energy intervention like this, you have to be wary of the backlash. Conversion concentrates are mighty potent stuff; therefore, you want to stay well away from a zoink when it blows. If you get a snootful, it won't hurt you, but you'll be feeling no pain for hours.

I'm still shaky from Boone's touch, hence slow on the cord's uptake. Sloppiness that might prove my undoing. Ah, shit, where's my head? I forgot to seal the thing off, and it's still too close to the—

Backlash, comin' at me, too late to clamp or compensate.

The feel-good infusion whammies into my solar plexus and shoots up through my chakras, nearly taking the top of my head off. But not in a bad way. Au contraire, it feels incredible, like knocking back a vat or two of Red Bull with a mega-caffeine chaser, but it's a massive jolt of happy I was neither prepared for nor expecting, and too much of anything, even a good thing, isn't necessarily great.

Bad news: goin' on my ass. Good news, not gonna care. Wheee!

Woohoo, maybe not! Strong hands, really strong, nice and warm hands on my arms, holding me fast, hard, firm chest against my back, propping me up, pushing me onto my feet.

"Hey! Are you okay? You're whiter than a sheet! What the hell just happened, here?"

Boone, that's Boone. Hey, Boone, good catch!

Oooh, feeling funky.

So, still on our feet? That's amazing. I can't believe I'm vertical. Now what? Oh, right! Hands! Feeling those hands all over me, turning me around, pushing ever-so-gently.

Leading me on?

Walk? Walk? You want me to walk? Sure, why not, I can walk. Apparently. Who knew? This is fun. Where are we going?

Who's giggling? Is that me? No way!

"Easy does it, Chuckles. One foot in front of other. Good boy. Almost there."

"I'm... I'm fine." I'm making a valiant stab at speech, but haven't a clue if I'm succeeding. My tongue feels funny. I gape stupidly around me, attempting to focus. The fuzzy blob floating just above me slowly resolves into a concerned face.

Boone's face. Boone's hunkering down beside me, eyeing me like I'm a recent escapee from a lunatic asylum. Wait a minute, what's going on here? I'm sitting on my bed. Why am I sitting on my bed?

Where in hell did the last five minutes of my life go?

"Funny, you don't look fine." Boone's face is a whole heap of "so not buying the 'I'm fine' story." "If I didn't know better, I'd swear you were stoned."

Funny, he's really funny. Must be, I'm giggling.

"Ellery," Boone gently prompts. "Is there something you're not telling me?"

"Plenty." I manfully repress my urge to emit more inappropriate humorous responses. "Something I suspect we have in common."

"I hope that's not all." He smiles crookedly, the corners of his eyes crinkling with indulgent resignation. "You're not going to tell me, are you?"

"I'm willing to negotiate an exchange of information. How about you?"

Boone eyes me thoughtfully, then abruptly pushes himself to his feet. He stands over me, his gaze intense but tempered with fond amusement. "Sure." He shrugs and extends a hand to me. "Sounds like fun."

Bemused, I stare at the open hand dangling so invitingly in front of me and then take it. His thick, strong fingers close around mine, drawing me up off the bed 'til I'm fully erect, swaying slightly, in front of him.

"Listen, I haven't eaten since some time yesterday, and I am seriously starving. You got a pizza place in this town? Or some other place that delivers? My treat."

"Yeah." I know my grin is goofy, but so what? "I could eat."

CHAPTER 9

"WHAT is that?" Boone casts a dubious eye at the forkful of lasagna en route to my mouth.

"Lasagna." Puzzled, I look down at the portion on my plate and then back up at him. "What, you've never seen lasagna before?"

"Sure I have! Even eaten some, in my time. It's never looked like that, though." He glares at my dinner suspiciously. "What's all that green crap in it? And where's the beef?"

Hopefully, still on the steer.

"Spinach. It's really good. You want some? There's plenty."

Boone gives me an over-the-top grimace. "No, thanks. I'll stick to this." He scans the huge slab of fully loaded deep-dish pizza he's hefting from his plate. "No spinach," he proudly announces, grinning like a cat of the Cheshire variety. "You want a slice? There's plenty."

"Thanks, I'm sure it's delish." I suppress a shudder. "Pepperoni and bacon and, wow, is that hamburger on there too?"

"Maybe." He squints at me and takes a huge bite. "What's wrong with that?"

"Aside from the cholesterol factor? A whole lot if you're a vegetarian."

"Ah." Boone nods sagely, comprehension dawning. "So I'm thinking although you make plenty, you don't eat a lot of bacon."

"Or anything else on that pizza." I try not to gag at the layer of grease glistening on Boone's slice. "But don't let me stop you."

Boone chews and ponders, his eyes sizing me up while that amazingly angular jaw moves rhythmically. "But weren't you having eggs for breakfast? That is, before I dragged you through them?" He finishes chewing, swallows, and smiles sheepishly. "I did apologize, for that, right?"

"You did," I acknowledge. "You're very observant. However, I'm a vegetarian. Not a vegan. I eat eggs and cheese, butter and milk. Some vegetarians eat fish too. But I don't."

"Oh." Boone takes another bite, followed by more contemplative mastication. "Do you have issues with hanging out with carnivores?"

Interesting question. One no one has ever asked me before. Putting up with what other people around me eat, no matter how personally objectionable I find it, is something I have to do all the time when I'm on tour. Max makes grudging allowance for my culinary limitations and ensures correct feeding instructions are included with all my travelling arrangements, but she's never been particularly gracious about it.

I've toyed with the idea of telling her I've converted to some weird fictitious religion only allowing me to travel on Tuesdays during a full moon when Mars is retrograde, in solar powered conveyances built in a month beginning with W. Fine, maybe the month thing is slightly over the top, but it would be fun to lay it all on her and watch her go simply ballistic.

I think I need another hobby. Perhaps I'm looking at it.

"Do I mind being around people who eat meat? Honestly?" He asked for it, I'm going to give it to him. "I'm not crazy about it, but I've learned to live with it. People who choose to consume the dead carcasses of animals still vastly outnumber we who have made a conscious choice not to exist at the expense of other life forms. Maybe someday that won't be the case, but for now...." I shrug and smile at him. "It is what it is."

Boone's flesh-coated slice lies abandoned on his plate while he focuses on me, his brow tightly furled. "Is your decision to swear off meat a moral choice, or does it have anything to do with what you can do?"

Wow. I can't believe he just asked me that! This guy is smart. I'm impressed he made the connection. And kind of excited he cared enough to ask.

"That would be a yes." I grin and have some more lasagna. "On both counts."

"No way!" Boone gapes at me. "Animals can be ghosts too?"

"Certainly. We're all energy. They're not self-aware, but they are sentient."

"And that means… what?"

He doesn't understand, but he wants to. This is getting better and better.

"Like us, they live because their physical body is inhabited and animated by a consciously controlled energy field capable of surviving the death of the body in a cohesive, perceivable form."

Boone blinks slowly, visibly processing.

I shut up and let him.

A comfortable silence settles between us. Our eyes engage, and suddenly his are smiling. A shade of fondness gentles the pensive line of his mouth. My eyes lock on his lips, in particular the swelling sensuality of the full lower one, lightly gleaming with grease from the pizza.

An electric pulse sings through me once more, this one of decidedly earthly origin. Startled by the sensation, my gaze jerks up to slam into the intense, green beams of his malachite orbs on the other side of the table as he is slowly, inexorably reeling me in. That's when I really feel it.

The most intense sense of connection I've ever experienced with anything.

Living—or dead.

I don't know what it means, but I like it. I want more. Lots more.

And just when I think it might be my turn to surrender to an inexplicable impulse to launch myself over a table and grab the guy on the other side, the moment passes.

Whoa....

If what almost made me go bananas all over Boone hit him the same way, he sure doesn't show it. He looks down at his plate, gives the pizza remnants residing there the once-over, then pushes it aside.

I guess it's just me. Oh well.

"Done?"

"The pizza, anyway." Boone nods. "I hope you don't mind, I'm gonna stick with the meat-eating thing for now, but I'm always open to new possibilities. And points of view," he concludes meaningfully.

And then again, maybe not. There's a lot going on behind those eyes. They're gleaming intently with a brand of hungry intensity I'm not entirely unfamiliar with. Just because I choose not to accept offers doesn't mean I don't get 'em. I've beat off my share of predators hailing from both sides of the fence.

Is it just me, or did that sound dirty? Must have something to do with the lust-colored lens through which I'm currently viewing the world. I blame it on the man across from me.

"Just taking a shot in the dark, here." Boone takes a slow sip of beer. "But getting back to the things that go bump in the night thing. If you don't mind me asking?" He pauses and looks at me expectantly.

"Not at all." I motion for him to continue. I wonder where he's going with this.

"You've mentioned dead people, and animals, but there's a lot more to it, isn't there?" He pauses and holds up his right hand, describing a vague circle in the air. "There's all sorts of weird stuff floating around out there we can't see and you can. Isn't there?" He rests the lip of the bottle against his bottom lip, watches me, and waits.

"What makes you say that?" The sharpness of my retort startles me. I thought I was okay with the idea of coming out from behind the Ouija board, but the sudden wave of insecurity sweeping over me shocks the hell out of me. But you know what? It shouldn't. It's only my gut telling me I'm being a fool. As much as I've enjoyed this momentary fantasy and flirting with Boone as well as the entire concept of closeness, it's about time I stopped kidding myself I can actually have any of it, and him, and came back down to Earth.

Because of what I am, engaging in any sort of intimacy must remain forever in the land of unattainable dreams and pointless fantasies. Although I long to reach out to him, I don't dare. He's smiling at me now, imagining he's fine with what little he knows, but he has no idea what it really means to be me.

If he could stand in my skin for one brief moment and truly experience even a small part of my reality, would he still be smiling? I doubt it. And let's get real here: why should he? Why should he be any different from anyone else I've ever known? There's a way to find out for sure, but I don't think my heart is up to risking the disappointment.

It's not easy to be me. Learning to pass for "normal" consumed most of my childhood. Although what was happening all around me was anything but. It took me years to come to terms with what I am and finally accept that my "normal" was a constantly schizophrenic existence requiring me to find a way to function with one foot firmly planted in each reality. Every waking moment.

I've learned how to walk the delicate line between this world and the next and not go crazy, given the potential for constant horror is a consistent thread woven into the very fabric of my mundane existence. What would probably drive your average person insane is just another day at the office to me. That's my world, and welcome to it, a whole lot of weirdness going on. I'm the ultimate package deal. If your idea of the ultimate package is a non-stop, all-you-can-scream buffet. A twenty-four-seven spookathon. When it comes to the macabre, we never close. Who in their right mind would want to take what I've got going on... on?

Never met him yet.

Or have I?

Do I have the guts to find out? That, I do not know.

"Why do I ask?" Boone's mild reply brings me back to the conversation. "I'm curious about the little show you put on upstairs."

Oh. That. Damn. I forgot about that.

"And don't tell me it was nothing. I have eyes, and I'm not stupid."

No, you're not. But are you strong enough to stand it? I want you to be, but I don't know if I can take it if you can't.

I stare at him. I don't know what to say. I want to tell him, but I'm too damned scared.

He watches me silently. Those eyes see everything and say nothing. What do I look like to him? What is he seeing?

"Tell you what, why don't I start. Here's a piece of information for you, for free." Strong, white teeth briefly gleam at me as those sensuous lips gently quirk in an engaging grin. "My life has often depended on my ability to swiftly observe and correctly assess my immediate surroundings. I don't often get it wrong." He grins again. "I'm here, aren't I?"

"So, what do you think you observed?" I latch onto the conversational thread he's tossed me and throw it back. God, I want to tell him, but I still don't know.

"I know what I saw. What I don't know is what it means."

And I'd like to.

He doesn't say it; he doesn't have to. I hear it but I still don't know if I can believe it.

I'm about to chicken out and return another yet ambiguous response when Boone sighs and sadly shakes his head. "Look, you have a lot at stake here, I get it. You've been playing the obfuscation game for so long you can do the misdirection dance in your sleep. Believe me, I can relate."

I believe you can.

"Listen, if you're not ready to give it up yet, I understand. I don't blame you for not trusting me. Why should you? I'm only the guy who busted into your house, stole your booze, threatened you at gunpoint, and ruined your shirt. I can't imagine why that wouldn't make you feel like you could trust me with your deepest, darkest secrets. It's cool. I won't ask for anything you don't want to give. And I do mean… anything." He pauses dramatically; his eyes holding mine while he drains his bottle of beer in several slow swallows.

Whoa.

"Although I won't lie to you and say I won't be deeply

disappointed if you can't... open up."

Oh, I want, I want, I want to very much. Open right up!

"I'm sorry!" I blurt and have a go at reeling my brains back in. "I'm weirded out. I admit it. I've never done this before."

"There's a first time for everything," he throatily observes, his eyes smoking with innuendo.

Omigawd. I have a slow-burning fuse in my shorts threatening to ignite. I think I need to get my mind out of there before it blows.

Okay, I'll do it. I'll talk.

"Well, if you really want to know about the upstairs incident—"

"Oh, I do, I do!" He nods vigorously.

"Okay, short version, I saved you from a free-roaming variety of psychic parasite I call a zoink."

Boone doesn't even blink. I'm impressed.

"Has a kind of a Scooby-Doo vibe to it," he finally comments.

"Got it in one. You're good."

He beams with the uncomplicated pride of a five-year-old. "I not only had kids, I was one."

Of that I have no doubt. Meanwhile, back at the explanation....

"Okay, I'll see if can I make this make sense."

"Don't worry about dumbing it down on my account," Boone dryly counters, a slightly defensive spin on his tone. "I can keep up just fine. I think pretty fast on my feet."

Aw, he thinks I just implied he was dumb. Maybe I'm not the only one nursing the odd insecurity or two.

I wonder if his are odder than mine.

Nah.

"The issue isn't your capacity for comprehension. It's my expositional talents I fear are not equal to the task."

"An odd statement coming from a writer." Boone waggles his eyebrows playfully at me. "What say we meet in the middle?"

He's laughing at me, but not in a mean way. And definitely still flirting.

I like it.

"Right." I take a deep breath and go. "You called it correctly. There are a whole lot more things populating the afterlife than ex-people. If you could see one tenth of what whiffs and wafts, swarms and squirms, floats and crawls and squirts in the ether all around you while you blissfully go about on your daily rounds, you probably wouldn't leave the house. And that still wouldn't keep 'em away from you."

"Really!" Boone's right eyebrow makes an impressive attempt to merge with his hairline. "It's a jungle out there, huh? And in here." He glares suspiciously at the empty air around him. Which really is entirely unpopulated. Situation normal for chez moi.

Everywhere else? Not so much.

"You have no idea. There's a lot of weird-ass shit floating around. Way too many varieties of roamers, floaters, screamers, and shakers for me to classify, but I used to try."

"You gave them names?"

"When I was a kid. It was a way of coping with it. Organizing the insanity by cataloging it."

Boone's eyes soften with sympathy. "Did it help?"

I shrug. "Some. Anyway, the type I dealt with upstairs I dubbed a zoink. And yes, you guessed it; I lifted the name from Scooby-Doo. Exactly what a zoink is and where it comes from, that's not as easy to explain."

"Take your time," Boone smiles encouragingly. "I'm not going anywhere."

Or having any problems with anything you're hearing so far. I am encouraged.

"You know the whole 'thoughts are things' thing? It's not just a New Age cliché. What you think, you get. And it can come back on you and literally bite you on the ass."

"Okay, I'm with you, I think." Boone's dubious expression says otherwise.

"Let me put this another way. We'll use light as an example. Light is a form of energy. I'm sure you're aware of the color spectrum and how each color has a specific frequency and vibration."

"I'm somewhat familiar with the concept," Boone nods.

"Well, energy is energy—whether it's light or heat or radiation or thought waves. Thoughts are more than electromagnetic impulses generated by your brain, they also exist in and affect the etheric and astral planes. Every single thought is energy and what you think has a real, tangible effect on the unseen realms. This isn't metaphysical mumbo-jumbo, it's as much an actual fact of astral physics as the rules governing the physical universe we can observe and quantify."

"Astral physics." Boone says it slowly, like he's trying it out for size. "Heavy. Please continue."

I grin. "Here's where it gets interesting. I used light as an example for a reason. Some of the properties we associate with light apply to the energy generated by thoughts. And emotions. Emotions can 'shade' the quality of energy associated with mental emanations. Positive thoughts and actions make good energy, and negative—"

"You're talking about frequencies. Good thoughts and feelings vibrate high, and bad—or negative—low-level nasty stuff."

"Exactly!" I'm excited by his acceptance. He knows. How cool is that? "Lower-level impulses and actions create really bad vibes. When stuff like that goes out into the universe, it isn't good for anyone. Most people don't have a clue how much what they think and feel affects them, their immediate surroundings, their personal realities and the one we all share. Every thought, both conscious and unconscious, sends out a field of energy with a specific charge determined by the emotional focus of the thinker. These fields interact with each other, shape our individual realities, and make an impact on the larger fabric of the universe. Our thoughts make things happen, draw all sorts of stuff to us, and sometimes, when the intent is strong and focused enough, can actually coalesce into artificially created entities capable of either helping us or haunting us. Quite literally."

Boone leans forward, listening intently. "I take it we're now talking zoink here."

"We are. For the bad things, anyway."

"So, a zoink is something someone thought up? For real? It came out of someone's head? That's a scary concept!"

"Now you're catching on." I have to smile. "'Right out of someone's head' is a damned good way of putting it. Everything, both things we can see and things we can't—"

"Or at least, I can't," Boone supplies with a grin.

"Right. Anyway, everything existing in the world right now started with a thought. So it is with a zoink."

"This is where you tell me the thoughts that make a zoink are bad." Boone isn't smiling anymore.

"Recipe for creating a zoink: concentrate intense emotion on one thought or concept and pour a massive amount of negative energy into it. You do it long enough, and habitually enough, and all that focused negative energy reaches a concentration point where it literally takes on a life of its own. People have no idea what they're doing when they harbor hate and envy and guilt and greed and all that other nasty stuff. You do enough bad thinking and feeling for long enough, and you create your own personal demon. That's when your troubles really start."

"I think I see where you're going with this."

Yes, I do believe you do. What's even better, although it's giving you much food for thought, it's not sending you screaming out the door.

I'm daring to hope. About a lot of things.

"A zoink has only one purpose—self-perpetuating. Not unlike everything else in this world and the next. In order to stay alive, it needs more of the bad stuff that made it in the first place. Its best source is the original one. You made it, you bought it. And you get to feed it."

Boone mulls this for a bit. He's doing very well keeping up with everything I'm telling him. Hope does more than float; right now it's dancing a jig.

"So, let me see if I get this. What you're saying is these things we can't see are hanging on us, sucking energy, like psychic mosquitoes?" He looks to me for confirmation.

"Exactly!" Ooh, that's good. Wish I'd thought of it. "Not everybody has 'em. But certainly if you're a hardcore, habitual emitter of negative emotions, I can almost guarantee you're hosting at least one. Maybe more. Once you do, the negative inclinations and emotions you indulged in to create it are only going to get worse."

Boone's face gets longer and grimmer. Yeah, he's smart. "And then what?"

"I think you already know." He does, but I'll spell it out for him anyway. "Once a zoink attaches, it will do everything it can to keep priming that negative energy pump. That means constantly upping the antisocial ante, inciting the host to think bad thoughts, do bad things, whatever it takes to ensure a constant supply of what it needs."

"The little demon sitting on your shoulder, whispering in your ear. That's for real?" Boone looks properly horrified. He should be.

"Oh, yeah. Whenever someone says they have no idea why they say or do stuff? They're closer to the truth than they know."

I wonder if he remembers he made a similar statement about an hour ago.

Boone's expression doesn't attempt to answer the question. "We make these things ourselves? By thinking?"

"The class Bs, yeah."

"That really sucks!"

"I know. So do they."

"That's the scariest thing I've ever heard." Boone's horrified eyes tell me he's not kidding. "These things must be all over the place. Every other person out there must have shit all over them!"

"Well, it's not quite as bad as all that. Most class B's aren't very powerful. They're like persistent subconscious nags and goads, and that's all they can do. Make suggestions. They can't actually compel you to do anything or override a person's free will. The capacity to make our own choices and decisions, despite outside influences and compulsions, very much remains with us. As well as ultimate responsibility for everything we do, no matter what influences surround us. Getting clear of all of it—and shot of your self-created demons—can be as easy as simply saying no."

"That's easy for you to say." Boone sighs and looks away. He understands what I've just told him, and he's connecting a few dots. I'm not sure where we go from here, if he's ready to deal with it or talk about it or if he'd rather pass on self-examination and fall back on denial.

When he turns back, the barrenness in his eyes has softened. "If there's a class B, I'm assuming the existence of a class A."

"You assume correctly." So, I'm assuming that's a "no" for talking about it. Fine. I'll back off for now. But I can't let him off the hook forever. For Carly's sake, we have to get to the root of Boone's emotional affliction.

That zoink he was packing didn't come out of nowhere. He knows it, and so do I.

"Ghostbusters?" The side of his mouth quirks.

Huh? Oh, the classes! He got that too.

"That would be a yes."

"Ah, the classics," Boone chuckles. "Okay, I have to ask. What is a class A?"

"They are sentients, actual etheric beings, not an artificially created, non-repeating thought form."

"Wow!" Boone emits a low whistle. "That's a lot of jargon. You really got into this whole otherworldly nomenclature thing."

"It passed the time." I shrug. "When I was a kid, as far as my this-world activities went, other than reading, watching a lot of TV, and keeping off Kevin Bradley's radar, I didn't have much else to do."

Ah, dear old Kevin. A story for another time.

"You see these things all the time? Since you were a kid?" Now he feels sorry for me.

I'm touched by his concern, but it's unnecessary. It's not like I walk around constantly averting my eyes to avoid being permanently traumatized by a steady stream of humanity filing past me with all-day suckers hanging all over them. It's not like that. At least, not now.

"Relax, it's not as bad as all that." I give him my best "hey, no big deal" expression. "I'm used to it, and anyway, it's not like every other person out there has a drinking problem."

"As in, something plugged into them doing the drinking, which would be a problem," Boone mutters. "I see."

"I try not to."

His eyes soften with concern once more, and I crack. Suddenly I want to tell him everything. All he has to do is ask.

"What do you mean?" he gently prompts.

"I mean, I literally try not to see them. Over the years I've learned how to… screen. I can't completely block out the other side, but I can tune out some stuff. Despite my best efforts, somehow the ghosts always get through, but when it comes to the low-frequency flotsam and jetsam, that I did teach myself how to block. I had to. Now when I look at people, I dial down the spectervsion, and what I don't want to see simply isn't there."

I don't know what's surprising me more, the fact I'm admitting way more than I originally intended or that he's still listening.

"I didn't always feel this way. When I was a lot younger and first realized what was going on, I suffered from a massive Don Quixote complex. Tilting at windmills was nothing compared to the task I set for myself. I was gonna save the world and everyone in it. I nearly wore myself to the bone zapping every zoink I saw. But I soon realized I had to stop. I was wasting my time."

"You knocked them off, and they would come right back!"

"Yep. The second my back was turned. Popping the pimple only addresses the symptom, not the cause. Unless you get all the roots, the weeds come back. So do the zoinks."

"But that doesn't sound fair!" Boone exclaims. "How can anyone fight something they can't see?"

Ah, that's the real question, isn't it? Let's see what you do with the answer.

"Anyone who's prepared to be honest with themselves knows if they have a problem. You don't need to be able to see your personal demons to exorcise them from your life. Free will counts for a hell of a lot more than anything I can do. Ultimately nothing and no one has the power to make anyone do anything they don't want to do, including me. I can't make anyone living let go of what's blighting their life or anyone dead let go of what's screwing up their afterlife. All I can do is make suggestions. We all are responsible for everything that happens to us, both here and there."

"That's heavy, dude." Boone gives his empty beer bottle a wistful glance.

Tell me about it.

"So, getting back to the zoink you dealt with upstairs," Boone at last starts down the conversational path I've been hoping he'd choose. Good, good, this is all good. If we can sit down and talk this out, maybe I can get enough information about what happened with him and Carly so when she comes back—

The LEDs implanted behind the painted eyes of Colonel Birchwood's third daughter Beatrice in the portrait hanging over the mantle start softly blinking.

Oh no! Not now!

Of course, Boone being the trained observer he apparently is, or so he says, immediately notices something different about the portrait.

"Either I'm seeing things, or the eyes in that portrait are blinking."

Damn, he's good.

"You're not, and they are," I sigh. "You'll have to excuse me. I have to take a call."

"You're kidding." He narrows his eyes as he takes another bead on me.

"I assure you, I am completely serious. Don't go away now, I'll be right back."

I don't wait for an answer but throw my napkin on the table, get to my feet, and head for the hall.

"I'll stay here, then, shall I? Hang out?" he calls after me. "Possibly with another beer. On second thought, make that probably."

I almost make it to the hall before he calls after me again.

"Thunderbirds, right?"

"Can't get anything past you," I answer over my shoulder.

"Got that right." His promissory taunt dogs me as I jog left and across the hall and into the library.

CHAPTER 10

I LOVE this room. When I was a kid during my golden-age English mysteries period, I fantasized about one day having a room exactly like this. Right out of the pages of Agatha Christie and Margery Allingham; my very own to the manor house born type library finally fully realized. Its rich, dark wood paneling, the huge leather-upholstered wingback chairs facing the ornately carved stone fireplace rampant with cherubs, some impishly grinning figures inspired by the other end of the Biblical spectrum, and an interesting rendition of the face of a Green Man smack in the middle. The plush chocolate carpet, reams of shelves groaning with the leather-bound, the gilt-edged, the old, comfortably creased and oft-perused, so many different species of my favorite thing. I could settle on the antique settee by the window and soak in all the exquisite details for hours. And often have. But not right now.

I bypass all the warm elegance vying for my attention, making straight for the aforementioned fireplace and the room's most amazing, unsuspected, and completely concealed feature.

I found the release, and the room, by accident, during the renovation portion of the acquisition, while cleaning the crud out of the fireplace figures. A tweak of the Green Man's nose and voila! Boy, did I get a surprise!

I know what I've done with it is way over the top, but it's just so gosh darn cool!

Another one of the colonel's deceased and departed descendents blinks at me from his mantel-side station. Quit nagging me, I'm coming, already.

I tweak the nose, and the bookcase to the right of the fireplace slowly swings toward me on its hidden pivot. Surprise! One honest to God, for real secret room I've appropriated to house my high tech and extremely anachronistic—as far as the décor is concerned—communication center. Is this not the coolest thing you've ever seen or what?

Now, you tell me Michael Crichton has one of these babies!

I slide into the comfortable lounger facing the screen and hit the satellite link.

"Incoming transmission from the Freedom Foundation," the computerized voice announces, the big, betraying FF logo bleeming all over the screen.

Another chunk of my cover bites the dust. All Boone has to do now is guess my weight, height, and shoe size and I'm fresh out of secrets.

"Hey Ellery," Paula French's sunny face displaces the displeasing logo. "Oooh, nice shirt!" Her face gleams with an infusion of impishness. "Makes you look so hot!"

Argh, gimme a break!

"Down, girl." I roll my eyes at her. "You and I both know you only have eyes for Joan. Quit fooling around and give me the latest. From your cheery demeanor, I'm presuming it's good."

"Isn't it always, Honeychile?" she dimples teasingly at me, her faux-Southern drawl cranked to the max. "All is booming on the financial front. Your investments are going through the roof. The money keeps pouring in," she finishes with a triumphant toss of her jet-black curls.

Excellent. For this, and so much more, once again, I thank you, my unseen friends.

"Good, the more we have, the more we can give away." I acknowledge her update with a pleased grin of my own. "And speaking of handing it out, how are you keeping up with fulfilling the UP grant applications?"

"Checks all cut and sent, boss," she curtly responds, now all business, no trace of the affected accent tinting her voice. "And as soon as we clear the slate, a whole bunch more are banging on the door. No matter how many we help, a lot of people out there are still pretty hard up."

"Well, hopefully, one day that won't be so. But until then, we'll keep doing what we're doing. Anything else?"

The "tell or bust" grin on her face says she's saved the best for the last.

"You know it. The PFP Project is a go. The groundbreaking ceremony is on the seventeenth. I don't suppose you'll make an appearance to do the honors?" she lightly teases.

I glare at her. "What, pray tell, would Ellery James, private citizen, temporary media curiosity, and noted recluse with no connection whatsoever with the Freedom Foundation be doing in attendance? I'm quite happy with Kent functioning as the Foundation's public face. I'm sure he'll continue to uphold his fine tradition as my stand-in. Oh, good work, by the way."

"I thought you'd be pleased." Paula looks smug. She's entitled. "I have to admit I'm still having a hard time getting my head around what we're about to do. The country's first completely green, energy self-sufficient and off-the-grid housing development. I get goose bumps just thinking about it. You're about to set one hell of an example, Ellery."

"That's the idea, Paula. And not me, the Freedom Foundation. I'm just an anonymous writer of fair to middling historical fiction, remember?"

She wrinkles her pert little nose at me, feigning disgust.

"More like a hardly anonymous but definitely overly modest writer who just might be standing at the leading edge of the next major green wave. Practical, everyday energy independence. We're not just talking about it, we're actually doing it."

"What can I tell you, I dream big." I've been lying awake nights dreaming about this for the better part of the last two years, and now that we're here and it's actually about to happen, I can hardly believe it.

"All this progress isn't going to come cheap." Paula gives me a rueful grin. "I hope you know what you're doing, hon."

"Now, Paula, it's only money. If I lived to be a thousand, I couldn't spend what I'm bringing in all by myself. Besides, what's the point of having it if you don't use it to do some good?"

There's no denying I'm rolling in it, but I don't honestly believe I'm actually entitled to any of it. I've gained my current monetary advantages because of a trick of fate I didn't earn and don't necessarily deserve giving me access to unsuspected realms and unusual allies. If I used it strictly for my own benefit, I literally couldn't live with myself.

"Ellery!" Paula frowns. "You know I'm with you all the way. I only want you to be careful. So far, it's been working for you, but I'm afraid one of these days you're gonna lose your shirt, darlin'."

"Not this one, I hope," an ironic voice sounds from directly behind me.

Ah, I knew he'd follow me in here. Betcha he hasn't missed a word.

Paula's eyes get wider than chocolate dinner plates when the tall, russet-haired drink of water behind me comes into her field of vision.

"Ooooh, Ellery," she gushes, "you've been keeping secrets. Who's your friend?"

"None of your business, Paula." I smile at her and reach for the link. "Bye now. Stay in touch."

I hang up on her; the FF sign-off logo abruptly replaces her pouting face.

"Transmission has been terminated," the canned computer voice informs me.

God, I hate that thing!

The screen goes blank; I take a deep breath. Damn. My involvement with the Freedom Foundation is another little detail I was hoping to keep under wraps for, oh, the rest of my life. The last thing I want and need is for the world to find out I've founded and am bankrolling what's swiftly becoming a sizeable and extremely public philanthropic organization.

Not exactly crazy about Boone Dantrell knowing about it either. Although one could argue since he already knows what I've been hiding behind door number one, what's the big deal about him uncovering my other big secret? Maybe nothing. Maybe everything. Call me crazy, but I would have liked the option of choosing if and when I came out to him about either.

Get real, Ellery, you've pretty much handed over control of practically every other aspect of your so-called life. Why should this be any different?

And now, for my next trick, watch me pull a rabbit out of my ass. I doubt it would distract him long, but it'd be a hoot to see the look on his face.

I spin me and my chair around to face the man behind me, and the music. The pole-axed stare greeting me causes me to wonder if I've sprouted ancillary limbs and an extra head or two.

"So, what do you think?" I grin at him. "Cool room, huh?"

He doesn't seem as interested in the location of the medium or messenger as he is in the message. "The Freedom Foundation?" he chokes.

Here we go.

"Ah." I paste on a bleak smile. "You've heard of us."

"The Freedom freaking Foundation." He slowly, incredulously enunciates each word. "The 'feed the hungry, heal the sick, help the poor' Freedom Foundation? You're hooked up with *that* freaking Freedom Foundation?"

That's a whole lot of Fs, dude.

"Yes," I sigh. "Um… actually, if you want to get technical, I *am* the Freedom Foundation. Surprise!"

Gah, he'd better not be going all weird on me. The entire tenor of our interaction so far has been refreshingly honest. He likes me. Not what I am, what I have, who I know, or what I do. I really hope it stays that way.

"You just keep getting better and better."

I have no idea what he means by that. The sudden, frank admiration in his eyes? Kind of embarrassing.

"It's no big deal," I grumble, painfully aware of a hot flush running rampant across my cheekbones. "It's just something I do because I can."

"Pardon me if I don't agree! I'd call it a huge deal. The Freedom

Foundation does a hell of a lot of good!"

Just my way of paying the world back for what it's given me. I can, so I do. That's all there is to it. Don't need to talk about it or go on about it.

"Fine, suit yourself. Whatever."

I probably should rein in the impending hissy fit lest I say something he'll regret, but talking about this is pissing me off. This is exactly why I don't want people to know anything about me and the Foundation. The focus should be on the work. Where it belongs.

I don't need any more spotlight action.

"Okay, okay, Scrappy, I give, don't get you ass out of joint." Boone holds up his hands in the universal gesture of surrender and takes a step back. "I get it. Consider the subject closed."

Did he just call me Scrappy?

"Did you just call me Scrappy?"

"Maybe."

"Don't do it again."

"Wow, do you always go berserk whenever anyone tries to pay you a compliment?"

"No."

Of course not! I don't do that. Do I?

Oh wait, he's actually got a point here. Maybe I do.

The bag of angry I've been pumping my indignation into is instantly punctured by the insightful barb he's nudged me with. Immediate deflation ensues.

"I'm sorry." I tender a shame-faced acknowledgement of my irrational outburst. "This is a touchy subject for me. The Foundation is my real work, and making it a happen and keeping it going is why I perform in the three-ring media circus I loathe and despise. Because of the public image I foster for the sake of selling books, a certain perception is attached to me I don't believe would reflect well on the reputation or integrity of the Foundation should it be known I have anything to do with it."

"You ask me, I think you're overreacting," Boone scowls. "You act like a bubblehead, not a psycho, and I think, if people knew you were involved with the Foundation, if anything, the public perception of you would improve, not—"

"You're entitled to your opinion," I cut him off. "But the Foundation is too important to me to take any chances. I don't care what people think of me. If balancing babies on the end of my nose sells books, then so be it. Whatever it takes to keep the money flowing. The Foundation is what matters. Me? I'm nothing—just the one-trick pony bringing home the bacon."

"I thought you didn't like bacon," Boone murmurs sadly.

"It's a metaphor." His gaze is compelling and strangely calming. Like the light of his eyes is wrapping around me, warming me. There's a good five feet between us, and yet I can feel his arms enfolding me, giving me a hug.

I feel better.

"A mixed one at that." Boone pauses and emits a huge yawn. "Listen, Mr. James, I'd love to further debate your interesting and somewhat disturbingly deprecating self-image, but I'm really beat." He wearily scrubs his face with his hands. "You mind if I borrow one of your couches and sack out for an hour or two? I'm sure you can spare one. You seem to have no shortage of them in this place."

He does look tired. Sounds like a good idea. He needs some rest; I need time to think.

"I can do better than that. Follow me."

"With pleasure," Boone softly replies in a low, silken tone giving me shivers. In a good way.

I might live here alone most of the time, but I've also got the room and resources to bivouac a regiment if required. Birchwood Manor was converted into an upscale bed and breakfast in the fifties, long before it came into my possession, and in its heyday, it hosted a healthy horde of affluent travelers before changing times, rising prices, and bypassing interstates gradually choked the tourist trade into oblivion. So when I got it, the place came with some pretty good bones to work with.

I kept the second floor as it was during the glory days of the

Boarding House, restoring the sizeable, self-contained suites along their original lines with the appropriate modern plumbing and lighting upgrades. I use the second floor suites for the occasional guests I rarely receive. I'm usually only required to house, feed, and entertain interlopers during those happily few and far between intervals when Max and her omnipresent entourage desert civilization and risk a perilous expedition into the unknown environs of deepest, darkest Birchwood, her flurry of flunkies descending upon me like a plague of Gucci locusts bearing bad tidings and mounds of designer luggage. Max and her luggage are happily housed—the flunkies too—and as long as they remain under my roof, they get to live in the luxury to which they are accustomed, and I never have to see them.

The third floor is mine, all mine. Moo ha ha.

Basically, what it boils down to is I've got a suite or several that should suit Boone just fine. All I have to do is lead him to a room, and hopefully he'll sleep.

Boone follows me up the stairs and down the breezeway toward the west wing.

"Where we going?" he finally asks as we near the door to the suite I've selected.

"Here." I indicate the door, step aside, and wave him through. "I think you'll be fine in here. Like I said, I can do a little better than a couch."

Boone gives me a wary once-over, then sidles by me and passes through. A few seconds later, I hear an appreciate wolf whistle emanating from the room's interior.

I thought he'd be pleased.

I smother a grin and follow him in.

I don't get very far, and neither did he. He barely cleared the doorway before halting, where he's now planted, frankly gaping at the unrestrained opulence of the emerald expanse all around him.

I've led him to the Green Room. I figured it would go well with his eyes.

Good call.

"Whoa, I feel like I'm in Disneyland."

"Yeah, I know. It does somewhat resemble an out of control rollercoaster ride, doesn't it?"

"Full of interior decorators on acid," Boone gulps.

"It's not my fault. I sacrificed the second floor to Max and let her and her insane interior designers run riot on this level so she'd leave the rest of the house alone. These rooms are strictly for company, and I don't spend any time here at all, so I wasn't too concerned with what they did to them."

"You obviously don't entertain much." Boone gives me some brow action. "Or you don't like the people you do. The wallpaper alone is so loud I don't know if I'm going to be able to sleep through it."

"Never know until you try." I gesture toward the bed. "So, if you think you'll be okay here, I'll leave you to it."

Boone catches my arm as I turn to leave the room.

"So you live in this big ol' over-decorated place by yourself? When you're not out there getting yourself plastered all over the tabloids? Just you?" He lets go of my arm and opens his wide in a broad, sweeping gesture. "All alone, in all of this?"

Sounds kinda sad when you put it like that.

"Yeah, so what?"

"And this Max you keep talking about, agent, friend, and sometime escort? That all she is?"

That's the second time he's asked me that. I gave him an answer before, but he obviously didn't believe me, or for some reason needs to hear it again. What would that reason be? And how do I feel about how he might or might not feel about me?

I have no idea. But I'd better soon find out.

I avoid the question and audaciously move him toward the bed by placing a hand on the small of his back. "That's enough of the third degree for now. You need some rest, and I need to get some work done today."

"Shit, I'm sorry!" Boone's contrite expression is almost my undoing. "I didn't mean to barge in here and mess up your schedule. But I guess I sure have, haven't I?"

"Well, I admit this isn't the way I usually spend an afternoon, but it's been a nice change. So far." I risk meeting his eye.

Leave, I should leave. Yup. Turn around; walk away. Any time now, gonna do it. Leave.

"So are you saying meeting me hasn't been an entirely negative experience?" Boone murmurs, moving closer.

My language skills have completely deserted me, and my common sense is also barely functional. There's not nearly enough space between us, and yet I wish we were even closer. This is happening way too fast. I can't think, can barely breathe, and I need to do both right now before he does something I may regret.

I stare helplessly at him, drowning in the magnetic malachite pools of his eyes, seconds from becoming a willing accomplice to whatever he wants.

Almost, but not quite.

"Make yourself at home." Somehow I force myself to take a step back and break the spell. "You'll find the bed very comfortable. You ought to, for what it cost me." I gesture towards the antique wardrobe claiming the west corner of the room. "If you want to shower, freshen up, there's a robe and pajamas, and a few other assorted items of apparel Max selected and stashed in there. There's an ensuite through there"—I indicate the doorway opposite the bed—"also stocked with a full range of toiletries. By Max. I don't know your personal preferences, so you'll have to make do with what we've got on offer for the moment."

"I'm sure what Max chose will be fine." Boone's grin fades to be replaced by wistful longing. I think I know what's responsible for the sudden mood shift, but I'll ask anyway.

"What is it?"

"Carly," Boone immediately responds.

I was right.

"Do you know when she's coming back?"

"When she's ready." It's not much of an answer, but it's the best I can do.

He nods, accepting it. "Would you wake me up if she… as soon as she…."

"The second she shows up. I promise."

"'Kay." He heaves an enormous sigh and glances toward the massive four-poster supporting a top-of-the-line king-sized mattress smothered by a thick emerald quilt and a forest of Kelly green pillows. "I guess I should try it out. The bed, that is. You off now to crank out another best seller?"

"Something like that."

"Have fun."

We'll see. Depends who turns up today.

I SHOULD head to my study and get to work, but I'm not ready to buckle down yet. I need some alone time, to think, to get my head on straight again. I'll get on with the rest of the day's regularly scheduled agenda, but first, a spot of clean-up and contemplation. Then down to business.

Clearing away the remnants of our recent repast won't take very long. It's not like we left a huge mess in the wake of our lunch, but tidying it up will give me something to do with my hands while I attempt to make sense of the latest turn my life has taken.

For me, anything involving other people is always complicated, but when you add emotions into the mix, there are no superlatives to adequately describe the degree to which I can potentially become fucked up. That is a word I do not use lightly, in fact, hardly at all, but it in this particular context, I can't think of a better one.

Big surprise coming, here: I don't do anything like anyone else, including how I feel. I'm not talking about moods, here, I mean how I literally—feel. The process, not the emotions. Let me elucidate.

Until I learned how to shield and shut down the emotional invasion, people gave me nothing but grief. I couldn't be within three feet of anything breathing without unconsciously absorbing and internalizing whatever strong emotion they broadcast. It made for some mighty confusing moments before Mrs. Sheridan diagnosed my dilemma and taught me how to head it off at the proverbial pass. Now I understand how susceptible I am to the emotional vagrancies of others and can protect myself from outside influences emanating from everyone around me; I don't need to put so much distance between me and everybody else, but self-sequestering has been working for me so far, and I'm used to it. Besides, constantly keeping the barriers up is tiring. Not necessary when there's no one in the hood but me.

When it comes to the set of emotions I'm most concerned with at the moment, while I'm inexperienced, I'm not entirely unaware. I've fended off my share of interest, offers, and advances. Definitely not talking in a literary context. Whenever I encounter amorous energies, I have to be particularly aware of my own thoughts and feelings and constantly on the alert for emotional infiltration from outside sources. Unfortunately, it's possible for anyone beaming heavy-duty desires in my direction to make me believe I want what they want. I have to keep on top of that sort of subliminal seduction attempt all the time lest I end up with someone on top of me without it being my idea.

Um....

Empathy is a great thing to have in small doses, but the extent to which I can experience it? It can really mess your head up, not to mention your entire life, if you allow yourself to become overwhelmed, lose your sense of self, and get sucked down in the undertow of alien emotions.

More than once I've been the unwilling object of unwanted desire, but I've never truly known it myself. I've never wanted anyone I've ever met.

Not until today.

But do I? What I'm feeling for Boone; is it real? Or am I simply absorbing and internalizing his growing fascination for me?

I don't know; I'm not sure. I should be. I know what outside emotional contamination feels like, and this isn't it. That is, I don't think it is. And yet, something is definitely passing between us. I've been aware of it more than once. I don't know what it is or why it's happening. My aura's clean; he hasn't sent any subliminal suckers my way. And I certainly haven't launched any at him. So that's not how we're connecting. And yet we are, which probably means my growing attraction to him is a direct result of him wanting me. But it's so strong, so real, coming from a place inside me, moving out, filling me, empowering me, instead of the other way around. It doesn't feel invasive, intrusive, like it's closing in on me, smothering, boxing me in.

I feel good, not scared; free, not confined. Liberated. Not trapped.

Definitely not the way it's always been in the past.

I finish loading the dishes in the dishwasher, no wiser than when I started, but I'm gonna have to live with it—and him—for the time being. Boone's not going anywhere until the unfinished business with Carly is concluded, so for good or bad, I'm stuck with him for however long that takes.

Hopefully by the time I've crossed his daughter over, I'll have figured out what's the deal—and how to deal—with Boone Dantrell.

All right, Tonto, our job is done, here. I'll make myself a cup of tea, and then we'd better hit the literary trail.

I ENTER my study, the late afternoon sun leaking through the south-facing windows after completing its mid-afternoon meander to this side of the house. Such a beautiful day to be alive. I put my steaming mug of chai tea on the low table beside the chaise and pick up the digital recorder resting beside it. After settling myself comfortably back into the cushions I close my eyes.

5… 4… 3… 2….

"Good afternoon, dear boy," Mrs. Sheridan's kind old voice emanates from a spot slightly behind me and to my right.

And there she is.

"How is your new friend?" she primly inquires.

I open my eyes and turn my head toward her, knowing exactly what I'll see. Those fuzzy pink slippers just never get old. She's standing by my desk, same as she ever was, her immutable appearance never altering an iota. But there's something incredibly comforting in that infallible constant—and her. She's the only one I've ever known who's never left me. I don't really understand how that's possible, how she can be here, with me, all these years, and still be her, but I've learned not to question it and simply accept.

"I don't know how he is. You tell me."

She's the one who can walk through walls. If she doesn't already know what Boone's up to, all she has to do is pop in on him and check.

It's not like he'd know.

"He is asleep and will remain so for several hours. We can begin now."

Good. I've been waiting for this all day.

This particular aspect of my "gift" is what makes all the rest of the accompanying baggage endurable. When this enigmatic dead old lady brings me the most special souls of all, the ones who make the long-gone past live and breathe for me once more with their wondrous tales, their words transporting me back to ages long forgotten.

The storytellers.

Though many of them have wandered the earth for millennia, these souls are different from the lost ones hopelessly trapped on this plane by their inability to let go of their cravings for more life. The storytellers do not linger here twisted and driven to slake their envy by tormenting the living. I don't know what sustains them; perhaps the living flame of the very truth they harbor and burn to impart.

They are self-appointed sentinels, testaments to eons long gone, archives of the essence of eras. They wait, patient and enduring through decades, centuries, and millennia until they find a way to pass on the precious treasure of time and knowledge they possess.

Until they find someone like me.

They come to me and I listen, becoming a vessel willing to accept their otherworldly transmissions, although, unlike the mediums of the days of tipping tables, Ouija boards and spirit trumpets, I channel in a very different way. I take their precious, recounted recollections and fashion them into the stories I present to an avid, waiting audience hungry for these tales of days, times, and people long gone by. Those now living read my gentle renderings of the storytellers' truths, never dreaming they've partaken not of a work of fanciful fiction, born in the imagination of a man, but of actual, real history. Someone who once lived, laughed, loved, dreamed, and died comes alive once more every time someone opens a book, turns a page, loses themselves in the clear, honest truth shining through the fictional smokescreen and thinks them real once more.

There could be a higher purpose for this supposed gift I've been given. But not as far as I'm concerned. For me, it doesn't get any more sublime than this.

Thank you for seeing me.

He's here.

"Thank you for trusting me with your truth."

My name is Stephano.

"I'm happy to meet you, Stephano. I'm Ellery. Shall we begin?"

I hit the record button on the digital recorder, take a deep breath, and begin to reiterate everything I hear Stephano say, my low, accompanying murmurs a quiet counterpoint to the mellow, melodious, otherworldly voice weaving a verbal tapestry transporting me to days and times my heart aches to know and feel and see.

CHAPTER 11

"OH DAVID, he's so little. He's going to be all alone now."

"Mommy? Mommy, is that you? Daddy?"

"David, it's so unfair! We can see him, but we can't... oh, I wish we could tell him we love him. One last time."

"Daddy! Mommy! You're here!"

"Elly? Can you see us?"

"Uh huh."

"Oh, my God, David, he can see us! Ellery, oh, my darling!"

"Mommy, what's wrong, why are you crying? Where am I? This isn't home. I want to go home!"

"I know, darling, I know you want to go home, but you can't right now. Please, sweetheart, I need you to listen to me. You're in the hospital, Elly. You're not sick, you're not hurt, thank goodness, but they brought you here after the accident because they had to make sure you were all right. You hit your head and were asleep for a little while. That's why you don't know what happened to your daddy and me."

"I'm not sick?"

"No, baby, you're fine."

"I'm okay! I don't need to stay here. We're all okay. We can go home now, right?"

"No, Ellery. We can't go home with you ever again. You... you have to stay here, and we have to.... Oh, David, how are we going to make him understand?"

"Mommy, you're making me scared."

"Ellery, listen to me now, son, this is very important."

"Yes, Daddy."

"You're a big boy now, aren't you, Elly?"

"Yes."

"And big boys aren't afraid. Your mother and I, we have to tell you something. You have to listen good, now, understand?"

"Okay, Daddy."

"We love you, sweetheart, forever and ever."

"And if we had a choice, we would never leave you."

"Leave me? Where are you going?"

"Think back, honey. We were in the car, remember?"

"Yeah."

"We were in an accident, Ellery. Your daddy lost control of the car, and we went over a hill and crashed into some trees. You weren't hurt, but your daddy and me, we... we—"

"You survived, honey. You're still alive, and we're so happy for that, but baby, we didn't make it. We're dead, Ellery. I'm sorry."

"No, you're not. You can't be dead. You're right here. I can see you. You're playing a game with me, right, Daddy?"

"No, honey, this isn't a game or a dream. I know you can see us, I don't know how or why, but we are dead, Ellery."

"No! No! You're lying!"

"Oh, honey, no, we would never do that to you!"

"We came to see you one last time before we left. We never dreamt we'd be able to say good-bye. But we must, sweetheart. Please try to understand."

"Nooooooo...."

"Now, Elly, you need to be a brave boy."

"No... no! You promised me you'd never leave me, and we'd be together forever and ever."

"Sue, we have to go."

"Oh, David, I can't do this, I can't leave him like this."

"*You need not fear for your son, Mrs. James. I will watch over him.*"

"*We love you, Ellery, we will always love you. We'll see you again someday. We want you to be a good boy and listen to this nice lady. Her name is Mrs. Sheridan, and she's going to look after you for us.*"

"*Hello, Ellery, I'm Mrs. Sheridan. You look like a fine young man. We're going to be good friends.*"

"*Good-bye, Elly. We love you. Please forgive us, and don't forget us.*"

NOOOOOOOOO!

"Easy, easy there, slugger, let's try waking up, now, how does that sound?"

I'm bolt upright on the chaise, screaming and shaking. Boone is beside me, gripping me firmly by the shoulders. I'm quivering in his grasp, quaking with rage, my eyes riveted on the image of the betrayer looking back at me from the foot of the chaise, goddamned pink poofy slippers and all.

"You!" I jab an accusing finger at her. "You were there! You were there in the hospital, after the accident. I remember you! I remember them!"

"Uh...." Boone looks nervously about. "Whazzup? Who ya talkin' to?"

I can feel his arm around my shoulders, still staunchly supporting me, but I'm barely aware of it or him. She's all I can see.

She's got a lot to answer for, and she's going to do it now!

"Yes, dear boy," she calmly replies and folds her hands primly in front of her. "You are correct. I was there with your parents. That was the day we met."

I feel light-headed with rage, all the fury and bewilderment of the long-forgotten betrayal boiling into my consciousness until it feels like the top of my head is going to fly off.

I can't believe I forgot this. I can't believe she did this to me!

"They came back for me. They came back for me, and you made

them leave!"

My face is wet. I'm shaking. Somewhere, Boone anxiously pleads for my attention, but I can't hear him, can't see him. I'm so *angry* at her!

"All these years, I thought you were my friend! You lied! You took them from me!"

"You know that's not true, my dear boy," she serenely maintains. "As soon as you calm down you'll realize that. We'll talk later, sweetheart, when you're in a better mood."

Don't you dare pop out on me! I'm not done with you yet!

"Come back here!" I howl at the empty air.

They left me. They left me, they left me. They left me with her. Why did they do that? Why did they go?

"Okay, Earth to Ellery. Come back, Space Cadet, you're creeping me out, here."

Boone?

What?

I blink, and his worried face, so close to mine, comes into focus. I'm back with him, sitting on the chaise, sheltered in the circle of his strong, supporting arm.

Omigawd, what just happened here? That insane, irrational rage, where did it come from? Why did I say that to Mrs. Sheridan? What's happening to me? Is this it? Am I finally losing my mind?

"Boone? What's happening to me?"

"I dunno, Scrappy, you tell me." He runs his thumb across my cheekbone, rubbing away the lingering damp traces of my recent rage. "I concluded a most restful nap. Very enjoyable, you were right about the bed, extremely comfortable, and worth every penny you paid for it. I was going through the house looking for you when I heard someone howling their head off. Figured it had to be you, followed the sound, found you passed out on the couch here, by all appearances having one hell of a nightmare. I get here, shake you out of it, you come to and start yelling at air. Or...." he sighs and shakes his head. "In your case, maybe not."

"I... I...." I still feel like I'm only half here, stuck somewhere between apparent reality and the wrenching residual awareness churned up in me by the stuff of bad dreams.

"Wanna talk about it?" Boone gingerly pokes me in the side.

A hysterical giggle explodes out of me. "You? You're offering me a shoulder? Don't I have enough problems already?" Increasingly exponentially every second you stay in my life.

"Hey!" He affects a lightly affronted expression. "Don't let my gun-toting exterior fool you, I am a deeply sensitive guy. I can pick a lock in less than thirty seconds; accessing my feminine side takes only slightly longer. Not as much practice, you understand. Besides," he sighs, gently rubbing my arm, "I figure I owe you one. For helping me with Carly."

"If that's the only reason you're here, don't trouble yourself. I don't need any help from you. I don't need anything from anyone. You know what, I'll tell you something, all right, I'll tell you where you can shove your shoulder and your... your—"

"Don't," Boone gently rebukes me, obviously undaunted by my irrational tirade. "I'm sorry, that didn't come out right. Listen, I don't know what's going on, but I recognize strung out when I see it. Whatever you need, here it is. I'm here because I can be and I want to be. No other reason. Okay?"

I believe him, what he's offering and why. It's sweet, and I appreciate the thought, but I can't. I can't, I can't, I can't. I can't possibly talk about this. Not now, not ever, and certainly not with him.

Can I?

I have to do something with this or I really will go insane. I've kept it inside too long. I don't know what to do. Mrs. S. would know. I need to talk to her so she can help me sort it all out, like she always has. When I was alone and scared, when the things relentlessly dogging me every waking moment would come for me, she would help me cope. The second I opened my eyes in the morning, coming to sweating and screaming in the night after being ripped from slumber by their ghastly whispering, she'd come to me and take my fears away. After my parents left me alone and I was constantly haunted by horrible things no one else could see and hear, she was there, she was always there, helping me understand what was happening to me and somehow find a way to live through it.

Now she's gone. Of all the times she could possibly pick to leave me, now, when I really need her, she's not here.

They left me; she left me.

He's all I've got.

"I saw them the day of the accident," I gulp out the explanation he's been so patiently awaiting. "My parents. I'd forgotten all about it, blanked it out somehow, but they were there, in my hospital room, that day after the accident, and so was she."

"I'm sorry," Boone frowns. "She? We're talking another ghost here? I gotta get me a program," he mutters.

It's all coming back to me in a sickening rush. The iron curtain sequestering the carefully hidden and long-repressed portions of my memory is dissolving, allowing them to finally flood free, filling in the blank spots in the fabric of my past, and forming the full picture of my life for the first time.

"That day, in the hospital, is when it all started." I'd forgotten this too.

Boone nods, his mouth set in a thin line of concern. "You mean the seeing and hearing dead people thing."

"Yeah. That. My parents were the first. I was eight years old. I didn't understand what had happened. I woke up in a hospital ward to them telling me I was the sole survivor of the car accident we'd just been in. They told me they were dead, and yet, there they were. Talking to me. Plain as looking at you. Even worse, not only were they saying they were dead, but they were going away forever and I'd never see them again. I realize now of course they had no choice, they had to cross over, but back then…. I was only eight goddamned years old, and I didn't understand any of it!"

Boone's face is a tight mask of compassion, and his eyes bleed concern. "Eight years old? God!" He shakes his head angrily.

A violent emotional resurgence starts me shaking again. I know my anger isn't rational, but it sure doesn't. It's been waiting way too long for its chance to rip the doors off and roar, and I think my odds of getting another lid on it are slim to none.

Boone's hand tightens encouragingly on my arm and then starts moving slowly, up and down, deeply reassuring stroking. It helps but doesn't halt the internal pressure. I'm gonna blow.

Tears tumble down my face, but I don't care. I've been holding them back since I was eight; it's more than time to let loose and wash this pain away. Like a cork being popped, a stream of words follows the fluid release. I haven't a hope of halting either tide, so I go with the flow.

"They said goodbye to me, and then they... they were gone. I freaked, I went running after them, trying to find them, tearing up and down the hospital corridors screaming at the top of my lungs for my folks. The doctors and the people from Child Services kept saying they were dead, but I didn't believe them. I knew they weren't, I'd seen them."

Boone doesn't say anything; he slowly massages my arm while I babble and blubber.

"I don't know what they would have done to me if she hadn't been there. I probably would have ended up in a psych ward somewhere, medicated to the gills. I wouldn't have stopped, wouldn't have let it go. I knew I was right, I'd seen them. I just wanted them back, and as far as I was concerned, the doctors and the people from Child Services were lying to me, keeping them from me."

"She?" Boone gently asks.

"A little old dead lady," I sniff and smile. "Barely this high, looks like she's about a hundred and ten, with an Estelle Getty hair-do, fluffy pink slippers, and this gawd-awful pink paisley housecoat that looks like it was made from some curtains left over from the sixties."

"Interesting image."

"Believe it or not, it's strangely comforting. So is she. She came to me after my parents left, said she was there to help me. Calmed me down, told me I had to accept my folks were gone. She kept me from that loony bin by making me understand I had to stop looking for them, stop telling people I could see them—and her and all the other ones—after that. She saved me, watched out for me, protected me, taught me how to deal with the dead, helped me stay sane."

"Sounds like a pretty nice lady to me," Boone kindly observes. "As dead old broads go."

I can't help it, I start laughing. Never in my wildest dreams could I conceive of calling Mrs. S. a broad, but he not only pulls it off, he gets away with it. God, I can't remember the last time I laughed, I mean, really broke down and yukked my guts out. I've been locked up so tight for so long, keeping so completely to myself, never letting anyone touch me, get close to me, because I can't. I have to be careful, can't let it slip, can't let anyone suspect.

I can't stand it.

The sobs spontaneously erupt out of me with shocking violence. "God, it hurts so much! Make it stop!"

"Hey," Boone soothes, gathering me into a fierce, protective embrace. "It's okay, Ellery, sometimes pain is good. Lets you know you're alive. And it gets better. You told me that, remember? Let it go, let it go, I'm here and I'm not going anywhere."

My mind is trying to absorb what he's saying; the words hit my ears but don't penetrate any further. I'm past comprehension; sobs rack me with rib-cracking ferocity. Alone, I've been so alone, my entire existence consumed with ameliorating this world and the next for everyone else, but for all my efforts, I've made no real place here for myself.

I've never let myself have anything or anybody. I've been too afraid.

I always thought this gift, curse, burden, blessing—whatever you want to call it, and the use I've put it to—was enough. I've spent my whole life telling myself I could find a way to be happy living to make everyone else's dreams come true. I tried to make it enough, convince myself it was working, but you know what? I lied. And now, held fast in the fortress of Boone's embrace, I come face to face with the falsehood I've been living.

It sucks. And it hurts so much.

He holds me; I let him. Gradually, my sobs subside. I feel bled dry of my anguish, cracked and broken, hollowed out and emptier than a desiccated reed. Now I know how much I want and need; I don't know what to do about it.

There is a quiet awareness humming in the echoing chambers of my heart. Boone's arms around me, so strong, warm, certain; this is good.

"Hey." Boone wipes my cheek with a callused thumb. "Feel better?"

I lift my head to see him looking down at me, his face gentle with concern. For me. In that tenuous instant, the pain and emptiness fall away; all that matters is him.

Eyes, such an amazing shade of green. Warm, compassionate, shining while they unashamedly devour me.

"Yeah." Mouth, lower lip full, moist and sensuous, hovering so close. "Much better. Thanks."

"Good," he nods, his intentions looming large in his eyes.

I wait.

Soft as a sigh, he touches his mouth to mine. I close my eyes, opening my senses to the brief, achingly tender caress. Moistness, the slick thrill of his tongue flicking out to taste my lips, darting between them. Intimate, wet intensity I've never experienced. Tastes good. Feels even better. I want more.

All too soon, it ends.

"I'm sorry," his mouth says, but contrition does not live in his eyes. "I don't know why I did that."

You lie, but I think I know why.

"Because you wanted to. I hope."

Thus perishes uncertainty. Now he knows what I want too, but not before he made this amazing advance and risked the kiss. I'm awed by his audacity.

"I did."

"I'm glad."

"Good. You're so hard to read. I wasn't sure."

"It was worth a try."

"So are you. Wanna try again?"

"Please."

Boone's mouth melts into mine once more, this time, not so gentle. His need shears through me, electric, urgent, hotter than hell. I'm more than ready for what he wants; I've been waiting for this and wanting him from the first moment I saw him, not understanding why or what, but I do, I want, I need....

Him.

He pushes me back, splaying me on the chaise, covering my body with his hard, heaving length, sucking and licking, his hot breath filling my lungs. I moan, open, take him in, clutch him fiercely, winding my legs around his waist, craving the power and passion crushing me into the yielding velvet beneath. My body thrums with need, every nerve ending screaming for his touch. I want him to touch me, want to feel him all over me, hands, his and mine reaching blindly and hungrily to peel away the maddening clothing barrier to get to slick and sweating skin, him on me, me on him.

His mouth is a relentless marauder exploring the side of my neck. He gasps harshly, groaning with pleasure when I fling back his robe and run my greedy fingers across his chest, along his ribs, down his back, drinking in his sweating skin. I cup his naked, bunching buttocks and squeeze hard, feel him shudder and thrust against me. Good, he feels so good, so strong, male, powerful and... and....

Alive.

Grunting, panting, his hands rough and impatient, fumbling with my shirt, ripping, tugging, buttons flying.

Another shirt bites the dust, but oh God, who cares?

He's working my zipper, pulling and yanking at my pants. Never losing contact with his searing mouth, I elevate my pelvis just enough for clearance and hear his happy grunt while he efficiently peels me like an eager banana.

Nothing. There's nothing between him and me.

His fingers curl around me so rough, yet so tender, gripping, stroking, squeezing, omigawd, omigawd, someone else... touching me... God! So good, never imagined it could be so good. God... God, that! Do that again, yes, yes, yes... don't, don't stop!

I groan deep and long, shivering with excitement, afire with sensation. His hands are everywhere, his mouth panting and murmuring and pleasuring mine while he heaves and bucks and shakes beneath my clutching, questing fingers.

I need to touch him too, feel the proof of his need. Hard to move, pinned down by his wildly thrashing pelvis, but I reach, grope, my fingers finding long, hard, pulsing slickness, and I grip him greedily, squeezing, sliding, eagerly pumping his swollen length.

"God!" he screams, and then comes in searing waves, hot semen pouring down my hand and across my heaving belly. His ecstasy blasts through me, pinwheels of insane, orgasmic brilliance exploding behind my eyelids, sending me high, higher, toward a blinding inner light. I see it, at last I see it, such pure, unfathomable brilliance beckoning, calling me toward it, a paradise hitherto denied me, the highest attainable pinnacle of mingling flesh and love.

So this is what all the fuss is about.

Whoa.

Still floating dreamily in the warm remnants of ecstasy, I cautiously open my eyes. I'm wantonly sprawled on my back on my chaise, sans attire, loosely wrapped around Boone. Draped limply atop me, he's equally spent and breathing like his lungs are about to collapse.

"Am I dead?" Boone groans, panting and pressing heavily on me.

"Wrong person to ask," I mumble, gently caressing the damp hollow of his back.

"Right," he amusedly snuffles against my chest. "You okay?"

"Yeah. I'm good. You?"

He thinks about it for a moment.

"Yeah," he finally responds. I can't see his face, but I hear the marveling bewilderment in his reply. "Strangely enough. I'd never have believed it possible, but I feel… I feel clear. For the first time since she died. I won't say I feel good, not quite there yet, but that constant chainsaw inside me churning up my guts is gone. I miss her; I still miss her like hell, but…."

He pushes himself up, propping his torso on his elbows, so he can see my face.

"I feel better." His expression becomes confused, mouth twitching with tension.

I wanna kiss it better.

"Ellery, is that bad?"

I know what he means. He's afraid if he doesn't bleed internally for Carly twenty-four seven, if he lets go of the loss and reaches for life, that he is betraying his girl. Abandoning her.

"No, it's not." I reach up and take his face in my hands. "It's what she wants you to do. That's why she stayed, to make sure you go on, live your life, be happy. She told you that, remember?"

"I remember." Boone's melting malachite eyes search my face. "A week ago, I would have sworn to you, what you just said? Being able to do any of it again? Not in this lifetime, but now, for the first time, I'm starting to believe it might actually be possible."

My heart lurches painfully in my chest. I haven't had time to think about what just happened, what it means to me, what this man is coming to mean to me.

I'll kiss now and think later.

Impulsively, I pull his head toward me and kiss him hard. He groans and folds willingly, opening to my questing tongue. We kiss deeply; I can feel his pulse in his neck racing against my splayed fingers.

"God, Ellery," he gasps after peeling his mouth off mine. "Not that I'm against finishing what you're starting, but this isn't the most comfortable.... We should probably retire to one of those large, comfy, expensive beds you've got upstairs. How's that grab ya?"

"Sounds like a plan."

"Lead the way," Boone grins and leaps off me.

CHAPTER 12

THAT scary man keeps staring at me. He doesn't look right. There's something wrong with him, something bad.

I've seen bad things around people before, sometimes even in them, but this is different. So is he. He looks like a man, but he's not. The colors around him are all wrong, and his body looks funny. Like it's going bad, or something. I don't understand.

He wants to hurt me.

I'm scared.

I'm being good, staying in Mrs. Burke's yard like she told me, so I should be safe, but I'm not. The bad man is opening the gate, coming in to get me. He's not supposed to do that, not supposed to come into the yard, but he is. Mrs. Burke doesn't know what he's doing. She's supposed to protect me, but she's not watching me. She never does. She knows I'll stay in the yard like she says, so she takes a nap instead of watching me like she's s'posed to. She always goes to sleep in the afternoon after she drinks her special coffee.

I should run away, go in the house, and then I'd be safe. He couldn't get me in the house, but then she'd get mad at me for coming inside, making noise and waking her up. She'd start yelling at me, and her colors would go all red and black and shoot at me, and it makes my head hurt real bad, and sometimes I throw up when that happens, and it makes her even madder. I can't go in. I can't go in until she says it's okay.

The man-thing is in the yard now, coming down the walk. His eyes are bad, and scary, and they're doing something to me. I can't breathe, my feet are stuck, I can't move, can't run away. The closer he *gets, I can feel how bad he is, how much he wants to hurt me.*

He wants to eat my soul.

Mommy, Daddy, I'm scared.

"Be still, now, dear boy."

"Mrs. Sheridan!" I don't see her, but I hear her, close to my right ear. She's here! She's here! All the grownups I know, they tell me to go away, to leave them alone, find something else to do. I know they don't want me and don't want to take care of me, so I stay out of their way, and they forget about me and stop making the bad colors. But that's okay, she never does. She's my friend. She always has time for me.

I don't need to be scared now. It's gonna be okay. She'll tell me what to do.

I'm so glad she's here. She's with me almost all time now. Whenever she is, the dead people don't scare me so much, and they don't bother me all the time. I think she makes them stay away. I'm glad. It's hard not to be scared of them, but I'm learning. I'm even getting used to the ones that look really bad, with blood all over them and their guts and brains and eyeballs hanging out. Mrs. Sheridan told me they don't have to look like that. Some of them do it on purpose, 'cause they're kinda mean and they want to look scary, and some of them don't understand they can change what they look like 'cause they're dead. She's teaching me how to talk to them, how to help them, how to make them not be mean and scary to me. I'm getting really good at making them change and helping them go to the nice place I feel but can't see. One day, I won't be ascared of anything dead. 'Cause no matter what they look like, they can't hurt me.

Dead things, and the things I see in people and around them, can't hurt me. Nothing dead can hurt me. That's what she said. I believed her. She's never been wrong before.

This man feels like a ghost, but he's not. He's not dead. But he's not like us, either.

Ghosts don't have colors, but he does. They're not people colors, they're not right. They're black, and icy, and dirty, they make his body look wavy and rippley, like it's not really a body, only looks like one. It would be really bad if he touched me. His eyes are glowing red, and they don't look like people eyes. He's staring at me like he hates me, and he's really, really hungry in a way that makes me scared.

He knows I can see! That's why he wants to eat me!

He's not a man, whatever he is. It's worse than being a ghost, and he can hurt me. If he catches me, he's gonna do something really, really bad to me. Worse than dying. The worstest thing that could ever happen.

"What's wrong with that man? He's not a ghost, but he looks like one."

I don't know, but I bet she does. She's really cool, she knows everything.

"Keep him away; don't let him hurt me!"

"Don't be afraid, sweetheart. I will protect you."

Oh, there she is. I can see her now; Mrs. Sheridan is in front of me! She looks all big and bright, like she's standing in the middle of a light bulb. She always makes good glows that make me feel nice and warm and safe whenever her swirlies touch me. Even though she can't hug me, not really, when she glows around me, it feels like she does.

Nice. Safe. She always keeps me safe. She has her glow all around me now. That's good. Now I know for sure nothing bad can touch me.

I'm not ascared now. Mrs. Sheridan won't let this bad thing get me. She'll kick its ass.

"Leave this to me, my darling. There will come a time when you will stand against such as this, but you are not yet ready."

Sometimes she says grownup stuff like this. I never understand what she's talking about, but I don't need to. Not right now. She told me someday when I'm big, I'll know lots of stuff. If she says so, it must be true. Right now, I just want her to make this scary man go away.

The man stops, the red in his eyes getting hotter, the bad black around him shooting towards me and bouncing off Mrs. Sheridan's glow. Hah, hah! Can't hurt me!

Her glow is so bright now I almost can't see her. She raises her arms and shoots light out of her hands at the bad man, and it flows all over him, covering up the black. I can't see him anymore; all I see is light. I hear growls, howls, screams, hurting my ears. I cover them to shut the sound out, close my eyes as the light flares, like a big huge sun....

Shit!

I rear up into full awareness, heart pounding, hyperventilating, every cell in my body screaming with sheer terror.

Holy crap! What the hell was that? The way my heart is racing, it feels like I'm barely this side of a coronary! Must have been a bad dream. Not just any unpleasant sleep experience, but the mother of all cauchemars.

Pardon my French.

Okay, scary sleep episode over, relax, restart heart, maybe go back to sleep.

I lie limply back, sinking into the welcome support of the mattress beneath, gulping and shaking while sweat streams off my trembling body. Almost have my breathing under control.

Hang on, something warm, and heavy, lying across my....

God! Arm! On me!

Sick with shock and terror, I fling it aside and scramble away from the unexpected embrace. I'm about to bolt off the bed and run screaming out of the room when my memory finally wakes up, joins the panic party already well in progress, and tosses a recollection my way.

It's okay, chill. There's supposed to be a man in my bed. He was there when I went to sleep. The fact he's still here several hours later should be cause for celebration, not screaming.

Well, there might be some screaming later on, when we both wake up again, only not terror-related.

We live in hope.

"Whoa, there, Scrappy, where's the fire?"

Boone pulls me back against his chest, wrapping both his arms around me. Shamefaced and still shaking, I just hang there and try to calm down.

"Bad dream." I force out the half-truth, willing my breathing to return to normal. No way I'm admitting to what really freaked me. I feel like an idiot. Scared out of my head by someone in my bed. I'm one sad puppy. "And will you stop calling me that!"

"Two in one day." Boone kisses the side of my neck, one of his large, warm hands describing comforting circles on my belly. "That's gotta be some kind of record. Definitely tops any of my recent experiences. Not that I keep track of my nightmares or anything like that. What you got to worry about keeping you up nights, Scrappy? Other than me, that is?"

I'm not answering that any more than I'm owning up to being spooked by a hairy arm on my chest. Nice arm, though. And the other one just like it. Like the hands even more.

"Gonna live?" Boone softly asks, still stroking. He keeps it up, I may start purring.

"Oh, I think so. Sorry for waking you. Believe me, I'm not usually like this. Normally I don't have any trouble sleeping at all. As for having nightmares? Doesn't happen."

That much is true. Which, if you think about it, is pretty surprising, considering how whacked my reality is.

"You're lucky," Boone murmurs and reaches around behind him. There's some movement in the dark; I feel the bedclothes being tugged, rearranged, hear the soft rustles of fabric and the muted thud of one pillow hitting another. We're not going back to sleep right away, are we? I sense some serious snuggling in my immediate future.

Sure, why not.

This feels good. Having someone touch me, hold me. All those years I told myself I was fine without it? I've been selling myself a bill of goods the size of the Brooklyn Bridge. And the sex. Oh. My. God. I had no idea it could be like that. With someone else, I mean. I'd be lying if I said I've never got myself off. Of course I have, but it's just, even though I thought making love alone felt pretty damned good, not having a basis for comparison, I had no idea how much better it is when it's someone else's hand doing the... offing.

Not just any other someone. Him.

Boone finishes his pillow wrangling and leans back against the pile.

"C'mere," he instructs, pulling me toward him. I willingly submit to his direction and in due course find myself nicely nestled between his legs, my back pressed into his chest.

Boone makes an excellent backrest.

He busies himself for several seconds arranging the bedclothes around us to his satisfaction.

This is nice. Snuggly.

"Feel better?" Boone nuzzles the side of my neck. I got tingles. Ooooh.

"Yeah, I'm… oh, that feels good."

Not very articulate right now. I'm no fortuneteller, but I'm predicting my linguistic ability will continue to deteriorate with a rapidity directly proportional to the rate of lippage being applied to my various body parts. God help me, I could get used to this. Really fast. My head is spinning, my heart thudding, and every inhibition and apprehension previously holding my libido at bay is rapidly heading for the border.

Bye-bye. Don't forget not to write.

I need to put a stop to this right now. There's too much at stake to let a little lust make me stupid. I've kept myself clear of every conceivable emotional attachment—intimacy being at the top of the list—and a mind-shattering orgasm or two later I'm on the brink of chucking every rule I've lived with, and by, ever since I was old enough to understand a normal life would never be mine.

You think it sounds nuts, try living it.

Darn him to heck.

One magic man marauds his way into my life, introducing himself by threatening to take it, and now, beyond all sense, reason, or rationale is making rapid, irreparable inroads into my heart. I don't know anything about him except he formerly did things for a living he's not proud of and once had a wife and a daughter. Oh, yes, his daughter and him, they both need my help. One to go on, the other to let go. And vice versa.

I think I'm falling for him. Wait. Upon further reflection, edit all uncertainty out of the previous statement. The falling thing? Already a fait accompli.

That's French for "I am so screwed."

"Hey?" Boone blows into my ear. "You still awake?"

"You kidding? You keep that up, parts of me are going to develop permanent insomnia."

Boone emits a throaty chuckle. "That's my boy. Hold that thought. Right now, though, I'm about to say two words as a guy you normally never want to either say or hear, but I think we should."

"And what words would those be?" I have no idea where he's going with this, but it should be interesting.

"Let's talk."

Ah. Not what I was expecting. Tell you what, let's not. That's not two words, either.

"Technically, that's three words."

"What?"

"Let's talk. Three words, not two. Let's is a contraction, combining 'let' and 'us', which means—ummph!"

Boone grasps my chin, turns my head, and firmly silences me with a deep, solid kiss.

"Writers. Don't be so damned pedantic," he mumbles into my mouth. Then he clamps his lips over mine again. Serious kissing ensues for several intoxicating seconds.

"What do you want to talk about?" I dreamily murmur after he peels his lips off mine.

"I dunno. What do you want to talk about? You're the one having issues here, not me."

"What?" I squawk. "Issues? What are you talking about? I so am not!"

"So you're telling me you're absolutely okay with what we've done and possibly wouldn't mind—"

Doing it again? Yes, please!

"Of course I am!" I answer far too quickly and loudly to add verisimilitude to my assertion. Even I know that.

"You are?" His reply reeks with fond skepticism. "I'd buy that, except for the whole waking up screaming thing. Kinda weakens your credibility."

He's got a point. Conceding it is not the same as admitting it.

My only response is several seconds of stony silence. Terminated by a soft sigh of resignation from the man behind.

"Okay," he says, and he pushes me up and away from him.

Shit, now I've done it, I've sent out the wrong signals and screwed it up. He's gonna get up, get dressed, and walk out on me, and it's my fault because I was too stupid to know what to do next. I'm about to start freaking, pleading, groveling but can't figure out which one to open with when I realize my expectations of abandonment are premature; he's only changing positions, not exiting stage gone.

He flattens the pillows, lies back down, then pulls me toward him and onto him. I pillow my head on his lightly furred chest, fascinated by the strong, regular tattoo of his heart beating beneath my cheek.

"Okay, fine, I'll start," he murmurs, pressing a kiss against my hair. "So tell me, M., why do you do that thing you do?"

I'm not exactly sure what he means, but I'm pretty sure it's not a reference to a Tom Hanks movie.

"The bubblehead thing. What's up with that? Why do you act like such a ditz in public?"

I gently raise my left hand, rest it on his chest. He doesn't seem to mind me touching him. Oooh. Skin. So soft. His chest hair tickles my fingers.

"You're really good at it, I'll give you that. I have to admit, after seeing you on more than one talk show, I'm pleasantly surprised to discover some actual substance behind that flashy exterior. You've got your blond impression down pat."

"And me being a brunette," I murmur. Skin. Feels nice. I could touch him all day.

"After catching your Oprah appearance...."

Ah yes. My stint on Oprah. Not my finest hour. Though it felt like the longest one at the time.

"I was even starting to believe the wacko who keeps popping up on your Facebook page claiming the man the world believes is Ellery James is only an attractive stand-in hired to front for him, and he is in fact, the real author of your books."

"Ah yes. The Genuine EJ. He's a hoot, isn't he?" I chuckle. "A ghostwriter for a ghost writer. Hey, wait a minute, what did you just say?"

Silence.

That's fine. I can wait.

"Nuthin'," Boone finally mutters.

You lying bastard!

"You've checked out my Facebook page?" I find the admission so astonishing I momentarily forget my fascination with the tactile qualities of the skin on Boone's chest.

"Maybe," he grudgingly admits. Finally. How interesting. What shall we make of this most intriguing nugget of information? Is it possible Mr. Dantrell was possibly not as only incidentally aware of me as he claims? Betcha he even read some of my books, the mendacious toad. But I'll let him cling to his flimsy falsehoods a while longer. I can afford to be magnanimous. Hell, I can even spell it!

"Why do I act like a bimbo in public?" It's a fair question. I have no problem with answering it, especially as he's probably already worked it out. "Misdirection. Smoke and mirrors. I have a couple of serious secrets that wouldn't bear up well under concerted media scrutiny or an examination of my private life. So I whenever I'm in public, I act like I haven't got two brain cells to rub together. If people think I have no depths to plumb, they won't go digging."

"So far it seems to be working well for you," Boone wryly observes.

"Fooled you, didn't it?"

"It did, indeed." Boone sighs and gives my ass a fond pat. "Like I said, you are nothing like I was expecting. Must really be a pain in the ass, though. Dumbing yourself down all the time. How long are you going to have to keep it up?"

"Not much longer. The buzz around *The Warrior's Tale* is starting to wane. A few more weeks and it'll settle down to mere background noise. They'll drop me like a stone-cold has-been the second the next installment in the Twilight saga comes out. Can't wait."

Boone snorts. "And I thought I had problems."

"I'd trade places with you in a heartbeat," I blurt without thinking, and then I want to swallow my tongue.

I've said stupider things in my time, but not by much.

"No," he sadly murmurs. "No, you wouldn't."

"I'm so, so sorry!" I hug him fiercely, choking with contrition. I really suck at this.

"It's okay, it's okay," he soothes, giving my back a gentle pat. "No harm meant, none taken. Do me a favor, though? When you're with me, check your 'I'm just a pretty face' thing at the door. You may act like a blond in public, but around here your dark roots are showing. All the way to your shoulders and then some," he smirks, fingering a hank of my hair.

"Don't get me started about the hair," I growl at him.

"What?" he feigns astonishment. "You don't like it?" He combs his fingers through its entire length. "I don't know, I kinda like it. It has a certain *je ne sais quoi*."

That's French for, "What the hell was I thinking, letting myself get talked into this?"

"Makes you look so…."

"Stupid?" I'm glad it's dark so Boone can't see the pout. Trust me, it's fierce.

"I was gonna say sexy."

"Whatever. I think it makes me look like the guy on *Friends* who almost ends up as Joey's roommate instead of Chandler."

"And that's… bad? I thought he was kinda hot."

So did I, which was truly weird, trust me.

"Anyway, I really hate it. It's way too high maintenance, for starters. I curse the day Max got the twisted idea to throw a longhaired wig on me and set up a photo shoot as a publicity stunt for the launch of *Scarlet Nights*. Me and a model who'd consumed a garlic-laden pasta dish for lunch prior to showing up for the shoot posing together—nose to nose—for hours re-enacting the cover. What a nightmare that was."

"You famous folk lead such fascinating lives." Boone chuckles and pokes me in the ribs. "Made for a really hot photo, though. And pretty much set you on your current path of 'looks like what he writes'. The hair that lurched a thousand hearts."

I can't believe he just said that. It was really good, though. Wish I'd thought of it.

"Shut up." I poke him back.

"You are, you know." Boone's breath tickles my ear.

"I… I'm what?" Oh, that feels good.

"Hot," he exhales all over the side of my neck. "And unbelievably adorable."

He chuckles, a deep, velvet sound resonating through his body. His chest rapidly expands and contracts, rocking me in time with the amused exhalations. The sounds and sensations tickle me, making me giddy with the delirious novelty of it all.

Lovin' every minute of it.

"Deal with it, Mr. James. You are a babe. The world thinks so, and so do I."

"Really?" I squeak.

"Really." He tenderly strokes my head. "I hate to break it to you, but I like the hair."

He thinks I'm hot. I'm grumbling on the outside, but giddy on the inside.

"This Max you keep talking about? Your agent? Is that all she is?"

"Why do you keep asking me that?"

"She makes all your appointments, hangs off your arm whenever you do the town, does your decorating. Does she buy your clothes too?"

Hmmmm, interesting. I'm no expert or anything, but if I didn't know better, I'd swear Boone's tone is green-tinged. And we're not talking in an ecological context.

"Well, yes, as a matter of fact, she was responsible for selecting most of my personal appearance wardrobe." It goes without saying that prior to my sudden success, while I'd certainly heard of Hugo Boss, Versace, and Gucci, I had very little actual experience of any of it either in my closet or on my person. "Why do you ask?"

"It's just—and I hope you don't mind me saying this—but she seems to make a lot of your decisions… for someone you're not related to, divorced from, or sleeping with."

"Well, better her than me." That's all I'm going to say about it. I hear what he's saying, and I know the way it looks. My relationship with Max is complex. And not something I'm going to explain to a stranger. Even a charming one with killer eyes, an even deadlier ass, and hands that sent me straight to heaven.

If he hangs around for more than a day, perhaps we'll talk.

Boone refrains from any further comment and gives my ass a friendly pat. I'm wondering if that's his signal the conversation portion of the evening has concluded and it's time now for returning to the sleep state.

Or not. My personal favorite.

"What are you doing here, Ellery?"

No, not more talking. I can think of better thing to do with both our mouths.

"Getting felt up." I'm being deliberately obtuse, hoping he'll take the hint and let us move on to more interesting ways to pass the rest of the evening. Twenty minutes, give or take, dedicated to divulging personal information is more than enough for one evening. I've pretty much maxed out my confessional capacity for this session.

"You know what I mean." He gives the cheek he was just stroking a gentle slap, setting my flesh to lightly tingling. In an unexpectedly interesting way. Oooooh! "What is someone like you doing in a one-horse town like this?"

"When I could be sniffing endless lines of cocaine in a ritzy Park Avenue pad while scores of young hopefuls plying me with sexual favors parade in and out of my bedroom? You're right, what the hell am I thinking?"

I hope he can hear the irony dripping in my voice.

"Hmmmm." Boone makes no further comment, evidently contemplating the picture I just painted him, his hand slowly, gently stroking my ass. He chuckles again. He has a nice laugh, deep, genuine and infectious. I'm really coming to like the sound of it.

"I take your point. Definitely not your scene." His voice is warm, laden with quiet admiration. "I can't see you on Park Avenue. Not this you, anyway." The stroking hand stops, perching lightly on the rounding swell of my rear. "The real you." He plants a soft kiss on my hair. "But why here? Buttwood, USA?"

"That's Birchwood!" I lightly slap him on the chest. "Don't diss my town. It's a very nice place. Quiet, picturesque. Very friendly. The people here have been very good to me!"

"They like you, that's for damned sure. Your name is on just about every public building in town. I was half expecting to see a statue of you in front of City Hall. Oh, by the way, before I forget, you might want to have a word or two with the helpful young lady in the Ellery James Public Library. The one with the red hair and freckles."

"Jolene? Why?"

"Tell her she might want to think twice before giving your address out to every smooth-talking stranger who wanders into her place and asks."

Ah ha. So that's how he found me. Bet it took him all of ten seconds to charm the info out of her. All he had to do was flash her that smile, and Jolene would have handed over the keys to the city and her firstborn, no questions asked.

Ask me how I know.

"I was wondering how you found this place so fast. Ironically enough, it's about the only building in town that *doesn't* have my name on it."

"Noticed that. So how did a hot guy like you end up in a one-horse town like this?"

"Long story short? I inherited, I came, I saw, got conquered, I reno-ed and refurnished and then stayed. Much to the chagrin of Max the Merciless, who to this day is still lobbying for the Park Avenue option or, failing to persuade me to vacate and relocate, she would accept a complete demo and rebuild."

"Eww." Boone's disapproval is palpable. "That would suck. This place and you? You're kinda made for each other, you know?"

Yeah, as a matter of fact, I do.

"You feel like you belong here. The old girl has a lot of character. Don't change a thing."

"Glad you approve." I really am. I love this place. It means a lot to me he can see how special it is.

"However you got here, I'm glad you did." Boone's arms tighten briefly, possessively, around me. "Never would have met you otherwise."

That sounds like a segue handed to me on a silver platter. There's no point avoiding this forever. Whatever brought him to Birchwood, ending up in my bed wasn't his original reason for coming to our sleepy little town. Our current condition is strictly serendipitous. A happy accident for me. For him too, I'm hoping, but I don't know for sure yet.

"So why are *you* here?" I ask him softly.

"Because you didn't have me arrested," Boone smoothly replies. "I thank you, again."

Nicely evaded. Well played.

Well, I had a feeling it wasn't going to be as easy as simply asking. You don't have to be a rocket scientist to work out one thing we have in common is being up to our respective asses in secrets. Only stands to reason he's as heavily invested in protecting his. He's not about to give them up to me simply because I recently showed him a good time. Or at least didn't make him laugh.

Whatever Boone does, he carries a gun while he's doing it. That could mean ex-military, law enforcement, private investigator, bounty hunter, CIA, FBI, ATF, or something else covert, to name but a few options. All of these could apply, as well as none. And lest we forget my least favorite line of conjecture, there's another reason why he might want and need to be armed. I can't afford to ignore this obvious alternative, no matter how much I'm coming to care for him.

Not everyone who carries a gun walks on the right side of the road. Every instinct I have tells me Boone's not a criminal, but feeling is not the same as knowing.

One way or another, I have to be absolutely sure.

Chapter 13

BACK up and try again.

"You know what I'm talking about. What are you doing in my neck of the woods, Mr. Dantrell? What brought you to Birchwood? Other than your truck."

It's probably a coincidence. Fate threw the dice and rolled me up a Boone. One thing is certain: whether his insertion into my existence is attributable to random chaos or divine design, Carly had nothing to do with it. She may have maneuvered Boone over to my table in the diner, but arranging for our paths to cross in the first place? I think not. The first time I saw her, when she was blasting through the intersection with her dad, she was as surprised as I was.

Boone silently considers the question for such a long time he might not intend to answer. I'm about to give him another verbal goad when he heaves a resigned sigh.

"I've been asking myself that ever since I walked over to your table. How the hell I ended up in this one-horse—"

"Hey! Don't diss my town!"

"Excuse me, pardon me, this quaint—"

"You can do better than that."

"This picturesque, and charming—"

"That's better."

"I'm glad you approve. Can I continue now? I forgot the question. Oh yeah, why am I here. It probably sounds like a cop-out, but the truck explanation is as good as any. Ditched my life in one afternoon, got in the damn truck, pointed it toward the interstate, and drove. Been on the road to nowhere ever since."

"And somehow, you ended up here?"

There's a quicksilver shift in his energy, a real blink-and-you'll-miss-it moment. He's not being entirely honest with me, but he doesn't know it. There was more intention than randomness in the direction he sent that truck than he's consciously aware of.

I'm not sure what it means, but it's very, very interesting!

He ghosts his hand up and down my back. His fingers tickle my spine. I can feel his mind working, almost hear his thoughts.

"Yup. What are the odds? I know it doesn't sound likely, but there it is. Seriously, I hit the highway with no plan other than putting as much distance between me and my former life as possible. Turned my back on everything and everyone. I didn't think of it that way at the time, but that's what it amounted to. I didn't just tell Palmer he could shove his dirty little organization and the crap they recruited me for—"

Aha! We got a name and confirmation he was involved in something covert. Possibly even illegal. But what? Listen and learn.

"I ditched Eve too."

Ah, yes. The wife.

"Your wife."

"Ex-wife." Boone sighs again. There's real regret in his voice, as well as true tenderness, every time he's mentioned her name. I've tried not to hear it, but it's there. Losing their child was undoubtedly the wedge cracking them asunder, but there was a time when things were good between them. But for the loss of Carly, would he still be with her?

Is Eve the one he really wants, but fears he can never have again? Even though I have no doubt he has... feelings... for me, am I simply a better-than-nothing substitute?

And if that's the case, what am I going to do about it?

I'd sooner have a root canal than proceed down this informational avenue, but I can't change who I am, even if it's probably already way too late to save myself from a thorough emotional hosing. I care about this man way more than I should. I want him to be happy. Whatever that means to him.

Go on, call me a schmuck. You know you want to.

"I'm sorry." I mean it.

"What are you apologizing for?" Boone pats my arm. "You didn't mess up my life. That was all me, baby. Anyway, it's a done deal. Ancient history. I left it all behind four months ago."

Four months? He and Carly have been driving around America for four months? Just Boone and his truck and his dead daughter and, lest we forget, his gun? Whoa, no wonder the guy went more than slightly medieval on me in Dinah's. Cooped up in that cab with no company he was aware of but his own self-loathing, he had ample opportunity to spend some quality time with the worst parts of himself.

This, folks, is how you make a zoink. Or several. Textbook.

What I can't get a take on yet is what's behind this monumental load of shit Boone is determined to shovel on himself. He's claiming full responsibility for tearing his family apart. Starting with what happened to Carly. To hear him talk, it's his fault. Carly's side of things—no way, José. Without details, I can't determine the real score, and it's driving me crazy!

What happened, dammit? Somebody throw me a clue!

Anyway, moving on to the next obvious question. You know you don't want to, but it has to be done.

I hear a light chuckle from the man beneath.

"You know, I can hear you thinking. To save you the trouble of asking: is it over between Eve and me, yes; do I have regrets, yes again, a whole fricking truckload. Do I want a do-over with her?"

He pauses, the strong arms cradling me fractionally tightening. "No. I'm not sure how I ended up here, but please believe me when I say this: meeting you is the only thing I've done in the past four months I don't regret. Eve is my past."

I want you to be my future.

He didn't say the words out loud, but I heard every syllable. Desire hovers between us, sharp, clean, and binding. Fierce, quiet joy swells inside me, and the audacious flaring of greedy hope. I've never asked for a thing for myself, never let myself believe I could have even the simplest of human pleasures. That was then. Now the never-hoped-for and never-dreamt-of is, against all improbability, actually within my grasp. I *want* it.

And him.

Please, universe, he followed me home, can I keep him?

"How about you?" Boone strokes my hair. "Has there ever been a Mrs. James?"

Because obviously there's not one now.

"No," I admit. "I have no experience of the matrimonial state. Not that I haven't had offers."

Oy. I'll say. Especially after the damn paparazzi and their stinking telephoto lenses peppered the tabloids with shots of me naively and very stupidly sunbathing in the buff in Bali on what I thought was a private beach. One of the more painful and embarrassing early reality checks issued to me along with the royalties for my first best-seller. The fame thing? Sounds great in theory. In practice, not so much. To those to whom much attention is given, pretty much everything personal and private is exacted.

Not to mention exploited.

I'm not ashamed of my ass, I simply don't appreciate seeing it in all its pasty glory plastered all over the front page of the Inquirer.

Boone emits a healthy snort. "I'll bet. A lot of people would kill to be in your shoes. Talk about your sexual smorgasbord. If even half the hookups the tabloids have attributed to you have some basis in actual fact, you've had some pretty famous tail. And the photos to go with."

This is interesting. The phrase is crude, his tone loaded with innuendo. If I'm reading the emotional shift right, he thinks I said I sleep with strangers all the time, ergo it follows I consider him nothing more than another notch on my bedpost. The deliberate crassness of his last comment is a cover-up, a smokescreen for shock, and something even more surprising.

Well, well, isn't this interesting. Mr. Dantrell has a strong streak of insecurity. Color me amazed.

"Don't get me wrong." Because I know you already have. "Just because people have an annoying habit of throwing themselves at me, doesn't mean I catch them. More like I throw them back."

Just so we're clear on that point.

The anxiety spike in the man beneath me stills. The emotions emanating from his warm body are mutating. There's still uncertainty, but his fear is banking down, shading into audacity. And hope.

"Why?" Boone's hand moves up to the nape of my neck, gently massaging the skin beneath my hair. It feels sinfully wonderful, the simple sensation of his stroking fingers, the warm hum of his affection flickering around them, kissing my skin.

"It's... it's complicated."

Fingers on me, the fire caressing me. I want to close my eyes, feel him touch me, drink in every sensuous sensation. I want to be totally in the moment, fully one with this enchanted interlude. Stop time for me, still its relentless march. No future, no past, there's nothing else, just him and me and what's happening between us.

Don't want to talk now, want to kiss.

I raise my head, straining forward, seeking his mouth.

To meet unexpected resistance.

"I'm sure it is," Boone's hand on my nape arrests my osculatory intention. "I'd still like to know."

More talking, no kissing. Wah.

"It's too risky to let anyone get close to me."

Honest and succinct. Can we kiss now?

"Oh, I get it. The whole things that go bump in the night deal. What's that got to do with boinking the living? Other than putting a spin on voyeurism I'll bet no one ever considered before."

Wow, me either. When it comes to contemplating even more bizarre takes on bizarre, evidently Boone's only getting warmed up.

"I'll never think of necrophilia in quite the same way either."

"Ew!" I slap him on the chest. "Don't even go there!"

"Sorry." He takes the hand I whacked him with and presses it to his lips. "Just trying to relieve the tension."

"Why? I'm not tense!" Even I can hear the defensive whine in my voice making a monkey out of my last statement. Wanna try kissing me better?

"This is a really touchy subject for you. How come?"

He doesn't understand. How could he? There's no way anybody could guess what a complete lie my carefully contrived playboy façade really is.

I card my fingers experimentally through the wiry chest hair beneath my hand, cataloging the crinkling texture. The enormity of this simple action has part of my mind chasing its tail in ever decreasing circles like a giant hamster freaking out on a wheel. Well, fasten your seatbelts, kiddies, we're about to take another trip on the "Things I Never Thought I'd Do" express. They say confession is good for the soul. Let's find out.

"Trust me, Boone, I can't risk anyone finding out about this. You've only seen a very small part of what I do. Dealing with the other side isn't always sweetness and light. There is some risk involved. But even if there weren't, let's get real here, for a sec. Asking someone to accept it's even possible to communicate with the dead, never mind claiming to be able to do it, is huge. Expecting the average person to be capable of wrapping their head around the concept? Not to mention the reality? Yeah, right! A lot of people couldn't do it. How do you determine who can or can't in advance? And lest we forget the constant irritant and annoyance of having a steady stream of dead people trooping through your life interrupting practically every aspect of it. That's what hanging out with me means, Boone. Everywhere else that isn't this house, I have no control over who shows up or when. It just happens, and it's going to keep on happening, probably until it's my turn to cross over. How weird is that? How many people are going to put up with that?"

"Well, if someone really cared about you, they would." Boone's reply is very quiet. "And despite what you think, you're not so different from the rest of us mere mortals. Lots of people have issues they wrestle with on a daily basis. This is just... different. It might take some getting used to, sure, but if they cared about you—I mean, really cared—"

"You'd think, wouldn't you?" I cut him off. "In theory it sounds great, but when it comes to actual practice I'm considerably less optimistic." I'm not talking through my hat, here. My deep-rooted skepticism is based in past, practical experience I'm neither admitting to nor explaining.

"This is a lot to expect anyone to take on faith. There's no way to know beforehand who can or can't deal with stuff like this." Even with my abilities. I can only read auras and emotions, I can't predict them. "It's a risk I'm not prepared to take. I don't want anyone treating me like I'm nuts. Patronizing me, telling me I'm imagining things. Medicating me and arranging impromptu exorcisms."

"That's a bit extreme, isn't it?" I can feel Boone's concern, hear it in his voice. Dammit, he's putting it together, sensing there's a hell of a story here. Just because he's right doesn't mean I'm going to tell him.

"You have no idea how far it could go. No idea."

"No," he murmurs. "You're right, I don't."

Yes, I have my reasons for staying away from people and love. Damned good ones. But they're mine, and I'm keeping them.

"Look how you reacted when you first found out."

The second the words leave my mouth, I want to pull them back. Boone doesn't make a sound, gives no outer indication of hurt, but I can feel it the instant my ill-considered verbal barb hits, pain spewing back out on me through the resulting wound.

I'm ashamed. He only meant me good; protecting a piece of my petty past isn't worth this.

"Ah, our first meeting." Boone takes a deep breath. "Not my proudest moment. But we were strangers at the time, and one of us was an asshole. It wouldn't be like that, not with someone you know and have built a foundation of trust."

"Who would that be? I've never let anyone get close to me. Not ever."

Oops.

Didn't mean to let that slip. Let's hope he missed it.

"Whoa!" Boone softly exclaims. "Back up here, are you saying what I think you're saying?"

So much for hope. It didn't take him very long to connect those dots.

"Yes, Boone, that's exactly what I'm saying." I roll off him and move away, shifting onto my left side. "You can say the V-word; it is appropriate and applicable. I freely admit it; I am—was—completely inexperienced and absolutely untouched previous to your arrival. You are the first."

The first in my bed, the first to touch me, to make love to me.

To make me love you.

"Ellery!"

Surprise!

I can't believe this is happening. The ghost stuff he handles without a problem. Discovering I was previously uncharted territory, that's grounds for panic?

"Jesus, I wish you'd said something, I wouldn't have...."

Taken advantage of me? Used me for a spot of catharsis? Engaged in a little sex therapy with the nearest, convenient warm body?

"Oh, Boone, relax, I'm not a baby," I airily retort. "Probably high time I found out what all the fuss was about. People do it all the time, no big deal; it's just sex, right?"

I need to stop talking now, before I say something really stupid. No point in making an even bigger fool of myself than I already have.

His fingers curve around my shoulder, imparting gentle concern shaded with amusement.

"You're not kidding; you really don't have a clue, do you? Come here."

He reaches for me again, wrapping his arm around my chest, pulling me to him, then spooning in tight behind me. Touching me, he never stops touching me. I like it, never want it to stop.

"What I was about to say was if I'd known, I'd have taken it much slower. Your first time, anyone's first time, is huge. Something special. You only ever have one, and if I'd known, I'd have tried to make it a better memory for you."

Now I feel stupid, but also insanely touched. I am mere moments from becoming total putty in this man's hands. If Eve ever shows up here looking for him, she's in for a hell of a whupping.

"Nothing wrong with the memory I already have."

Boone chuckles. "You say that now because you don't know any better. Wait 'til you have a larger sample group to extrapolate from."

Oooh, sounds like a plan! Can we start now?

"I can't get my head around how it's been for you. Dealing with this spirit thing completely solo since you were eight? Eight frigging years old? Other than an old dead lady dressed in pink, in all that time you haven't encountered one single soul you could trust? No one? How the hell is that possible?"

I took a chance once. Only once. Once was enough.

"I can't even imagine what that would be like." He gives me a fast, hard hug. "Don't you get lonely?"

Of course I do, but after awhile, you learn to not mind it so much. Kind of like all the other stuff you learn how to live with, because what other choice do you have, really?

None. Or so I thought, until today.

"This has got to be freaking you out," Boone whispers into my ear. "I have to go really slow with you, don't I?"

His hot breath against my skin makes me tremble. Almost as much as the terrible tenderness in his voice.

"You can do whatever you want with me." I twist in his embrace until we're face to face, heart to heart, mouth to mouth.

THE next thing I'm aware of is the incessant nagging of the morning sun beating aggressive reveille against my closed eyelids. Snarling and surly, I'm being booted back into the waking world, and I don't wanna go. I feel sluggish, spaced, not quite hung over, but close enough. It's as if I'm slightly out of phase with reality.

Drinking. I hate drinking. Why do I do this to myself?

Hang on. There's another reason why this morning in particular I'm waking up on the wrong side of the night before.

A most excellent reason.

Woo hoo!

I got laid last night. Just thinking about it is making me spontaneously alliterate.

Eagerly anticipating visual confirmation of the intimate recollections flooding my awareness, I turn over and open my eyes to the first morning of a whole new life.

Wait a minute, this isn't right. The other side of the bed is empty. There's no one there. Just like every other morning. Then again maybe not. There is one important, essential difference between this particular dawn and every other I've greeted alone in this bed. Cold, rumpled, smelly, stained sheets. Rats.

Evidently the only thing I'm waking up to is the odiferous, messy residue of the night before.

Surprise.

Boone sure knew how to call me. He got it right when he said I didn't have a clue. What I don't get is how completely I messed up reading him. I really thought he cared about me. Shows you how much I know.

Alone again, naturally. Welcome to the human race, Ellery. This is how it's done in the twenty-first century. Hook up, get 'er done, and get out. Boone is obviously extremely accomplished in all three areas. Especially the getting out part.

Didn't even stick around long enough to leave me a note. "Thanks for the orgasm?" "Sorry to come and come, and then go, but that's life?" Maybe notes are optional. Along with consideration. Not like I have the first clue what the proper "love him and leave him" protocol is these days. I'll Google it later.

There's a first and a last time for everything. So it is with me and all things carnal. I'll consider the alpha and omega of my intimate experiences in this incarnation as encapsulated in one hell of a night to remember. I can finally say I did it. Several times, but now it's over and done. Thanks for all the fish, pack it away and move on.

Disgruntled and despondent, I throw off the covers and shuffle to the ensuite to empty my bladder. First pee of the morning. Whee. Followed hard upon by another unaccustomed sight and unwelcome reminder of what I'd never done before and now never will again.

A discarded towel and bathrobe hanging over the edge of the hamper.

Ah, he might not have the guts to say good-bye to my face, but he's not all bad. Evidently he picks up after himself.

Tidy. That's nice.

One short shower, shave, and blow dry later, I'm feeling less like slashing and more like my usual sanguine self. But I'm still not entirely back on an unemotional keel. Twenty minutes of yoga and I should be busting into song.

The hills are alive....

Sing it, Maria.

I pad naked into my closet, select some briefs and a pair of shorts. I feel no pain. I feel no pain. I feel no pain.

My new mantra for the day. So far it's working.

I exit my suite and make the short journey to my meditation room. Inner peace. I could sure use some right now.

Having a second sanctuary within a structure entirely devoted to reclusion might seem redundant to the extreme, but the ambient atmosphere I've managed to establish in this space exclusively dedicated to serenity has saved my sanity more than once. Trust me, I need this place. Today more so than ever before.

I light a stick of incense, the clean, sweet jasmine smoke immediately swirling up my nostrils. A scent I deeply relish, usually a potent emotional balm, and for me, a never-fail feel-good.

At least, until today.

Maybe forty minutes of yoga will do the trick.

I breathe deeply, attempting to clear my mind, and start into the sun salutation sequence. I've enacted this familiar dance so many times I've internalized it down to the molecular level, but today every motion feels strained, studied, and unbelievably awkward. I can't find the rhythm, have completely lost the flow. As for the effect my less than stellar efforts are having on calming the chaotic state of my mind? I'd be better off popping a Valium.

So much for inner peace.

Dang. This getting over it and getting on with it stuff might be harder than I thought. Come on, Ellery, it's only a broken heart. What's the big deal? Not like you were using it or anything.

Start again. Focus. We can do this.

Flow, down into the lunge, breathe, nice stretch, work it, move up into uttanasana, ooh, baby, now we're talkin', stretch, feel the burn, now we're getting it, that's more like it.

"Wow." A low, masculine, appreciative growl behind me. "That's really impressive. I had no idea you could bend over like that! Mother of God, you're flexible! I don't mind telling you, this unsuspected talent is giving me plenty of ideas. Not to mention the current attitude of your ass being so convenient for some serious fantasy fulfillment."

"Jesus!" I'm still in uttanasana, bent over damned near double, my forehead pressed to my shins. I grab my ankles, striving for balance, now seriously compromised by having the crap scared out of me.

Too late; I'm going over.

This is gonna hurt.

And then I don't fall. Boone's strong, supporting hands averting total disaster at the last possible second. Saved!

He steps in behind me, holding my hips, his rock solid groin butting invitingly against my butt.

And we do mean rock solid.

Hello!

"You okay down there? Must have a hell of a head rush going."

He's here! He's still here! He's... he's... he didn't leave me, he's still here! I don't understand but I'm not complaining!

"Um... thanks!" Head rush, body rush, it feels like every red corpuscle I own is flooding my face, and it's not because of my inverted position. I'm also aware of how comfortably Boone's pelvis fits into my rearing rear.

Like we were made for each other.

"Listen." Fingers gently squeeze my hips. "You can come up now, but you should probably take it slow. Easy does it. I'm good." He thrusts gently, teasingly against me. "I've got your ass. I mean... back."

I love yoga. This position especially. But I think I'll come up for air now, or perhaps something even more interesting.

I slowly uncurl my spine and achieve an upright position. I've barely had time to adjust to my new orientation when my support system spins me around with dizzying enthusiasm.

"So, how flexible are you, anyway?" He leers and swoops in for some serious face sucking. I'm so shocked, happy, and dizzy I'm completely compliant with being thoroughly, deliciously osculated.

I don't know how long we suck, lick, bump, and moan, but it's over way too soon.

"Mornin' M.," Boone breathes after coming up for air. "Hope you didn't mind waking up alone, but I decided I needed to start repaying you for your kindness and hospitality. I intended to open with fixing you a fantastic breakfast, but after I checked out your larder, I discovered some serious deficiencies. So I went shopping."

He cooks?

"You cook? And shop?" I stare at him through an irrational haze of insane happiness. He's still here. And he cooks.

"Yup." He nods and beams with enormous satisfaction. "I picked up enough supplies to see us through today, but you need to stock up, dude."

"You're still here!" I blurt like a total boob. Is it too late to swallow my tongue?

"Yeah." Boone cups my jaw with his large, warm hands, his eyes so close and tender. "I'm still here, M. I definitely did not ditch you, and I'm sorry for giving you the impression I did. Maybe booking before you woke up, even if my intentions were good, was a bone-headed thing to do."

"No!" I blurt again. "I'm cool, I didn't think you… you…."

I lie like a frugal rug.

"Yeah, you did."

I could curl up inside his gaze and stay there forever.

"Maybe I did. A little bit."

"More than a little. I hurt you, and that's not cool. I will make it up to you. Here's the first installment."

His warm, moist mouth expertly covers mine, fitting so familiarly, like it's finally found a home. He kisses me confidently, carefully, and thoroughly.

Apology definitely accepted.

Just when things are starting to get interesting, he abruptly breaks the clinch. "Oh, baby, as tempting as you are, I've already got something cooking in the kitchen."

He pulls me in for a quick peck on the mouth, winks, and then turns away. "Come on, M., shake a leg."

"What did you just call me?"

M. He's been calling me M. ever since he walked in here.

"M. for Maestro." Boone pauses in the doorway. "Hey, I'm also a huge fan of Lee and Dannay. What, you prefer Scrappy?"

"Definitely not!"

"All right," he grins. "M. it is. Now, move that shapely ass of yours. Breakfast awaits, and we don't want it to get cold."

"Whatever you say, V."

"Huh?" It's his turn to be clueless.

Gotcha!

"V. for Velie."

"I get it," he grins. "Cute."

CHAPTER 14

"WHERE do you keep your coffee maker?" Boone's perplexed frown is especially endearing while he stares at the mechanical lineup on my marble countertop, noticeably shy of the aforementioned appliance. I savor his consternation along with my mouthful of the most incredible Belgian waffles I've ever tasted.

This man can cook. He's fairly talented in the kitchen as well.

His eyes cut to my mouth. "Are they okay?" He sounds anxious. Why? "I didn't know what you like. Other than Eggs Benedict, that is, and I don't know how to make it."

Oh! He means the waffles!

"Are you kidding, they're great!" I swallow and enthuse. "I don't have one, by the way."

"One what?"

Blank expression. Dude, keep up!

"Coffee maker. I don't have one."

"Why not?"

"I don't need one."

God, these waffles are good. I'm on the verge of an oral orgasm. I can't believe I just said that. Good grief, one night of sex and I've become a total degenerate.

Go, me!

"I don't drink coffee." I would have thought that was obvious, but apparently not.

His eyes narrow suspiciously. "Why not?"

What do you mean, why not? Why do you think?

"I don't like it," I carefully enunciate, then cram my waffle-laden fork into my mouth. "It's nasty, icky, bitter brown stuff. Blech."

I probably shouldn't have said that last mouthful while I had one.

"You're not serious?" He's truly horrified. "You are serious! Who doesn't like coffee?"

"Um... me?" I flash him an impudent grin, grab my mug o' chai tea, and salute him with it. "Can't stand the stuff. Never could. I do, however, have an extensive herbal tea selection in my pantry, but since you've previously rifled it, you already know that. Feel free to re-peruse and pick out an agreeable caffeine substitute."

"I'll pass." Boone shudders. "Well, that explains why you had no coffee. I thought you were out, as in—temporarily not in stock, not—but you plain didn't have any, period. Ever." He gives me a sour look.

Hey, nobody's perfect!

"Surprise."

"What am I going to do with this?" He casts a mournful glance at the package of Folgers Ground Roast in his right hand. I'm tempted to suggest it would make a great doorstop, but the look of tragic loss on his face invokes a warm feeling of compassion and restraint within me.

Besides, even though I'm pretty sure he wouldn't, if I really piss him off, he's quite capable of whupping my ass, and not in a good way. Best not to antagonize a man who hasn't had his morning coffee.

Tee hee.

"Well, you could stand there and hold it, but then your food will get cold."

"Tea," Boone grumbles. "Even worse, herbal tea. Blech." He plunks the unopened package of coffee on the counter, picks up his plate, and shuffles over to the breakfast bar to come to roost on the stool beside me. "I can't believe I'm hanging out with a *tea* drinker. It's a good thing you've got a great ass."

So I've been told. Quite frequently over the course of the night and the evening before. His isn't too shabby either. Let's not even talk about the shoulders. Ooh, mama!

"Get over it," I heartlessly advise, and I shovel in another forkful.

Boone crosses his arms and affects a fierce pout. "The man doesn't like coffee. Are we talking simply not partial to the taste, or have you also sworn off because of some obscure moral or spiritual objection to the substance not immediately obvious to the rest of us caffeine swillers?"

This is so surreal. I'm sitting at my breakfast bar having waffles with a side order of banter with the handsome and charming man I slept with the night before.

Cue the theme of *The Twilight Zone*. Omigawd. Rod Serling! He could actually show up right now. In the non-flesh. That is, if he's still hanging around and wants to talk. It's not likely, but it is theoretically possible.

Okay, enough of the ridiculous, let's get back to the sublime.

I slept with a man. In my bed. Me. Honest and for true. And now it's the morning after, and he's still here. We're here. Sitting side by side. Eating.

He even made me breakfast!

Somebody pinch me!

"For a man who makes waffles like this, I think I can live with a coffee maker in my kitchen."

"For that, the waffle maker thanks you." Boone grins and tucks in to his own repast. "You'll notice I held the bacon on the side."

"For that, the vegetarian thanks you." I return the smile.

We fill the next few minutes with some contented mastication, but it isn't long before Boone gets an expression I realize—with an accompanying "omigawd" moment for doing so—is his "I got something to say" look.

Wow.

"I figured it out," Boone swallows and announces.

Hah! Told ya!

"What?"

"Why those stories of yours seem so real."

You lying bastard, I knew it! You *have* read my books!

"You don't say." Hell, yeah, I'm gonna call him on it! "I find myself wondering how that could be. You told me you were personally unacquainted with my work."

Talk your way outta that one, smartass!

"I know what I said," he ripostes with a rakish grin. "Perhaps I wasn't being entirely truthful when I said it."

"Perhaps?" I arch a brow at him.

"Okay, I lied. But I'm right, aren't I?"

"About what?" I'm playing dumb. I know he knows, but I want to hear him say it.

"Your books. You didn't make them up. You took dictation from some dead guy."

Five of them, to be exact. But geez, when you put it like that, it sounds like all I did was listen and type. Which is neither flattering nor accurate.

"Well, I wouldn't put it quite that way." I scowl at him.

Boone blinks, light apprehension springing into his wary gaze. He's sensing a shift in the way the conversational wind is blowing, and he's already battening down the hatches.

This guy was married, all right. He's good.

I'm gonna keep this going for awhile. Some payback for the "taking dictation" crack.

"For your information, I didn't just 'take dictation'."

I have a go at faking affront. It's a piece of cake. I've made a career of playing a high-strung, high-maintenance, temperamental, overly-demanding, over-the-top, sensitive artistic type subject to frequent fits of pique and the vapors. I'm very, very good at it.

All the better to keep people away, my dear.

"Hang on, I didn't mean anything by it; it was just an

expression," Boone frowns.

I'm good. He's buyin' it. Sucka.

"Anyone can regurgitate the facts of their life, but making them interesting? Not as easy. I contribute a definite and not inconsequential stylistic enhancement to the source material."

And we're workin' it. And him. This is fun!

"I never said you weren't a good writer. If that's what you heard, it's not what I meant!"

That's enough. I'll let him off the hook, now.

"Relax!" I throw my arms around his neck. "I'm yanking your chain."

"I knew that." He swallows and slumps against me with relief. "You, sir, are an evil man," he chuckles.

"Thanks. I'll get even better with practice."

"God help me." Boone wraps a warm hand around my nape and squeezes. "I've created a monster."

"What can I say, I was having fun. I've never done this before."

"No, it's okay, I'm fine." His smile and energy coincide with his assertion, so I believe him, and yet there's something oddly out of kilter about him, suddenly. Like a weird aftertaste in my mouth.

Ah, it's nothing. Compared to what I'm used to, everything about this morning is completely off the wall, so outside my box of morning normal I should be flipping out all over the first floor.

Chill and enjoy the new sensations, dude.

"But getting back to your original, most astute observation, you're right about where my books came from. It's been a hell of a ride from anonymously passing on personal messages to having an entire shelf in my office dedicated to books with my name on the outside of the cover and the dust jacket instead of inside on the book plate."

Boone leans forward with obvious interest. I'm vaguely disappointed when the hand massaging my neck withdraws.

"Personal messages?"

Whoa, hold the phone. This man doesn't miss a dammed thing. One unconsidered utterance and once again we're in unexplained territory. Dammit!

I've never told anyone any of this. Who was there to tell? The nitty-gritty details of my life, how I got from point then to point now, just happened. One day I was there, and now I'm here. All the steps in between are a blur. The whole process was more than slightly surreal.

The story of my life according to my official bio as routinely trotted out to placate pushy talk show hosts is very different from the one I actually lived. But even though I was there for every moment and lived to tell the tale, it doesn't seem real.

"When I was a kid, dead people used to literally swarm me. They scared the living heck out of me until I learned the rules."

"There are rules?" Boone is clearly astonished by the concept. His right hand, formerly resting quiescent on his thigh, begins to describe small, slow circles against the denim encasing his leg.

"Sure there are. There are rules for everything. As above, so below. Visible universe, invisible universe. The one we live in is governed by clearly defined physical laws. Same thing goes for everything spooky-side."

"What goes up must come down," Boone weighs in. "Etcetera, etcetera." Right hand, palm down on his thigh, still slowly circling. Something very strange about the hand and the motion.

"Yup." I jerk my eyes away from it. They keep wanting to go there, and I'm not sure why. The movement, and my inexplicable fascination with it, is distracting. "Once I began to understand the way things worked in the unseen universe, and consequently how to better protect myself, life became more tolerable. A lot less terrifying."

That's so odd. The way he keeps rubbing his thigh. He doesn't strike me as a fidgeter. I don't think that's a word.

Oh, so now you're an expert on Boone and whether or not he fidgets. That is a word. Based on what, exactly? Your exhaustive store of up-close and personal knowledge obtained during an observation period of a whopping twenty-four hours? No, less than that, even.

Has that really been all it's been? Not even a full day? Really?

"So how did you get the hang of it? Trial and error? I know there was a rulebook in Beetlejuice, but I hardly think it's that easy. I'm guessing the afterlife doesn't come with an instruction manual."

Rub, rub, rub. Why is he doing that?

"I wish. Certainly would have helped. Thank God for Mrs. S.!"

Stop staring at the hand! Eyes up and front!

"Nice little old pink lady?"

"That's her. She taught me what the spirits could and couldn't do, and when I found out their threats were a bunch of otherworldly hot air? It was very empowering."

"I'll bet," Boone nods. I'm warming to the subject now, and his obvious interest. "But why would they want to scare you in the first place? Sounds like a really mean thing to do to a little kid."

The idea obviously bothers him. The concept in general or as pertaining to me specifically, I'm not sure, but what seems clear is that if it were possible to go back and kick some phantom ass on my behalf, he's up for it.

That's... sweet.

"Well, they didn't, not really; they were just desperate. But I didn't understand that. I was only a little kid who could do something no one around me could, and as long as I was ignorant of the ways of the otherworld, I was victimized on a constant basis. That stopped once I learned how to protect myself and found out I didn't have to put up with the supernatural scare tactics. I read them the riot act and the spook was on the other foot. We communicated. When they realized I was listening and they didn't need to come on so strong and scary to get me to do what they wanted, most of them calmed down and turned out to be quite nice. All the bluster and fury was based on frustration. They had unfinished business, and they needed someone—namely me—to help them sort it out."

"Unfinished business. You mean like Carly."

Grief floods his eyes; his hand stills on his thigh and clenches.

"Yeah, like Carly."

"They must have been on you like white on rice."

I appreciate Boone's intelligence and insight. It's gonna cut way down on the exposition.

"Oh, you have no idea." I risk a swift glance down. His right hand is unclenched, lying loosely on his thigh. Not moving. Thank God.

He pauses, cants his head to the side.

"So you did what they wanted. Passed on their messages. But how could you? You obviously didn't walk up to the next of kin—or whomever—and say, 'Hello, you don't know me, but your dead Uncle Bill wanted me to tell you have a nice life.' Or whatever."

Not until yesterday, that is.

"Hell, no! That's what the post office is for. If I had a dollar for every anonymous letter I've sent out in the last twenty or so years, it still wouldn't cover the postage. Previous to my performance of yesterday, I had a strict policy of never delivering a post-mortem message in person. I broke that rule not once, but twice, by speaking directly to the lovely lady who owns the diner and, of course, you. You saw how that turned out."

"Not my finest hour," Boone admits, his eyes suddenly, hauntingly tender. "But from where I'm sitting, it ultimately turned out pretty good."

My throat suddenly constricts with a surge of affection so intense it's strangling me. "Me too."

Boone leans forward, his green eyes dancing with lust. His lips are warm, sticky, and sweet with syrup. I lick the taste of it, and him, from my mouth.

The waffles are good, but he tastes way better.

"You were saying." His eyes never leave mine while he touches his thumb to the corner of my mouth, gently wiping something from the crease.

"Um…." I got nuthin', here.

"I asked you how you went from solving spooks' problems to…."

"Writing best-sellers. Right." That mouth is mesmerizing. As much as I'm flattered by his interest, I can think of several things I'd rather be doing with mine. All of them not involving talking.

Whoa, lookit me, I'm definitely on the slippery slope to full-fledged moral turpitude. Excellent.

"When I got comfortable dealing with the spirits crossing my path during the course of my ordinary day, Mrs. S. began expanding my horizons. They started showing up from all over the world."

"You mean she was sending out for more spooks?" Boone briefly considers this. "How would you do that? Personal ads? Dead letter office?"

"Oh, that's hysterical." I glare at him.

"I can think of more."

"Please don't." I roll my eyes at him. "The first storyteller—that's what I call them—came to me in university. He wasn't recently dead, by any means, meaning all his people had passed over, but he knew that. He hadn't joined them because he had something he wanted to say, but there was no one living I could deliver it to. That was fine with him; he didn't want me to pass the message on to anyone, his unfinished business was finding someone to listen."

"He wanted to tell his story. That's why you call them… what you call them." Boone nods, resting his chin on his cupped hand. He's listening intently, by all appearances intensely interested in what he's hearing. Maybe some of that raptness is due to what he's seeing, too.

I'm hopeful.

"I listened. It was easy. The stories were utterly fascinating. I started taking notes and then recording the sessions. Something in me didn't want the details to get lost. They needed to be set down, made permanent. Preserved for posterity. It started like that, but as my fascination with the people and what I was hearing grew, I wanted to take it further. I came up with the idea of turning their past life recollections into actual books. We were talking authentic history here; I couldn't keep it all to myself. My plan was to take my transcripts and turn them into manuscripts, stockpile them somewhere secure, like in a safety deposit box, or something, until after I died, and then—"

"Sonofabitch, you were gonna sit on them! And then pass them on to posterity as real biographies after you were gone!"

"Yeah. Once I snuffed it, it would have been safe to 'out' myself and admit where the stuff came from. My gift would have done something good, the storytellers would live on, their legacy preserved and transmitted, and as for me, well, it wouldn't matter anymore whether people knew my secret, would it?"

Boone doesn't say anything, his gaze bordering uncomfortably on pity.

"You were going to spend the rest of your life hiding? All by yourself, working on something you'd never see the benefit of? Nobody knowing about you or what you can do, no one ever suspecting how many people you'd helped without ever asking or getting anything for yourself? Just you and a bunch of... ghosts? Until you became one of them?"

Geez, the way he's talking, you'd think I was some kind of pathetic escapee from a Dickens novel. Or even worse, a bad Gothic romance.

Ellery Eyre. That's me.

"Hey." His sympathy is settling around me like a cheap suit. Making me feel equally uncomfortable. "It's not as bad as all that. Here's a thought. If I put my life in a book, do you think anyone would buy it?"

"Better that than living it," Boone responds fervently. "Thank God fate intervened and denied you the lovely, desolate future of obscure anonymity you had all lined up for yourself."

"Yeah, lucky me," I glare at him. "The alternative is so much better." There is more than a shade of sarcasm in my retort.

"All right, I'll concede that with the size of the secret you're sitting on, being subject to the degree of public scrutiny you've had thrown at you might occasionally be inconvenient."

"I'm not even going to dignify that with a response."

"Seems like you just did." Boone grabs my hand, raises it to his lips. "Sorry, sweetie, I'm starting to understand how much you hate living in a fishbowl and why, but you gotta admit, even too much attention is better than no attention at all."

I see his point, and really, deep down, I don't disagree with him.

Day before yesterday? Totally different story, but now I know what I came so close to missing....

Funny; my assertions to Max to the contrary, garret-languishing doesn't sound nearly as much fun now as it did yesterday morning.

I snatch my hand back, but I can't quite suppress a smile of grudging agreement. "No, I don't have to admit any such thing," I mutter.

"Your mouth may say no, no, no," Boone chuckles. "But your eyes...."

His voice trails off suggestively, and he licks his bottom lip, green eyes sparking with desire.

I'm really ready to stop talking now.

The subtle serpent of desire uncoiling in my shorts is abruptly snuffed out when Boone recommences the hand-to-thigh action.

Not again!

The resumption of the rubbing also seems to divert Boone's intentions from seduction back to conversation. Me, I'm trying to understand what's bothering me so much about a simple repetitive action.

As soon as I figure it out, I'll let myself know.

"So." Boone starts talking again. Unfortunately. "How were you saved from the aforementioned fate? What happened to change your plans?"

"Ah, that. It was my misfortune... or not." I grin at him. "Depending on your point of view, to be assigned a college roommate who had an extremely curious and nosy fiancée also happening to be Max's niece. I won't bore you with the details. Long story short, for some reason she got it in her head to poke into my private papers when I was at class one day, found one of the transcripts, read through it, went berserk, ratted me out to her aunt, and the next thing I know, I've got Max-zilla on my case, dogging my steps night and day, waving contracts in my face and swearing if I sign she'll make me an overnight sensation."

"She didn't lie about that," Boone observes, rubbing. "So why did you?"

"It was the only way to make her go away. Temporarily, anyway. Besides, I didn't see the harm in it. I didn't believe her."

"So you didn't see any of this coming?"

"Are you kidding? Would you have?"

"If I were as good as you, I might have."

"You don't have to flatter me to have your way with me."

I lean forward to plant a nice, wet one on him. He stops rubbing long enough to subtly but definitely fend me off and put me back in my place.

This is getting as weird as the rubbing. Why does he keep coming on to me like he's interested in starting something I'd be as interested finishing and then….

Excitus interruptus?

"As long as I'm finding out where all your bodies are buried—"

"Oh, hah, hah," I groan.

"Told you I had more. Like I was saying, as long as I'm asking: as if you hadn't given yourself enough to do already, how did the Freedom Foundation come about?"

"It came from the shock of me suddenly making insane amounts of money and not having expensive tastes, an extravagant partner, or an insatiable drug addiction upon which to squander it."

"Nor, I would think, the desire," Boone insightfully observes.

"Let's just say no matter how I feel about what's happened to me, I'm very grateful for what I have and mindful I don't deserve it."

Boone draws back, his brows colliding with consternation. "Why would you say that?"

"I'm not laboring under the delusion I possess any great literary talent. I got lucky—or not, depending on how you look at it—in somehow acquiring an ability that dropped these stories into my lap, but they're not mine. I'm essentially writing biographies and passing them off as fiction."

"And it doesn't hurt the cause you look like you just jumped off the cover of a romance novel."

"Please don't remind me. Anyway, this money I've made from these stories, because I didn't really earn it—well, not entirely—I can't keep it all for myself."

Boone looks at me like I'm nuts. Maybe I am, but it's the way I feel.

"Well, it's not like they can spend it!" he protests.

"You know what I mean."

"Yeah," he nods, admiration gleaming in his eyes. "I do. You want to make a difference. And fate, for whatever reason, handed you the means on a gold-plated platter. So you ran with it."

He does understand.

"So, here we are now," Boone says. "From 'talks to the dead guy' to best-selling writer, media sensation, and darling of the talk show circuit."

"That foolishness only happens whenever a new book comes out. The Ellens, Oprahs, and Lettermans remember they haven't used me recently to help boost their ratings, and the harassment begins anew. For a few months I have to put up with the publicity tours and the media hype, but after I show my face, make the requisite rounds, and prove to be as boringly reclusive as the last time out, they quickly forget about me and go back to badgering Britney and Paris."

"Then you run back here and hide for another couple of years." Boone throws me a rueful smile. "How's that been working for you?"

"It is what it is." I shrug it off. "Not like I've had a lot of choice."

His malachite eyes narrow like they're drilling tiny holes straight into my soul. It hurts how well he already knows me. How much he sees. I burn beneath his searing gaze as he peels back layer after layer of the superfluous parts of me.

I don't mind losing them. Or myself.

Not to him.

"You always had choices, Ellery," he gently murmurs. "Far more than you ever gave yourself. And now you have another one."

I can't stand it anymore.

"Dude, if you don't stop talking and start kissing, I won't be responsible for my actions."

CHAPTER 15

BOONE actually averts his eyes. "I'm sorry about that," he mutters.

All I can do is gape, mouth flapping open in the breeze. I know what I'm seeing, but it can't be happening. I watch with rapidly escalating incredulity, a subcutaneous red stain sprawling across his cheekbones. Blushing? The man is blushing. Are you kidding me?

Blushing and apologizing. I have no idea where any of this is coming from, but I should probably find out.

"About what?"

"The kissing, and… and…." He's not actually stuttering, but he's close. "Stuff. Believe me, right now nothing would make me happier than hauling you off that stool, throwing you to the floor and—"

Now we're talking!

"Hey, don't let me stop you." I hop off my stool, grab two handholds of his shirt, and pull him toward me.

"No! No, we can't!" His eyes bulge with panic, and he rears back like I'm Freddy Krueger coming in for a one-blade landing. He almost does back flips in his apparent haste to backtrack, and just when it seems he's headed all the way out of the kitchen in his frantic effort to evade me, he screeches to a spectacular stop, rooting himself ten feet away, breathing heavily and whipping his head apprehensively from side to side like he's waiting for kitchen ninjas to leap out of the cabinets and Ginsu him to death.

If he doesn't give me a damned good explanation for what I just saw, I might help them.

"Can't?" I'm doing my best not to sound as hurt as I feel. Which is pretty darned offended. And confused. I don't understand his sudden seeming aversion to my company. He didn't seem to have any issues with intimately interfacing last night, but now he has to sit here and talk to me in the rosy glow of the morning-after sunshine, or, God forbid, even more shocking, touch me, now he has problems?

Calm down, calm down, no point in both of us going berserk. Something else is going on here. I've known it ever since we sat down to breakfast, but the still, small, annoying voice of intuition lurking in the background of my awareness, patiently waiting for me to acknowledge it? I've been so consumed with gleefully basking in the unaccustomed normalcy of these past few moments I've pretty much been telling it to piss off.

I knew this was too good to last. So was he.

"You're gonna think this is weird." Well, to his credit, he is trying to explain.

"Weird? Me?" You forget who you're talking to, son. "Weird is my middle name."

"I thought it was Joyce." Boone stops giving himself whiplash and looks my way for the first time since the commencement of his freaking fit.

Fine time to be pedantic! Who cares what my middle name is! What's up with you?

"Whatever! Weird and me," I hold up my left hand, first two fingers intertwined. "We're like that. Stop stalling and pissing me off!" I bark at him.

"Carly!" he snaps back at me, bright blotches of red erupting on his cheeks.

Huh?

"You said she's still around, and she's coming back." Feet planted firmly apart, hands on his hips, Boone juts out his chin and glares at me. He seems to be getting over his momentary difficulties with self-expression.

"Yeah, that's right. In fact, I'm a little surprised we haven't seen her already." Hmmm. I can only think Mrs. Sheridan has something to do with it.

Oh, wait; I get it. Not something we need to worry about, but he doesn't know that.

I should probably fill him in.

"Relax, Boone, it's not going to happen." I move toward him.

"What?" He eyes my approach dubiously but doesn't make any overt moves to either escape or fend me off.

"Anyone, including Carly, popping in while we're in the middle of each other. So to speak." I grin at him. "If that's what you're worried about, don't be."

He skeptically scopes the kitchen. "What's to stop them?"

"L'il ole pink lady again. She controls access to my personal environment for all things otherworldly. She does a very good job."

"Granny Good Ghost? Seriously?"

"I promise you, nothing gets by her."

I wait while he mulls.

"So, no spooks popping in while we're...."

"In flagrante delicto? Nope. That goes for Carly too."

"Oh!" His face is abruptly transfixed with an expression of joyous comprehension. Followed by a rush of lust. "Well, that changes things!"

He starts toward me, arms opening wide. I sense some serious kissing in my immediate future. This could be good.

Or maybe not. That splotch. On the heel of his right palm. What the hell is that?

He didn't have it yesterday. I'm sure of it.

"Boone, hang on." I grab his hand, turn it palm up to get a better look. Wow! His hand is like ice. That's weird. Why is his hand so cold? I don't know. One problem at a time.

First impression: a cut? Or bite? More like a bite. Definitely a puncture wound. Puffy and red. Kind of nasty. Infected? Already?

That's not right. And there's something about the wound. The edges are odd. Blurry. If I didn't know better, I'd swear this was an insertion area.

No, it can't be! Not possible. Can't be an IA. Not on actual flesh. Zoinks can only affect energy fields, not—

Second impression slamming in to me, hard on the first. Whatever did this was flesh and blood. It also wasn't human.

Shit!

"It's nothing." Boone's denial is abrupt and terse, the afflicted appendage yanked from my grasp with frightening abruptness. He steps back, folds his arms defensively across his chest, his right hand tucked protectively into his armpit.

No lust on his face now. What's going on behind the expressionless mask currently confronting me is anybody's guess. No mistaking his body language, though. That long, lean form is screaming, "Keep away; mind your own business" in big, bold letters. Punctuated with "mess with me at your peril."

Sorry, no can do, compadre. What I'm seeing and sensing doesn't leave me a lot of options. I have to examine his damned hand whether he likes it or not.

Bright side, at least he no longer has a gun. That is, I don't think he does. The one I relieved him of yesterday is still stashed in my liquor cabinet, isn't it?

I'm hoping, yeah. Why me?

Okay, fortune favors the bold. Or is it the foolish? Whatever, I'm going in.

"Come on, Boone, if it's nothing, what's the harm in letting me see? Humor me," I grin at him.

Boone takes another step back, the hostility on his face notching up to DEFCON Two. So not good. Anger swirls around him, rapidly escalating, spiking out from his field like the quills of a pissed off crimson porcupine.

Wow, that didn't take long. Also renders the whole "it's not possible" issue extremely moot. I can't deny the evidence of my eyes.

My former-assailant-turned-lover stands before me, aiming enough defensive animosity in my direction to ward off a pack of guys twice my size. Giving every indication he's about to recant his lover stance and revert to his previous role of menacing, life-threatening thug. Simply because I asked to see the boo-boo on his hand.

I think the IA premise is more than proven. Great, now what do I do?

"It's a scratch," he growls, eyes narrowed and snarling. "Caught it on something in my truck while I was stashing the groceries. Or something. What's the big deal?"

I thought as much. Boone was attacked and infected after he left the house. While I was sleeping. Memories of the man from the night before briefly and bitterly assail me. They're especially bitter juxtaposed with the current reality.

When I woke up alone this morning, I thought the worst thing I had to deal with today was being loved and left. I had no idea I'd be facing a bite and switch.

"It looks infected." I cautiously inch closer. "Chill, I'm only trying to help."

"If I wanted your help, I'd ask for it!" he spits out from between clenched teeth. "It's fine! Leave it alone!"

This is bad, this is really bad. He's only a hair away from homicidal. Why does this suddenly seem so heartbreakingly familiar?

Wow, shades of déjà vu! Surprise, here we are again, staring into the eyes of Mr. Big and Scary. I'm so over this Alpha Male thing. Thought he was too.

I have to get close enough to determine what I'm dealing with and then deal with it, but if I go for it, there's a very real chance he'll go for me. And not in a good way.

Nobody ever told me relationships were this complicated. Or potentially hazardous.

"Boone, listen." I take another step toward him, hoping he will.

The instant I touch his energy field, a stinging, repulsive whammy slams into me, rocking me back on my heels. The reverse effect on

Boone is equally spectacular.

Newton's Third Law is also applicable on the etheric planes.

"Stay away from me!" he howls, eyes bulging, skin mottling black and crimson with the force of his trumped-up rage. "Back off! I don't want you touching me, you goddamned weirdo!"

I know it really isn't him saying it, but that hurt. It was supposed to. It was supposed to make me turn tail and run, driven away by either fear or disappointment, and if I didn't know what I know, it might have worked. All the same, I can't help flinching slightly with the blow.

He knows he hurt me; I can see it in his eyes. I can also see he didn't mean it, doesn't know why he said it, and doesn't have a clue how to fix it.

I could throw him one, as long as he doesn't reciprocate by throwing a punch.

"You know what?" he falters, dragging the back of his hand across his mouth, his eyes hunted, face wracked with regret. "I don't have to stick around for this bullshit."

That's an exit line if ever I heard one. He said it, I heard it, but I can't help noticing he's not moving.

"Fine!" I holler at him. "Neither do I!"

"Fine!"

"Fine!"

We stand there, staring each other down, breathing hard. He hovers on the cusp of flight, eyes screaming he wants to stay. I grab his gaze with everything I've got, pumping positive vibes into his field, hoping I can hold him.

Whatever the hell you are, you can't have him. He's mine!

"Boone." I'm unashamedly imploring. "Can we start again?"

Don't do this. If you go, I can't help you. Stay with me. Stay with me. You know you want to.

"I...." His eyes glisten with uncertainty and longing. His right hand twitches and rises from his side, palm up and opening toward me as if reaching and offering.

Please don't leave me.

Hope unfurls and flames between us. I can feel the subtle shift in his field, edging over to my side. He's still being pushed and pulled away from me, but he's bucking the insistent inner traction. Me. He does want me; he wants to stay with me. Have him, I almost have him....

"*Khnumhotep.*" A reedy wisp of a female voice floats down the breezeway, coming between us.

No! You have to be *kidding* me! Dammit, why is this happening now? Can't those people keep a little old lady confined? There are a dozen or so of them and one of her. Why is this so hard?

I throw Boone a despairing look and dash from the kitchen. I don't want to leave him literally hanging, but I have no choice. I haven't had time to contemplate the implications of a corporeal non-human psychic parasite somewhere in our midst, never mind speculate on what its abilities and range might be. If someone as fragile and psychically defenseless as Mrs. Potts got entangled in the mix? I have no idea what would happen to her. I won't risk her doddering into the kitchen in order to find out.

God, grant me strength. And a really big butterfly net.

I've barely made it into the hall when I have to backpedal furiously in order to avoid crashing into the befuddled dear doddering out of the library, her ancient talon of a right hand wrapped around the battered metal handle of a decrepit watering can that probably came into being around the same time she did. I've never seen it before; lord only knows where she found it. Or why she brought it. Yet another of the unfathomable mysteries constantly accompanying her. Unfortunately, I am unable to attempt to unravel it at the moment. Perhaps another time.

"Good morning, Khnumhotep," she quavers, her fissure-ridden face creaking beneath a blurry smile. "I'm off to water the plants."

Ah, that explains the can. Plants, huh? How sweet. Wish I had some.

Boone. Boone needs me. I have to get back to Boone. Now. And on the other hand, we have her. Normally I wouldn't mind her wandering around the place, but at the moment, "normal" is strictly a distant dream. I have to get my faded lady back where she belongs. And so I will, eventually, but for the moment I must settle for containing her somewhere safe until her keepers—and I use the term extremely loosely—come for her. She means no harm and, as a rule, does none. Well, not much anyway.

Little old ladies. I'm surrounded by them on both sides of the here and now and the hereafter. If this is the universe trying to tell me something, it's gonna have to speak up.

Mrs. Potts benignly regards me with the placid wisdom of the utterly innocent.

"Beware," she sternly admonishes. "You must not let love blind you."

Excuse me?

Startled by the solemn authority in her wavering voice, I stare down into her ancient, crinkled face. She is the absolute incarnation of immaculate incomprehension, her rheumy eyes shimmering like faded shadows of sapphires, vacuous, completely bereft of any hint of awareness.

I must be hearing things. There isn't even the slightest spark of intelligence in those dear old eyes. No lights on, no one home. Same old, same old, and so, alas, is she. Poor sweet lady, who were you, before you moved away? I wish I knew.

And what keeps bringing you back to my door?

"Mind my words, Khnumhotep," she unexpectedly intones once more. "Don't let the Evil in."

Okay. Hair, back of neck, standing to serious attention. My nape feels like a pincushion on steroids. What-what-what made her say that?

And to what is she referring? The unclassified icky that somehow got a stinger in Boone? But how would she know about it? Creepy. Thanks for the heads up—if that's what it was—but I already know about the UI, and I'd already be dealing with it if I hadn't been called out to deal with you!

And what's love got to do with it? Besides being both an

excellent song and movie. I'm just asking.

Not a clue to be seen in the diluted blue irises beneath me. Was the substance of her enigmatic address manufactured by well-intentioned but completely directionless dementia? I should be so lucky.

Evil? Her use of that specific term has thrown me for a loop. I'm not a huge believer in the concept, in spite of everything I've seen. In fact, it's due to what I've seen that I can't subscribe to the notion of anything that absolute. I know a lot of people believe in it, but the reality, in my experience, is a lot less dire. There are some seriously screwed up entities out there, but absolute evil? Never encountered it.

And yet to dismiss the notion so cavalierly, on the heels of one seeming impossibility and an enigmatic improbability….

Maybe not the smartest course of action.

A strange sliver of dread slices through me. Mrs. Potts blinks, emits an eerily incongruent, almost elfin giggle, then breezes past me and totters into the library with surprising rapidity. Still toting her damned can. Wait, I should check to see if it's loaded. The last thing I want is her on the loose in my lovely library swinging a fully charged water-dispenser.

No. I can't. I can't spare the time. I'm going to have to throw the fate of my books over to the vicissitudes and vagaries of the universe. And in so doing exhaust my quota of obscure 'V' words for the day.

Enough fooling around. Back to the kitchen and the man I left behind.

Boone.

All right, I'm here, but he's not. Where did he go? He didn't come past me while Mrs. Potts and I were shooting the breeze in the breezeway, but there is more than one way out of the kitchen. He could have gone up the back stairs or exited through door number two. My least favorite option.

Using the back door to leave the house and hit the road. Even if I hadn't been distracted by the dear, demented lady currently toddling around in my library and hopefully not watering the indigenous literature, it's highly unlikely I'd have heard him leave. This is a big house. Seriously huge. If a person has a mind to vanish into it or depart surreptitiously from it, either way, easily done.

I have to find him. He can't have gone far. If he's in the house, all I have to do is mount a room-to-room rummage and I'll turn him up inevitably, but if he's already flown my coop? Every second I waste running around in here means he's out there, getting farther and farther away.

So what do I do, go or stay? Root or route?

Calm down, don't panic. We can figure this out.

You know who'd come in handy right about now? Mrs. S. I could send her out after him. She's better than a bloodhound. And you don't have to clean up after her.

I've got to get her to give me a pager.

"Ellery."

Mrs. Sheridan pops in directly in front of me, a vision of pink rebuke, her wrinkled old lips clamped in a mildly disapproving moue.

"Shit!" I shriek. I hate it when she does this. Hate it, hate it, hate it. Twenty and then some years on of having the spit scared out of me on a daily basis, you'd think I'd become inured to the nerve-shattering effects of the unexpected pop-in.

You'd think that. Know what? You'd be wrong.

"Please don't do that!" I howl at her, only a hair away from hyperventilating. "Thanks for finally showing up, by the way." Where were you when I really needed you?

Yeah, I'll admit it; some assistance with Boone earlier, insight, input, information, a clue as to what the hell was going on, would have been appreciated. But her not being around when she could do the most good seems to be par for the course ever since Boone arrived. Funny, I hadn't really made that connection until now. Can't imagine why. Possibly I've had other things on my mind.

"Ellery, you must listen to me, my dear."

"Look!" I feel no remorse for being short with her. "I need you to find Boone. Now!"

Mrs. Sheridan stoically stares me down. "No." She mournfully shakes her silvery head.

I want to wring her scrawny spectral neck. "No? What do you mean, no? Find him! Find him now!"

"It would serve no purpose. Where he has gone, you cannot follow."

Good God, what does that mean? "Don't start with me! I'm not kidding!"

She and I have had this thing going on for years. She pulls out the cryptic card, then throws an abstruse oral puzzle in my path, and I try to not go insane while piecing together her annoyingly inscrutable clues in order to reason my way through whatever obscure point she's endeavoring to impress upon me. It's a fun game, it really is, barrel o' laffs, and any other time I'd be all in, but right now, not a good time.

"I don't think you understand," I carefully explain. "I need to find him, now."

"I understand you perfectly, my dear boy." She has such a pleasant, gentle smile. Especially when she's playing cat's cradle with my patience. "It simply isn't possible."

I'd kill her if she weren't already dead.

"Will you... just... for... for—" I'm sputtering, I'm so frustrated. "I need you to knock off the Yoda routine for once in your life!"

"I'm not insensitive to your concern, dear boy." She calmly ignores my escalating hissy fit. "Or unaware of your affection for your new friend."

That's one way of putting it.

"Well, then you'll understand why I want to find him. I can't do that and stand here and talk to you too. You got something to say to me, you're going to have to tag along. Or, and this would be incredibly helpful, you can stop being you, for once, and just go and find him, for god's sake! We both know you can! Don't tell me otherwise, because I know it's not true!"

So there.

Her dark old eyes aren't smiling. "Yes, I can find him," she quietly confirms. "But I'm not going to look for him. Neither are you."

"That's where you're wrong!"

"Don't use that tone of voice with me, young man!"

The rebuke is so strong and sudden I'm staggered. Maybe if she'd actually, physically slapped me, she'd top the shock factor of the verbal whupping she just handed me, but not by much.

"You will be quiet, you will listen, and you will do it now!" she thunders.

Yes, ma'am.

CHAPTER 16

FINE, I'm listening. All ears. Talk. Make it quick. I've got an itchy, scratchy feeling of impending doom inching up my spine that is neither cliché nor imaginary. Boone is in serious trouble. I can feel it in my bones.

I always wondered what that felt like. Now I know.

"I am truly sorry."

An apology? She's kidding. She yelled at me and is holding me back from helping Boone so she can dispense some contrition? What's even weirder, I have no idea why she's apologizing.

"You must understand."

And awaaaaaay we go. Five bucks says she's not about to say anything I want to hear. Trust me, this is nothing new. Our customary dynamic was established when I was eight years old and has not significantly changed over the years, although I have. It goes something like this: she shows up pretty much whenever she pleases, does a fair impersonation of a female Master Po in pink, and after pontificating at length about the day's portion of universal knowledge she's so graciously meted out to me, she verbally chucks me under the chin and leaves.

That may have flown when I was I was twenty years younger and three feet shorter, but the last time I literally looked up to her was a long time ago.

When I get a minute, I need to take a good, hard look at what it is with me and women. And why I roll over and do whatever they say every time one muscles into my life and prods me down a path I neither imagined nor intended. So far, every major fork my life has taken I've been shoved onto by a female.

"Stop treating me like I'm eight years old!" It's never too late to put your foot down. However, the distinct edge of juvenile petulance in my protest might be costing me credibility. Perhaps heading down tantrum alley isn't the way to go right now.

"Don't be childish, dear boy."

Oh, what the hell, why not?

"Newsflash for you, ma'am, I'm all grown up now! Things have changed! Yeah, and just so you know, if you haven't already figured it out, there's someone else in my life now, so you'd better get used to it!"

So there! Neener, neener!

Wait a minute. Back up. Did I hear what I just said? No way, it couldn't be that simple! Is that what this is all about? Boone invading her territory? Is she pulling rank on me because she feels threatened? Holding out and refusing to help me—and Boone—because she's... she's....

This is just too weird.

Is Mrs. Sheridan jealous?

Shut up!

I feel light-headed, almost sick, my knees threatening to fold up under me like a house of cards as waves of doubt smash against the crumbling bastions of my beliefs. This can't be happening. Not now. Not her. She's my friend, the only real one I've ever had. She's always been the one I've turned to for guidance, for wisdom, help, and comfort. Never doubted her, never once thought she meant me anything but good.

But what if I'm wrong?

The strict isolation policy I've adhered to all these years—and she's encouraged—what was it really all for? Why? Why did it have to be that way? Was it absolutely necessary for me to be so alone for so long? If I'd let the world in, occasionally, would it have been so bad?

I feel like I'm hovering on the brink of utter madness, nothing short of the dissolution of my entire world as the enormity of her potential duplicity sprawls out in front of me like an ugly parody of the truth she claimed to represent. The entire, awful deception revealed to me for the first time because I dared to become what I've been misled into denying.

A fully functioning human being.

Boone is the first major challenge to her monopoly of me. If she can't deal with that, or him, if she wants to cut him out of my life so she can resume unilaterally running it, then this blind strike of fate is a lucky break for her. Mighty serendipitous indeed.

No, I won't believe it. I can't. It's too awful. If I got her this wrong, then I can't trust anything I see, think, feel, or know.

I can't trust her or anyone else.

Even him.

"Please tell me you're not trying to take him away from me!" The anguished cry erupts from me.

I love you both. Don't make me chose between you.

Her stern expression immediately softens, those old, oh-so-familiar eyes misting with sad comprehension. "My poor, darling boy. Is that what you think?"

She raises her wizened hand toward my cheek like she means to touch it, if only she could. "Of course I do not wish your dear one harm. I won't deny I've had a hand in arranging certain circumstances in your lives, but I assure you, everything I've done has been to help you, my boy. Both of you. I give you my word."

I simply stare at her, bewildered and battling both my tears and a bevy of conflicting emotions. I so want to believe her, but I don't know what to think.

"You've been so alone. It hurt me to stand by you, witness your suffering, and do nothing. The fault is not in you, my child. You've never failed us. You've held to your sworn, solitary path. But you don't know—you don't remember what we made you do. Even the faintest memories of the one you were compelled to forsake, we took them from you along with him."

Wow. The listening thing? Totally riveted, here. Don't understand any of it, but I'm not budging until I hear her entire confession. Something tells me this particular unburdening has been a long time coming.

Her ancient eyes glisten with affection so profound it startles me. But I no longer doubt her or fear her motives. All I see before me is love.

That's so creepy.

I know how that sounds, but you have to understand, the quality of affection between me and Mrs. Sheridan, the way she's always been with me, has been not so much sentimental as practically supportive. With a heavy emphasis on the practical. I'm not saying she hasn't shown me kindness, but as personalities go, she's not exactly the emotionally demonstrative type, and certainly never doting or tender.

That is, until now.

"My darling." Her old, familiar voice is so laden with unaccustomed affection my throat closes over.

Hair—back of nape thing. It's happening again. Accompanied by a herd of goose bumps erupting over my arms. Chills playing leapfrog on my vertebrae. The whole creepy catalogue of physical red flags? I got 'em all going on.

"I could no longer watch in silence and allow your ordeal to continue. I intervened. Can you forgive me my weakness? Because I loved you too much, I may have undone you both."

"I don't understand."

I feel I needed to say something at this point, no matter how obviously inane.

"Of course you don't," she smiles benignly at me. "How could you? It's clear to me, now, how poorly you have both been served. You should have been together from the beginning. Compelling you to part was the mistake. Your bond would not have diminished you, as the Tribunal feared. Quite the opposite. Quite the opposite," she sadly intones. "If only we had trusted love and not been swayed by haste and fear, it would not have come to this. But now, even though my intentions were good, I fear what I've done to you has only compounded the original error and made things so much worse."

I'm helplessly bewildered by her obvious distress and almost overwhelmed by the mountain of mystery she's heaping at my feet. Nothing I've heard makes the slightest sense, although I believe she believes what she's saying. Meanwhile, what's messing with Boone isn't sitting around waiting for me to catch up. The sense of time ticking down, the certainty the sands in Boone's hourglass are swiftly trickling out, mounts with every second I stand here doing nothing. As interesting as all of this is, her timing really sucks. Another enigma is not what I need from her right now.

I'm feeling an overwhelming urge to throw up my hands and throw in the towel, forever abandoning her to her eternal obfuscations.

I don't know what to do.

"Your friend is in grave peril. As are you. More than you could possibly imagine. Because I allowed you to come together."

Wait! Wait! Is she finally getting to the point? Yes!

At last, something I understand. I think.

What does she mean? Is she talking meeting, or coming? Together? Is she saying what I think she's saying? And how does she figure us doing it had anything to do with her?

Let's not even go there.

"Boone and me together? As in… having sex? With each other?" I can't believe I just said the 'S' word to Mrs. S. I cross my arms and glare at her. "Forgive me for thinking it was our idea!"

"In part." She peers at me over the tops of her glasses, smiling subtly. "Acting upon the impulse to reunite was indeed your idea, as you say. Yet how do you think you found each other in the first place?"

"What are you saying? Now you've branched out into match-making?"

Why not, I've heard weirder things today.

"Not precisely." Her bittersweet smile bleeds affection tinged with sorrow. "The bond between you never changes, no matter how many times you do. He always looks for you. He can't help it; his desire to be with you is too strong. The Tribunal feared this, that he would be driven to defy the Interdict. Therefore, one of the most important duties I was given when I was appointed your Watcher was to ensure he never found you."

All of a sudden I'm riveted again.

"It has never been easier for him to do so than now."

Because of the damned publicity machine. I'm everywhere.

"Although it was necessary for you achieve your current prominence and power, it increased the likelihood he would see your face and be drawn to you by the forces he didn't understand but could not resist. I was to ensure that did not happen."

"I guess he showed you."

I don't know why, but the notion he, or maybe even we, somehow stuck it to a shadowy bunch of stuck-up know-it-alls by doing a twenty-first century gay version of star-crossed lovers seriously appeals to me.

Although I'm hoping for a happier ending than Romeo and Juliet.

"No, my dear." She gives me a pitying look. "Your Boone would not have come to Birchwood had I not chosen to do nothing to stop him. That was my first mistake."

"But... you said we should be together!" Make up your mind!

"The rightness of your union was never the issue. Where I failed you both was its timing. I should have kept him from you until he mastered the flaw that delivered him to the enemy. But I was afraid he would be unable to conquer his darkness without you, as he has failed to do so many times before."

This does not sound good. Especially the darkness part. Already met a noisy little piece and it was no big deal, but what's messing with him now? I don't need her to tell me we're talking a whole different kettle of dark.

"The crossing of the child changed everything. With her loss, he was drawn to you all the more. Frustrating his need for you yet again made him desire his own death. I couldn't let that happen. I couldn't stand by and do nothing while he immolated himself once more. Not this time. You needed him. I refused to allow you lose your chance to be together in this life too."

"Thank you." I don't know what else to say. I'm not exactly sure how she managed it, but however it happened, however he found me, was led to me, or was allowed to come to me and what she did to facilitate, I'm extremely grateful.

"I didn't realize the child was being stalked," she ruefully admits. "That was my second mistake."

Carly. Now she's talking about Carly. Stalked? By whom? Or what?

What do I get if I guess right?

Please say Boone.

"Now we're getting to the point, right? You know where Boone is and what's going on?"

Please, please tell me you know!

"Have you never wondered about the spirits who come to you seeking your help, how they find you?" She smiles enigmatically.

Sure, but I don't need to know this very moment.

"You bring them?"

"Oh, no," she lightly chuckles. "I merely ensure you are not overwhelmed by their demands. They find you because they are drawn to your light."

"I assume we're not speaking in a metaphorical sense."

"Not at all. You are somewhat familiar with the concept of varying frequencies of energy fields."

"You could say that," I dryly return.

"Then it should come as no surprise to learn your abilities and what you do with them leave a considerable impression on the fabric of the universe."

"You mean I stick out like a universal sore thumb."

"As you wish." She chuckles again. "You must also know your ability to communicate with the dead is not unique."

Thank God!

"I had hopes," I admit.

"Translators are always amongst the living. You are a necessary part of the universal order, for through you and others like you, the lost ones can be put back on the path. They can sense your unique energy and are drawn to you. The Outcast knew this."

Outcast? Who or what is that? And what does all and any of this have to do with Boone?

"It sought a Translator to further its own vile ends and knew if it followed the child, it would find one."

What it? What are we talking about, here?

"The misfortunate befalling your Boone has been a terrible accident. I'm sorry."

God, give me strength!

"Okay, you're sorry, I got that. Apology accepted. Can we stop apologizing for how we got Boone in the shit pile and do something to get him out?"

Please!

Mrs. Sheridan folds her hands, arranges her features in a serenely stonewalling expression. "There's more," she calmly informs me.

Of course there is.

"Your identity in each incarnation has been kept a careful secret. You have been hidden from Him over the millennia, awaiting the moment when you must finally confront Him, and now, because of my carelessness, He has found you before the Time."

Holy Apocalypse, Batman. Is she kidding? Seriously, this has gone far enough. She had me right up until the millennia business. I know for a fact I'm not nearly that old. It just feels that way sometimes.

Like right about now.

"You're making this up!"

"I have never been more serious." She gives me a gimlet glare. Yikes. Those eyes could freeze a volcanic eruption in mid-belch. "Because I have failed in my sworn duty, the Outcast has found both of you, together, your bond rekindled. Before you were fully prepared and ready to face him."

I still think she's making this up.

"And that's bad because…?" I cross my arms and glare at her.

"You don't understand," she sighs. "This isn't a joke, my boy.

You have no idea what you're up against. You're not ready to fight Him, and yet you must. You're the only one who can. I don't know if either you or Boone will survive the encounter."

Survive. Did she just say—survive?

Survive?

"Your bond will give Him access to you. That's why He's taken him. To save your dear one and yourself, you must oppose Him. If you don't, you'll both die, but if you do, you probably won't defeat Him."

I'm getting a bad feeling about this. Not to mention totally confused by a whole heap of misplaced pronouns.

"The bond is the key. It makes you uniquely vulnerable to psychic invasion and attack. What hurts one, hurts the other. It's why the Tribunal originally decreed you should be separated. You know this is so. You know you are different. You've always known you could not live and love as others. This is why I always taught you to guard your energy and emotions. To seek solitude and cultivate seclusion. Why the Outcast can now use Boone to defeat you."

I feel numb with shock and a growing, sick sense of dread. She's right. I know she's right. This talk of Tribunals and tribulations is still way over my head, but the bond between Boone and me?

That's real. I've been aware of something different about me ever since I woke up this morning. A sense of Boone. Growing stronger. Something not quite right about it, though. Even now, if I concentrate I can feel an inner irritant, a subtle background buzz, as if the air around me is filling with noxious fumes. My chest hurts, like something's knocking on my ribcage from the inside.

We're in really deep shit. And I haven't got the first clue what to do about it or how to deal with it.

"I'm not afraid," I blurt with way more bravado than brains.

Please don't say, "You will be." That's a Yoda moment I can do without right now.

"You have always been the most courageous of fools," she smiles sadly at me.

I'm not sure whether to be encouraged or insulted. Not that it matters either way.

"I don't know what else to tell you, my boy. You and your dear one are together once more. For good or bad, it is what it is, and it can't be undone. However, the bond between you is true and strong as it ever was. That single fact could be your final undoing or your ultimate salvation. Whether it shall prove to be a curse or a blessing is not for me to say."

"Why not?" I bleat. Even though she's scaring the crap out of me, I've got to give her major points for one cracking recapitulation.

"Your fate is in your hands, not mine."

Yup, she's good. She's right too.

"So what do I do now?" It's a fair question. I hope she can tell me.

"It's much too soon," she mournfully observes. "I'd hoped for more time to prepare you. But it can't be helped. The bond is the key. Love conquers all. Never forget that, my dear."

You kidding? I've engraved it in my brain.

She takes a step toward me and raises her hand as if she means to touch my forehead. Instinctively, I lean down toward the ascending phantom palm.

"Before you forget, you must remember. Your destiny is upon you. Forgive me, my darling."

The aged agates of her eyes blaze, and incandescent energy streams from her upturned palm, slamming into the middle of my forehead.

Drilling dead center through my third eye.

That's when the lights go out.

I'LL never get used to the color of the sky. Blue. So very strange. So unlike the viridian skies of home I will never see again.

Home. It serves no purpose to think on it. This is our place now. What we were, where we came from, all of it is no more. Memory is a curse; soon it will be stripped from me. I am not afraid to forget. Oblivion will only serve to accomplish what must be done.

The only thing of which I am unsure: will the surrender of all I am deliver me from my need for him? Can such love as ours ever be truly denied or forgotten? Though all of time should come between us?

How can I leave him? How can I not?

"Eternity itself will not keep me from you. How can these fools hope to accomplish what all of time will not?"

Ah, my beloved, so brash, so defiant. I should have known you'd find a way to be with me one last time.

He comes to me, sweeps me into his arms. Hard, corded muscles wind about me; I clutch him to my breast, as if I could pull him under my skin and keep him there forever. He is my very heart, my soul. Dearer to me than my own life. How can I survive without him?

"They have not parted us yet."

"You should not be here!" I scold him, but I will not leave him with lips sullied with the taste of a final rebuke. I nuzzle the side of his face, the harsh stubble of his chin branding my mouth with his rough texture. The smell of him, the taste of him. Precious sensations I will never know again. I must have all of him, sear him into my very flesh. Now, while I still can.

There is so little time left to us.

"Do you wish me to go?" he teases me, stroking his hand along the side of my face. My heart sighs with every caress. I must harden it; and break his.

"I wish you to promise you'll obey the Interdict."

He draws back from me, the deep malachite hue of his eyes blazing.

"I will do no such thing!" he rages. "Ask me anything, my love, anything but that."

"But it has been decided. We must obey!"

"You must obey!" he thunders, his eyes aflame with anger and desire. "You are the Chosen. You alone can deny the Nameless One. But you must not do so without me."

"The Tribunal decrees otherwise."

"The Tribunal is wrong!"

Tears mar his visage. Please, do not weep for me. I can endure anything but this.

I try to avert my gaze, but he will not permit it. He takes my face in his hands, turns my head, lifts my chin until I must meet the glowing wonder of his gaze.

"It makes no sense to sunder us. We are Bond. Parts of one other. My heart beats in your chest, as does yours in mine. My strength is yours to command, my life yours to use. You are the Chosen. I am your Bondman, as you are mine. I must be at your side in all things, most especially this." His smile is tremulous and heart-rending. "I can do nothing without you. How can you hope to prevail without me?"

He speaks the truth. If we allow this to happen, we are doomed before we've even begun. As long as I strive singly, I must fall. It is inevitable. I have known it from the beginning.

And yet the Tribunal does not agree. They have decided we must part for all time. Though my heart knows it is wrong, I will do my duty and everything required of me.

As will he.

"Promise me," I implore.

"I promise I will find you. They will not keep me from you."

His fingers tangle in my hair, clutching the back of my head, holding me fast while his mouth descends upon mine, bruising, claiming, kissing me deep, hard, avidly. I answer back with equal ardor and desperation. This kiss, in all its sweet glory and ecstasy, shall be our last. The only moment left to us is the only one of which we may be certain.

"I'm sorry, my dear ones, I cannot give you any more time."

Mother!

Startled by the sound of her voice, I tear my mouth from his and spin in his arms. She stands before us, tall, slender, and ageless, her long, silver hair gleaming against the golden glow of her official robes.

She is fully garbed, her ceremonial mantle heavy upon her graceful frame, the Great Eye gleaming grandly from its nest in the sacred headpiece adorning her regal brow.

Goddess, no. Not yet. It is too soon.

"You must come with me, my boy." Her melting, agate eyes are liquid with sorrow. The glance she turns upon my beloved carries a message I do not understand.

"Do it now," she softly commands.

"My lady." He closes his eyes and bows his head to her.

He takes my arm, whirls me around, and catches me about the waist, holding me fast to his chest while placing the palm of his right hand on mine.

Too late, I comprehend his purpose.

"We are one!" he cries, the heat of the hand on my chest searing the naked flesh beneath. "This cannot be undone. This we must never forget. Now we never will!"

His strength flows into me, along with his life. God, no! I can't see, can't stand, no longer know the supporting strength of his arms around me. His essence fills me, his body dissolving and returning to the wind and waves, departing this life and yet still in me, with me, a tiny, constant, eternal flame.

Falling, farther and farther away. From life, from memory, from the touch of his lips, the light of his eyes.

The sound of her voice, growing ever fainter, fading, following me into the cleansing mists of time.

"Remember...."

CHAPTER 17

WOW, check out that chandelier. Got crud all over it. Funny, I never noticed it before, but it could definitely do with a whole heap of dusting.

Yuck.

Why am I staring at my chandelier? Could it be because I'm flat on my back on the couch in the parlor, and it happens to be overhead?

Could be.

What the—what the hell am I doing here? Last thing I remember, I was... somewhere else. With Mrs. Sheridan. We were chatting. Yeah, that's it, having a chat. I needed her help. That sounds about right. Help. Help with what?

I've got nuthin', here.

I don't believe this; I'm far too young to be senile. Screw it, I'm not going to lie here and lament my mental disintegration, I'll head to the kitchen, find Boone, he'll know.

Boone!

Memory sluices back into my brain in a sickening rush. Boone, breakfast, bite mark. Something bad going down.

I surge into a sitting position with a rapidity I instantly regret. The nausea and dizziness I immediately experience are my first clue maybe all is not quite right with me. I feel disconnected, disoriented; I swear my head is three times its normal size. The room tilts like it's on a huge pivot, and I have to clutch the couch before I'm flipped on the floor.

I know the room isn't really rolling like a drunk seaman, it just feels that way. What I want to know is why. If I didn't know better, I'd swear I was coming back from one hell of a bender, which for me isn't saying much. Half a bottle of wine and I'm anybody's. One of the main reasons why I never drink in public.

But what does my low alcohol threshold have to do with anything? I certainly haven't been drinking today. Why do I feel like I have? Not to mention waking up on the couch I must have passed out on, only I know damned well I did no such thing.

Or do I?

"There you are."

Boone! He's here! Thank God! Wait! How? What about....

What? The danger I thought he was in? What if there isn't any? I don't remember drinking, but if I have been more than a few fumes to the wind after all, got stonk, and passed out on the couch, then all this Boone in peril stuff is only an alcoholic hallucination. I'm better now, and so is he.

I like that story, I'm sticking to it.

My heart doing anticipatory somersaults in my chest cavity, I turn toward where I last heard the sound of his voice. There he is, propped in the doorway, larger than life as usual. Shoulder pressed into the lintel, his long, lanky form on casual, comfortable display, he accepts the wooden support like the whole house owes him, arms crossed, his mouth stretched wide in an arrogantly confident grin.

Everything's all right now, and so is he. That's right, isn't it?

Wait. He looks so pale. Almost transparent. That's weird. What's with the shades? He wasn't wearing any when he left.

Was he?

My head must still be out to lunch. Boone is back. Everything's fine. So is he.

"Hey, whatcha got for me?"

His voice sounds funny too. Scratchy. Is he catching a cold? Probably shouldn't kiss him, then.

I'll risk it.

I'm so happy to see him. Hysterically, deliriously happy. Almost euphoric. I don't understand the force of the emotional rollercoaster urging me onward, but I'm more than happy to go with it. Without a single inhibition or reservation, I'm off the couch, making for him at a dead lope. Screw funky dreams and semi-ominous symbolism, to hell with weird vibes and the eerie aftertaste of uncertainty, and hasta la vista to the half-assed premonitions nibbling on the edges of my awareness. It can all take a hike. Good riddance to bad recollections. All I want is him.

I gallop toward him; he laughs and pushes off the doorframe, bracing to receive me. He opens his arms, and I crash into his chest. My mouth impacts on his with enough force to draw blood, our lips mashing together over hard, unyielding teeth. I want to crawl inside him, kiss him until I can't breathe, smear him over every square inch of me. Want him, want him, want him, him, just him, more, can't get enough, the feel of him, the taste, his mouth hot, wet, and wanton, lips rampaging greedily across my face, licking, nipping, biting.

His breath, hot and steamy against the side of my neck, searing the skin all the way to my ear. His voice, low, skewed, scratchy.

Like dusty bones rattling inside an abandoned tomb.

Wrong.

"This is too easy."

The twisted, inhuman voice slithering out of Boone's throat into my ear winds around my heart and cruelly squeezes. "You have grown soft and careless, Arkon. But then, you never were a match for me. Shall I spare us both the wait and end it now? I could do it so easily."

I don't even have time to draw a breath before Boone's hand clamps around my neck, squeezing hard while he whirls, hoists me high, and slams me against the wall. I'm splayed, suspended, my feet dangling, helplessly pinned, Boone's familiar yet suddenly strange face looming large in my wavering vision.

This is not Boone. Might be a dead ringer for my guy, but wearing his face doesn't make it him. The alien eyes beneath me are utterly empty. We're talking seriously devoid of even the slightest scintilla of any indication of life behind them. Cadaver-eyes. I'm not kidding. I could be looking at an animated corpse. A living, breathing dead body wearing a gleeful death's head grin while it slowly, serenely throttles me.

What are you, and what did you do with my Boone?

Oh, my God, I kissed that?

Ewww.

Ellery, get a grip, right now you've got bigger problems than possibly contracting a major case of ectoplasmic cooties from tall, blech, and hostile, here. Whatever it is. An energy construct imitating Boone? Has to be, but how is it possible? I'd better get out of its grip fast, or I'm not going to live long enough to find out.

My world is scarily, speedily contracting to a single, desperate point of concentrated consciousness, my brain rapidly succumbing to oxygen deprivation. My windpipe being slowly collapsed by something faking my lover's face, while undoubtedly one hell of a howling cosmic irony, is definitely not a figment of my imminent expiration.

It's time to speak up or forever rest in peace.

"You kill me, you'll be sorry," I manage to gasp out. Hey, I figure opening with a touch of bravado couldn't hurt. It definitely worked for me during my recent initial encounter with the real Dantrell.

The improbable thing in front of me emits a scratchy, incomprehensible, but oddly rhythmic sound. Like a rusty bellows from hell. Lungs falling out? I wish.

Laughing. The damned thing is laughing at me.

"Fear not, Arkon, I shall not kill you so swiftly and cleanly," my Boone-shaped nemesis slavers at me. "Where is the sport in that?"

What's with this "Arkon" stuff? Is it a name or a title? It's not ringing any bells for me. Some additional informational input would be appreciated. However, as much as I can tell, from my limited perspective, I am once again noticeably bereft of my usual otherworldly ally. No joy of any kind forthcoming from that quarter. Probably have to rely on Chuckles here to handle the exposition. As for getting my ass out of this sling, I think I'm on my own.

The hand around my neck loosens its lethal clutch. I'm still being held aloft and squashed against the wall, but my ability to breathe has improved a whole bunch.

I quickly fill my lungs a few times, mentally preparing to pull some chokehold-busting moves out of my ass to use against this thing to get it off me. I realize the odds are slim I'll be able to pull it off, but nothing ventured, nothing strained.

I'm also more than slightly disturbed to realize there were at least three inappropriate double-entendres in that last thought. I blame oxygen deprivation.

Never mind.

Cagily anticipating my attempt to make a break for it, or perhaps simply because he can, my adversary casually lifts me off the wall and slams me back again with easy, disdainful violence. I bounce off the sheetrock, teeth clicking, eyeballs rattling in their sockets, pyrotechnics pinwheeling before my stunned senses.

"Behold the mighty Arkon!" Boone's simulacrum sneers. "The ages have not been kind to you, my brother. Where is your power now? Why do you not smite me down where I stand? Is that not what you are sworn to do?"

I assume this is a rhetorical question. Okay, a couple of rhetorical questions. But please, don't let my let my pathetic inability to do anything to resist stop you from expositionally running your mouth and filling me in.

Do go on, I'm all ears.

"I had not thought to find you so soon." The voice issuing from the counterfeit of Boone's mouth hits my ears sideways, like gravel scraping across my skin. "I hungered for a Translator. So tasty!" I suppress a shudder while I watch it lick Boone's lips. "I knew the child could find one. I had not thought she would lead me to you instead."

That's exactly what Mrs. Sheridan said. This wasn't an intentioned attack, it was an accident. A stroke of dumb luck.

Mrs. Sheridan? Where did that come from?

"So one of us got lucky," I wheeze. "Or not."

So not liking what I'm hearing, but I better get over it and keep listening.

"A prize indeed!" it gloats. "No mere mortal Translator, but the great and glorious Arkon! In the flesh," it ominously rumbles.

Not so great or glorious, apparently. And excuse me, last time I looked, most definitely mortal. You know something I don't know?

"The mighty Arkon," the sim sneers, spraying small flecks of disdainful spittle across my face. The fine, cold drops pepper my skin like tiny Tasers. Chilling me straight to the bone.

That was spit. Real spit. Oh, no. Another detail I missed.

This thing isn't an energy construct. It's actual, real flesh and blood. Boone's flesh and blood. My senses have been so suspended from being in a state of strangulation it hasn't hit me until now that I'm looking at the impossible. This isn't Boone. Yet it is. It feels like him, smells like him, even tastes. But it's not. It's not him. It's not even human.

But it is alive.

Oh, God.

I got it all wrong. It's not some new kind of mega-zoink using him to making a supersized energy knockoff, it's… it's….

I can't say it, it's too weird. It's also not possible.

It should not, cannot exist. Maybe someone should tell *it* that; it doesn't seem to know or care. For sure the ludicrous improbability of its existence isn't cramping its yapping style. Or interfering with its ability keep me off my toes and slapped to this wall like a longhaired, dumbass butterfly.

"You are so sunken in this wretched flesh you've been repeatedly forced into that you have all but lost yourself. Twice on the streets of this miserable town you encountered the emanation tracking the child, and you failed to recognize your danger. You let me pass unchallenged. You did not know me," it leers, grinning ghoulishly.

I'm momentarily out to sea, and then a face dances impudently across my inner eye. Twice spotted, once questioned, and summarily dismissed as insignificant.

The Peter Lorre lookalike. You have got to be kidding!

"I should have known your precious Bondman would defy the Interdict. I thank him for his disobedience and his diligence. Had he not sifted through all time to find you and finally succeeded, and had you not so predictably succumbed to your weak need for him, I would not have gained the means to destroy you both. The ecstasy I experience, even now, as I savor him, drop by succulent drop, will be nothing compared to the pleasure consuming you will bring me. Soon this vessel I am reshaping him to create will be complete. When my latest emanation is fully enshrined in its new temple, I will do the same to you."

Say what?

"Consume you and transform you into a host for another portion of my greatness. That is your fate. How does it make you feel, my dear once-brother, to know you have lost? You will go to your doom knowing you were helpless to prevent me from reducing the Tribunal's last hope—and his most beloved—to mere vessels of my will. You will be nothing more than parts of the whole enabling me to at last escape my prison and reign in this place, as is my right."

It leans forward and brushes the mockery of Boone's mouth against mine. "The power I will acquire on this side when I absorb your essence will greatly advance my ability to create more vessels for my emanations. What a delicious irony. Caught unawares, betrayed by your lover and the lure of the flesh, your very defeat will hasten the day you are sworn to prevent. Sweetness, my dear, doomed brother. Such joy your imminent defeat brings me as you could not possibly imagine."

Are we done yet? Wow. Whole lot of crap in that last information byte. Most of it being stuff I simply cannot use right now. I've pretty much maxed out my blather tolerance levels. Besides, if what's happening under my nose is anything to go by, I can't afford to hang around here any longer. I'm not the only one who's rapidly running out of time.

The Xerox of Boone's face is becoming disconcertingly more stable with each passing second. His features are losing their funky, slightly indistinct edges, and his skin color is practically normal. I almost can't tell this from the real thing. Except for the eyes. They're still dead and flat and several shades too dark. I'm wondering if they'll ever be completely right. I have no idea how this transformation, or substitution, or transfiguration—or whatever—is happening. But I have a horrible feeling I know what it will mean for the real Boone if I let this unnatural process continue to its inevitable conclusion.

So we're just gonna have to make sure it doesn't! Great, now that's settled, all I have to do is somehow outsmart my loquacious nemesis, find my lover, unplug this parasite, and send it packing!

Lover. That's so cool. I'm never gonna get sick of saying that. But I digress.

Where was I? Oh yeah, getting this sonofabitch to let me go. How? I know! When in doubt, lead with something you're really good at.

I excel at pissing people—and otherworldly assholes—off.

"Wow, you dream big." I blink benignly at the sim. "Sorry, you seem to have slipped my mind at the moment, mind telling me who you are? And please don't say 'your worst nightmare'. That's so been done to death."

The simulacrum's off-color eyes narrow to squinty, suspicious slits.

"You do not know me? Not even now?" it growls with obvious disbelief and escalating annoyance.

Score one for the Jamester. Apparently it's not as much fun for the fugly if I'm unaware of its true identity. Let's rub some more salt in this most interesting wound.

"Nope, sorry. Can't say as I do. You got a card? Facebook page? References? Resume?"

"You mock me!" it roars.

No, really. That's what it said. I wouldn't make something like this up.

Some things never change. These wacky, apocalyptic entities with Cthulhu-esque delusions of grandeur are so damned predictable. *So* saw the ranting in clichés thing coming.

"Hell, yeah! Why should you be the one having all the fun? What are you going to do about it? Kill me?"

The all-too-solid fingers circling my neck bite slightly into my skin, a mockery of a caress. The pressure continues. My windpipe starts to constrict. The sim schools his stolen features into a huge, sick, happy grin.

That last shot may have been a taunt too far.

"You truly do not remember," the rasping, screeching parody of Boone's velvet baritone reeks with gloat. Color me confused. Now the stinking thing seems happy. I have no idea why. But there is some good news mixed in with all this bad.

Except for the eyes, it's now almost a perfect copy, but it doesn't sound anything like him. The voice is still off. That's good. I think that means there's still time.

I'm hoping.

The shit-eating grin on the face below me almost swells off the smug-meter. The fingers compacting my throat back off. Normal breathing resumes.

And there was dancing in the streets. Metaphorically speaking.

"You do not understand. How delicious."

I'm sorry, I can't let that last Doctor Evil-esque comment go.

"And you don't use contractions. Apparently. That's a literary cliché, you know. Aliens and assorted otherworldly types are often represented in the popular media with a peculiar inability to use oral short cuts. Who knew there was actual truth behind a seemingly arbitrary fictional convention?"

Yes, I'm babbling, but there is a method to my apparent madness. Now I'm not being choked and repeatedly slammed through the sheetrock, I can focus on the energy patterns flowing into and around my captor. I immediately hate what I'm seeing.

Exactly what I was afraid of. Damn. I knew this had to be happening, but while suspecting it is one thing, actually seeing it quite another.

Oh, Boone, how did you get yourself into this mess?

As it boasted and I surmised, the sim's transformation is being fuelled by a massive influx of energy of a very specific, familiar sort, rapidly and greedily siphoned from a single source.

Boone. I can feel him, his essence, the scent of his soul, pooling within this obscene, unnatural, entirely impossible thing. Consuming him, to become him. It shouldn't be possible. And yet it's happening right in front of me.

If I could squirm out from under this hand and peel myself off my wall, I'd kick my ass around every block in Birchwood for being such a moron! I was so fixated on the entry wound in his hand—which is exactly what it was, my reluctance to acknowledge the possibility aside—I didn't even look for the cord. That would have told me everything I should have known.

I am a schmuck!

This cannot be happening. "Impossible" isn't a word I normally use, but this—is. It just does not work like this. Flesh is flesh and spirit is spirit, and the two only meet and blend together in one way.

This is not it.

I have to get off this wall. We're running out of time. I need a distraction. Something, anything. Not asking for much, but hey, a miracle would be nice!

Now, if it's not too much trouble.

Ask and ye shall receive. Hallelujah.

Even though I can't see what from here, something must be yanking this thing's cord, because I can feel a disturbance in the transfer. As in, it's slowed right down to a trickle. Hello! One old Pink Lady finally heard from? I'm hoping. Of course it's her. Who else could it be?

About time! She'll kick this thing's ass. I feel better already.

A frenzied roar interrupts my internal victory dance. Ah, somebody's pissed. Boo hoo.

"Who dares to interfere!" the sim shrieks.

Wouldn't you like to know? Heh, heh! You might think you're hot shit, but you haven't met my Granny!

Hey! Wait! Ow!

My antagonist roars again, finally ripping me off the wall. Which, okay, was what I wanted, but not quite like this. Before I can seize the moment and pummel my way to freedom, it forces me to my knees with, you guessed it, superhuman strength, knots its hand in the back of my shirt, and swiftly and violently hauls me along behind while it double-times out of the parlor, snorting and snarling, hopefully bound for where it's stashed Boone.

I'm choking again. This time my rucked-up shirt is constricting my windpipe. The breezeway is a blur for several nightmarish seconds while I'm dragged down it with enough force to snap my neck, scuffling, stumbling, and completely under the control of the thing propelling us both mercilessly forward. Wherever we're going, I hope we get there before my air gives out.

Our transit couldn't have taken more than a few seconds; even so, my vision is graying out by the time we reach our destination.

Kitchen. We're in the kitchen. My new location barely registers when I go from slowly strangling on the end of arm to hurtling through space. The sim hauls back and tosses me halfway across the room like I'm a hacky sack. The thing so casually setting me on my current trajectory might be defying every known law of the here and hereafter, but I enjoy no such special abilities or dispensation. To one such as I, all the regular rules still apply.

In short, what goes up must come down.

Including me.

After an extremely brief flight, I crash into the tile floor. Hard.

"Behold your precious Bondman," the sim snarls. "Take a last look at your love—and your betrayer."

I know what I'm going to see when I lift my reeling head from the floor and peer at the unmoving shape beside me, but it doesn't make it any easier to accept or believe.

What little remains of Boone sprawls motionless barely an arm's length away, insensate and completely unaware of what's happening to him. He's way past knowing anything anymore. He's so close to me. I could reach out and touch him, and believe me, nothing would make me happier right now, but I'm too terrified to try.

Damn. It's even worse than I thought. His body is actually transparent. I can see the pattern of the floor tiles he's lying on. Through him. I'm looking at a Boone-shaped see-through ice sculpture. Without the ice. A human soap bubble.

Shit.

He's almost gone. And what's sucked him nearly dry, using what it stole from him to literally duplicate him down to the last hair follicle in impossible flesh and blood detail, stands over us, grinning with hideous glee and exulting in how comfortably it fits in Boone's stolen skin.

Zoinks don't do this. Zoinks *can't* do this. They can't empty their host completely of their life essence, and they can't use stolen soul energy to make themselves a flesh suit they can move into. Nothing can do that.

That is, nothing up until now. The proof of that pudding is snarling derisively and staring at me through Boone-shaped eyes. Hello, Zoinkzilla?

You know what? I don't think we're talking zoink at all. My bones are talking to me again, and they're saying there's more going on here than meets the human eye. Even mine. If I'm to have any hope of sussing out the real score and hopefully successfully fighting this thing, I need a different perspective.

But first, if things weren't already ridiculously complicated and practically hopeless enough, now I'm here and have discovered the identity of our previously unknown ally?

Why can't I do things the easy way? Just once. I'm not greedy; one lousy time's all I'm asking.

The new entry into the lists isn't Mrs. Sheridan, as expected: it's Carly.

Honey, you picked a fine time to finally show up. I know you mean well, but if you really want to help, fly this coop as fast as your little phantom legs can carry you and fetch Mrs. Sheridan. Clear out, now, sweetie, while you still can, and leave the fighting to the men and the grannies.

Oh, no! What is she doing? No, Carly, you have to stop!

The valiant little girl-ghost is hunched protectively by her father's side, her hands resting lightly on his chest, over his heart. She's trying to buy her dad more time by giving him an energy transfusion. What she hopes to accomplish with this endearingly selfless but utterly futile action—beyond providing a brief distraction, for which I'm grateful—I have no idea. She doesn't have enough energy to replace what Boone has lost, even if it were possible. What he really needs is for the entire process to be put in reverse. For all her love and will, that's something she can't do for him. I don't know if I can either, but I'm prepared to die trying.

I guess so is she.

"You're not getting my dad." Carly juts out her little chin with endearing bravado and gives our loathsome opponent enough attitude to power a small city. She's not backing down one iota. Bless.

"Ah, the offspring," the sim sneers at Boone's infant champion. "What a tasty morsel you are. Thank you for the snack."

This isn't an idle threat. While energy, even hers, cannot be destroyed, it can be consumed. And transformed. If this thing laps her up, she won't survive the digestion process. Everything she is will be assimilated and become part of that noxious thing, and the entity once known as Carly Dantrell will cease to exist.

This isn't sci fi, it's serious Borgification. For real.

Absolute, utter, complete, irrevocable, total, eternal oblivion. Not gonna happen.

The thing wearing her father's stolen face stares down at us, deliberately drawing its tongue across its purloined lips with obscene lasciviousness.

"Yum," it taunts.

Chapter 18

SHIT. The voice issuing from the sim's pseudo-throat is still slightly off, but it's improving. Sounding more like human than unearthly talons scraping across a gravestone.

Carly's gutsy intervention is slowing it down some but not stopping it. She's bought us some time, maybe another minute or two. Certainly no more. What I'm going to do with those precious, hard-won seconds, I haven't the first clue.

The sim raises its right hand, extending it toward Carly, its revolting intentions rampant across its gloating face. I can't let him start on her too. Time to draw his fire.

"Stop it!" I scream at him. "Leave her alone. Leave them both alone! I'm the one you want!"

Well, that's what it said. Why would it lie? Aside from it obviously can.

The sim's slimy fake eyes round on me, dripping with triumph. So that much was true, I am what it really wants. He only took Boone to get to me.

But why?

I'm missing something here.

I can see the logic of using Boone to gain access to the house. The way this place is protected, as long as I'm inside, I'm untouchable. There's no way it could get past my wards unless it literally had an in with someone who could. Like my brand new lover. But that doesn't make sense; why do things the hard way? Why wait until I was in my place of power before making a move on me, when by its own admission it had two clear opportunities to get me when I had no idea it was within scratching distance? Why didn't it strike then? Boone wasn't even in the picture; we hadn't met yet, but so what? I was open. So why wait? What prevented it from pressing its advantage when it had easy access and clear opportunity?

Because it didn't?

Hmmm. Then what did Boone give it that I haven't? At least, not yet.

Snap. Oh, shit. The sound of the other shoe dropping.

Permission. He gave it permission. Opened the door of his soul and asked it in.

That's it. That has to be the answer. I don't know why he gave it carte blanche to move in and take over; it must have tricked him somehow. Snuck in under his radar and offered to give or do something for him in line with his "I'm not worthy" agenda.

He was walking around out there, unprotected and unsuspecting, with a giant Achilles heel I knew about, and I let him do it.

Great.

This is my fault. Instead of letting myself get sucked in by the sexual Pandora's box and all its resident yummy distractions recently presented to me, I should have made my libido take a number and moved solving Boone's guilt issues to the top of my "to do" list. Instead of him. If I'd first got to the bottom of what needed to be settled between him and Carly, instead of giving him free and easy access to mine, none of us would be in this mess right now. Way to go, Ellery, you've probably doomed us all.

That's cheerful! And not very helpful. Besides, I'm not ready to capitulate. Still holding out hope for a certain Pink Lady to show up.

Any time, lady! Now would be really good!

"Ellery, don't worry about me! Save my dad!"

Bless you sweetheart, you're so brave. A real chip off the old soldier. You'd both throw yourself under the bus to save the other without even blinking, but there's no way that's going to happen. Not while I'm around. I made your dad a promise I'd see you safe to the other side. I've never gone back on my word, and I don't intend to start now.

"You heard me." I scramble to my feet and face it down, deliberately interposing my body between it and them. "Yoo-hoo, over here! Come on, forget about them, pick on someone your own size."

"With pleasure, Arkon." The sim's dead eyes reek with greed, and it licks its lips again. "Your pathetic Bondman and his loathsome whelp are nothing. You are what I covet."

The feeling is so not mutual. Bondman? Does he mean Boone? What does that mean?

Argh. Another dangling puzzle I don't have time to pursue.

"So, let me see if I understand this correctly," I answer my adversary. "I hand myself over and let you have your nasty way with me, and in exchange for getting free rein to suck me dry, you'll put Boone back and let him and the child go free."

"I will." The dead eyes narrow, lips pulling back from glistening teeth in an obscene simulation of a smile. "You have my word."

Oh, really? Do I look that stupid to you? Guess again, spook breath.

You, sir, are a lying sack of shit. You'll take me for everything I am and then turn around and squash them both flat, because you can. On my own, I'm not sure I can stop you. At least, not from harming both of them. One I can keep away from you, but both?

I know what Boone would want me to do.

I hear the voice of a long-awaited angel sounding sweetly in my ear.

"I have the power to intervene on the behalf of one. Only one. You must choose the one I am to save."

Mrs. Sheridan! I'm so happy to hear you I could kiss you! Carly! Help Carly! Take her in tow and get her out of harm's way, now!

I have no idea where my Pink Lady is, but I don't need to see her to know I can trust her to deliver. She's trickier than this twisted, sick thing could ever hope to be. I can confidently hand my Carly concerns over to my invisible fairy grandmother. She's got Boone's baby covered.

Now it's my turn to pull a few rabbits of out my hat. Prepare to have your party thoroughly pooped, my fine, fugly friend. Surprise!

Thanks to the arrival of the amazing Mrs. S., the odds we might all walk away from this intact and my optimism quotient have improved immeasurably.

Woo hoo!

The sim glares and gloats, obviously completely unaware the battle has been joined. That's right, pay no attention to the old lady behind the curtain. Keep your eyes on me, only on me.

"So what do you want me to do?" Like I don't know.

"Give yourself to me. Completely. Of your own free will."

You wish. Be careful of that, by the way, 'cause you're gonna get it.

"You got it!" I flip it the bird, close my eyes, and shoot my soul straight out of my body.

One soft, small word, like an ancient invocation, in me, around me, ushering me into the blue. "Remember…"

"WHAT have you done?" The sim tilts back its head and marks my exit with howls of unremitting rage, infuriated by the sight of its coveted prize crumpling to the ground. It just figured out I stiffed it and left it holding an empty shell. Which it doesn't want. The body's not where it's at; it hankers for the soft, chewy center. That would be me, free and clear on the astral, giggling up a storm and dancing rings around Boone's doppelganger, serene in the knowledge I'm completely out of its reach as long as it clings to its current carnal state.

Surprise! You honestly didn't think I was going to make it easy for you, did you? You can't have your Boone and eat me too!

You want me? You're gonna have to come out and get me!

Come on, you inhuman asshole, let Boone go and come out and play with the big boys. Bring it! You know you want to. Let's see how you do against someone who knows how to fight back.

Oh, I have no doubt as soon as it gets over itself and its hissy fit, it'll come howling out of Boone's throat and straight for mine. I only have seconds before I'll have more ugly on my hands than I might know what to do with, so I'd better use what little time remains to scout around.

"Return to your form!" my still-incarnate adversary rails at me. Completely ineffectually, I might add. "You will obey me!"

That's what you think, sucka.

Perhaps I spoke too soon.

"Obey me! I will wipe him and his brat from existence this instant if you do not return and submit yourself to me. I warn you, I will not hesitate to sacrifice this emanation to accomplish this! I can afford to lose it. Can you say the same of them? You cannot hope to save them!" it cackles, drooling.

Damn. That might not be an idle threat. Now I see the full scope of the situation from my wider astral vantage point; I finally comprehend the true size of the pile of cosmic shit we are all in.

This is bad; this is really, really bad. This changes everything.

All the time I thought the sim was the real enemy, the animating intelligence driving the transformation, and the worst thing I had to deal with. I was wrong. What is the term it keeps using? "Emanation"? God help me, I think I know what that means now.

I cast my astral vision upward to see something I never thought possible hovering over us like an actual crack of doom. A narrow rift in the continuum, a fracture in reality resembling a swollen, obscenely winking eye hangs in the ether overhead, and peering out from behind its ragged lids is a vast, whirling, howling knot of hate and chaos possessing, in its darkest part, a writhing core of something I've never believed existed, but now I'm floating here, staring dumbly at it, completely unable to refute its reality....

Dang. That's Evil all right. Well, this is awkward.

I've gravely underestimated the enemy. Here's hoping those words won't be my epitaph.

Carly is safe, the one good thing in all of this. Boone is now my sole concern. I think I can save him, but it won't be easy. There's a very good possibility this extra-corporeal journey will be a one-way trip and I won't be walking away from this one. Anywhere. Ever.

That's okay; Boone's worth it. We've all got to go sometime. I just didn't think my time would be quite so soon. Especially in the light of recent events.

Well, damn. It's always something. After a lifetime of isolation and abstinence, I find the guy of my dreams and finally get some, and now it's all over before it's even begun.

Huh. I'm truly a hopeless case. Here I am, in probably the last few moments of not only my life but possibly my entire existence, about to throw myself into the breach most likely to get killed and maybe even completely, absolutely and utterly obliviated, and what am I thinking about? Sex!

I really am a guy.

But back to the problem at hand. The sim isn't the one calling the shots here. Boone's essence depletion and creation of the physical duplicate is being directed from above. What was my first clue? Not one, but two cords, the first rearing its ugly self from the anchor point in Boone, the other plugged into the sim. They converge, combine, and intertwine to form a thick, boiling etheric energy column driving up into the rift and beyond, forming a turbulent, tumescent connection between Boone, the sim, and the roiling heart of evil.

There's where the real threat resides.

Attacking the problem at the sim level is pointless. Cutting off a finger won't stop the fist. The emanation is only an extension of the greater Ick on the other side of the rift. Like a probe. Or something. But an imperfect and incomplete one.

From my astral position floating above everything I'm leaving behind, I've got the whole picture. It's not a pretty one. The rift is closing. Good news and bad news. When it does it'll definitely cut the cord, bringing this whole suck and reshape thing to a screeching halt. Unfortunately the rate at which the rift is collapsing won't be fast enough to help Boone; he'll be gone long before the crack is corked and the evil genie is once more sealed in its bottle.

The "emanation" spewed out by the rift entity isn't stable. Because it's part of a being from another dimension, its energy isn't compatible with this one. On its own it can only exist here as long as it's connected to the RE. When the rift closes and cuts it off from its source, it will go poof. Disassociate and return to the universe. It isn't like a zoink; it can't exist for any length of time as a disembodied, coherent, independent energetic mass. It needs to inhabit a physical body. But because of the incompatibility issue, it can't possess an extant one. The RE has to make it one using the raw materials readily available. A living denizen of this dimension. Like Boone. It uses them to create a new corporeal home for its obscene "baby" in the exact image of the donor that is compatible with its alien energy matrix, destroying the original in the process. Then it moves in. Tah-dah.

I don't know how many times this… thing—whatever the heck it is—has been "emanating" itself or exactly how many of these peek-a-body knock-offs are already out there. Out of its own borrowed mouth, this one isn't the first. Once I make it spit Boone out and give him back to me, I'd give anything to make sure he'll be the last.

My mouth to the gods' ears. It might come to that.

Speaking of saving Boone, I know what I have to do. It's simple, really. Just like dealing with a zoink, only on a much bigger scale. Cut the cord. Once that happens and both sim and victim are separated from the RE, what was taken from Boone will return to him, and the sim will literally fall apart. He'll be free, the sim will revert to whatever it becomes when it doesn't get to finish—probably something really nasty—and that will be all she wrote.

Piece of cake? In theory, yes, but there's one teeny, tiny little catch. Simply cutting the cord isn't going to cut it. As long as the rift is open, that thing can throw out another line and start the whole process up again. In order to make sure the sim stays dead and the emanation dries up and blows away, I have to entirely block the RE's access to this side until the rift closes.

Easier said than done. Especially as the only thing I've got to work with is me. I have no idea what's going to happen to me when that thing catches on to my cunning plan, takes exception to my interference, and tries to drill right through me to get to its loathsome offshoot. I'm fairly sure it won't take me messing it over lying down.

Oh well, who wants to live forever? I've got to do this. There's no other way.

God.

Regrets, I've got a few. A little more time with Boone would have been nice. I hope he'll be happy. Maybe Mrs. S. will keep an eye on him. Now that she won't have me to kick around any more, she's going to need a new job.

I love you. Please remember me.

Thought of another one. No last good-bye. That sucks. Ah, I begin to understand the intensity of the longing of the many who've sought me out over the years for this lost opportunity. Always so desperate for me to pass their final farewells on for them. I get it now. How's that for irony? It really hurts to want it so much and know you can never have it. An interesting perspective and insight for my final moments.

Hey! Screw this, defeatist crap! I'm not dead yet!

Let's do this thing.

I think of Boone, only of Boone, and let love lift me up. The higher my vibrational level, the better. Ain't nothing more powerful than love.

This is me doing my best impression of the Little Dutch Boy, only I won't be using a finger to stop up this dike.

Look out, ugly. Here I come.

I'm overflowing with positive energy and glowing like a mega happy face when I intersect the column connecting the RE to my lover and his wannabe. My high-flying astral body severs the black, seething energy conduit like a precision laser, the massively positive level of my field instantly repelling the truncated stump, sending it hurtling back through the rift.

Take that, you muthasucka.

Boone is safe. I don't dare split my concentration to look behind me to be absolutely sure, but it's not necessary. I feel the sim cease the instant its lifeline is severed, its purloined energy immediately flooding back into Boone. He's going to be okay now. His strength will return with his life force and he'll wake up soon with a whole pile of questions. Maybe no one to give him answers, but he will wake up.

That's worth dying for in my book.

Maybe it won't come to that. Maybe it will. I hate to be a doomsayer, but so far, this has been way too easy. The RE is in shock, rolling and thrashing around in its cosmic prison, trying to work out what just happened. It's not going to stay confused very long.

It will figure it out, and it will fight back. Better brace myself for the backlash.

I've no sooner speculated when a massive wall of mega-nega mighty-honked-off energy comes screaming straight for me, loaded for bear and itching for a fight. It hits me like a P-O'ed pile driver, the hungry, howling terminator of the attacking uber-tendril bristling with a gazillion hungry spikes. All with my name on them. The psychic pitons dig deep into my astral form and anchor in me like adamantium.

It's got me good. Right where I want it. Me against him. Mano a icko.

It's okay. I can do this. Keep it focused on me and hold it back from Boone. Just… hold until the rift closes. I may have more barbs in me now than an acupuncture addict, but it won't matter then. I'll be free.

We both will. Free and alive.

Together. All I have to do is hold on.

Think of Boone. Think of Boone.

I do, and the spontaneous surge of love I feel infuses me with new strength, shriveling the first wave of pointy intruders burrowing deeper into my astral essence in an attempt to start sucking. No, I don't think so. You don't get to walk into me and move in. You're not dealing with a babe in the woods, here. I know how the game is played.

Round to me. So far, so good. Rift is closing. This is working. I just might pull this off.

And we're holding.

No, you don't! Can't go through, so you think you can go around?

Sneaky!

I concentrate and flare out my field, heading off the tendrils attempting an end run around me. Inundated by the pure white light of my much higher vibes, the suckers smoke and shrivel.

Nice!

Good, we're doing good, the rift is closing. Hold, I only need to hold a little longer.

I'm about to commence some serious back patting when I feel the first tug.

Oh, my God, I've been suckered by the suckers! Damn!

In my preoccupation to save Boone at all costs, I forgot two things. The sim wasn't the real threat. Boone wasn't the real target.

Holy shit, I'm screwed. Here's me thinking I was soooo clever, foiling the sim by going extra-corporeal, when in truth, getting me out of my body was what the real foe wanted all along. The tendril attacks? Feints. Dealing with them diverted my attention from the RE's true objective. Not sucking me. At least not yet. No, it needed me to look the other way while it sank the hook deep enough so I couldn't wriggle off. And now it has. It's hooked me, suckered me, and now it's going to reel me in. It intends to pull me back through the rift, trapping me with it on the other side, where it'll have all of eternity to have its way with me and make me wish I'd never been born.

The horror has barely taken hold when the terrifying traction begins and I'm hauled inexorably forward, remorselessly pulled ever closer to the shrinking rift and the whirling maw waiting on the other side. Hungry, slavering, and anxious to receive me.

Sonofabitch!

I want to dig in, drag my heels, claw back, but it's like trying to get traction on quicksand. There's nothing to hang onto, no way to wriggle off the hook, and nowhere to go but up.

Then through.

Maybe I should simply let it take me. I'm not saying I want to spend the rest of eternity in a little cosmic box with a trillion tons of pissed off evil sucking me through a straw, but what choice do I have?

Wait a minute, am I nuts? Let it take me? I don't think so!

Boone!

A burst of warm, white love thrills through me, as if suddenly liberated from a secret internal reserve. I feel its power singing inside me, pumping me up, pushing my vibrational level uber-positive and unstoppable, higher, higher, no holding me now. I don't know where this second wind has come from, but it just might save my bacon. For sure it's repelling my nasty invaders like pouring salt on a slug. I'll burn the barbs right out of me, make this thing let go before it pulls me through.

No!

A snaking, slithering tendril makes straight for my etheric jugular. The slender, silver umbilical binding my astral form to my physical body, my only connection to life, and my way back home. Damn, this thing is cagey; I never saw that coming, though I damned well should have. It's been a long time since I've done anything like this. Like excuses are going to help me now. "He let his guard down." I wonder how that'll look on my tombstone. I might not have long to find out. My obsolete astral skills may have cost me the game—and my entire existence. If I don't head this thing off at the pass and stop it from snapping my life line—

I'm sunk.

Shit.

Damn, it just stuck the proverbial fork in me. I'm done.

No, really. This is no joke. It cut my cord. Even if I slip the hook before I'm pulled through the rift, I've got nowhere to go. I'm dead. *Dead.* Officially a resident of the other side.

Hey, I guess that makes me a ghost writer.

I still got it.

But I haven't managed to unhook myself; therefore, my cord issues are irrelevant. Ghost or no, my unwanted journey into the rift continues, even faster now with the severing of my earthly tether, but hey, there's a bright side. Everyone I leave behind will be safe, because the unholy barn door will finally close right behind me.

That's me, the eternal optimist.

Boone.

I don't want to leave you.

Remember.

"*Help me.*"

I'm here.

A supernova roars from deep within me, flaring bright and clear, rapidly expanding outward, filling every particle of my being. Neither constrained nor slowed by the frontiers of my astral form, the mega-wave swells onward and outward to suffuse my surrounding field with its pure, cleansing light. Encapsulated in a bubble of brilliant resistance, I feel strong, safe, anchored in an unfailing cradle of unbreakable bands of corded eternity, like arms holding me forever, never ceasing, never tiring, never letting go, his arms... his...

Love.

What feels like my lover and yet can't possibly be winds lovingly around me, anchoring me against the malevolent tow. Boone. Somehow he's reaching out to me, giving me his strength to help me fight this thing. But that can't be; he's down there, and I'm up here, and yet it is, it's him, he's all around me, tethering my soul with unbreakable bonds, halting my advance toward that ravenous, unclean thing. Our spirits mingling, our power combined, we hold firm against the vast, measureless determination of that ancient, implacable obscenity.

One final, unearthly howl of frustration shudders through the rapidly dwindling slit of reality allowing our adversary fleeting access to our dimension, and then the rift slams shut.

I'm free!

We did it, we did it together. I called, he came, and we did it. I'm safe, so is he, the danger is past, and now I can go to him. We can be together.

Wait. What the....

I see something there, approaching me. Or me, it. What is that? That... that light? So... pretty....

What's happening to me? I feel strange, confused. I was going to do something. Go somewhere. A second ago it was so important, more important than anything but now, for the life of me I can't remember. What it was. Where I was going. There was something else. No, someone. Someone who meant a lot to me. I can almost see his face.

No, it's gone.

I'm having a hard time remembering. It's the light. It's

distracting. Making me forget.

Ellery, wait! Please don't leave me.

I thought I heard something. A voice. I remember it, I think. I feel it inside me. It feels like love. Part of me wants to go to it, follow the voice and the love, but the light, coming closer, is so much brighter. It wants me too.

He wants me, it wants me. I don't know what to do.

Ellery. Come back to me.

Ellery. Who is that? Is that me? Come back? Where did I go?

I stand on the edge of the brilliant envelope of beautiful light, the cascading corona swirling, beckoning, inviting me in. In a part of my awareness even now rapidly receding, I know I once belonged somewhere else. I'm sad to leave what I once was and knew behind, but hovering on the brink of embracing this wonderful light, it's becoming increasingly difficult to remember anything but the fascinating radiance before me.

If I step inside the light, it'll all be gone. Everything, everyone.

Even him.

No.

I can't go. Not yet.

"Ellery! Oh God, no, he can't be dead, he can't be dead. There isn't a mark on him, what's going on? Breathe, dammit, breathe! Don't you die on me, you bastard! You hear me?"

I will myself away from the light, and suddenly I'm somewhere else. I know this place. I've been here before. I think.

Well, as long as I'm here, I might as well take a look around. Oh look, two men, over there. The one spread-eagled on the floor, not breathing? He looks familiar, but I can't be sure. What's with the hair? Could use a good cut, dude. I wouldn't be caught dead with hair like that.

Forget about him, it's the other man I can't take my eyes off of. He's bent over bad hair guy, breathing into his mouth. The red-haired man is really upset. Why? It hurts me to see him so sad. I want to make him feel better, but I don't know how.

He's desperate, full of fear and anger. Sobbing, yelling at bad hair guy, badgering him to wake up. Not gonna happen. Someone should tell the poor man to give it a rest. He's wasting his time. I can tell from here, the guy on the ground will never breathe again.

I don't know who I feel worse for, the dead guy with the bad hair or his heart-broken companion. Him. The one with the amazing eyes. He keeps talking to the man in his arms, begging him to breathe. I can tell he loves him a lot. A sliver of envy tugs at my heart. I wish those glorious green eyes would look at me that way.

Then suddenly, impossibly, they do.

He raises his head and sees me. His grief-laden eyes widen; he clutches the limp man he holds tightly to his chest.

He loves him, and yet he's looking at me... like....

I never want him to stop.

"Ellery, Ellery, please don't leave me!"

Me? You mean me? He's talking to me. Ellery? Is that who I am? Why can't I remember?

Wait! We're not alone. There's someone else in the room. I've been so focused on the men, I didn't see the older woman and the little girl behind them. Maybe they weren't here before. But they're here now.

The little girl is crying. What, another one? Boy, you could irrigate half the planet with the waterworks happening in this room. At least the old lady in the ridiculous pink slippers is dry-eyed. She's not crying, but she's giving me bug-eyes. Why? What did I ever do to her?

"I don't understand, ma'am. Why doesn't he go back?"

What? Why are you asking me? How should I know?

No, sorry, got it wrong. The little girl isn't talking to me, she's talking about me. Me? She's asking the old lady why I'm not going back? Not going back where? What's that supposed to mean?

"Hush, child," the old lady admonishes, her hand resting firmly on the little girl's shoulder. The child looks like she wants to run over to me, but the old lady's not letting her. Odd. I wonder why. I'm a nice guy. Wouldn't hurt a flea. At least I don't think I would.

Who am I again?

"He could return to his body. There is a way to restore his sundered bridge. But first he must choose."

Choose? What? Sounds interesting. I want to hear more.

Ow! Something nagging, pulling at me. A glow on the edge of my peripheral vision.

Oh, right. The light. I'm keeping it waiting.

Yeah, yeah, I hear you. I'll be right there. I need a minute. I'm not done here yet.

"Come on, Maat, look at him! The fight scrambled him up good. He doesn't even remember his own name. At least the one he's using this life."

A silvery, elfin giggle accompanies the bright female voice sounding behind me. I turn to see another woman standing there, this one much younger than the one with the child. Way prettier too.

Her hair is amazing. So long, so blonde. Where did she come from? I know she wasn't here before. I'm sure I don't know her. A face like that I would remember. And yet, like everyone else in this room, there's something frustratingly familiar about her. I just can't put my finger on what.

"Don't hurt yourself, honey." She emits another amazing giggle. "You'll never get it. I've changed a lot since you last saw me."

She bestows a melting smile upon me and then turns stern eyes on the older woman.

"Come on, Maat, throw him a clue. We have to help him work it out."

"I can't." The wizened woman in pink shakes her head. "I've meddled enough. He has to work it out for himself or not at all."

"Oh, that's just great!" my blonde champion fumes. "You picked a fine time to fall back on the rulebook. What's the point? We've already bent so many of them bringing these boys together, what's one more? Especially now! We can't let it end like this; we can't let him go to the other side, it's too soon!"

"It's only the end of this incarnation, not of his task. The

Bondman saved him from eternal oblivion. He can return when another suitable vessel is made available."

"Pooh on that! What about *this* incarnation? And our poor boys? After everything we went through to get them together? The strings we've pulled? The favors we've called in? They've only just found each other, and you're going to let a technicality split them up again? That's hardly fair!"

The women bicker back and forth, their words a meaningless buzz in my ears. I feel something tugging at my heart. Not the light, although that's still around. It doesn't seem nearly as important now. It might want me, but the feeling's no longer mutual.

Not while I'm looking at him. And he at me.

He sees me. Part of me knows that's not right and shouldn't be possible, but he does.

"Ellery, you can't go. You can't leave me. Not now. Not you too."

He clutches the other's limp body, cradling him in his lap and rocking him like a child. He stares at me with drowning eyes, unashamed of the acid tears coursing down his cheeks.

"Ellery!" he entreats. "I can see you. There has to be a reason why. It must mean something. Come back to me. You can do it. Try. Just… try. Don't leave me. Please don't go. Ellery! Say something!"

His head drops despairingly; he buries his face in the dead man's neck.

My neck.

Ellery.

That's me.

He's Boone.

"That's Boone!" I excitedly point at the weeping man.

The women on either side of me stop arguing and immediately make me the center of their attention.

"Maat?" the golden woman prompts her older companion.

Wait, I know her too! The old lady—that's Mrs. Sheridan!

"What do you want to do, dear boy?"

Boone holds my body close, still rocking me and weeping into my shoulder. The white light waiting for me continues to subject the atoms of my phantom form to persistent but gently coercive traction, but the strong love burning within me for this man defiantly resists the brightness beckoning.

Bottom line, his pull on me is a hell of a lot stronger. The light and every promise of eternity it's offering? I'll pass. No offense, but I'll see you around. Better luck next time?

Nothing matters but him. Screw the light. I want him; I want to be with him.

I point toward my inert body. "I want to go there."

"Sounds like a choice to me!" the golden woman whoops.

Who is she again?

"Here, honey, let me help you."

She takes me by the hand and leads me to Boone. We stand over the two men, one living, one dead. The man I love, holding my earthly remains, sensing my approach lifts his head.

"Ellery?" he quavers, his wet eyes glowing with fierce hope.

Meanwhile, back to the out-of-body guy. Now I'm here, what do I do? Houston, we have a problem. As in, how do I effect re-entry? Astral cord, completely severed? Sort of a tough technicality to work around, no matter how much I want to go back.

The spirit is willing, but the cord is cut.

Well, this sucks. Now what?

The golden woman giggles. I'm really getting to like the sound.

"You're so cute. You've forgotten almost everything, haven't you? Believe me, I know how that feels."

I haven't been able to follow a thing she's said, but she has such pretty eyes. So blue. I must know her. Ah, it'll come to me. If we can't figure out how to shoehorn me back into my bod, I'll have the rest of eternity to work on it.

"Sorry, I shrug. "No lo comprendo."

"You don't have to understand," she smiles. "Just look."

She points toward Boone. Instantly I'm aware of a warm spot in the middle of my chest, pulsing with life, getting stronger, pulling me toward him.

A compulsion I definitely don't intend to resist.

"He is your bridge," the golden woman softly explains. "Your Boone is connected to both your body and your soul. It was done of his own volition in ages long forgotten. Because of his willing sacrifice, the bond between you can never be broken."

That's handy. Hope it didn't hurt.

"Go to him, dear boy, and he will see you home," Mrs. Sheridan softly instructs.

Thank you! And you too, lovely lady, whoever you are!

You're welcome, Khnumhotep.

Home, I'm going home.

Chapter 19

ELLERY, come back to me. Please.

Ow, ow! My head hurts! What was I doing out there?

The familiar, frequently nauseating instant of reentry is mercifully brief. Corporeal reinsertions can be real bitch. Although I enjoy haring about on the astral plane, I hate the aftertaste. Hopefully the usual accompanying energy hangover will be brief.

Yup, I'm back. I know where I am, but I'm not sure why. I'm lying across Boone's lap. He's cradling me in his arms, hugging me. Tight, really tight, almost—ow!

He's saying something, but I can't quite make it out over all the blubbing.

Yeah, that's blubbing, all right. Boone's the one doing it. That's disturbing.

I reach up and tap him gently on the back. "Hey? What's going on?"

Boone abruptly ceases sniffing and muttering. He's still holding me tight; in fact, my request for enlightenment makes him hug me even harder.

My chest hurts like a sonofabitch. Like someone has been pounding the snot out of my sternum.

Someone like Boone?

Only one reason I can think of why he would need to do that. Couple it with me coming back not from unconsciousness, but being out of my body....

"Hey?" I have a go at getting my unresponsive companion to respond. I need to know why he needed to give me CPR.

Although I'm extremely relieved he succeeded.

"Sorry, I...." He snuffles into my shirt. "I need a minute, here."

"No problem, take your time." Blow away to your heart's content. It's only a shirt. Plenty more where it came from.

"I need to... to hold you." He's still doing all his talking to the side of my neck, but his voice sounds steadier and less squishy.

"No, it's fine. Honest. I'll just lie here and...."

Stare at the ceiling. We seem to be in the kitchen. Why are we in the kitchen? There's no chandelier in the kitchen. Why do I have a weird feeling there should be?

And I want to dust something. While I'm lying around waiting for an explanation, I glance over the wall clock. Shut up! It can't possibly be that late! Last thing I remember, we were finishing breakfast, and now that demented digital monstrosity on the wall says it's three thirty in the afternoon?

It lies. I've always hated that clock. Max's idea. First thing tomorrow, it's going to the Good Will.

Three thirty? How can that be? I've lost a fair chunk of my day. Now I know what abductees feel like. Missing time, my ass. I want answers, and I want them now.

"You were dead." Boone finally raised his head. He looks like hell. Red-rimmed eyes, streaky, blotchy face, still slightly runny nose. I guessed as much from the way he sounded, but still, seeing the undeniable evidence of his distress etched all over his face? Disturbing.

But not nearly as much as what he just said.

"Dead?" I stare at him in disbelief. I knew I'd been out of my body, evidently needing—and getting—a bit of a jump-start... but dead? I was thinking a temporary cessation of functions, but... dead? "As in—pushing up the daisies, six feet under, bereft of life, he breathes no more—dead?"

"Dead," he confirms with a curt nod. "You stopped breathing, your heart wasn't beating. No signs of life whatsoever. For almost ten minutes. Kinda hard to interpret those symptoms any other way."

I'll say! "But obviously, I got better."

"Yeah," he sighs, hanging his head. "Thank god for that."

"So I assume I owe you my life?" I smile and slowly stroke his arm. I can think of quite a few ways to express my gratitude.

"What?" He stares back at me like he doesn't understand. "What are you talking about?"

Now it's my turn to be confused. "The CPR. You got me going again, obviously. Thank you?"

"Oh, that." Boone's eyes flood with grief. "I tried, but it didn't help. You were gone, and I couldn't bring you back."

"Wait a minute. That doesn't make sense. If I was dead, and the CPR didn't have anything to do with bringing me back…."

"What did?" Boone's eyes narrow. I'm starting to know what he means when he does that. "You don't know? You don't remember?"

He sounds as surprised by this as I am.

"And you do?"

His eyes contract until they are slender, unreadable slits. I definitely know what that means. He's holding something back.

"Maybe."

"Ellery, you okay now?"

Carly! Where did she come from?

"He's fine, honey." Boone glances quickly toward the little girl hunkered down beside us, looking us over with melting, caring eyes. The little dead girl. The girl he can't possibly see or hear. Not only is he quite clearly doing both, but he's also matter-of-factly addressing her like having a conversation with his dead daughter is something he does every day.

Business as usual.

Hey! That's my job!

"Hey!" I blurt. "Can you… are you… is she…?"

I sound like a blathering idiot.

Father and daughter quickly exchange glances. It's ever so cute.

"Yes," they simultaneously reply.

Seriously adorable. And totally freaking me out.

"How?" I squeak.

Further quick visual by-play ensues between what is starting to look suspiciously like two co-conspirators. Conspiring to keep something from me.

"Dunno." Boone overdoes the casual shrug and also fails miserably to convince with his overly studied attempt at innocence. The kid isn't any better at faking nonchalance. "But I'm not complaining."

There is something going on here. Over and above the obvious impossibility of Boone's new abilities. I immediately suspect the involvement of a certain pink-shod granny. A quick glance around fails to turn her up. Means nothing. She might not be here now, but she has been.

I want to press the point and make them both 'fess up, but the look on Boone's face softens my heart. He's obviously torn between two loves, if I can be so bold as to attribute that quality to the affection he obviously feels for me. I can nail him to the wall—literally and figuratively—later. The dispensation he's currently enjoying, his puzzling ability to see and hear his daughter, might not last long. And Carly certainly can't, and shouldn't, hang around much longer.

He's been given a great gift, an opportunity most people will never receive. I should back off, give them some space, and let them take full advantage of whatever last time they have together.

I put on a stern front and give Boone a rebuking glare. "You, sir, are holding out on me, but we'll sort it out later. Right now, I'll settle for a hug."

"I can do that," Boone's eyes glisten, his supporting arms tightening around me with rib-cracking relief.

"Ow!"

"Sorry. I didn't mean to...."

"It's okay. Sternum's still a bit sore. Ribs too."

"I'm sorry. I was scared. You okay?"

"Think so. Don't think anything's cracked. Bent, but not broken. It doesn't hurt to breathe."

"How about laugh?"

"I dunno, say something funny."

"Um… maybe later."

Fair enough.

"Can we get up now?" I ask as the fervent embrace continues. Not that I mind having the crap hugged out of me, it's just, this floor is hard and I can't feel my ass any more.

"I could get up," Boone murmurs into the side of my neck. Then plants a soft kiss on my skin. Oooh. Nice.

Chuckling, we haul each other up and stagger toward the nearest sitting surface, the chairs around the kitchen table.

Carly follows us, her eyes pooling with liquid love for her father. Boone's hands are heavy and solicitous upon me while he helps me to sit, but the longing glances he shoots her way are not lost on me.

I'm definitely superfluous to requirements. Not a feeling I'm used to in situations like this, but I'm totally fine with it. I will keep to my intention of making myself scarce and leave them to their last goodbyes.

"Boone, listen, my head is really killing me right now. I want to lie down, and I'm sure I can find my way to my bedroom on my own. Besides, I think there's someone else you'd rather be talking to at the moment, and since you don't need me to do it, if you don't mind, I'll disappear and leave you to it. Sound like a plan?"

"You're gonna be okay?" Boone eyes me anxiously.

I don't believe it. Even now, even with the gift of quality time with his departed daughter handed to him on a silver platter, I say the word, he'd come with me. I think I love this man.

No, I lied. I don't just think, I know.

"I'm fine. I'll be upstairs. Go, be with your daughter."

Boone's eye fill with an emotion he can't articulate. He hangs his head, blinking fiercely, grabs my hand, and squeezes it hard.

"You're welcome." I squeeze back, then gently break his grateful grasp. "Catch you later."

I wheel about and start to traverse the tile, nearly making it out of the kitchen when the unexpected stops me in my tracks, mere footfalls from the breezeway and freedom.

Just inside the doorway and spilling out into the hall is a huge pool of—I have no idea what it is—an odd, viscous black liquid. Like lumpy molasses. And the smell? Try rotting fruit soaked in garlic.

Nasty.

I don't even want to think about what this might be or where it came from.

"What the hell is this?" I whirl and demand of the other two occupants of the room.

Boone looks to Carly. She looks to him. This silent collusion thing would be adorable if they both weren't holding out on me!

"Why are you asking me? It's your house!"

We are so gonna talk later!

I'VE somehow managed to clean the crud off my kitchen floor, crawl upstairs, change the bedding, shed my clothes, and slip into some lovely silk jammies, bottoms only. Urinate, wash my hands, splash water on my face. Brush my teeth.

That does it, I'm good. Time to hit the sheets. I know it's early for bed, but between being dead, amnesiac, mopping up a considerable quantity of indeterminate, unexplained, possible otherworldly excrement, and who knows what all else may have happened to me I can't remember or am not being told about, I've had an extremely full day.

I can hardly wait to lose myself in that mattress. So it is with much surprise and no small degree of annoyance that I exit my ensuite to discover I may have to postpone my close encounter with my big comfy bed.

I am not alone.

A beautiful woman stands at the foot of my bed. Apparently

awaiting me. Her petite form draped in an elegant white robe, a cascade of hair sitting heavily on her shoulders, spilling down her back like a golden shawl, enormous blue eyes set like living sapphires in an exquisitely featured porcelain face. Gorgeous eyes. Simply breathtaking. Something familiar about them. And her.

Or not.

Oh yeah, she's dead. Bet you saw that one coming.

"Can I help you?" I stamp down the tsunami of annoyance bubbling up within. I could give her attitude, but that would only prolong the process. Let's find out who she is and what she wants and get her gone soonest so I can get some sleep.

Next time I see Mrs. S., she's got some 'splainin' to do. Apparitions in my bedroom, male or female, are not supposed to be allowed. Either she's falling down on the job or she booked off on holidays and neglected to inform me. Whatever, this is the last thing I need right now.

Those glorious sapphire eyes light up when she sees me. Like she knows me. I know I don't know her.

"You don't recognize me, do you?" She giggles. A silvery, almost elfin sound. Coy, coquettish. Familiar.

No, it can't be.

She giggles again, her eyes glowing mischievously.

It can't be her. It can't!

"Mrs. Potts!"

"In the flesh, honey." She dazzles me with her smile. "Or maybe not so much anymore." She emits an exuberant, trilling laugh. Utterly entrancing. "I was quite the hotsie totsie in my day, wasn't I?" She dimples teasingly.

"Stunning," I gasp, enchanted by the transformation. So this is what she truly was, once upon a time. Before today, I'd only seen flashes of this grand, glorious woman, like ghostly memories of magnificence struggling to manifest even briefly through the ruin she had become, but now, to see her like this, with her beauty, grace, and intelligence restored to her....

By death. Ah… damn.

"You're dead." Realization and concurrent grief silence me. She's gone. But… but I saw her, talked to her, only this morning. Damn. I wonder how it happened. I probably won't have to wait long to find out. Only as long as it takes for someone at the Shady Rest to ring and give me the news.

Damn. I wonder if she has any family. I never found out. What if there isn't anyone to claim the body? To bury her? She was so old. The last birthday she remembered, she claimed to be a hundred and five, but no one at the home knew for sure.

I'll bet that's why she's here. To ask me if I'll take care of her.

"Yes, darling, I'm deader than a doornail," she proudly beams. "Happened right after we had our last chat. You remember the one." Her little rosebud mouth contracts into a disapproving moue. "You naughty boy, you didn't tell me you don't have any plants! And what did you do with the cat?"

Don't look at me like that; the imaginary felines and the non-existent interior foliage were your ideas!

"Next mind that now," she tsks, brushing my incipient protest aside with an airy wave of her slim hand. "I have to run soon, but before I go, I thought you should know I left my body in the cupboard under the back stairs. You might want to take me out of there before I start to smell."

She's kidding!

She's not.

"You what!?" I shriek. "How did you end up in there?"

"Who knows?" She shrugs and casually tosses a sheaf of her long, blonde hair over her left shoulder with a gesture oddly evoking a young, blonde, much shorter Cher. "I was loony tunes, remember? I probably crawled in there to take a nap. Or change the litter box. It doesn't matter now, does it?"

"No, I guess it doesn't."

Litter box?

"I also wanted to thank you." She folds her hands in front of her, an equally familiar mannerism I've seen performed many times before. Not by her, however. "For enduring my constant intrusions with such good grace and being so kind to an addled old lady. This place was an important part of my life. It was also my home for over fifty years. It brought me great comfort to be allowed to come here and visit whenever I wanted."

And your keepers at the Shady Rest were taking a nap.

"Don't mention it. It was my pleasure. I enjoyed your visits. Really. Please believe me."

"I do," she beams. "But I won't be dropping by any more."

No. I guess you won't.

"I'll miss you." I mean it. I really will.

She giggles. "Why, you slick young charmer, I believe you mean that. What a sweet boy you are. I swear, if I were eighty years younger and still breathing...." She dimples, her eyes sparkling mischievously. "It wouldn't do me any good. You're spoken for."

"I believe I am." That's something I never thought I'd ever say, but it sounds good.

Feels even better.

"You are a good boy, dearie. But now I really need to leave you and go into that pretty light." She blows me a kiss and waves. "Bye, now, Khnumhotep! Give your Boone a kiss for me!"

Thanks, I will. Hang on. That name. She called me that name again. I should—this might be my last chance to find out why. And actually get an answer!

"Wait!" I call out to her. "Why do you keep calling me that?"

"That's for me to know and you to find out." She giggles, blows me a kiss, and fades forever out of my life.

Enchanting.

Ah, that wasn't so bad. Didn't take long to send her off, either. Now she's gone and I can finally get some sleep.

Wait. She did it to me again. She probably didn't mean to, but she did it anyway.

I can't go to bed; I've got a dead old lady in my closet. I can't leave her there. Not like she'd know or care if I got in a few hours shut-eye before we retrieved her. But I would.

I have to get her out of there and properly taken to her final rest. Now, not later. I should phone the sheriff, and the Shady Rest, and the Coroner? Or maybe just the sheriff. He'll know what to do.

Dammit.

I grumble my way into my closet in search of a fresh set of clothes.

Why me?

TIRED, I'm so tired.

I drag myself down the breezeway, following the faint lilt of voices issuing from the parlor. I'm reluctant to interrupt what will probably be their final conversation, but I realized on my way downstairs I probably should.

I get one foot inside the room, intending to immediately announce my presence, and see something nearly stopping my heart.

Again. This time, for a good reason.

Boone is comfortably ensconced in the overstuffed armchair beside the south-facing window. He's hasn't noticed me, his attention fully occupied by the wee slip of a ghostly girl curled up in his lap, her phantom head making no impression on the broad, sweater-covered chest cushioning it. There they sit, gazes inextricably interwoven, their rapt adoration for a brief moment arresting all time in their immediate vicinity while they bask inviolate in the small pocket of love they've woven about themselves.

It's adorable, precious. They look so good together. So natural and, dare I say it, normal. If I didn't know she was dead, no way I could tell by looking.

I should let them know I'm there, but I can't bring myself to break this up.

"Daddy," the little girl says to her father. "You'll tell Mommy what I said?"

"I promise, baby," Boone duly vows.

Oh. I might be walking into the middle of something none of us want me to hear.

I quickly clear my throat.

Two heads turn toward the sound, and twin grins fly my way.

"Hi, Ellery!" Carly brightly greets me. "My dad and I have been having the bestest time. You done sleeping already?"

I wish.

Boone is quicker on the uptake.

"What's happened?" He takes his eye off me only as long as it takes to murmur something to Carly. She nods, blinks out, and then instantly reappears beside me. Boone only takes a half a second longer to lever his long length out of the armchair and stride over to my side. He's already in full alert, on-duty mode by the time he arrives.

I know, I know. How do I know that? Not like I've ever seen him like this before, but I know.

Trust me.

"Nothing, not anything serious, anyway." Relax, stand down, it's okay. "Just a slight logistical problem I've recently been made aware of."

"Meaning?"

"Follow me," I sigh.

I figure it would be easier to show him. I'm sure he can handle it. Something tells me poor Mrs. Potts won't be the first dead body he's ever seen.

Not the first one today, even.

Man, I need to get some sleep.

I lead the procession to her last resting place, open the closet door, stand aside, and wave him through. Boone pokes his head past the doorframe and takes a look.

"Ellery, there's a little old dead lady in your closet."

"Tell me about it."

"What is she doing in there?"

"The backstroke? What do you think? She's dead! Don't bother asking me how she got here, I don't know. She stopped off on her way to the hereafter and gave me the good news."

"Considerate," Boone nods.

"I thought so."

"Not to sound insensitive or anything, but what's this got to do with me?"

"I have to call someone to come and get her, and I'd rather they didn't see you."

"Ah." Boone's face shuts down, his expression unreadable.

"No, I don't mean it that way." I sigh and roll my eyes. "It would just be easier. Not to have to explain you. Right now. I will, later, but right now...."

I know I'm floundering, but just as I'm going down for the third time, I am rescued by the dawning of comprehension.

"I get it." Boone nods. "Small town, everybody knows everybody's business and spends half their lives discussing, distorting and disseminating it. It'll move things along if you don't have to answer any unnecessary questions."

"Exactly." I exhale my relief. I'm not ashamed of you, it's just, right now I'm really tired and I don't want to have to explain you to George and Bernie and Vern and anyone else who may show up in response to my summons. Might be half the damned town, for all I know.

"Right!" Boone points upward. "I'll go upstairs, find something to keep me busy, and wait for you to be done dealing with this. Your bedroom okay?" He grins, green eyes exhibiting a slightly lustful gleam.

Not in front of the children.

"My bedroom's fine. I'll see you later."

"Sooner than later, I hope. Coming, sweetheart?"

"In a minute, Daddy," Carly tells her father. "I want to say bye to Ellery. I won't be seeing him again."

The playful gleam in Boone's eyes freezes over. He forgot. This small state of grace he and Carly have been floating in is finite. Soon she has to take her leave of him and the earthly plane forever.

This day, this moment in time, is all they get.

He rebounds almost instantly, strong-arming his way past his distress. He's determined to be brave, for Carly's sake.

"Okay." He goes for chipper and almost makes it. "Come find me when you're ready, sweetheart. You too," he tells me with a shy grin.

I'll do my best.

"I want to thank you for what you did for my daddy," she solemnly announces the instant Boone is out of earshot.

"You're welcome. Happy to help."

I sense we're not exactly on the same page. She may be referring to whatever went on during that chunk of missing time. Here's a thought. If she's thanking me for it, it follows she knows something about it. Maybe everything.

If I pump her, will she spill?

"I know he's going to be okay now."

That small statement brings me up short and forces me to put my curiosity, and any hopes I had of satisfying it through her, permanently aside. She's reminded me she's almost done here, and as her remaining time on this plane is far more finite than mine, I'd be a selfish toad to waste hers pursuing a personal agenda.

So I won't. The mystery of the missing time will have to wait. But not forever. I will find out what went on today. Carly isn't my only avenue of information.

"You will look after him, for me, won't you?"

"Of course," I assure her.

"He's much better now. Ever since he met you. He thinks I'm too young to understand, but I can tell. He loves you. Like he loved my mom."

Wow. What in the heck did they talk about while I wasn't there? It was nice of her to tell me how she thinks he feels about me. Not that I needed her to, but still… nice. In a weird sort of way. Not creepy weird, unusual weird.

I'm not sure why she wants me to know she knows. Especially considering the comment I inadvertently overheard about her wanting Boone and her mother to reconnect.

"And… you're okay with that?"

She sighs. "My mommy found someone to help her feel better. He makes her laugh and smile again. I think that's nice."

Did she tell Boone this? And if so, how does he feel about it? If she didn't, should I?

"Mommy's getting better, and now Daddy will too. I don't need to worry about them now."

If I write one very special letter to help Boone keep his promise to this special little girl, then both her parents won't have to worry about her either. They'll be able to celebrate her life and know with unerring certainty one day, they will hold her again. I'll run the possibility by her, offer to be the messenger, see what she says.

Closure is not only a beautiful thing, it is a very special gift. In this instance, I'll take great pleasure in bestowing it.

Godspeed, little girl. Safe journey. So very glad I got to know you.

Chapter 20

THE ambient light in my suite is attenuating, absorbing the approaching evening shadows, the atmosphere heavy and silent, when I enter ten minutes shy of two hours later. Boone's in bed, resting on his side, his face to the wall. Meaning the part of him presently presenting to me is his back. I can't see if he's awake or asleep, but I don't need to see to know.

He's awake. Waiting for me.

Something else I know, because I can feel the way he feels.

She's gone. This time for good.

I take another step forward, then stop.

Hey! He's on my side. I don't remember saying he could sleep on my side of the bed! Why is he doing that?

Well, we'll just have to find a way to shift him.

I'll get on it right now.

I quickly shed my clothes, and by the time I reach the wrong side of the bed, I'm fully shucked. I hesitate, unsure how to proceed. Should I be polite and give him a verbal warning? Go for the stealth approach and sneak in under his radar by burrowing beneath the sheets, or opt for the aerial assault option, take a flying leap, and announce my presence by bouncing off his chest?

Who knew this stuff could be so complicated?

Boone beats me to the clutch.

"C'mere, I need a hug." He rolls over to face me, smiles invitingly, grabs the bedclothes, and lifts them to reveal the empty space beside him.

I can do that.

Wrong side be damned, I'll learn to adapt. Besides, I'm flexible.

I slide in beside him, falling willingly into his waiting embrace. He drops the covers, arranging them around us, sighs, and snuggles. For a time I'm content simply to lie with him, feeling his arms around me, listening to the sound of his breathing, enjoying the comforting touch of his strong, warm hand stroking my back.

"Hell of a day," he murmurs after several minutes of stroking.

"Yup."

"Glad you're still here."

"Me too."

"Figured you would be."

"Yup."

This is nice. Laconic, but nice. I could sleep now.

"You probably have a few questions."

You could say that.

"Yup."

"I might have a few answers."

"Oh?"

Yippee! Finally! Someone's going to tell me something! I might expire from the shock.

Bad analogy.

"Little old pink lady at nine o'clock," Boone enigmatically observes in the same mild, almost mesmerizing tone he's been using since the conversation began.

"What? What does that mean?"

"Behind you. Little old lady. See for yourself."

Shut up!

I sit up, turn over, and immediately grab the covers and pull them up to my chin.

Boone wasn't kidding. There she is, standing beside my bed, the last place I would ever expect to see her, especially here. And now.

Mrs. Sheridan.

"I thought you said she didn't invade your privacy. As a rule."

Says the naked man occupying my side of the bed.

"Usually, she doesn't. Although I'm starting to wonder if maybe it was because, as a rule, there wasn't anything to interrupt! Wait a minute." I cease freaking as comprehension dawns. "You can see her?"

"Obviously."

So the phenomenon isn't strictly Carly-related.

Interesting.

"Perhaps you should ask her what she wants? Then maybe she'll go away."

"Why does it have to be me? You can see her too. You ask her."

"She's your grandma. Obviously she came to speak to you."

"I don't see why that's necessarily so obvious. Maybe she wants to introduce herself to you. Although she could have waited for a better time." I glare at her.

Mrs. Sheridan enters the verbal fray before Boone can launch his next oral salvo. "Actually, I'm here to speak to you both."

She smiles again, that kindly, oh-so-warm and familiar smile, the one saying safety and love and understanding to me when I was so alone and there was no one in my life who cared about me but her. I don't know if it's because my eyes are suddenly misting with the emotion gathering inside me, or if she actually *is*....

Glowing, lightly golden, like a fine mist has been sprinkled in the air above her, filtering down, covering her, making her sparkle.

Pretty.

"Blessed boy," she softly murmurs. "I will always be here for you. You as well, Boone Dantrell. I stand to serve you both, as it has always been."

I'm expecting him to respond immediately with some flip comeback or a demand for her to elaborate upon that most cryptic comment. But he doesn't do either. He doesn't say a word, simply accepts her commendation without comment.

I lie beside him, trying to fathom the underlying meaning encrypted in the meaningful glances passing between my new lover and my oldest friend. Something pops in my head, a completely offside notion. I have no idea where it came from, but there it is, and it's so out there I can't keep it in.

"You're… you're not a ghost, are you?" I blurt, as all the mysteries of my life embodied in this enigmatic, disembodied old lady suddenly crystallize into unsubstantiated certainty.

"Of course I am, darling," she smiles sweetly at me. "What else could I be?"

I don't know, but just like everything else I don't understand that's happened to me today, I'm going to find out.

"All right, let's go with something easier. In all the time I've known you, I never learned your first name. Do you have one?"

"Yes," she primly responds.

"Why did you never tell me?"

"You've never asked me, dear."

"Fine. I'm asking now."

"Maat." She smiles sweetly at me. "I am Maat."

Are you indeed?

"The goddess of truth, justice, and the Egyptian way," Boone unexpectedly quips. "Pleased to meet you, ma'am."

"She's not the actual goddess!" I protest. "Not for real."

"Of course not," she immediately supplies.

"Of course not, there's no such thing," Boone agrees. "But you have to admit, it is apropos."

Yeah, come to think of it, as names go, it does sort of fit her. But how would you know?

"Don't worry about it now, dear," she smiles indulgently at me once more. "One day, all this and more will be clear to you."

"And what day would that be, pray tell?"

"Get some sleep now. You need your rest."

And softly, sweetly, twinkling like a comforting and yet slightly frustrating star, she fades from sight.

"Is she always like this?" Boone yawns.

To my credit, exercising admirable restraint, I do not slug him right in the face.

I want to, but I don't.

"This seeing and hearing spooks thing? Will it shut off any time soon, or is it going to turn into a full-time gig?"

"You're asking me?"

"You see anyone else in the room?" He leans over and kisses the tip of my nose.

"Nope, and hopefully neither do you. Seriously, I can't explain why it started in the first place so how long it's going to last? Your guess is as good as mine."

"I guess we'll sleep on it and see how things look in the morning."

"Welcome to my world."

"We'll see," he chuckles, kissing the top of my head. "The jury may still be out on my upgrades, but there is one thing I know for sure."

"What's that?" I sigh, snuggling.

"Your days of dealing with this shit alone are officially over." He busses me firmly on the mouth. "From now on, anything coming after you will have to get through me first."

"*Yea, though I walk through the valley of the shadow of death, I will fear no evil, for thou art with me,*" I softly murmur.

"Hmmm?" Boone dreamily echoes.

"It's from the Bible. The twenty-third Psalm."

"Actually, I knew that," he chuckles.

"Although David was referring to Jehovah."

"Tough act to follow, but I'll do my best. Say, doesn't the next line mention something about a rod and a staff?" He gives me an unsubtly suggestive nudge. "And… comforting?" he leers, licking the side of my face.

"Now that you mention it." I gasp when his hand moves across my stomach, then starts south.

"And if we rub 'em together, do you think we can start a fire?"

Count on it.

His creeping, questing hand suddenly, maddeningly stops.

Now what?

"Mind if I ask you something?" he parks his hand on my belly and quips.

"What? Now?" I never noticed it before, but I squeak when I'm excited. Voice spontaneously skips an octave and goes straight to "freak."

"No big deal, idle curiosity. Just occurred to me if anyone would know, you would."

He gazes at me expectantly. What does he want, an engraved invitation?

"All right, I'll play. What do you want to know?"

"You don't have to get all pissy." He pouts and rolls back into his pillow. "It's only one lousy little question."

Argh!

"I'm not...." I take a deep breath and struggle to mean what I'm about to say. "Pissy. Ask your question."

"Elvis!" He brightens and rolls back to face me. "Is he really dead?"

He has got to be kidding.

"How should I know?"

"I just thought, maybe, when he was on his way to... wherever, he might have, you know, dropped by to say 'hi'."

This is a joke. He's not serious.

"Why would he do that? It's not like we knew each other or anything!"

"Does everyone who comes to see you know you previous to

passing on?"

"No, practically none of them, but I don't see what this has to do with...."

"So you don't know?"

"Didn't I just say that?"

"Can you guess?"

"I'm a writer, not a fortuneteller!"

"Star Trek, right!" He grins triumphantly. "Original Series, not the reboot."

"Can we *please* get some sleep now?" I whine.

"Ever been to Graceland?"

"As a matter of fact, no."

"Me either. Tell you what. Let's make plans to go there someday soon. Settle the question once and for all. Deal?"

"Deal."

EPILOGUE

I SURFACE slowly, painlessly, swimming languidly upward through a sea of serenity. Attaining awareness by sweetly effortless increments. The closer I draw to wakefulness, the better I feel. For the first time in a long time, I'm more than ready to greet the day, because what's waiting for me in it is far better than anything I've ever dreamt.

Love carried me to sleep, and now it welcomes me back once more. I wake to the feeling of strong arms surrounding me and the sweet, hungry stirrings of my body to a touch it will never get enough of.

His.

I lie motionless in the circle of his arms, drinking in the sensations. Drowning in the softness of his hand moving slowly down my back, stroking me tenderly, desire burgeoning within me as gently as the touch invoking it.

His hand trembles with his own need; his hard, insistent length gently prods my side.

I'm still too drowsy to do much more than submit willingly to the incredible sensations surging through me, so I give him a low "ummmm" of encouragement and press into him. When his hand freezes, I moan again. This time with disappointment.

He resumes stroking me with wordless intensity. Still softly, slowly, gently, but the strokes get longer, start to range farther afield upon my tingling, hungry skin.

He's starting to chart me in earnest. Exactly what I had in mind.

Not just hands now. Warm, moist lips explore my neck, moving across my chest, incited by the evidence of my escalating receptivity. The hand on my back moves, a tongue rasps hotly over my right nipple.

The intensity of the stimulation sheers through me with an unexpected jolt, making me gasp, arch toward him, and beg for more.

I don't have to ask twice.

Strong fingers cup my buttocks, kneading the flesh with delicious avidity. He licks the nipple again before taking it in his teeth and gently nipping.

My dick thumps impatiently against my belly, aching and weeping for attention while he kisses an excruciatingly pleasurable path down the length of my torso. He's having a mighty good time getting wherever he's going. His right hand takes a simultaneous meander around my hip, bound, I am hoping, for the Promised Land. I'm not sure which traveler I'm rooting for to get there first. Just so long as they don't take much longer.

He rests his hand on my hip and moves slowly over me, back up to take a long, lingering taste of my mouth. He rubs his cheek against mine. His lips hover close to my ear, hot breath banking my inner fire.

"Ellery," he whispers, making my name sound like a prayer. "Are you awake?"

I take his hand and place it firmly upon the firmest part of me.

"What do you think?"

His tongue slips into my mouth; his fingers wrap around me. I can't believe how exciting it is to be touched... like this. To feel him holding me, exploring me while he's kissing me, making me moan and buck and beg for more. He nibbles my lower lip, licking it teasingly before diving down, sucking urgently, hotly, tongue thrusting, swirling, tasting. His hand tightens and pumps and sends me jolting, writhing, higher, closer—

—over the edge into bliss. Sobbing, screaming for him, I shudder uncontrollably, my body blissfully wracked and singing with completion.

He gathers me into his arms. I'm fainting, laughing, crying, and half-unconscious with the pleasure he's just given me. He murmurs soothingly, stroking my hair and petting me with amused affection while I come back down to earth.

"So are you gonna live?"

"God, I hope so," I gasp. "How you doing?" I look over, tracing his twitching, turgid length with my eyes. "You up for some reciprocation?"

He takes my hand and places it on his primary area of interest.

"What do you think?"

"I think I'm ready to try something new."

"Don't let me stop you." He rolls on his back, raises his arms, and pillows his head on his hands, leaving himself wide open for my pleasure.

And his.

I drape myself over him and rest my elbow on his stomach, addressing his crotch.

"I think I see your problem," I gravely inform him, taking him firmly in hand. "But I have the solution."

"I'm all ears," he croaks, groaning with pleasure when I gently squeeze.

"Not from what I'm seeing," I reply, and lick my lips.

PHOENIX EMRYS began her writing career at age seven when she penned her first opus, a supernatural thriller about a green porcelain horse and her favorite Barbie. She continued to write vociferously into her twenties, producing several fantasy tales featuring two male characters of the intensely bonded, brothers-in-arms variety. The book she slaved over and submitted for publication utterly failed to impress, whereupon she chucked the writing and got on with her life.

In 1999 her first computer and a shiny new obsession for two hot guys in a certain sci fi series led her into the world of fan fiction, where she discovered two hot guys who really liked each other could do way more than hug... a lot. Not only did this exciting new arena rekindle her atrophied desire to write, but the slash revelation inspired her to significantly expand her literary horizons.

Ahem.

Ten years of fan fic writing ensued. During which she wrote—a lot—and learned some too.

Phoenix is a Canadian south paw and lives in British Columbia with her daughter, the world's largest cat, and his psycho Siamese nemesis. She loves to knit and write about hot guys in love, with happy endings.

Phoenix tweets at http://twitter.com/phoenix_emrys. Visit her blog at http://phoenixemrys.wordpress.com/. You can contact her at olorien56@gmail.com.

Supernatural Romance from DREAMSPINNER PRESS

http://www.dreamspinnerpress.com